Everyman, I will go with thee,
and be thy guide

THE EVERYMAN LIBRARY

The Everyman Library was founded by J. M. Dent in 1906. He chose the name Everyman because he wanted to make available the best books ever written in every field to the greatest number of people at the cheapest possible price. He began with Boswell's 'Life of Johnson'; his one-thousandth title was Aristotle's 'Metaphysics', by which time sales exceeded forty million.

Today Everyman paperbacks remain true to J. M. Dent's aims and high standards, with a wide range of titles at affordable prices in editions which address the needs of today's readers. Each new text is reset to give a clear, elegant page and to incorporate the latest thinking and scholarship. Each book carries the pilgrim logo, the character in 'Everyman', a medieval morality play, a proud link between Everyman past and present.

Arnold Bennett

ANNA OF THE FIVE TOWNS

Edited by
PETER PRESTON
University of Nottingham

EVERYMAN
J. M. DENT · LONDON
CHARLES E. TUTTLE
VERMONT

First published in Everyman Paperbacks 1997

J. M. Dent
Orion Publishing Group
Orion House, 5 Upper St Martin's Lane,
London WC2H 9EA
and
Charles E. Tuttle Co., Inc.
28 South Main Street,
Rutland, Vermont 05701, USA

Printed in Great Britain by
The Guernsey Press Co. Ltd, Guernsey, C. I.

British Library Cataloguing-in-Publication Data
is available upon request.

ISBN 0 460 87653 8

CONTENTS

NOTE ON THE AUTHOR AND EDITOR

ENOCH ARNOLD BENNETT was born in Hanley, Staffordshire in 1867, the oldest of the nine children of Enoch and Sarah Bennett. His father, formerly a potter, draper and pawnbroker, qualified as a solicitor in 1876 and Bennett's first job, after he left secondary school in 1883, was in his father's office. He attended night school at the Wedgwood Institute in Burslem and although he passed the London University matriculation examinations he twice failed his legal examinations. In 1889 he moved to London, where he worked as a shorthand clerk in a solicitor's office and started writing to earn extra money. In 1893 he began his career as a full-time writer, becoming first Assistant Editor and then Editor of *Woman*, at the same time as publishing a wide range of stories and short articles.

His first novel, *A Man from the North*, appeared in 1898, and in the same year he decided to make his living from fiction, although it was not until 1902 that his next two novels – *The Grand Babylon Hotel* and *Anna of the Five Town* – were published, establishing the broad directions his fiction would take over the next thirty years. He quickly gained a reputation as the chronicler of life in the Potteries, and *Anna* was succeeded by a number of works set in the area: *Tales of the Five Towns* (short stories, 1905); *Whom God Hath Joined* (1906); *The Grim Smile of the Five Towns* (short stories, 1907); *The Old Wives' Tale* (1908); *Clayhanger* (1910), which initiated a trilogy completed by *Hilda Lessways* (1911) and *These Twain* (1915); *Helen with the High Hand* (1910); *The Card* (1911) and *The Matador of the Five Towns* (1912). Some of these Five Towns books, together with the grimly naturalistic *Riceyman Steps* (1923), are generally regarded as his best works, but he also achieved wide popularity with novels, sometimes with sensational plots, set in a more opulent and metropolitan world. As well as *The Grand Babylon Hotel*, these include *Leonora*

(1903), *Sacred and Profane Love* (1905), *The Regent* (1913), *The Pretty Lady* (1918) and *Imperial Palace* (1930).

Between 1902 and 1913 he lived mainly in France where in 1907 he met and married Marguerite Soulie. By 1914 he had returned to England and from 1915 engaged in war work, rising to be Director of Propaganda at the Ministry of Information. After the war he travelled a good deal, often spending whole summers sailing his own yacht off the coasts of England and continental Europe. He was formally separated from his wife in 1921 and in 1922 met Dorothy Cheston, an actress, with whom he had a daughter, born in 1926.

Although best known as a writer of novels and short stories, Bennett published a good deal of non-fiction, including practical handbooks (*Journalism for Women*, 1898; *How to Become an Author*, 1903), autobiography (*The Truth About an Author*, 1903), criticism (*Fame and Fiction*, 1901; *Literary Taste*, 1909), popular philosophy (*How to Live on Twenty-Four Hours a Day*, 1908, *The Feast of St Friend*, 1911; *How to Make the Best of Life*, 1923; *The Savour of Life*, 1928) and travel sketches (*Paris Nights*, 1913; *Mediterranean Scenes*, 1928). He was fascinated by the theatre and wrote, often in collaboration with Edward Knoblock or Eden Phillpotts, both original plays and stage adaptations of his own novels, which were produced in theatres in London and the provinces, several of them enjoying long and profitable runs. He was also in great demand as a journalist, writing for a wide variety of newspapers and journals, including *T. P.'s Weekly*, *New Age*, the *New Statesman* (of which he was a director from 1915) and *John Bull*. In the 1920s his articles in mass-circulation newspapers such as the *Daily Express* and the *Sunday Pictorial* brought his work to an even larger public, while his series 'Books and Persons', which appeared in the *Evening Standard* from 1926, was highly influential in establishing, confirming or casting doubt on a number of literary reputations.

In January 1931 Arnold Bennett contracted typhoid fever while on a visit to France, and he died in London in March of that year. His *Journal 1929* had been published in 1930 but the appearance in 1932 of the *Journals 1896–1928* allowed his admirers further insight into the career of a committed, hard-working and variously talented author.

PETER PRESTON is Senior Lecturer in Literature in the Department of Continuing Education and Deputy Director of the Humanities Research Centre at the University of Nottingham, where he has worked since 1973, first as Resident Tutor in Lincoln and, from 1980, as Staff Tutor in Literature. He has a special interest in the literature of region and place and has published essays on Arnold Bennett and Elizabeth Gaskell as well as co-editing two volumes of critical essays, *The Literature of Place* (1993) and *Writing the City* (1994). His other main interest is in the work of D. H. Lawrence, and since 1991 he has been Associate Director of the University's D. H. Lawrence Centre. He is the author of *A D. H. Lawrence Chronology* (1994) and co-editor of *D. H. Lawrence in the Modern World* (1989) and of three student editions, published in Italy: *The Fox* and *The Virgin and the Gipsy* (1993) and *'Sun' and Selected Short Stories* (1995). The Penguin edition of Lawrence's *Mr Noon*, with his introduction, appeared in 1996. He has also co-edited *Raymond Williams: Education, Politics and Letters* (1993) and edited *Literature in Adult Education: Reflections on Practice* (1995).

CHRONOLOGY OF BENNETT'S LIFE

Year	*Age*	*Life*
1867		Enoch Arnold Bennett born 27 May in Hanley, Staffordshire; first of nine children of Enoch and Sarah Ann Bennett

CHRONOLOGY OF HIS TIMES

Year	*Arts, Science and Technology*	*History and Politics*
1867	Marx, *Das Kapital* Ibsen, *Peer Gynt*	Second Reform Bill; Dominion of Canada founded
1868	Browning, *The Ring and the Book* Wilkie Collins, *The Moonstone* William Morris, *The Earthly Paradise*	(February) Disraeli (Conservative) Prime Minister; (December) Gladstone (Liberal) Prime Minister
1869	Matthew Arnold, *Culture and Anarchy* R. D. Blackmore, *Lorna Doone* J. S. Mill, *On the Subjection of Women*	Suez Canal opened; Girton College for women opened in Cambridge
1870	Death of Dickens Spencer, *Principles of Psychology*	Married Women's Property Act; Forster's Education Act introduces elementary education for 5–13-year-olds; Franco-Prussian War
1871	George Eliot, *Middlemarch* (–72) Thomas Hardy, *Desperate Remedies* Darwin, *The Descent of Man*	Religious tests abolished at Oxford and Cambridge; Trade Unions legalized; Paris Commune suppressed
1872	Samuel Butler, *Erewhon* Hardy, *Under the Greenwood Tree*	Secret ballots in national elections
1873	Tolstoy, *Anna Karenina* Walter Pater, *The Renaissance*	Death of David Livingstone

Year	*Age*	*Life*
1875	8	Moves to Burslem; becomes pupil at Wesleyan Infants School
1876	9	Father qualifies as solicitor
1878	11	Family moves to Cobridge
1882	15	Attends Middle School at Newcastle-under-Lyme
1883	16	Leaves school and begins work in father's office

Year	*Arts, Science and Technology*	*History and Politics*
1874	Hardy, *Far from the Madding Crowd* Trollope, *The Way We Live Now* (–75) First Impressionist Exhibition in Paris Modern bicycle introduced	Disraeli Prime Minister; Factory Act restricts working week to 56½ hours
1875	Trollope, *The Prime Minister*	Britain buys Suez Canal shares
1876	Eliot, *Daniel Deronda* Mark Twain, *Tom Sawyer* Spencer, *Principles of Sociology* Invention of telephone	Queen Victoria Empress of India; Battle of Little Bighorn and death of General Custer
1877		Transvaal annexed by Britain
1878	Hardy, *The Return of the Native* Henry James, *The Europeans*	Foundation of Salvation Army; Irish Land League formed (Parnell)
1879	George Meredith, *The Egoist* Dostoevsky, *The Brothers Karamazov*	Somerville College and Lady Margaret Hall for women founded at Oxford; Zulu Wars in South Africa
1880	Death of George Eliot George Gissing, *Workers in the Dawn* Hardy, *The Trumpet-Major* Zola, *Le Roman expérimental*; *Nana*	Gladstone Prime Minister; women admitted to degrees at London University; compulsory elementary education; Boer uprising in Transvaal
1881	Gilbert and Sullivan, *Patience* Ibsen, *Ghosts* James, *Portrait of a Lady*	Irish Land Act; Social Democratic Federation founded; US President Garfield murdered
1882	Deaths of Darwin and Trollope Maupassant, *Une Vie* R. L. Stevenson, *Treasure Island*	Phoenix Park Murders, Dublin; Married Women's Property Act;
1883	Moore, *A Modern Lover* Nietzsche, *Also sprach Zarathustra* Trollope, *Autobiography*	Fabian Society founded; death of Marx

Year	*Age*	*Life*
1884–5	17–18	Student at night-school in Wedgwood Institute, Burslem
1885	18	Passes London University matriculation examination
1887–8	20–21	Twice fails legal examinations; begins to write for the *Staffordshire Knot*
1889	22	Moves to London; works as solicitor's shorthand clerk

Year	*Arts, Science and Technology*	*History and Politics*
1884	Gissing, *The Unclassed* Work begins on *Oxford English Dictionary* (completed 1928) Twain, *Huckleberry Finn*	National Socialist League founded; Third Reform Bill extends vote to country householders
1885	Rider Haggard, *King Solomon's Mines* Moore, *A Mummer's Wife* Stephen (ed.), *Dictionary of National Biography* (vol. 1) Zola, *Germinal*	Salisbury (Conservative) Prime Minister; fall of Khartoum: death of General Gordon
1886	Rider Haggard, *She* Hardy, *The Mayor of Casterbridge* James, *The Bostonians* Kipling, *Departmental Ditties* Stevenson, *Dr Jekyll and Mr Hyde*	Irish Home Rule crisis; (February) Gladstone Prime Minister; (August) Salisbury Prime Minister
1887	Conan Doyle, *A Study in Scarlet* Hardy, *The Woodlanders* Rutherford, *Revolution in Tanner's Lane* Strindberg, *Miss Julie*	Queen Victoria's Golden Jubilee; Independent Labour Party founded; 'Bloody Sunday' – three killed at peaceful demonstration of unemployed in Trafalgar Square
1888	Death of Matthew Arnold; Arnold, *Essays in Criticism*, 2 Kipling, *Plain Tales from the Hills*	County Councils established
1889	Death of Browning Charles Booth, *Life and Labour of the People in London* Gissing, *The Nether World* Shaw, *Fabian Essays*	London dock strike
1890	William Booth, *In Darkest England* Ibsen, *Hedda Gabler* Morris, *News from Nowhere* Stanley, *In Darkest Africa* First underground railways in London	Beginnings of municipal housing; Parnell disgraced after O'Shea divorce

Year	*Age*	*Life*
1891	24	Lives in Knightsbridge and Victoria, then lodges with Frederick Marriott in Chelsea; first piece in *Tit-Bits*
1893	26	Gives up working in solicitor's office
1894	27	Becomes Assistant Editor of *Woman*
1895	28	'A Letter Home' in *The Yellow Book*
1895–6	28–9	Writes *A Man from the North*; becomes Editor of *Woman*
1897	30	First visit to Paris
1898	31	Moves to Fulham; *A Man from the North*; *Journalism for Women*; first signed article in the *Academy*; decides to live by writing fiction and begins a sensational novel (*The Ghost*); rents a house in Witley, Surrey for country weekends
1899	32	*Polite Farces*, three one-act plays

Year	*Arts, Science and Technology*	*History and Politics*
1891	Gissing, *New Grub Street* Hardy, *Tess of the D'Urbervilles* Shaw, *The Quintessence of Ibsenism* Wilde, *The Picture of Dorian Gray*	Elementary schooling free; Yeats founds National Literary Society; International Copyright Act
1892	Ibsen, *The Master Builder* Kipling, *Barrack-Room Ballads* Shaw, *Widowers' Houses* Diesel's internal combustion engine	Gladstone Prime Minister; Keir Hardie first Independent Labour Party MP
1893	Gissing, *The Odd Women*	Gladstone's Irish Home Rule Bill defeated
1894	Moore, *Esther Waters* Shaw, *Arms and the Man* Wilde, *Salome* *The Yellow Book* Henry Ford's first motor car constructed	Rosebery (Liberal) Prime Minister
1895	Joseph Conrad, *Almayer's Folly* Hardy, *Jude the Obscure* H. G. Wells, *The Time Machine* Wilde, *The Importance of Being Earnest* Marconi's wireless telegraph	London School of Economics founded; Jameson Raid, South Africa
1896	Chekhov, *The Seagull*	Nobel Prizes instituted
1897	Conrad, *The Nigger of the 'Narcissus'* Shaw, *Candida*	Queen Victoria's Diamond Jubilee; Indian revolt on north-west frontier
1898	Hardy, *Wessex Poems* James, *The Turn of the Screw* Shaw, *Plays Pleasant and Unpleasant* Wells, *The War of the Worlds* Curies discover radium	Death of Gladstone
1899	James, *The Awkward Age*	Boer War begins

Year	*Age*	*Life*
1900–1	33	Becomes Pearson's literary adviser; resigns as Editor of *Woman*; moves to Bedfordshire
1901	34	*Fame and Fiction*; appoints J. B. Pinker as his literary agent
1902	35	Death of his father; *The Grand Babylon Hotel*; *Anna of the Five Towns*; begins weekly series, the *Savoir Faire Papers*, in *T. P.'s Weekly*; gives up reviewing for *Academy*
1903	36	Moves to Paris; lives in France until 1912, with frequent visits to England; *The Gates of Wrath*; *The Truth About an Author* (anonymously); *How to Become an Author*; *Leonora*; new series of essays in *T. P.'s Weekly*, *A Novelist's Log-Book*; forms idea for *The Old Wives' Tale*
1904	37	*A Great Man*; *Teresa of Watling Street*
1905	38	*Tales of the Five Towns*; *The Loot of Cities* (short stories); *Sacred and Profane Love*; begins *Savoir Vivre Papers* in *T. P.'s Weekly*
1906	39	Briefly engaged to Eleanor Green; *Hugo*; *Whom God Hath Joined*; *The Sinews of War* (with Eden Phillpotts); *Things That Interested Me* (privately published journal extracts)

Year	*Arts, Science and Technology*	*History and Politics*
1900	Deaths of Nietzsche, Ruskin and Wilde Conrad, *Lord Jim* Freud, *Interpretation of Dreams* Planck's quantum theory	Reliefs of Mafeking and Ladysmith; British Labour Party founded; Commonwealth of Australia founded
1901	Chekhov, *Three Sisters* James, *The Sacred Fount* Kipling, *Kim* Thomas Mann, *Buddenbrooks*	Death of Queen Victoria and accession of Edward VII; US President McKinley assassinated
1892	Death of Zola Conrad, *Heart of Darkness* Henry James, *The Wings of the Dove* William James, *The Varieties of Religious Experience*	Boer War ends; Education Act – secondary schools established in England and Wales; Balfour (Conservative) Prime Minister; Sinn Fein founded
1903	Death of Gissing Butler, *The Way of All Flesh* James, *The Ambassadors* Shaw, *Man and Superman* Wright brothers' first flight	*Daily Mirror* launched; Emmeline Pankhurst founds Women's Social and Political Union; split between Bolsheviks and Mensheviks in Russia; Lenin becomes leader of Bolsheviks
1904	J. M. Barrie, *Peter Pan* Chekhov, *The Cherry Orchard* Conrad, *Nostromo* Freud, *Psychopathology of Everyday Life* James, *The Golden Bowl*	Franco-British *entente cordiale*; Russo-Japanese War breaks out
1905	E. M. Forster, *Where Angels Fear to Tread* Shaw, *Major Barbara* Wells, *A Modern Utopia*; *Kipps* Wilde, *De Profundis* Einstein's special theory of relativity	Abortive revolution in Russia; Japan defeats Russia
1906	Galsworthy, *The Man of Property* Years, *Poetical Works*	Campbell-Bannerman (Liberal) Prime Minister; Labour Party wins 54 seats in election

Year	*Age*	*Life*
1907	40	Meets (in January) and marries (in July) Marguerite Soulie; *The Ghost*; *The Reasonable Life*; *The Grim Smile of the Five Towns*; *The City of Pleasure*; *Things Which Have Interested Me, Second Series* (privately); begins *The Old Wives' Tale* (finished August 1908).
1908	41	In spring, moves to villa near Fontainebleau; *Cupid and Commonsense* (dramatization of *Anna of the Five Towns*) at Shaftesbury Theatre; *The Statue*; *Buried Alive*; *How to Live on Twenty-Four Hours a Day*; *The Old Wives' Tale*; *The Human Machine*; *Things Which Have Interested Me*, *Third Series* (privately); as 'Jacob Tonson' begins series 'Books and Persons' in *New Age*
1909	42	*What the Public Wants* at the Aldwych and Royalty Theatres; *Literary Taste*; *The Glimpse*
1910	43	Lives in Brighton from January to March and begins *Clayhanger* (finished in June, published in October); spends two months in Switzerland and Italy and six weeks in Brittany before taking flat in Paris; *Helen with the High Hand*
1911	44	*The Card*; *Hilda Lessways*; *The Feast of St Friend* (pocket philosophy); gives up villa near Fontainebleau; *The Honeymoon* at the Royalty Theatre; spends six weeks in America and at end of year four months in Cannes
1912	45	*Milestones* (with Edward Knoblock) at Royalty Theatre; runs for over 600 performances; returns to live permanently in England, first in Brighton, then Putney; *The Matador of the Five Towns*; *Those United States* (travel sketches); buys yacht, *Velsa*
1913	46	Moves to Comarques, Thorpe-le-Soken, Essex; *The Great Adventure* (dramatization of *Buried Alive*) begins long run at Kingsway Theatre; *The Regent*; *The Plain Man and His Wife* (pocket philosophy); *Paris Nights* (travel sketches)

Year	Arts, Science and Technology	History and Politics
1907	Kipling wins Nobel Prize Cubist Exhibition, Paris Conrad, *The Secret Agent* Forster, *The Longest Journey* Synge, *Playboy of the Western World*	Defeat of Labour's bill to give women the vote
1908	Forster, *A Room with a View*	Asquith (Liberal) Prime Minister
1909	Death of Meredith Wells, *Tono-Bungay* Diaghilev's Russian ballet visits Paris	Old age pensions introduced for those over seventy
1910	Death of Tolstoy Forster, *Howards End* Wells, *The History of Mr Polly* First Post-Impressionist Exhibition, London	Death of Edward VII; accession of George V
1911	Copyright extended to fifty years after author's death Conrad, *Under Western Eyes* D. H. Lawrence, *The White Peacock* Rutherford's theory of the atom	Lloyd George's National Insurance Bill; Suffragette riots in London
1912	Jung, *Theory of Psychoanalysis* Lawrence, *The Trespasser* Futurist Exhibition in Paris	Women's Franchise Bill rejected by Commons; sinking of *Titanic*
1913	Lawrence, *Sons and Lovers* Proust, *Du côté de chez Swann* Mann, *Death in Venice* Einstein's general theory of relativity First Morris Oxford car	War in Balkans; Irish Home Rule Bill passed by Commons but rejected by Lords; Panama Canal opens

Year	*Age*	*Life*
1914	47	Dramatization (by Richard Pryce) of *Helen with the High Hand* at Vaudeville Theatre; sails for two months near France and Italy; begins political articles for *Daily News*; death of mother; *The Price of Love and Liberty!* (essays); *From the Log of the 'Velsa'* (in United States; England 1920).
1915	48	Begins war work and tours the battle front; becomes a director of the *New Statesman*; *The Author's Craft*; *These Twain* (in United States; in England 1916); *Over There* (war reporting); film of *The Great Adventure* shown
1916	49	Adopts his nephew Richard Bennett as his son; *The Lion's Share*; starts anonymous series of 'Observations' in *New Statesman*
1917	50	Living mainly in London; *Books and Persons*
1918	51	Becomes Director of British Propaganda in France and then Director of Propaganda at the Ministry of Information; *The Pretty Lady*; *Self and Self-Management*; starts series of articles in *Lloyd's Weekly Newspaper*; *The Title* at Royalty Theatre
1919	52	Publishes *The Roll-Call*; *Judith* and *Sacred and Profane Love* at Kingsway and Aldwych Theatres
1920	53	Adaptation of *The Beggar's Opera* begins three-year run at Lyric Theatre, Hammersmith; buys new yacht, the *Marie Marguerite*; *Our Women* (essays)

Year	Arts, Science and Technology	History and Politics
1914	Conrad, *Chance* Joyce, *Dubliners* Lawrence, *The Prussian Officer*	Assassination of Archduke Ferdinand and outbreak of First World War
1915	Death of Rupert Brooke Conrad, *Victory* Ford Madox Ford, *The Good Soldier* Lawrence, *The Rainbow* Somerset Maugham, *Of Human Bondage* Richardson, *Pilgrimage* Virginia Woolf, *The Voyage Out*	Failure of Gallipoli campaign; sinking of *Lusitania*; Zeppelins bomb London; Coalition Government formed
1916	Death of Henry James Joyce, *Portrait of the Artist as a Young Man*	Battles of Verdun and Jutland; Easter Rising in Dublin; Lloyd George Prime Minister
1917	T. S. Eliot, *Prufrock* Freud, *Introduction to Psychoanalysis*	United States enters war; battle of Ypres; revolution in Russia, followed by civil war
1918	Lytton Strachey, *Eminent Victorians* Wilfred Owen killed Rutherford splits the atom	First World War ends; vote granted to women in England over thirty and men over twenty-one; first woman MP elected to Parliament
1919	Hardy, *Collected Poems* Keynes, *Economic Consequences of the Peace* Shaw, *Heartbreak House* Woolf, *Night and Day* First transatlantic flight	Treaty of Versailles
1920	F. Scott Fitzgerald, *This Side of Paradise* Jung, *Psychological Types* Lawrence, *The Lost Girl* Weston, *From Ritual to Romance* Edith Wharton, *The Age of Innocence*	League of Nations established

Year	*Age*	*Life*
1921	54	*Things That Have Interested Me* (essays); spends much of summer sailing off the French and English coasts; begins to write articles on theatre for the *Daily Express*; formal separation from his wife
1922	55	Meets Dorothy Cheston; film versions of *The Old Wives' Tale* and *The Card* screened; *The Love Match* and *Body and Soul* at the Strand Theatre and the Euston Theatre of Varieties; *Mr Prohack*; *Lilian*; begins series of articles (for next year) in *John Bull*; begins work on *Riceyman Steps*; moves to Cadogan Square, London
1923	56	*Things That Have Interested Me, Second Series*; *How to Make the Best of Life*; *Riceyman Steps*; *Don Juan* (play); spends most of summer sailing near England and the Continent
1924	57	*London Life* (with Edward Knoblock) at Drury Lane; *Elsie and the Child* (stories); begins series of articles in *Sunday Pictorial*; again spends summer sailing
1925	58	Production of *The Bright Island* by the Stage Society
1926	59	Daughter Virginia (by Dorothy Cheston) born; *Things That Have Interested Me, Third Series*; *Lord Raingo*; from now until his death writes 'Books and Persons' essays in *Evening Standard*; *Riceyman Steps* (dramatized by Michael Morton) at Ambassadors Theatre
1927	60	Spends much of first half of year in continental Europe; *The Woman Who Stole Everything* (stories); *The Vanguard* (in United States; in England as *The Strange Vanguard*, 1928); *Flora* at Rusholme Theatre, Manchester and *Mr Prohack* (with Edward Knoblock) at Court Theatre

Year	*Arts, Science and Technology*	*History and Politics*
1921	Aldous Huxley, *Chrome Yellow* Lawrence, *Women in Love*	Red Army wins Russian civil war
1922	Death of Proust Eliot, *The Waste Land* Joyce, *Ulysses* Lawrence, *Aaron's Rod* Woolf, *Jacob's Room* BBC makes first broadcasts	Bonar Law (Conservative) Prime Minister; Irish Free State established; civil war in Ireland; Mussolini marches on Rome and establishes dictatorship
1923	Yeats wins Nobel Prize Lawrence, *Kangaroo*	Hitler's failed Nazi coup in Munich; Baldwin (Conservative) Prime Minister; women granted equality in divorce proceedings
1924	Deaths of Conrad and Kafka Forster, *A Passage to India* Mann, *The Magic Mountain*	First (minority) Labour government: Ramsay MacDonald Prime Minister; (November) Baldwin Prime Minister; death of Lenin; Stalin comes to power
1925	Shaw wins Nobel Prize Eisenstein, *Battleship Potemkin* Scott Fitzgerald, *The Great Gatsby* Kafka, *The Trial* Woolf, *Mrs Dalloway* J. L. Baird experiments with TV	Hitler, *Mein Kampf*; British Unemployment Insurance Act
1926	Lang, *Metropolis* William Faulkner, *Soldier's Pay* Kafka, *The Castle* Lawrence, *The Plumed Serpent* T. E. Lawrence, *The Seven Pillars of Wisdom*	Withdrawal of British troops from the Rhineland; General Strike in Britain; British Commonwealth established
1927	Forster, *Aspects of the Novel* Last part of Proust, *A la recherche du temps perdu* published Woolf, *To the Lighthouse* First talking film Lindbergh's solo Atlantic flight	Trotsky expelled from the Communist Party

Year	*Age*	*Life*
1928	61	*The Savour of Life* (essays); *Mediterranean Scenes* (travel sketches); *The Return Journey* at the St James's Theatre
1929	62	*The Religious Interregnum* (essay); *Piccadilly* (film story); *Judith* (opera libretto with music by Eugene Goossens) at Covent Garden; visits Russia with Max Beaverbrook
1930	63	*Journal, 1929*; *Imperial Palace*; begins *Dream of Destiny* (unfinished); moves to Chiltern Court, Baker Street
1931	63	In January contracts typhoid fever in France; dies at Chiltern Court on 27 March

Year	*Arts, Science and Technology*	*History and Politics*
1928	Death of Hardy Eisenstein, *October* Huxley, *Point Counter Point* Lawrence, *Lady Chatterley's Lover* Evelyn Waugh, *Decline and Fall*	Voting age for women in England lowered to twenty-one
1929	Mann wins Nobel Prize Faulkner, *The Sound and the Fury* Robert Graves, *Goodbye to All That* Ernest Hemingway, *A Farewell to Arms* Woolf, *A Room of One's Own*	Collapse of New York Stock Exchange (Wall Street crash); minority Labour government (MacDonald Prime Minister); Nazis win Bavarian elections
1930	Death of Lawrence W. H. Auden, *Poems* Freud, *Civilisation and its Discontents* Lawrence, *The Virgin and the Gipsy* Waugh, *Vile Bodies*	End of allied occupation of Germany; Nazi gains in German general election; Mosley forms New Party; MacDonald forms National Government; Gandhi begins campaign of civil disobedience
1931	Ivy Compton-Burnett, *Men and Wives* Faulkner, *Sanctuary* Anthony Powell, *Afternoon Men* Woolf, *The Waves*	Financial crisis in Britain; unemployment reaches 2.8 million; Means test introduced; National Governments (MacDonald Prime Minister) elected in August and November; Britain leaves Gold Standard; Japan invades Manchuria

CHRONOLOGY OF THE COMPOSITION AND PUBLICATION OF *ANNA OF THE FIVE TOWNS*

The information set out here is drawn from Bennett's letters and journals, the relevant volumes of which are abbreviated as *L*i, *L*ii and *J*i (see Suggestions for Further Reading for publication details). Arnold Bennett is referred to as AB.

18 February 1896	hopes to begin his second novel ('*moeurs de province* [provincial manners], it will be, utterly unliterary') 'next October' (*L*ii 36)
16 March 1896	'I am positively anxious to begin the new novel, which will have some such title as *The Strange Woman* (being a study of a *femme incomprise* [misunderstood or unappreciated woman] whom I know well)' (*L*ii 39).
August–early September 1896	visits Belgium with James Brown and describes to him plot and some of characters of next novel
28 September 1896	has been gathering material while in Potteries; title 'Sis Marigold' (*L*ii 63)
29 September 1896	writes 200 words; main outline settled; uses 'old sketch'; 'I had done enough to reassure myself' (*J*i 15–16)
21 October 1896	'I have written 2 chapters once & one twice, & the third and fourth are forming themselves, & the 7th is quite formed.' Having problems with tone and point of view (*L*ii 66)
18 November 1896	'temporarily at a standstill' (*L*ii 69)
12 January 1897	'I took up my neglected novel "Sis Tellwright", and sketched out a chapter, with difficulty re-creating the atmosphere. The portions already drafted seemed good, more than satisfactory as the result of the "first process" in the manufacture of my fiction' (*J*i 29).

30 January 1897	writes 2,300 words; 'began actually to have a dim vision of some of the characters – at last' (*J*i 31)
31 January 1897	'it hasn't seriously been touched this year . . . henceforward to be known as *Anna Tellwright*' (*L*ii 75)
8 February 1897	drafts 1,500 words (Chapter 8), making 7,000 words (35 pages) altogether; 'I have lifted the thing up to a certain height, whence it can't possibly fall down' (*L*ii 79)
21 March 1897	bicycle accident; *Anna* abandoned (*J*i 36)
10 October 1897	tells H. G. Wells that he's trying to 'shove . . . notions' about 'the romance of manufacture' into his next novel (*L*ii 90)
6 December 1897	wants to get on with 'my Staffordshire novel, treating it in the Conrad manner' (*J*i 64)
23 January 1898	returns to 'serious fiction', 'after an interval of about nine months' (*J*i 70)
28 March 1898	hopes to start again 'after Easter' (*L*ii 107)
by 18 April 1898	fails to return to novel (*J*i 76)
12 September 1898	'Anna Tellwright' 'with which I have made some progress' is 'put aside indefinitely' in favour of popular fiction (*J*i 80)
5 January 1899	'I am dying to get on with my Staffs novel . . . I could write that novel in six months' (*L*ii 116)
24 January 1899	'two short sensational stories – and then to my big novel' (*J*i 87)
7 February 1899	'on Thursday' (i.e. 9 February) will read through what he has written 'and see if I feel drawn to it' (*L*ii 119)
29 March 1899	'I have finished the draft of my Staffordshire novel.' Plans to return to it after Whitsuntide and rewrite it in six months (*L*ii 121)
by Easter 1899	draft finished 'just before Easter', written at rate of 8,000–10,000 words per week (*J*i 91)
Easter 1899	(Easter Day 2 April) in Potteries, collecting further material

after Easter 1899	has to resist temptation to begin at once on next version (*J*i 91)
6 July 1899	hopes to return to 'serious novel' in October (*L*ii 123)
18 October 1899	'I hope to devote at least three whole days a week to "Anna Tellwright"' (*J*i 95)
6–7 November 1899	reading through draft; needs much work (*J*i 98)
7 November 1899	fails to make start on rewriting (*J*i 99)
9–10 November 1899	decides on opening sentence and arrangement of first paragraph (material eventually used in Chapter 7) (*J*i 99)
16 November 1899	'. . . to-night . . . I made the first real start on the final writing of "Anna Tellwright". I worked from 5 to 12 p.m. and wrote 1,000 words, first-rate stuff' (*J*i 100)
by 31 December 1899	'the whole draft (80,000 words) of my Staffordshire novel "Anna Tellwright"' (*J*i 101)
13 February 1900	'My novel, I grieve to say, has been laid aside, but I am at it again now' (*L*ii 130)
by 1 January 1901	records that in 1900 he wrote 'the draft of my Staffordshire novel, "Anna Tellwright". 80,000 words, and part of the final writing' (*J*i 106)
10 February 1901	restarts *Anna Tellwright*; going smoothly, but may get stuck; hopes to finish by end of April (*L*ii 145)
21 February 1901	'began it fifteen days ago'; has written 16,000 words, 'about one-fifth of the whole'; hopes to finish by 30 April (*L*ii 147)
22 April 1901	writes 1,000 words (*L*ii 150)
23 April 1901	half 'irrevocably complete'; writes 2,500 words; hopes to finish in six weeks (*L*ii 150)
14 May 1901	'the . . . novel of Staffordshire life which I am just finishing' (*L*ii 154)
16–17 May 1901	seventeen hours' continuous work on last 5,000 words; 74,000 in total (*J*i 111)
1 June 1901	H. G. Wells tells AB 'I shall be glad indeed to read that SERIOUS novel'

26 December 1901	novel 'not yet published or announced' (*L*ii 163)
10 March 1902	tells Edward Garnett (who has read and commented on the novel for Duckworths) that he cannot alter the ending; Garnett recommends publication, but AB demands a higher royalty than Duckworths prepared to pay (*L*ii 166)
3 July 1902	McClure to publish novel in United States (*L*i 33)
9 September 1902	H. G. Wells has received his copy of *Anna* and writes to AB about it later the same day
c. 15 September 1902	*Anna of the Five Towns* published in London by Chatto & Windus
15 September 1902	George Sturt writes to AB about *Anna* (*L*ii 171–4)
20 September 1902	responds to H. G. Wells's comments on novel (*L*ii 170–1)
4 October 1902	responds to Sturt's comments on *Anna* (*L*ii 174–5)
9 May 1903	plans for French translation (*L*i 37)
1903	McClure Phillips publishes *Anna* in United States
by 8 April 1904	sells French translation to *Le Temps* (*L*i 46)

INTRODUCTION

'By the way', Bennett wrote to his friend and fellow-novelist George Sturt on 18 February 1896, 'I know a good lot about my second novel already – *moeurs de province* it will be, utterly uniliterary' (*L*ii 36).[1] In September of the same year Bennett told Sturt that on a recent visit to Staffordshire he had gathered 'good stuff about my native heath' (*L*ii 63). A day later, on 29 September, he noted in his journal that the novel would be 'a study of parental authority' (*J*i 15). Thus we can see Bennett establishing a style, a setting and a subject matter for the novel which was to become *Anna of the Five Towns*. And in describing or defining *Anna*, Bennett was also defining the kind of novelist he hoped to become.

Bennett's progress towards a settled vision of his material and his treatment of it was not, however, to be straightforward or rapid. Six and a half years passed between his first mention of the novel and its publication (see Chronology, pp. xxviii–xxxi). For Bennett, this was an unusually protracted period of gestation and composition, involving several false starts and much hesitation and indecision. To some extent the delay was caused by practical considerations. Bennett felt that, in order to give his literary career a firm foundation, he needed to write popular novels and non-fiction books and to undertake a good deal of journalism and occasional writing. This would keep him in the public eye and ensure a regular income. But where *Anna* was concerned, his failure to complete the novel in good time has other causes, which relate to Bennett's developing sense of the kind of writer – or writers – he hoped to become. He felt it both necessary and possible to maintain a distinction between fiction that was popular and pot-boiling and something altogether more serious. From its very inception, he firmly placed *Anna* in the latter category.

Indeed, as his work on the novel progressed, he came to regard it more seriously and think of it as carrying considerable weight in determining his distinctive subject-matter, setting and manner of writing. On 8 February 1897 he told Sturt that he knew he lacked the 'creative impulse necessary for a big theme, but I fancy I can, by sheer force of concentration & monotony do something effective in a small way' (*L*ii 77). This is entirely in keeping with his earlier description of the novel as '*moeurs de province* . . . utterly uniliterary'. In subject matter it will be something on the lines of Balzac's *Eugénie Grandet* (1834), which Bennett admired and to which *Anna* clearly owes a good deal.[2] In calling the novel 'utterly unliterary' Bennett does not mean that he believes stylistic or aesthetic considerations to be unimportant, but that he is aiming for a degree of restraint and distance, so that the novel may not conform to prevailing expectations about action and emotions. By October 1897, however, this view was partly modified and Bennett told H. G. Wells that his view of the Staffordshire landscape needed treating 'on a Zolaesque scale' (*L*ii 90). During 1898 and 1899 he more than once calls *Anna* 'my serious novel', and by January 1899 is able to tell Sturt that it has 'lately in my mind . . . assumed a larger & more epical aspect' (*L*ii 116). In his journal later that month it is simply 'my big novel' (24 January 1896; *J*i 87), and in the final stages of composition it becomes 'my serious Staffordshire novel' (21 February 1901; *L*ii 147). What is clear is that Bennett had a good deal invested in *Anna*, not only in terms of time, research and anxiety, but also in developing his own confidence in what he could achieve as a novelist.

It is also important that Bennett calls *Anna* his 'Staffordshire novel', a description that signals his occupation of what he increasingly regarded as his rightful literary territory. Bennett had come to believe that the Potteries offered an apt setting and subject-matter for fiction; further, that he could become *the* novelist of the Five Towns; and that, in aesthetic terms, he had a mission to reveal to readers aspects of the industrial landscape that had been neglected by previous writers. This 'discovery' of the Five Towns took place over a number of years, and is related to Bennett's developing ideas about the role and function of the artist.[3] In his first novel, *A Man from the North* (published in 1898 but completed by May 1896), the central character, Richard Larch, who has escaped from the Potteries to pursue a literary career in London, becomes aware of a special quality in a London suburb: 'It seemed to him that the latent poetry of the suburbs arose like a beautiful vapour and filled these monotonous and squalid vistas with the scent and colour of violets, leaving nothing common, nothing ignoble'.[4] Beauty, Bennett was to argue over the next few years, may be discovered in the most apparently unpromising locations, and can be released by the artist's powers of perception and imagination.

Such insights seem to have been intensified and given specific reference to the Potteries in September 1897, when Bennett returned to Burslem on receiving news that his sister's fiancé had drowned:

> During this week ... the grim and original beauty of certain aspects of the Potteries ... has fully revealed itself for the first time. ... It is *not* beautiful in detail, but the smoke transforms its ugliness into a beauty transcending the work of architects and of time. ... it thrills and reverberates with the romance of machinery and manufacture ... (*J*i 46–7).[5]

Clearly, the views he saw on this visit were a kind of revelation, as is confirmed by his letter to H.G. Wells of 10 October 1897:

> I am very glad ... to find that the Potteries made such an impression on you. ... only during the last few years have I begun to see its possibilities. Particularly this year I have [been] deeply impressed by it. It seems to me that there are immense possibilities in the very romance of manufacture. ... I am quite sure there is an aspect of these industrial districts which is really *grandiose*, full of dark splendours, & which has been absolutely missed by all novelists up to date (*L*ii 90–1).[6]

Bennett's use of the word 'romance' is significant; by it he means something stern and grand, almost sublime, transcending the appreciation of natural 'beauty' and related to the struggle between humanity and the rest of the natural world. And discovering that romance, that dimension of beauty, is for Bennett a central function of the artist. 'To find beauty, which is always hidden', he was to write in January 1899, 'that is the aim. ... All ugliness has an aspect of beauty. The business of the artist is to find that aspect' (*J*i 84–5).

Bennett's motives in adopting the Potteries as a literary subject are not, however, simply philosophical or aesthetic; they also relate to the development of his literary career. When Bennett writes of Burslem that he 'sort of synthesised the entire place, imprisoned it in one comprehensive impression' (*L*ii 63) he is, in part, referring to an act of colonization, by means of which he established his proprietorial rights to a literary territory, much as Hardy had staked his claim to Wessex. Bennett's admiration for the shrewd manner in which his friend and collaborator Eden Phillpotts managed his literary career was in part based on his awareness of how effectively Phillpotts had exploited Dartmoor as a setting for his fiction. Bennett was also conscious of rival claimants to the Potteries and while writing *Anna* he read and commented on a number of fictional works set in the area.[7]

Bennett's comprehensive and comprehending vision appears early in the novel, when Anna, Agnes and Henry Mynors survey the landscape from Bursley's new park: a view which Bennett invites his readers to share and understand: 'Look down into the valley from this terrace-height . . . embrace the whole smoke-girt amphitheatre in a glance, and it may be that you will suddenly comprehend the secret and superb significance of the vast Doing which goes forward below' (pp. 13–14). Bennett here brings into a single perspective his sense of the simultaneous grandeur and destructiveness of large-scale manufacture. This perspective is also present in what seems to have been the first fruit of Bennett's enlarged vision, his essay 'The Potteries: A Sketch', published in March 1898 and reprinted in this volume (see pp. 200–202). A few days after its publication, Bennett told George Sturt, 'I deem it the best prose I have done' (15 March 1898; *L*i 106). In both wording and outlook the essay is closely related to the passage in *Anna*. In the 'Sketch', however, the final image of a landscape ringed by furnaces that seem to signal to one another across a valley filled with 'acres of burning ironstone' suggests a victory for industry. This sentence is removed to another context in the novel (see pp. 57, 176) and the description in Chapter 1 ends with the image of sooty sheaves which, while it may not suggest a victory for nature, at least indicates its fragile survival in the face of the worst that humanity can do.

The tone of both passages shows how distant Bennett is from that vein of English anti-industrial writing that runs through Blake, Wordsworth, Ruskin, Morris and Lawrence. In an essay written in 1910 Bennett said of Ruskin that he 'gorgeously inveighed against the spectacular horrors of industrialism. But he would probably have been very cross if he had to drink his tea out of the hollow of his hand, in default of a cup'.[8] Lawrence's description in Chapter 12 of *The Rainbow* (1915) of the new coal-mining town of Wiggiston rests on no such paradoxical yet comfortable and mutedly elegiac image as 'sooty sheaves'. Rather, Lawrence finds in the mechanical nature of the industrial world a quality which penetrates the very being of the workers and reduces them to ghost-like creatures, mere cogs in a machine, identified only in terms of their jobs. He makes no concession to industrialism, or even to the domestic importance of coal. For Ursula Brangwen, through whose consciousness the scene is recorded, the only possible reaction is repugnance, and the only course of action escape. Bennett, however, sees the pottery industry as an example of historical, even evolutionary inevitability: 'The Potteries are the Potteries because on that precise spot of the surface of the British Empire there were deposits of clay and quick-burning coal close to the surface. If this was not an invitation on the part of Nature to make pots, what was it?'[9]

When Bennett began to write *Anna* he was, like his central character and 'like many women, and not a few men, in the Five Towns ... wholly ignorant of the staple manufacture' (p. 38). In the essay 'Clay in the Hands of the Potter' (published in 1913 and reprinted in this volume) Bennett wrote about the research he undertook to repair his own ignorance and, in a muted way, Anna makes a similar journey of discovery. In Chapter 6 she looks out of her bedroom window:

> The entire landscape was illuminated and transformed by [the] unique pyrotechnics of labour atoning for its grime, and dull, weird sounds, as of the breathings and sighings of gigantic nocturnal creatures, filled the enchanted air. It was a romantic scene, a romantic summer night, balmy, delicate, and wrapped in meditation. *But Anna saw nothing there save the repulsive evidences of manufacture, had never seen anything else* (p. 57; my italics).

Here there is a gap between the perceptions of the author and those of his character – and the gap is important because of the novel's title. Anna is *of* the Five Towns yet she is remote from and ignorant of its principal industry (which, ultimately, is the source of her own large fortune), and blind to the evidence of beauty and grandeur around her. Anna and the author look at the same landscape, but they see different things.

This theme is further developed later in the novel, when Anna visits Mynors' works. Bennett writes of the supremacy and antiquity of the potter's craft as part of 'the secret nature of things'. Clay becomes the element of the workers' lives: they touch it, inhale it and their skin is coloured by it; some, like the paintresses, are killed by it. As Anna moves through the factory, witnessing the progress from raw clay to finished product, she is 'awed by the sensation of being surrounded by terrific forces always straining for release' and aware that her presence makes little difference to men and women caught up in 'mad creative passion' (pp. 97–8). At the climax of the passage she comes close to the heart of these processes when, challenged by a worker who is emptying a cooling kiln, she steps inside:

> A blasting heat seemed to assault her on every side, driving her back; it was incredible that any human being could support such a temperature.
>
> 'There!' said the jovial man, apparently summing her up with his bright, quizzical eyes. 'You know summat as you didn't know afore, miss.' (pp. 100–101).

Yet, although the visit has an impact on Anna, Bennett makes no attempt to develop her character in the light of what she sees at the factory. Her grandmother was a paintress but Anna's wealth places her at a great distance from any industrial process, a distance which will no doubt be increased by her marriage to Mynors: she will never be more than a spectator to industry, and it is impossible to tell whether her brief glimpse of the true heat of manufacture will make any permanent change in her outlook on life.

If clay is one prevailing medium of the novel, the other is money. In terms of action the book begins with Anna's assumption of her inheritance; and in the second half of the novel events are propelled by a forged bill of exchange and an act of embezzlement. In one way or another almost every character is seen in terms of wealth or poverty, getting or spending, generosity or meanness, success or failure in business. They range from Mr Lovat, the bank manager who 'irrigate[s] the whole town with fertilizing gold' (p. 33), to Sarah Vodrey, whose meagre savings, enough to pay for her own funeral, are all she has to show for a lifetime of drudgery.

The 'parental authority' that Bennett insisted on as the theme of the novel is exercised by Ephraim Tellwright, a character largely defined by his tight control over his own and Anna's money. When he comes into conflict with Anna the issue usually concerns the exercise of economic power: Anna's scant and tightly regulated responsibility for the household expenses; Ephraim's insistence that she should demand more money from the Prices; and his sense that her marriage to Henry – satisfactory though it is in many ways – will place her, and her investments, irrevocably beyond his control. Anna's rare acts in defiance of her father also concern money. To Ephraim, even *asking* for money, especially for pleasurable or charitable purposes, constitutes an act of rebellion, which is exacerbated when she insists that she is only asking for what is her own. Anna is thus driven to subterfuge and deceit: she conceals from Ephraim the arrival of a cheque so that she can buy clothes for her holiday on the Isle of Man, and she retrieves and destroys Willie Price's forgery. The latter act enrages Ephraim so much that he punishes and humiliates her in the only way left to him – by passing control of the meagre weekly housekeeping allowance to her younger sister.

Anna's independence and sense of identity are money-related, but in a highly qualified manner. A central symbolic moment occurs when she visits the bank on her twenty-first birthday and has to invent an ordinary signature in order to obtain access to her bank account. But this necessary self-naming, by which she appears to acquire a formal, public identity and status, is already undermined by an incident, equally symbolic and significant, earlier in the day, when Ephraim formally hands her the documents relating to her investments and then immediately takes them back. Towards the end of the novel, when she continues to press Ephraim for some of her money to buy household linen he signifies that he has washed his hands of her financially by angrily surrendering her bank books, thus giving her, for the first time, total control over her property. Within a page of this scene she is telling an avid Henry that she wants him to take charge of her fortune as soon as they are married. In both cases she is willing, even eager, to cede financial control, and with it part of her status and identity, to the men who dominate her life.

Money is also deeply implicated in the novel's religious dimension. Much of the chapel activity has to do with cash: the school-building fund; the bazaar; even the Revival, the account of which ends with a glimpse of the notice 'that cabinet photographs of the revivalist could be purchased on application at one shilling each' (p. 56). Ephraim Tellwright, even at the height of his work for the chapel, was not 'much smitten with either the doctrinal or the spiritual side of Methodism'; rather it is 'in the finance of salvation that he rose supreme' (pp. 20–21). Business and social activities had come to dominate Methodism at the time the novel is set (see Appendix 2), and the Suttons are examples of the kind of Methodists in whom prosperity could sit comfortably with faith. In some respects, however, the 'mysterious begetting of money by money' (p. 89) constitutes an alternative belief system. The bank, 'an opulent and spacious erection which stands commandingly at the top of St Luke's Square', is one of Bursley's most imposing and frightening buildings. Its manager enjoys wide-ranging powers which seem to place him above ordinary mortals:

> By a single negative he could have ruined scores of upright merchants and manufacturers. He had only to stop a man in the street and murmur, 'By the way, your overdraft—,' in order to spread discord and desolation through a refined and pious home. His estimate of human nature was falsified by no common illusions; he had the impassive and frosty gaze of a criminal judge. Many men deemed they had cause to hate him, but no one did hate him: all recognized that he was set far above hatred (p. 33).

Anna's relationship with the Prices confers on her a similar kind of power, about which she is very ambivalent. When Ephraim first tells her the extent of Titus's debt she is deeply shocked by his failure and hypocrisy – 'That he, debtor and promise-breaker, should have the effrontery to pray for the souls of children, to chastise their petty furtive crimes, was nearly incredible' (p. 32) – and she is surprised when Ephraim actually *defends* Titus. Her shock is quickly succeeded by guilt that Titus's problems might have been brought about by the shortcomings of the premises he rents from her. This feeling is confirmed when she visits the Edward Street works the same afternoon, but faced with Titus's combination of defiance and obsequiousness Anna finds in herself unsuspected reserves of strength and obduracy. Yet her determination to make the Prices meet their financial obligations is always mitigated by her maternal and protective feelings towards Willie Price. The increasingly forceful demands that Ephraim insists on are at odds with Anna's attempts, especially after the Revival, to live a more Christ-like life and extend to both Prices (but particularly to Willie) a wider understanding and compassion. This feeling is intensified by her sense of the difference in status and affluence between herself and the Prices: 'Here were she and her father, rich, powerful, autocratic; and there were Willie Price and his father, commercial hares hunted by hounds of creditors, hares that turned in plaintive appeal to those greedy jaws for mercy' (p. 70). After Titus's death, Anna's sympathy for Willie increases, and she finds herself best able to express her feelings through acts of financial generosity: indirectly by destroying the forged bill of exchange and joining with Henry to make good the money embezzled by Titus from the chapel funds; directly by giving him the £100 note. Yet even here the situation is equivocal, for as she hands him the money, they both realize, too late, that they love one another. The novel says little about the motives for Willie's suicide, but it seems clear that financial restitution is not sufficient to allay his sense of shame; indeed, the very source of that restitution may serve only to intensify the shame. And a final irony is that Anna and Henry begin their married life in the Prices' old house. Anna, inexorably rising beyond Willie on the social scale, supplants him even as she succours him.

In a different way, the link between money and sexual feelings is demonstrated by the relationship between Anna and Henry Mynors. The uncertain depth of Henry's feelings for Anna is made an issue early in the novel when Anna herself speculates about how the community will regard them as a couple:

> Many people would say, and more would think, that it was her money which was drawing Mynors from the narrow path of his celibate discretion. She could imagine all the innuendoes, the expressive nods, the pursing of lips, the lifting of shoulders and of eyebrows. 'Money'll do owt'; that was the proverb. But she cared not. She had the just and unshakable self-esteem which is fundamental in all strong and righteous natures; and she knew beyond the possibility of doubt that, though Mynors might have no incurable aversion to a fortune, she herself, the spirit and body of her, had been the sole awakener of his desire (p. 12).

The narrative, however, throws doubt on Anna's certainty. As events turn out, Anna becomes Henry's sleeping partner in a business sense before she does so in a sexual sense, and is thus joined to him in a way that certainly her father and perhaps many other members of her society would regard as more solemn, binding and even mystical than the bond of marriage. Although she is happy at the prospect of her coming marriage, she anticipates more keenly its duties and modest powers (over Agnes's future, for instance) than its joys. Henry's kisses may be passionate, but Anna is coolly aware of and seemingly undeflected by 'her dispassionate frigidity under [his] caresses' (p. 178). When Henry learns the true extent of Anna's fortune we are allowed a rare access to his feelings: he is 'astonished and enraptured beyond measure. . . . The fifty thousand danced a jig in his brain that night' (pp. 192–3). It may be that Anna's 'spirit and . . . body' awaken Henry's desire, but the real nature of that spirit and body in his eyes is by no means certain. And the dutiful but unresponsive surrender of Anna's body to Henry's caresses will be accompanied by the equally important surrender of her cheque book.

Money also plays a part in family relationships, and here the central contrast is between the Tellwrights and the Suttons, the simplicity of the house on Manor Terrace being set against the comfort and materialism of Lansdowne House. For Alderman Sutton and his wife, the material comfort in which they live is the just reward of a life of honest diligence. In Beatrice's willingness to spend her father's money and in her reactions to the comforts that money brings, everything spells excess. In her we see the conspicuous consumption of feelings as well as of the chocolate creams she carries in her pocket; Anna's reaction suggests the contrasting limitation of her own experience:

> 'I simply dote on them. I love to eat them in bed, if I can't sleep.' Beatrice made these statements with her mouth full. 'Don't you adore chocolates?' she added.
>
> 'I don't know,' Anna lamely replied. 'Yes, I like them.' She only adored her sister, and perhaps God; and this was the first time she had tasted chocolate.
>
> 'I couldn't *live* without them,' said Beatrice (pp. 74–5).

Similarly, during the holiday on the Isle of Man, Anna is astonished not only by the amount of money the Suttons spend on food and drink, but also at the ease with which Beatrice and her mother extract money from Alderman Sutton:

> He opened the left-hand front pocket of his trousers – a pocket which fastened with a button; and leaning back in his chair drew out a fat purse, and passed it to his wife with a preoccupied air. She helped herself, and then Beatrice intercepted the purse and lightened it of half a sovereign.
>
> 'Pocket-money,' Beatrice said; 'I'm ruined.'
>
> The Alderman's eyes requested Anna to observe how he was robbed (p. 133).

There is an openness here that is quite foreign to Anna's experience with her father: Alderman Sutton's 'preoccupied air' is in marked contrast to Ephraim Tellwright's fierce attentiveness in financial matters, while his comical complaisance at Beatrice's interception of the purse is quite different to the aggrieved reluctance with which Ephraim surrenders two shillings for the Sunday-school treat.

Anna's trip to the Isle of Man is significant in other ways. At the age of twenty-one, she is enjoying her first holiday, her first taste of economic independence, her longest ever spell of freedom from her father's direct influence. Standing with Henry on the deck of the steamer, she experiences a moment of pure being: 'a feeling of intense, inexplicable joy, a profound satisfaction with the present, and a negligence of past and future. To exist was enough, then' (p. 126). She is entranced with the idea '"of being out of sight of land – nothing but sea"' (p. 127), and is for the first time liberated from the imperatives of family responsibilities and religious and social expectations. The journey finds her free-floating, borne towards 'the island, mysterious, enticing, enchanted . . . a remote entity fraught with strange secrets' (p. 127), which releases her imagination and gives her a sense of power and possibility. She finds herself in a wilder and grander natural landscape than any she has known, and climbing Bradda with Henry she is in a setting where 'to the furthest eternity of civilization more and more intricate, simple, and strong souls would always find solace and repose' (p. 130).

But for Anna the real outcome of her holiday is not a permanent change to her outlook on life: she is no Jane Eyre or Catherine Earnshaw, who finds in her relationship with nature a powerful philosophical and emotional solace; nor can she carry over to her relationship with Ephraim any of the easiness she enjoys with Mr Sutton. In the end what is important for Anna, the Suttons and Henry about the episode on the island is her behaviour during Beatrice's illness, which occurs just as her relationship with Henry is reaching a critical point. When Beatrice is out of danger Anna reflects on the lessons she has learnt from her days in the sick-room: she feels that 'events had lifted her to a higher plane than that of love-making', is 'filled with the proud satisfaction of a duty accomplished' (p. 145), and is glad that she has thus earned the Suttons' gratitude and respect. Yet she is not fully aware of what has happened: 'She was in an extremely nervous and excitable condition. . . . She had not begun to realize the crisis through which she had just lived' (p. 145), and it is while she is in this state that Henry proposes.

The circumstances suggest a release from the usual constraints under which Henry and Anna live: they are at 'the limit of the path' in 'intense gloom' amid 'strange night-noises' in a place where 'the imagination [is] stimulated by the appeal of all this mystery and darkness' and where the sea seems 'wonderful, terrible, and austere' (p. 145). But Anna is conscious that although the setting may be appropriate for Henry's imminent proposal, it has actually been impelled by 'the thought of her vigils, her fortitude, her compassion' (pp. 145–6). The narrative emphasizes her self-knowledge and, above all, her knowledge of Henry: 'The actual question was put in a precise, polite, somewhat conventional tone. To Anna, he was never more himself than at that moment' (p. 146). Even as Henry proposes to her Anna feels he dominates, and her vision of 'her career as his wife' (she knows that she is marrying the rising manufacturer as much as the man), although described as 'her freedom', seems desirable largely because it will offer her the opportunity to 'release Agnes from the more ignominious of her father's tyrannies' (p. 146). Characteristically, she is occupied not with the raptures or even the social standing that marriage might bring her, but with what it will enable her to do for others.

The episode on the Isle of Man is important and revealing for what it tells us about the kind of novel this is and how Bennett conceives of his central character. The title of *Anna of the Five Towns* specifically invites the reader to consider Anna in relation to her environment, and the first description of her suggests that this relationship is problematical:

> It seemed a face for the cloister, austere in contour, fervent in expression, the severity of it mollified by that resigned and spiritual melancholy peculiar to women who through the error of destiny have been born into a wrong environment (p. 8).

Anna is 'of' the Five Towns in that she was born and lives there, yet, this description seems to say, she is not entirely comfortable in her environment, not wholly shaped by its values; she finds herself there 'through the error of destiny'. In this paragraph the novel briefly promises a narrative of a woman's frustration and liberation – attempted or achieved – such as is often found in English fiction of the nineteenth and early twentieth centuries. In Charlotte Brontë's *Jane Eyre* (1847) the heroine defies social expectation and eventually finds happiness in a marriage of both passion and companionship, albeit with a suitably disabled man. In the work of George Eliot, Maggie Tulliver in *The Mill on the Floss* (1860) chafes against the restrictions placed upon women's freedom of movement, while Dorothea Brooke, the heroine of *Middlemarch* (1870–1), finds herself similarly at odds with her environment and seeks a fitting opportunity for intellectual and social action. Maggie is destroyed by her misguided attempts at rebellion and Dorothea's St Theresa-like ambitions are eventually adapted to the non-heroic scale of modern life. Hardy's strong women characters – Eustacia Vye in *The Return of the Native* (1878) or Sue Bridehead in *Jude the Obscure* (1895) – attempt to live beyond the usual codes and are destroyed or cowed into submission.

In a later generation, both rebellion and liberation seem more possible, for the central character of H. G. Wells's *Ann Veronica* (1909) and even more so for Lawrence's women in *The Rainbow* (1915) and *Women in Love* (1920). When Lawrence read *Anna* he was an Englishman in exile, to whom the novel seemed an unwelcome reminder of a culture he had abandoned, for ever as he then thought. Typically, however, he sees Bennett not just in terms of an English hopelessness, but as an exemplar of a larger failure in modern literature, a hateful defeatism which Lawrence's own work was always to challenge:

> I have read *Anna of the Five Towns* today . . . I hate Bennett's resignation. Tragedy ought really to be a great kick at misery. But *Anna of the Five Towns* seems like an acceptance – so does all the modern stuff since Flaubert. I hate it. I want to wash again quick, wash off England, the oldness and the grubbiness and despair.[10]

Lawrence's response to Bennett's novel was to come in 1920 when he published *The Lost Girl*, a novel which shows a young woman from a stifling and potentially destructive environment challenging the values in which she has been brought up and making the crucial break which – though she seems 'lost' to her family and neighbours – enables her to find and maintain her own integrity. Alvina Houghton makes false starts and is more than once drawn back to her home town of Woodhouse before she leaves England with Ciccio, an Italian circus artist. Yet the novel by no means has a happy or settled ending: the final chapter is called 'Suspense', and the last page finds Alvina in a remote and primitive village in Italy, with Ciccio about to depart for the First World War:

> 'I'll come back,' he said.
> 'Sure?' she whispered, straining him to her.[11]

The tension and uncertainty suggested by these closing words and the events that precede them are quite foreign to the world of *Anna of the Five Towns*. Anna's story, by contrast, is one of accommodation and adaptation. She knows that she will never experience religious fervour or sexual ecstasy or even the creative passion of the artist-potter. Furthermore, once she has overcome her anxiety about her lack of deep faith and accepted her sexual indifference towards Henry, she is untroubled by these absences. Anna submits to the demands of duty and the inevitabilities of social mobility, but although she experiences moments of self-doubt and one flash of insight about her feelings for Willie Price, her submission is preceded by no profound rebellion or dreams of departure.

Two of the earliest responses to *Anna* came from H. G. Wells and George Sturt, and they both criticized the book on similar grounds. Wells told Bennett that his general impression was 'that of a photograph a little underdeveloped',[12] while Sturt accused him of being 'unwilling to let the reader be emotional', and went on to complain that the description of Anna's kitchen in Chapter 7 occupies more space than the encounter between Anna and Henry during which it occurs. Therefore 'the reader feels dished, because something must have happened which you have said nothing about'; the scene lacks 'an atmosphere of excitement and thrill and emotion and impending change' (15 September 1902; *L*ii 172–3).

Bennett was stung to an immediate and vigorous defence of his method and showed that he knew very well what he was doing in *Anna of the Five Towns*, telling Sturt that

> [t]he book is impassioned & emotional from beginning to end. Every character ... is handled with intense sympathy. But you have not perceived the emotion. Your note on the description of Anna's dresser is a clear proof of this.... I 'let myself go' to the full extent: but this does not mean that I shout and weep all over the place (*L*i 175).

He also refuted Wells's remark about the underdeveloped photograph, warning him not to mistake a carefully measured degree of literary restraint for lack of feeling: 'I trust you understand that the degree of development to which I have brought the photograph, is what I think the proper degree. It is Turgenev's degree, and Flaubert's. It is *not* Balzac's. Anyhow it is the degree that comes natural to me.'[13] Bennett's achievement in *Anna of the Five Towns* derives precisely from his sense of the 'proper degree' of development for his subject matter. He has a secure knowledge and understanding of the setting in which he places his story. In particular he understands and sympathizes with Anna's situation: how the emotional tenor of her home and the constraints and expectations of the society in which she lives shape her personality. He also understands how Ephraim Tellwright, whose treatment of his daughter contributes to that shaping, is himself the product of a particular history and emotional background: he remembers his own father as 'a grim customer, infinitely more redoubtable than himself' (p. 105). A household tyrant, he creates in Manor Terrace a melancholy atmosphere that affects his spirit whenever he enters the house, and he has 'never known that expansion of the spirit which is called joy' (p. 106). Anna does not inherit the full legacy of her father's narrow joylessness; instead she develops her own kind of integrity and self-esteem, but unlike Lawrence's Alvina she never escapes her environment. Driven by duty and her sense of 'the profound truth that a woman's life is always a renunciation, greater or less', she agrees to marry Henry, even though she knows she does not love him, and faces the future 'calmly and genially' (p. 199). Bennett may not 'shout and weep all over the place', but it is his very restraint, his ability to make us believe that Anna achieves that degree of freedom allowed by her character and circumstance, that makes his story both convincing and moving.

References

1. See Suggestions for Further Reading for full publication details of Bennett's letters and journals, the volumes of which are referred to in the text as *Li*, *Ji*, etc.

2. Louis Tillier, Georges Lafourcade and Margaret Drabble have discussed the relationship between the two novels. See Suggestions for Further Reading for full publication details.

3. For further discussion of this issue, see Peter Preston, '"A grim and original beauty": Arnold Bennett and the Landscape of the Five Towns', *Geography and Literature: a Meeting of the Disciplines*, ed. William E. Mallory and Paul Simpson-Housley (Syracuse, New York: Syracuse University Press, 1987), pp. 31–55, and 'Rediscovered Country: Arnold Bennett and the Five Towns as Literary Subject', *Literature of Region and Nation*, 4 (1), Autumn/Winter 1993: 1–16.

4. *The Man from the North* (London: Methuen, n.d.), p. 106.

5. The journal entry is printed in full on pp. 229–30.

6. A fuller quotation from this letter can be found on p. 230.

7. It was a reading of H. G. Wells's short story 'The Cone' (1895), which is set in the Potteries, that first led Bennett to write to Wells (30 September 1897; *Lii* 89). In his next letter to Wells, Bennett refers to W. N. Tirebuck's novel *Miss Grace of All-Souls* (1895) and *In the Valley of Tophet* (1896), a collection of short stories by Henry W. Nevinson, both set in coal-mining districts (10 October 1897; *Lii* 90–1). In December 1898 he reviewed (*Academy* 17 December) *A Deliverance* by A. N. Monkhouse, which deals with Midlands life. Writing to Monkhouse on 23 December, he told him that George Moore had 'touched the edge' of the 'beauty beneath the squalor & ugliness of these industrial districts' in *A Mummer's Wife* (1885) (*Lii*

114). Bennett also acknowledged Moore's formative influence on his work: 'it was the first chapters of *A Mummer's Wife* which opened my eyes to the romantic nature of the district that I had blindly inhabited for over twenty years. You are indeed the father of all my Five Towns books' (24 December 1920; *L*iii 139).

8. 'The People of the Potteries', *Sketches for Autobiography*, ed. James Hepburn (London: Allen & Unwin, 1979), p. 138.

9. *Ibid.*, p. 136.

10. D. H. Lawrence to Arthur McLeod (4 October 1912), *The Letters of D. H. Lawrence*, vol. I, ed. James T. Boulton (Cambridge: Cambridge University Press, 1979), p. 459. 'Elsa Culverwell', Lawrence's earliest version of the novel that became *The Lost Girl*, was begun and abandoned in December 1912, soon after he read *Anna*. 'The Insurrection of Miss Houghton' was begun in January 1913 and abandoned in March of the same year. He retrieved the manuscript in February 1920 and completed the final version of *The Lost Girl* by May. It was published in November 1920.

11. *The Lost Girl*, ed. John Worthen, with an introduction and notes by Carol Siegel (Harmondsworth: Penguin, 1995), p. 339.

12. *Arnold Bennett and H. G. Wells*, ed. Harris Wilson (London: Rupert Hart-Davis, 1960), p. 86.

13. *Ibid.*, p. 89.

NOTE ON THE TEXTS

Anna of the Five Towns was published in London by Chatto & Windus on about 15 September 1902. An American edition was published by McClure Phillips in 1903. When Chatto & Windus's rights to the novel expired in 1910, they were transferred to Methuen, and the American rights to Doran. Bennett made no changes to the text for subsequent editions by either of these publishers. This edition reproduces the text of the first edition, with some silent alteration of punctuation, according to Everyman house style. Subsequent impressions of that edition introduced a textual error in Chapter 8 (p. 101), which is here corrected (see Notes, p. 222).

'The Potteries: A Sketch' was published in *Black and White* on 12 March 1898. 'Clay in the Hands of the Potter' was published in the American magazine *Youth's Companion* in October 1913 and in England in the *Windsor Magazine* in December 1913. 'My Religious Experience' began publication in the *Evening Standard* on 14 October 1925 and was published in America in the *Century Magazine* in March 1926. It was reprinted in *Things That Have Interested Me, Third Series* (1926).

ANNA OF THE FIVE TOWNS

I DEDICATE THIS BOOK
WITH AFFECTION
AND ADMIRATION
TO
HERBERT SHARPE*
AN ARTIST
WHOSE INDIVIDUALITY
AND ACHIEVEMENT
HAVE CONTINUALLY
INSPIRED ME

'Therefore, although it be a history
Homely and rude, I will relate the same
For the delight of a few natural hearts.'*

CHAPTER ONE

The Kindling of Love

The yard was all silent and empty under the burning afternoon heat, which had made its asphalt springy like turf, when suddenly the children threw themselves out of the great doors at either end of the Sunday-school – boys from the right, girls from the left – in two howling, impetuous streams, that widened, eddied, intermingled, and formed backwaters until the whole quadrangle was full of clamour and movement. Many of the scholars carried prize-books bound in vivid tints,* and proudly exhibited these volumes to their companions and to the teachers, who, tall, languid, and condescending, soon began to appear amid the restless throng. Near the left-hand door a little girl of twelve years, dressed in a cream coloured frock, with a wide and heavy straw hat, stood quietly kicking her foal-like legs against the wall. She was one of those who had won a prize, and once or twice she took the treasure from under her arm to glance at its frontispiece with a vague smile of satisfaction. For a time her bright eyes were fixed expectantly on the doorway; then they would wander, and she started to count the windows of the various Connexional buildings* which on three sides enclosed the yard – chapel, school, lecture-hall, and chapel-keeper's house. Most of the children had already squeezed through the narrow iron gate into the street beyond, where a steam-car was rumbling and clattering up Duck Bank, attended by its immense shadow. The teachers remained a little behind. Gradually dropping the pedagogic pose, and happy in the virtuous sensation of duty accomplished, they forgot the frets and fatigues of the day, and grew amiably vivacious among themselves. With an instinctive mutual complacency the two sexes mixed again after separation. Greetings and pleasantries were exchanged, and intimate conversations begun; and then, dividing into small familiar groups, the young men and women slowly followed their pupils out of the gate. The chapel-keeper,* who always had an injured expression, left the white step of his residence, and, walking with official dignity across the yard, drew down the side-windows of the chapel one after another. As he approached the little solitary girl in his course he gave her a reluctant acid recognition; then he returned to his hearth. Agnes was alone.

'Well, young lady?'

She looked round with a jump, and blushed, smiling and screwing up her little shoulders, when she recognized the two men who were coming towards her from the door of the lecture-hall. The one who had called out was Henry Mynors, morning superintendent of the Sunday-school and conductor of the men's Bible-class* held in the lecture-hall on Sunday afternoons. The other was William Price, usually styled Willie Price, secretary of the same Bible-class, and son of Titus Price, the afternoon superintendent.

'I'm sure you don't deserve that prize. Let me see if it isn't too good for you.' Mynors smiled playfully down upon Agnes Tellwright as he idly turned the leaves of the book which she handed to him. 'Now, do you deserve it? Tell me honestly.'

She scrutinized those sparkling and vehement black eyes with the fearless calm of infancy. 'Yes, I do,' she answered in her high, thin voice, having at length decided within herself that Mr Mynors was joking.

'Then I suppose you must have it,' he admitted, with a fine air of giving way.

As Agnes took the volume from him she thought how perfect a man Mr Mynors was. His eyes, so kind and sincere, and that mysterious, delicious, inexpressible something which dwelt behind his eyes: these constituted an ideal for her.

Willie Price stood somewhat apart, grinning, and pulling a thin honey-coloured moustache. He was at the uncouth, disjointed age, twenty-one, and nine years younger than Henry Mynors. Despite a continual effort after ease of manner, he was often sheepish and self-conscious, even, as now, when he could discover no reason for such a condition of mind. But Agnes liked him too. His simple, pale blue eyes had a wistfulness which made her feel towards him as she felt towards her doll when she happened to find it lying neglected on the floor.

'Your big sister isn't out of school yet?' Mynors remarked.

Agnes shook her head. 'I've been waiting ever so long,' she said plaintively.

At that moment a grey-haired woman with a benevolent but rather pinched face emerged with much briskness from the girls' door. This was Mrs Sutton, a distant relative of Mynors – his mother had been her second cousin. The men raised their hats.

'I've just been down to make sure of some of you slippery folks for the sewing-meeting,'* she said, shaking hands with Mynors, and including both him and Willie Price in an embracing maternal smile. She was short-sighted and did not perceive Agnes, who had fallen back.

'Had a good class this afternoon, Henry?' Mrs Sutton's breathing was short and quick.

'Oh, yes,' he said, 'very good indeed.'

'You're doing a grand work.'

'We had over seventy present,' he added.

'Eh!' she said, 'I make nothing of numbers, Henry. I meant a *good* class. Doesn't it say – Where *two or three* are gathered together . . . ?* But I must be getting on. The horse will be restless. I've to go up to Hillport before tea. Mrs Clayton Vernon is ill.'

Scarcely having stopped in her active course, Mrs Sutton drew the men along with her down the yard, she and Mynors in rapid talk: Willie Price fell a little to the rear, his big hands half-way into his pockets and his eyes diffidently roving. It appeared as though he could not find courage to take a share in the conversation, yet was anxious to convince himself of his right to do so.

Mynors helped Mrs Sutton into her carriage, which had been drawn up outside the gate of the school yard. Only two families of the Bursley Wesleyan Methodists kept a carriage, the Suttons and the Clayton Vernons. The latter, boasting lineage and a large house in the aristocratic suburb of Hillport, gave to the society monetary aid and a gracious condescension. But though indubitably above the operation of any unwritten sumptuary law, even the Clayton Vernons ventured only in wet weather to bring their carriage to chapel. Yet Mrs Sutton, who was a plain woman, might with impunity use her equipage on Sundays. This licence granted by Connexional opinion was due to the fact that she so obviously regarded her carriage, not as a carriage, but as a contrivance on four wheels for enabling an infirm creature to move rapidly from place to place. When she got into it she had exactly the air of a doctor on his rounds. Mrs Sutton's bodily frame had long ago proved inadequate to the ceaseless demands of a spirit indefatigably altruistic, and her continuance in activity was notable illustration of the dominion of mind over matter. Her husband, a potter's valuer and commission agent,* made money with facility in that lucrative vocation, and his wife's charities were famous, notwithstanding her attempts to hide them. Neither husband nor wife had allowed riches to put a factitious gloss upon their primal simplicity. They were as they were, save that Mr Sutton had joined the Five Towns Field Club and acquired some of the habits of an archaeologist. The influence of wealth on manners was to be observed only in their daughter Beatrice, who, while favouring her mother, dressed at considerable expense, and at intervals gave much time to the arts of music and painting.

Agnes watched the carriage drive away, and then turned to look up the stairs within the school doorway. She sighed, scowled, and sighed again, murmured something to herself, and finally began to read her book.

'Not come out yet?' Mynors was at her side once more, alone this time.

'No, not yet,' said Agnes, wearied. 'Yes. Here she is. Anna, what ages you've been!'

Anna Tellwright stood motionless for a second in the shadow of the doorway. She was tall, but not unusually so, and sturdily built up. Her figure, though the bust was a little flat, had the lenient curves of absolute maturity. Anna had been a woman since seventeen, and she was now on the eve of her twenty-first birthday. She wore a plain, home-made light frock checked with brown and edged with brown velvet, thin cotton gloves of cream colour, and a broad straw hat like her sister's. Her grave face, owing to the prominence of the cheekbones and the width of the jaw, had a slight angularity; the lips were thin, the brown eyes rather large, the eyebrows level, the nose fine and delicate; the ears could scarcely be seen for the dark brown hair which was brushed diagonally across the temples, leaving of the forehead only a pale triangle. It seemed a face for the cloister, austere in contour, fervent in expression, the severity of it mollified by that resigned and spiritual melancholy peculiar to women who through the error of destiny have been born into a wrong environment.

As if charmed forward by Mynors' compelling eyes, Anna

stepped into the sunlight, at the same time putting up her parasol. 'How calm and stately she is,' he thought, as she gave him her cool hand and murmured a reply to his salutation. But even his aquiline gaze could not surprise the secrets of that concealing breast: this was one of the three great tumultuous moments of her life – she realized for the first time that she was loved.

'You are late this afternoon, Miss Tellwright,' Mynors began, with the easy inflections of a man well accustomed to prominence in the society of women. Little Agnes seized Anna's left arm, silently holding up the prize, and Anna nodded appreciation.

'Yes,' she said as they walked across the yard, 'one of my girls has been doing wrong. She stole a Bible from another girl, so of course I had to mention it to the superintendent. Mr Price gave her a long lecture, and now she is waiting upstairs till he is ready to go with her to her home and talk to her parents. He says she must be dismissed.'

'Dismissed!'

Anna's look flashed a grateful response to him. By the least possible emphasis he had expressed a complete disagreement with his senior colleague which etiquette forbade him to utter in words.

'I think it's a very great pity,' Anne said firmly. 'I rather like the girl,' she ventured in haste; 'you might speak to Mr Price about it.'

'If he mentions it to me.'

'Yes, I meant that. Mr Price said – if it had been anything else but a *Bible* – '

'Um!' he murmured, very low, but she caught the significance of his intonation. They did not glance at each other: it was unnecessary. Anna felt that comfortable easement of the spirit which springs from the recognition of another spirit capable of understanding without explanations and of sympathizing without a phrase. Under that calm mask a strange and sweet satisfaction thrilled through her as her precious instinct of common sense – rarest of good qualities, and pining always for fellowship – found a companion in his own. She had dreaded the overtures which for a fortnight past she had foreseen were inevitably to come from Mynors: he was a stranger, whom she merely respected. Now in a sudden disclosure she knew him and liked him. The dire apprehension of those formal 'advances' which she had watched other men make to other women faded away. It was at once a release and a reassurance.

They were passing through the gate, Agnes skipping round her sister's skirts, when Willie Price reappeared from the direction of the chapel.

'Forgotten something?' Mynors inquired of him blandly.

'Ye-es,' he stammered, clumsily raising his hat to Anna. She thought of him exactly as Agnes had done. He hesitated for a fraction of time, and then went up the yard towards the lecture-hall.

'Agnes has been showing me her prize,' said Mynors, as the three stood together outside the gate. 'I asked her if she thinks she really deserves it, and she says she does. What do you think, Miss Big Sister?'

Anna gave the little girl an affectionate smile of comprehension. 'What is it called, dear?'

'*Janey's Sacrifice or the Spool of Cotton, and other stories for children*,'* Agnes read out in a monotone: then she clutched Anna's elbow and aimed a whisper at her ear.

'Very well, dear,' Anna answered loud, 'but we must be back by a quarter past four.' And turning to Mynors: 'Agnes wants to go up to the Park to hear the band play.'

'I'm going up there, too,' he said. 'Come along, Agnes, take my arm and show me the way.' Shyly Agnes left her sister's side and put a pink finger into Mynors' hand.

Moor Road, which climbs over the ridge to the mining village of Moorthorne and passes the new Park on its way, was crowded with people going up to criticize and enjoy this latest outcome of municipal enterprise in Bursley: sedate elders of the borough who smiled grimly to see one another on Sunday afternoon in that undignified, idly curious throng; white-skinned potters, and miners with the swarthy pallor of subterranean toil; untidy Sabbath loafers whom neither church nor chapel could entice, and the primly-clad respectable who had not only clothes but a separate deportment for the seventh day; housewives whose pale faces, as of prisoners free only for a while, showed a naïve and timorous pleasure in the unusual diversion; young women made glorious by richly-coloured stuffs and carrying themselves with the defiant independence of good wages earned in warehouse or painting-shop; youths oppressed by stiff new clothes bought at Whitsuntide, in which the bright necktie and the nosegay revealed a thousand secret aspirations; young children running and yelling with the marvellous energy of their years; here and there a small well-dressed group whose studious repudiation of the crowd betrayed a conscious eminence of rank; louts, drunkards, idiots, beggars, waifs, outcasts, and every oddity of the town: all were more or less under the influence of a new excitement, and all with the same face of pleased expectancy looked towards the spot where, half-way up the hill, a denser mass of sightseers indicated the grand entrance to the Park.

'What stacks of folks!' Agnes exclaimed. 'It's like going to a football match.'

'Do you go to football matches, Agnes?' Mynors asked. The child gave a giggle.

Anna was relieved when these two began to chatter. She had at once, by a firm natural impulse, subdued the agitation which seized her when she found Mynors waiting with such an obvious intention at the school door; she had conversed with him in tones of quiet ease; his attitude had even enabled her in a few moments to establish a pleasant familiarity with him. Nevertheless, as they joined the stream of people in Moor Road, she longed to be at home, in her kitchen, in order to examine herself and the new situation thus created by Mynors. And yet also she was glad that she must remain at his side, but it was a fluttered joy that his presence gave her, too strange for immediate appreciation. As her eye, without directly looking at him, embraced the suave and admirable male creature within its field of vision, she became aware that he was quite inscrutable to her. What were his inmost thoughts, his ideals, the histories of his heart? Surely it was impossible that she should ever know these secrets! He – and she: they were utterly foreign to each other. So the primary dissonances of sex vibrated within her, and her own feelings puzzled her. Still, there was an instant pleasure, delightful, if disturbing and inexplicable. And also there was a sensation of triumph, which, though she tried to scorn it, she could not banish. That a man and a woman should saunter together on that road was nothing; but the circumstance acquired tremendous importance when the man happened to be Henry Mynors and the woman Anna Tellwright. Mynors – handsome, dark, accomplished, exemplary, and prosperous – had walked for ten years circumspect and unscathed amid the glances of a whole legion of maids. As for Anna, the peculiarity of her position had always marked her for special attention: ever since her father settled in Bursley, she had felt herself to be the object of an interest in which awe and pity were equally mingled. She guessed that the fact of her going to the Park with Mynors that afternoon would pass swiftly from mouth to mouth like the rumour of a decisive event. She had no friends; her innate reserve had been misinterpreted, and she was not popular among the Wesleyan community. Many people would say, and more would think, that it was her money which was drawing Mynors from the narrow path of his celibate discretion. She could imagine all the innuendoes, the expressive nods, the pursing of lips, the lifting of shoulders and of eyebrows. 'Money'll do owt';* that was the proverb. But she cared not. She had the just and unshakable self-esteem which is fundamental in all strong and righteous natures; and she knew beyond the possibility of doubt that, though Mynors might have no incurable aversion to a fortune, she herself, the spirit and body of her, had been the sole awakener of his desire.

By a common instinct, Mynors and Anna made little Agnes the centre of attraction. Mynors continued to tease her, and Agnes growing courageous, began to retort. She was now walking between them, and the other two smiled to each other at the child's sayings over her head, interchanging thus messages too subtle and delicate for the coarse medium of words.

As they approached the Park the bandstand came into sight over the railway cutting, and they could hear the music of *The Emperor's Hymn.** The crude, brazen sounds were tempered in their passage through the warm, still air, and fell gently on the ear in soft waves, quickening every heart to unaccustomed emotions. Children leaped forward, and old people unconsciously assumed a lightsome vigour.

The Park rose in terraces from the railway station to a street of small villas almost on the ridge of the hill. From its gilded gates to its smallest geranium-slips it was brand-new, and most of it was red. The keeper's house, the bandstand, the kiosks, the balustrades, the shelters – all these assailed the eye with a uniform redness of brick and tile which nullified the pallid greens of the turf and the frail trees. The immense crowd, in order to circulate, moved along in tight processions, inspecting one after another the various features of which they had read full descriptions in the *Staffordshire Signal* – waterfall, grotto, lake, swans, boat, seats, faïence, statues – and scanning with interest the names of the donors so clearly inscribed on such objects of art and craft as from divers motives had been presented to the town by its citizens. Mynors, as he manoeuvred a way for the two girls through the main avenue up to the topmost terrace, gravely judged each thing upon its merits, approving this, condemning that. In deciding that under all the circumstances the Park made a very creditable appearance he only reflected the best local opinion. The town was proud of its achievement, and it had the right to be; for, though this narrow pleasaunce was in itself unlovely, it symbolized the first faint renascence of the longing for beauty in a district long given up to unredeemed ugliness.

At length, Mynors having encountered many acquaintances, they got past the bandstand and stood on the highest terrace, which was almost deserted. Beneath them, in front, stretched a maze of roofs, dominated by the gold angel of the Town Hall spire. Bursley, the ancient home of the potter, has an antiquity of a thousand years. It lies towards the north end of an extensive valley, which must have been one of the fairest spots in Alfred's England,* but which is now defaced by the activities of a quarter of a million of people. Five contiguous towns – Turnhill, Bursley, Hanbridge, Knype, and Longshaw – united by a single winding thoroughfare some eight miles in length, have inundated the valley like a succession of great lakes. Of these five Bursley is the mother, but Hanbridge is the largest. They are mean and forbidding of aspect – sombre, hard-featured, uncouth; and the vaporous poison of their ovens and chimneys has soiled and shrivelled the surrounding country till there is no village lane within a league but what offers a gaunt and ludicrous travesty of rural charms. Nothing could be more prosaic than the huddled, red-brown streets; nothing more seemingly remote from romance. Yet be it said that romance is even here – the romance which, for those who have an eye to perceive it, ever dwells amid the seats of industrial manufacture, softening the coarseness, transfiguring the squalor, of these mighty alchemic operations. Look down into the valley from this terrace-height where love is kindling, embrace the whole smoke-girt amphitheatre in a glance, and it may be that you will suddenly comprehend the secret and superb significance of the vast Doing which goes forward below. Because they seldom think, the townsmen take shame when indicted for having disfigured half a county in order to live. They have not understood that this disfigurement is merely an episode in the unending warfare of man and nature, and calls for no contrition. Here, indeed, is nature repaid for some of her notorious cruelties. She imperiously bids man sustain and reproduce himself, and this is one of the places where in the very act of obedience he wounds and maltreats her. Out beyond the municipal confines, where the subsidiary industries of coal and iron prosper amid a wreck of verdure, the struggle is grim, appalling, heroic – so ruthless is his havoc of her, so indomitable her ceaseless recuperation. On the one side is a wresting from nature's own bowels of the means to waste her; on the other, an undismayed, enduring fortitude. The grass grows; though it is not green, it grows. In the very heart of the valley, hedged about with furnaces, a farm still stands, and at harvest-time the sooty sheaves are gathered in.

The band stopped playing. A whole population was idle in the Park, and it seemed, in the fierce calm of the sunlight, that of all the strenuous weekday vitality of the district only a murmurous hush remained. But everywhere on the horizon, and nearer, furnaces cast their heavy smoke across the borders of the sky: the Doing was never suspended.

'Mr Mynors,' said Agnes, still holding his hand, when they had been silent a moment, 'when do those furnaces go out?'

'They don't go out,' he answered, 'unless there is a strike. It costs hundreds and hundreds of pounds to light them again.'

'Does it?' she said vaguely. 'Father says it's the smoke that stops my gillyflowers* from growing.'

Mynors turned to Anna. 'Your father seems the picture of health. I saw him out this morning at a quarter to seven, as brisk as a boy. What a constitution!'

'Yes,' Anna replied, 'he is always up at six.'

'But you aren't, I suppose?'

'Yes, I too.'

'And me too,' Agnes interjected.

'And how does Bursley compare with Hanbridge?' Mynors continued. Anna paused before replying.

'I like it better,' she said. 'At first – last year – I thought I shouldn't.'

'By the way, your father used to preach in Hanbridge circuit* – '

'That was years ago,' she said quickly.

'But why won't he preach here? I dare say you know that we are rather short of local preachers – good ones, that is.'

'I can't say why father doesn't preach now:' Anna flushed as she spoke. 'You had better ask him that.'

'Well, I will do,' he laughed. 'I am coming to see him soon – perhaps one night next week.'

Anna looked at Henry Mynors as he uttered the astonishing words. The Tellwrights had been in Bursley a year, but no visitor had crossed their doorsteps except the minister, once, and such poor defaulters as came, full of excuse and obsequious conciliation, to pay rent overdue.

'Business, I suppose?' she said, and prayed that he might not be intending to make a mere call of ceremony.

'Yes, business,' he answered lightly. 'But you will be in?'

'I am always in,' she said. She wondered what the business could be, and felt relieved to know that his visit would have at least some assigned pretext; but already her heart beat with apprehensive perturbation at the thought of his presence in their household.

'See!' said Agnes, whose eyes were everywhere. 'There's Miss Sutton.'

Both Mynors and Anna looked sharply round. Beatrice Sutton was coming towards them along the terrace. Stylishly clad in a dress of pink muslin, with harmonious hat, gloves, and sunshade, she made an agreeable and rather effective picture, despite her plain, round face and stoutish figure. She had the air of being a leader. Grafted on to the original simple honesty of her eyes there was the unconsciously-acquired arrogance of one who had always been accustomed to deference. Socially, Beatrice had no peer among the young women who were active in the Wesleyan Sunday-school. Beatrice had been used to teach in the afternoon school, but she had recently advanced her labours from the afternoon to the morning in response to a hint that if she did so the force of her influence and example might lessen the chronic dearth of morning teachers.

'Good afternoon, Miss Tellwright,' Beatrice said as she came up. 'So you have come to look at the Park.'

'Yes,' said Anna, and then stopped awkwardly. In the tone of each there was an obscure constraint, and something in Mynors' smile of salute to Beatrice showed that he too shared it.

'Seen you before,' Beatrice said to him familiarly, without taking his hand; then she bent down and kissed Agnes.

'What are you doing here, mademoiselle?' Mynors asked her.

'Father's just down below, near the lake. He caught sight of you, and sent me up to say that you were to be sure to come in to supper tonight. You will, won't you?'

'Yes, thanks. I had meant to.'

Anna knew that they were related, and also that Mynors was constantly at the Suttons' house, but the close intimacy between these two came nevertheless like a shock to her. She could not conquer a certain resentment of it, however absurd such a feeling might seem to her intelligence. And this attitude extended not only to the intimacy, but to Beatrice's handsome clothes and facile urbanity, which by contrast emphasized her own poor little frock and tongue-tied manner. The mere existence of Beatrice so near to Mynors was like an affront to her. Yet at heart, and even while admiring this shining daughter of success, she was conscious within herself of a fundamental superiority. The soul of her condescended to the soul of the other one.

They began to discuss the Park.

'Papa says it will send up the value of that land over there enormously,' said Beatrice, pointing with her ribboned sunshade to some building plots which lay to the north, high up the hill. 'Mr Tellwright owns most of that, doesn't he?' she added to Anna.

'I dare say he does,' said Anna. It was torture to her to refer to her father's possessions.

'Of course it will be covered with streets in a few months. Will he build himself, or will he sell it?'

'I haven't the least idea,' Anne answered, with an effort after gaiety of tone, and then turned aside to look at the crowd. There, close against the bandstand, stood her father, a short, stout, ruddy, middle-aged man in a shabby brown suit. He recognized her, stared fixedly, and nodded with his grotesque and ambiguous grin. Then he sidled off towards the entrance of the Park. None of the others had seen him. 'Agnes dear,' she said abruptly, 'we must go now, or we shall be late for tea.'

As the two women said goodbye their eyes met, and in the brief second of that encounter each tried to wring from the other the true answer to a question which lay unuttered in her heart. Then, having bidden adieu to Mynors, whose parting glance sang its own song to her, Anna took Agnes by the hand and left him and Beatrice together.

CHAPTER TWO

The Miser's Daughter

Anna sat at the bay-window of the front parlour, her accustomed place on Sunday evenings in summer, and watched Mr Tellwright and Agnes disappear down the slope of Trafalgar Road on their way to chapel. Trafalgar Road is the long thoroughfare which, under many aliases, runs through the Five Towns from end to end, uniting them as a river might unite them. Ephraim Tellwright could remember the time when this part of it was a country lane, flanked by meadows and market gardens. Now it was a street of houses up to and beyond Bleakridge, where the Tellwrights lived; on the other side of the hill the houses came only in patches until the far-stretching borders of Hanbridge were reached. Within the municipal limits Bleakridge was the pleasantest quarter of Bursley – Hillport, abode of the highest fashion, had its own government and authority – and to reside 'at the top of Trafalgar Road' was still the final ambition of many citizens, though the natural growth of the town had robbed Bleakridge of some of that exclusive distinction which it once possessed. Trafalgar Road, in its journey to Bleakridge from the centre of the town, underwent certain changes of character. First came a succession of manufactories and small shops; then, at the beginning of the rise, a quarter of a mile of superior cottages; and lastly, on the brow, occurred the houses of the comfortable – detached, semi-detached, and in terraces, with rentals from £25 to £60 a year. The Tellwrights lived in Manor Terrace (the name being a last reminder of the great farmstead which formerly occupied the western hill side): their house, of light yellow brick, was two-storied, with a long narrow garden behind, and the rent £30.* Exactly opposite was an antique red mansion, standing back in its own ground – home of the Mynors family for two generations, but now a school, the Mynors family being extinct in the district save for one member. Somewhat higher up, still on the opposite side to Manor Terrace, came an imposing row of four new houses, said to be the best planned and best built in the town, each erected separately and occupied by its owner. The nearest of these four was Councillor Sutton's, valued at £60 a year. Lower down, below Manor Terrace and on the same side, lived the Wesleyan superintendent minister, the vicar of St Luke's Church, an alderman, and a doctor.

It was nearly six o'clock. The sun shone, but gentlier; and the earth lay cooling in the mild, pensive effulgence of a summer evening. Even the onrush of the steam-car, as it swept with a gay load of passengers to Hanbridge, seemed to be chastened; the bell of the Roman Catholic chapel sounded like the bell of some village church heard in the distance; the quick but sober tramp of the chapel-goers fell peacefully on the ear. The sense of calm increased, and, steeped in this meditative calm, Anna from the open window gazed idly down the perspective of the road, which ended a mile away in the dim concave forms of ovens suffused in a pale mist. A book from the Free Library* lay on her lap; she could not read it. She was conscious of nothing save the quiet enchantment of reverie. Her mind, stimulated by the emotions of the afternoon, broke the fetters of habitual self-discipline, and ranged voluptuously free over the whole field of recollection and anticipation. To remember, to hope: that was sufficient joy.

In the dissolving views of her own past, from which the rigour and pain seemed to have mysteriously departed, the chief figure was always her father – that sinister and formidable individuality, whom her mind hated but her heart disobediently loved. Ephraim Tellwright† was one of the most extraordinary and most mysterious men in the Five Towns. The outer facts of his career were known to all, for his riches made him notorious; but of the secret and intimate man none knew anything except Anna, and what little Anna knew had come to her by divination rather than discernment. A native of Hanbridge, he had inherited a small fortune from his father, who was a prominent Wesleyan Methodist. At thirty, owing mainly to investments in property which his calling of potter's valuer had helped him to choose with advantage, he was worth twenty thousand pounds, and he lived in lodgings on a total expenditure of about a

† *Tellwright*: tile-wright, a name specially characteristic of, and possibly originating in, this clay-manufacturing district.

hundred a year. When he was thirty-five he suddenly married, without any perceptible public wooing, the daughter of a wood merchant at Oldcastle, and shortly after the marriage his wife inherited from her father a sum of eighteen thousand pounds. The pair lived narrowly in a small house up at Pireford, between Hanbridge and Oldcastle. They visited no one, and were never seen together except on Sundays. She was a rosy-checked, very unassuming, and simple woman, who smiled easily and talked with difficulty, and for the rest lived apparently a servile life of satisfaction and content. After five years Anna was born, and in another five years Mrs Tellwright died of erysipelas.* The widower engaged a housekeeper: otherwise his existence proceeded without change. No stranger visited the house, the housekeeper never gossiped; but tales will spread, and people fell into the habit of regarding Tellwright's child and his housekeeper with commiseration.

During all this period he was what is termed 'a good Wesleyan', preaching and teaching, and spending himself in the various activities of Hanbridge chapel. For many years he had been circuit treasurer. Among Anna's earliest memories was a picture of her father arriving late for supper one Sunday night in autumn after an anniversary service, and pouring out on the white tablecloth the contents of numerous chamois-leather money-bags. She recalled the surprising dexterity with which he counted the coins, the peculiar smell of the bags, and her mother's bland exclamation, 'Eh, Ephraim!' Tellwright belonged by birth to the Old Guard of Methodism; there was in his family a tradition of holy valour for the pure doctrine: his father, a Bursley man, had fought in the fight which preceded the famous Primitive Methodist Secession of 1808 at Bursley, and had also borne a notable part in the Warren affrays of '28, and the disastrous trouble of the Fly-Sheets in '49,* when Methodism lost a hundred thousand members. As for Ephraim, he expounded the mystery of the Atonement* in village conventicles and grew garrulous with God at prayer-meetings in the big Bethesda* chapel; but he did these things as routine, without skill and without enthusiasm, because they gave him an unassailable position within the central group of the society. He was not, in fact, much smitten with either the doctrinal or the spiritual side of Methodism. His chief interest lay in those fiscal schemes of organization without whose aid no religious propaganda can possibly succeed. It was in the finance of salvation that he rose supreme – the interminable alternation of debt-raising and new liability which provides a lasting excitement for Nonconformists. In the negotiation of mortgages, the artful arrangement of appeals, the planning of anniversaries, and of mighty revivals, he was an undisputed leader. To him the circuit was a 'going concern', and he kept it in motion, serving the Lord in committee and over statements of account. The minister by his pleading might bring sinners to the penitent form, but it was Ephraim Tellwright who reduced the cost per head of souls saved, and so widened the frontiers of the Kingdom of Heaven.

Three years after the death of his first wife it was rumoured that he would marry again, and that his choice had fallen on a young orphan girl, thirty years his junior, who 'assisted' at the stationer's shop where he bought his daily newspaper. The rumour was well-founded. Anna, then eight years of age, vividly remembered the home-coming of the pale wife, and her own sturdy attempts to explain, excuse, or assuage to this wistful and fragile creature the implacable harshness of her father's temper. Agnes was born within a year, and the pale girl died of puerperal fever.* In that year lay a whole tragedy, which could not have been more poignant in its perfection if the year had been a thousand years. Ephraim promptly re-engaged the old housekeeper, a course which filled Anna with secret childish revolt, for Anna was now nine, and accomplished in all domesticity. In another seven years the housekeeper died, a gaunt grey ruin, and Anna at sixteen became mistress of the household, with a small sister to cherish and control. About this time Anna began to perceive that her father was generally regarded as a man of great wealth, having few rivals in the entire region of the Five Towns. Definite knowledge, however, she had none: he never spoke of his affairs; she knew only that he possessed houses and other property in various places, that he always turned first to the money article in the newspaper, and that long envelopes arrived for him by post almost daily. But she had once heard the surmise that he was worth sixty thousand of his own, apart from the fortune of his first wife, Anna's mother. Nevertheless, it did not occur to her to think of her father, in plain terms, as a miser, until one day she happened to read in the *Staffordshire Signal* some particulars of the last will and testament of William Wilbraham, JP, who had just died. Mr

Wilbraham had been a famous magnate and benefactor of the Five Towns; his revered name was in every mouth; he had a fine seat, Hillport House, at Hillport; and his superb horses were constantly seen, winged and nervous, in the streets of Bursley and Hanbridge. The *Signal* said that the net value of his estate was sworn at fifty-nine thousand pounds. This single fact added a definite and startling significance to figures which had previously conveyed nothing to Anna except an idea of vastness. The crude contrast between the things of Hillport House and the things of the six-roomed abode in Manor Terrace gave food for reflection, silent but profound.

Tellwright had long ago retired from business, and three years after the housekeeper died he retired, practically, from religious work, to the grave detriment of the Hanbridge circuit. In reply to sorrowful questioners, he said merely that he was getting old and needed rest, and that there ought to be plenty of younger men to fill his shoes. He gave up everything except his pew in the chapel. The circuit was astounded by this sudden defection of a class-leader, a local preacher, and an officer. It was an inexplicable fall from grace. Yet the solution of the problem was quite simple. Ephraim had lost interest in his religious avocations; they had ceased to amuse him, the old ardour had cooled. The phenomenon is a common enough experience with men who have passed their fiftieth year – men, too, who began with the true and sacred zeal, which Tellwright never felt. The difference in Tellwright's case was that, characteristically, he at once yielded to the new instinct, caring naught for public opinion. Soon afterwards, having purchased a lot of cottage property in Bursley, he decided to migrate to the town of his fathers. He had more than one reason for doing so, but perhaps the chief was that he found the atmosphere of Hanbridge Wesleyan chapel rather uncongenial. The exodus from it was his silent and malicious retort to a silent rebuke.

He appeared now to grow younger, discarding in some measure a certain morose taciturnity which had hitherto marked his demeanour. He went amiably about in the manner of a veteran determined to enjoy the brief existence of life's winter. His stout, stiff, deliberate yet alert figure became a familiar object to Bursley: that ruddy face, with its small blue eyes, smooth upper lip, and short grey beard under the smooth chin, seemed to pervade the streets, offering everywhere the conundrum of its vague smile. Though no friend ever crossed his doorstep, he had dozens of acquaintances of the footpath. He was not, however, a facile talker, and he seldom gave an opinion; nor were his remarks often noticeably shrewd. He existed within himself, unrevealed. To the crowd, of course, he was a marvellous legend, and moving always in the glory of that legend he received their wondering awe – an awe tinged with contempt for his lack of ostentation and public splendour. Commercial men with whom he had transacted business liked to discuss his abilities, thus disseminating that solid respect for him which had sprung from a personal experience of those abilities, and which not even the shabbiness of his clothes could weaken.

Anna was disturbed by the arrival at the front door of the milk-girl. Alternately with her father, she stayed at home on Sunday evenings, partly to receive the evening milk and partly to guard the house. The Persian cat with one ear preceded her to the door as soon as he heard the clatter of the can. The stout little milk-girl dispensed one pint of milk into Anna's jug, and spilt an eleemosynary* supply on the step for the cat. 'He does like it fresh, Miss,' said the milk-girl, smiling at the greedy cat, and then, with a 'Lovely evenin',' departed down the street, one fat red arm stretched horizontally out to balance the weight of the can in the other. Anna leaned idly against the doorpost, waiting while the cat finished, until at length the swaying figure of the milk-girl disappeared in the dip of the road. Suddenly she darted within, shutting the door, and stood on the hall-mat in a startled attitude of dismay. She had caught sight of Henry Mynors in the distance, approaching the house. At that moment the kitchen clock struck seven, and Mynors, according to the rule of a lifetime, should have been in his place in the 'orchestra' (or, as some term it, the 'singing-seat')* of the chapel, where he was an admired baritone. Anna dared not conjecture what impulse had led him into this extraordinary, incredible deviation. She dared not conjecture, but despite herself she knew, and the knowledge shocked her sensitive and peremptory conscience. Her heart began to beat rapidly; she was in distress. Aware that her father and sister had left her alone, did he mean to call? It was absolutely impossible, yet she feared it, and blushed, all solitary there in the passage, for shame. Now she heard his sharp, decided footsteps, and through the glazed panels of the door she could see the outline of his form. He stopped; his hand was on the gate, and she ceased to breathe. He pushed the gate open, and then, at the whisper of some blessed angel, he closed it again and continued his way up the street. . . . After a few moments Anna carried the milk into the kitchen, and stood by the dresser, moveless, each muscle braced in the intensity of profound contemplation. Gradually the tears rose to her eyes and fell; they were the tincture of a strange and mystic joy, too poignant to be endured. As it were under compulsion she ran outside, and down the garden path to the low wall which looked over the grey fields of the valley up to Hillport. Exactly opposite, a mile and a half away, on the ridge, was Hillport Church, dark and clear against the orange sky. To the right, and nearer, lay the central masses of the town, tier on tier of richly-coloured ovens and chimneys. Along the field-paths couples moved slowly. All was quiescent, languorous, beautiful in the glow of the sun's stately declension. Anna put her arms on the wall. Far more impressively than in the afternoon she realized that this was the end of one epoch in her career and the beginning of another. Enthralled by austere traditions and that stern conscience of hers, she had never permitted herself to dream of the possibility of an escape from the parental servitude. She had never looked beyond the horizons of her present world, but had sought spiritual satisfaction in the ideas of duty and sacrifice. The worst tyrannies of her father never dulled the sense of her duty to him; and, without perhaps being aware of it, she had rather despised love and the dalliance of the sexes. In her attitude towards such things there had been not only a little contempt but also some disapproval, as though man were destined for higher ends. Now she saw, in a quick revelation, that it was the lovers, and not she, who had the right to scorn. She saw how miserably narrow, tepid, and trickling the stream of her life had been, and had threatened to be. Now it gushed forth warm, impetuous, and full, opening out new and delicious vistas. She lived; and she was finding the sight to see, the courage to enjoy. Now, as she leaned over the wall, she would not have cared if Henry Mynors indeed had called that night. She perceived something splendid and free in his abandonment of habit and discretion at the bidding of a desire. To be the magnet which could draw that pattern and exemplar of seemliness from the strict orbit of virtuous custom! It was she, the miser's shabby daughter, who had caused this amazing phenomenon. The thought intoxicated her. Without the support of the walls she might have fallen. In a sort of trance she murmured these words: 'He loves me.'

This was Anna Tellwright, the ascetic, the prosaic, the impassive.

After an interval which to her was as much like a minute as a century, she went back into the house. As she entered by the kitchen she heard an impatient knocking at the front door.

'At last,' said her father grimly, when she opened the door. In two words he had resumed his terrible sway over her. Agnes looked timidly from one to the other and slipped past them into the house.

'I was in the garden,' Anna explained. 'Have you been here long?' She tried to smile apologetically.

'Only about a quarter of an hour,' he answered, with a grimness still more portentous.

'He won't speak again tonight,' she thought fearfully. But she was mistaken. After he had carefully hung his best hat on the hat-rack, he turned towards her, and said, with a queer smile:

'Ye've been day-dreaming, eh, Sis?'

'Sis' was her pet name, used often by Agnes, but by her father only at the very rarest intervals. She was staggered at this change of front, so unaccountable in this man, who, when she had unwittingly annoyed him, was capable of keeping an awful silence for days together. What did he know? What had those old eyes seen?

'I forgot,' she stammered, gathering herself together happily, 'I forgot the time.' She felt that after all there was a bond between them which nothing could break – the tie of blood. They were father and daughter, united by sympathies obscure but fundamental. Kissing was not in the Tellwright blood, but she had a fleeting wish to hug the tyrant.

CHAPTER THREE

The Birthday

The next morning there was no outward sign that anything unusual had occurred. As the clock in the kitchen struck eight Anna carried to the back parlour a tray on which were a dish of bacon and a coffee-pot. Breakfast was already laid for three. She threw a housekeeper's glance over the table, and called: 'Father!' Mr Tellwright was re-setting some encaustic tiles* in the lobby. He came in, coatless, and, dropping a trowel on the hearth, sat down at the end of the table nearest the fireplace. Anna sat opposite to him, and poured out the coffee.

On the dish were six pieces of bacon. He put one piece on a plate, and set it carefully in front of Agnes's vacant chair, two he passed to Anna, three he kept for himself.

'Where's Agnes?' he inquired.

'Coming – she's finishing her arithmetic.'

In the middle of the table was an unaccustomed small jug containing gillyflowers. Mr Tellwright noticed it instantly.

'What an* we gotten here?' he said, indicating the jug.

'Agnes gave me them first thing when she got up. She's grown them herself, you know,' Anna said, and then added: 'It's my birthday.'

'Ay!' he exclaimed, with a trace of satire in his voice. 'Thou'rt a woman now, lass.'

No further remark on that matter was made during the meal.

Agnes ran in, all pinafore and legs. With a toss backwards of her light golden hair she slipped silently into her seat, cautiously glancing at the master of the house. Then she began to stir her coffee.

'Now, young woman,' Tellwright said curtly.

She looked a startled interrogative.

'We're waiting,' he explained.

'Oh!' said Agnes, confused. 'I thought you'd said it. "God sanctify this food to our use and us to His service for Christ's sake, Amen."'

The breakfast proceeded in silence. Breakfast at eight, dinner at noon, tea at four, supper at eight: all the meals in this house occurred with absolute precision and sameness. Mr Tellwright seldom spoke, and his example imposed silence on the girls, who felt as nuns feel when assisting at some grave but monotonous and perfunctory rite. The room was not a cheerful one in the morning, since the window was small and the aspect westerly. Besides the table and three horse-hair chairs, the furniture consisted of an armchair, a bent-wood rocking chair, and a sewing-machine. A fatigued Brussels carpet* covered the floor. Over the mantelpiece was an engraving of 'The Light of the World',* in a frame of polished brown wood. On the other walls were some family photographs in black frames. A two-light chandelier hung from the ceiling, weighed down on one side by a patent gas-saving mantle* and a glass shade; over this the ceiling was deeply discoloured. On either side of the chimney-breast were cupboards about three feet high; some cardboard boxes, a work-basket, and Agnes's school books lay on the tops of these cupboards. On the window-sill was a pot of mignonette in a saucer. The window was wide open, and flies buzzed to and fro, constantly rebounding from the window panes with terrible thuds. In the blue-paved yard beyond the cat was licking himself in the sunlight with an air of being wholly absorbed in his task.

Mr Tellwright demanded a second and last cup of coffee, and having drunk it pushed away his plate as a sign that he had finished. Then he took from the mantelpiece at his right hand a bundle of letters and opened them methodically. When he had arranged the correspondence in a flattened pile, he put on his steel-rimmed spectacles and began to read.

'Can I return thanks, Father?' Agnes asked, and he nodded, looking at her fixedly over his spectacles.

'Thank God for our good breakfast, Amen.'

In two minutes the table was cleared, and Mr Tellwright was alone. As he read laboriously through communications from solicitors, secretaries of companies, and tenants, he could hear his daughters talking together in the kitchen. Anna was washing the breakfast things while Agnes wiped. Then there were flying steps across the yard: Agnes had gone to school.

After he had mastered his correspondence, Mr Tellwright took up the trowel again and finished the tile-setting in the lobby. Then he resumed his coat, and, gathering together the letters from the table in the back parlour, went into the front parlour and shut the door. This room was his office. The principal things in it were an old oak bureau and an old oak desk-chair which had come to him from his first wife's father; on the walls were some sombre landscapes in oil, received from the same source; there was no carpet on the floor, and only one other chair. A safe stood in the corner opposite the door. On the mantelpiece were some books – Woodfall's *Landlord and Tenant*, Jordan's *Guide to Company Law*, *Whitaker's Almanack*, and a Gazetteer of the Five Towns.* Several wire files, loaded with papers, hung from the mantelpiece. With the exception of a mahogany what-not* with a Bible on it, which stood in front of the window, there was nothing else whatever in the room. He sat down to the bureau and opened it, and took from one of the pigeon-holes a packet of various documents: these he examined one by one, from time to time referring to a list. Then he unlocked the safe and extracted from it another bundle of documents which had evidently been placed ready. With these in his hand, he opened the door, and called out:

'Anna.'

'Yes, Father?' her voice came from the kitchen.

'I want ye.'

'In a minute. I'm peeling potatoes.'

When she came in, she found him seated at the bureau as usual. He did not look round.

'Yes, Father?'

She stood there in her print dress and white apron, full in the eye of the sun, waiting for him. She could not guess what she had been summoned for. As a rule, she never saw her father between breakfast and dinner. At length he turned.

'Anna,' he said in his harsh, abrupt tones, and then stopped for a moment before continuing. His thick, short fingers held the list which he had previously been consulting. She waited in bewilderment. 'It's your birthday, ye told me. I hadna' forgotten. Ye're of age today, and there's summat for ye. Your mother had a fortune of her own, and under your grandfeyther's will it comes to you when you're twenty-one. I'm the trustee. Your mother had eighteen thousand pounds i' Government stock.'* He laid a slight sneering emphasis on the last two words. 'That was near twenty-five year ago. I've nigh on trebled it for ye, what wi' good investments and interest accumulating. Thou'rt worth' – here he changed to the second personal singular, a habit with him – 'thou'rt worth this day as near fifty thousand as makes no matter, Anna. And that's a tidy bit.'

'Fifty thousand – *pounds*!' she exclaimed aghast.

'Ay, lass.'

She tried to speak calmly. 'Do you mean it's mine, Father?'

'It's thine, under thy grandfeyther's will – haven't I told thee? I'm bound by law for to give it to thee this day, and thou mun give me a receipt in due form for the securities. Here they are, and here's the list. Tak' the list, Anna, and read it to me while I check it off.'

She mechanically took the blue paper and read:

'Toft End Colliery and Brickworks Limited, five hundred shares of ten pounds.'

'They paid ten per cent last year,' he said, 'and with coal up as it is they'll pay fiftane this. Let's see what thy arithmetic is worth, lass. How much is fiftane per cent on five thousand pun?'*

'Seven hundred and fifty pounds,' she said, getting the correct answer by a superhuman effort worthy of that occasion.

'Right,' said her father, pleased. 'Recollect that's more till* two pun a day. Go on.'

'North Staffordshire Railway Company ordinary stock, ten thousand and two hundred pounds.'

'Right. Th' owd North Stafford's getting up i' th' world. It'll be a five per cent line yet. Then thou mun sell out.'

She had only a vague idea of his meaning, and continued: 'Five Towns Waterworks Company Limited consolidated stock, eight thousand five hundred pounds.'

'That's a tit-bit, lass,' he interjected, looking absently over his spectacles at something outside in the road. 'You canna' pick that up on shardrucks.'*

'Norris's Brewery Limited, six hundred ordinary shares of ten pounds.'

'Twenty per cent,' said the old man. 'Twenty per cent regular.' He made no attempt to conceal his pride in these investments. And he had the right to be proud of them. They were the finest in the market, the aristocracy of investments, based on commercial enterprises of which every business man in the Five Towns knew the entire soundness. They conferred distinction on the possessor, like a great picture or a rare volume. They stifled all questions and insinuations. Put before any jury of the Five Towns as evidence of character, they would almost have exculpated a murderer.

Anna continued reading the list, which seemed endless: long before she had reached the last item her brain was a menagerie of monstrous figures. The list included, besides all sorts of shares English and American, sundry properties in the Five Towns, and among these were the earthenware manufactory in Edward Street occupied by Titus Price, the Sunday-school superintendent. Anna was a little alarmed to find herself the owner of this works; she knew that her father had had some difficult moments with Titus Price, and that the property was not without grave disadvantages.

'That all?' Tellwright asked, at length.

'That's all.'

'Total face value,' he went on, 'as I value it, forty-eight thousand and fifty pounds, producing a net annual income of three thousand two hundred and ninety pounds or thereabouts. There's not many in this district as 'as gotten that to their names, Anna – no, nor half that – let 'em be who they will.'

Anna had sensations such as a child might have who has received a traction-engine to play with in a back yard. 'What am I to do with it?' she asked plaintively.

'Do wi' it?' he repeated, and stood up and faced her, putting his lips together: 'Do wi' it, did ye say?'

'Yes.'

'Tak' care on it, my girl. Tak' care on it. And remember it's thine. Thou mun sign this list, and all these transfers and fal-lals, and then thou mun go to th' Bank, and tell Mester Lovatt I've sent thee. There's four hundred pound there. He'll give thee a cheque-book. I've told him all about it. Thou'll have thy own account, and be sure thou keeps it straight.'

'I shan't know a bit what to do, Father, and so it's no use talking,' she said quietly.

'I'll learn* ye,' he replied. 'Here, tak' th' pen, and let's have thy signature.'

She signed her name many times and put her finger on many seals. Then Tellwright gathered up everything into a bundle, and gave it to her to hold.

'That's the lot,' he said. 'Have ye gotten 'em?'

'Yes,' she said.

They both smiled, self-consciously. As for Tellwright, he was evidently impressed by the grandeur of this superb renunciation on his part. 'Shall I keep 'em for ye?'

'Yes, please.'

'Then give 'em me.'

He took back all the documents.

'When shall I call at the Bank, father?'

'Better call this afternoon – afore three, mind ye.'

'Very well. But I shan't know what to do.'

'You've gotten a tongue in that noddle of yours, haven't ye?' he said. 'Now go and get along wi' them potatoes.'

Anna returned to the kitchen. She felt no elation or ferment of any kind; she had not begun to realize the significance of what had occurred. Like the soldier whom a bullet has struck, she only knew vaguely that something had occurred. She peeled the potatoes with more than her usual thrifty care; the peel was so thin as to be almost transparent. It seemed to her that she could not arrange or examine her emotions until after she had met Henry Mynors again. More than anything else she wished to see him: it was as if out of the mere sight of him something definite might emerge, as if when her eyes had rested on him, and not before, she might perceive some simple solution of the problems which she had obscurely discerned ahead of her.

During dinner a boy brought a note for her father. He read it, snorted, and threw it across the table to Anna.

'Here,' he said, 'that's your affair.'

The letter was from Titus Price: it said that he was sorry to be compelled to break his promise, but it was quite impossible for him to pay twenty pounds on account of rent that day; he would endeavour to pay at least twenty pounds in a week's time.

'You'd better call there, after you've been to th' Bank,' said Tellwright, 'and get summat out of him, if it's only ten pun.

'Must I go to Edward Street?'

'Yes.'

'What am I to say? I've never been there before.'

'Well, it's high time as ye began to look after your own property. You mun see owd Price, and tell him ye can na accept any excuses.'

'How much does he owe?'

'He owes ye a hundred and twenty-five pun altogether – he's five quarters in arrear.'

'A hundred and—! Well, I never!' Anna was aghast. The sum appeared larger to her than all the thousands and tens of thousands which she had received in the morning. She reflected that the weekly bills of the household amounted to about a sovereign, and that the total of this debt of Price's would therefore keep them in food for two years. The idea of being in debt was abhorrent to her. She could not conceive how a man who was in debt could sleep at nights. 'Mr Price ought to be ashamed of himself,' she said warmly. 'I'm sure he's quite able to pay.' The image of the sleek and stout superintendent of the Sunday-school, arrayed in his rich, almost voluptuous, broadcloth, offended her profoundly. That he, debtor and promise-breaker, should have the effrontery to pray for the souls of children, to chastise their petty furtive crimes, was nearly incredible.

'Oh! Price is all *right*,' her father remarked, with an apparent benignity which surprised her. 'He'll pay when he can.'

'I think it's a shame,' she repeated emphatically.

Agnes looked with a mystified air from one to the other, instinctively divining that something very extraordinary had happened during her absence at school.

'Ye mun'na be too hard, Anna,' said Tellwright. 'Supposing ye sold owd Titus up? What then? D'ye reckon ye'd get a tenant for them ramshackle works? A thousand pound spent wouldn't 'tice a tenant. That Edward Street property was one o' ye grandfeyther's specs;* 'twere none o' mine. You'd best tak' what ye can get.'

Anna felt a little ashamed of herself, not because of her bad policy, but because she saw that Mr Price might have been handicapped by the faults of her property.

That afternoon it was a shy and timid Anna who swung back the heavy polished and glazed portals of the Bursley branch of the Birmingham, Sheffield, and District Bank, the opulent and spacious erection which stands commandingly at the top of St Luke's Square. She looked about her, across broad counters, enormous ledgers, and rows of bent heads, and wondered whom she should address. Then a bearded gentleman, who was weighing gold in a balance, caught sight of her: he slid the gold into a drawer, and whisked round the end of the counter with a celerity which was, at any rate, not born of practice, for he, the cashier, had not done such a thing for years.

'Good afternoon, Miss Tellwright.'

'Good afternoon. I – '

'May I trouble you to step into the manager's room?' and he drew her forward, while every clerk's eye watched. Anna tried not to blush, but she could feel the red mounting even to her temples.

'Delightful weather we're having. But of course we've the right to expect it at this time of year.' He opened a door on the glass of which was painted 'Manager,' and bowed. 'Mr Lovatt – Miss Tellwright.'

Mr Lovatt greeted his new customer with a formal and rather fatigued politeness, and invited her to sit in a large leather armchair in front of a large table; on this table lay a large open book. Anna had once in her life been to the dentist's; this interview reminded her of that experience.

'Your father told me I might expect you today,' said Mr Lovatt in his high-pitched, perfunctory tones. Richard Lovatt was probably the most influential man in Bursley. Every Saturday morning he irrigated the whole town with fertilizing gold. By a single negative he could have ruined scores of upright merchants and manufacturers. He had only to stop a man in the street and murmur, 'By the way, your overdraft – ,' in order to spread discord and desolation through a refined and pious home. His estimate of human nature was falsified by no common illusions; he had the impassive and frosty gaze of a criminal judge. Many men deemed they had cause to hate him, but no one did hate him: all recognized that he was set far above hatred.

'Kindly sign your full name here,' he said, pointing to a spot on the large open page of the book, 'and your ordinary signature, which you will attach to cheques, here.'

Anna wrote, but in doing so she became aware that she had no ordinary signature; she was obliged to invent one.

'Do you wish to draw anything out now? There is already a credit of four hundred and twenty pounds in your favour,' said Mr Lovatt, after he had handed her a cheque-book, a deposit-book, and a pass-book.

'Oh, no, thank you,' Anna answered quickly. She keenly desired some money, but she well knew that courage would fail her to demand it without her father's consent; moreover, she was in a whirl of uncertainty as to the uses of the three books, though Mr Lovatt had expounded them severally to her in simple language.

'Good-day.'

'Good-day, Miss Tellwright.'

'My compliments to your father.'

His final glance said half cynically, half in pity: 'You are naïve and unspoilt now, but these eyes will see yours harden like the rest. Wretched victim of gold, you are only one in a procession, after all.'

Outside, Anna thought that everyone had been very agreeable to her. Her complacency increased at a bound. She no longer felt ashamed of her shabby cotton dress. She surmised that people would find it convenient to ignore any difference which might exist between her costume and that of other girls.

She went on to Edward Street, a short steep thoroughfare at the eastern extremity of the town, leading into a rough road across unoccupied land dotted with the mouths of abandoned pits: this road climbed up to Toft End, a mean annexe of the town about half a mile east of Bleakridge. From Toft End, lying on the highest hill in the district, one had a panoramic view of Hanbridge and Bursley, with Hillport to the west, and all the moorland and mining villages to the north and north-east. Titus Price and his son lived in what had once been a farmhouse at Toft End; every morning and evening they traversed the desolate and featureless grey road between their dwelling and the works.

Anna had never been in Edward Street before. It was a miserable quarter – two rows of blackened infinitesimal cottages, and her manufactory at the end – a frontier post of the town. Price's works was small, old-fashioned, and out of repair – one of those properties which are forlorn from the beginning, which bring despair into the hearts of a succession of owners; and which, being ultimately deserted, seem to stand for ever in pitiable ruin. The arched entrance for carts into the yard was at the top of the steepest rise of the street, when it might as well have been at the bottom; and this was but one example of the architect's fine disregard for the principle of economy in working – that principle to which in the scheming of manufactories everything else is now so strictly subordinated. Ephraim Tellwright used to say (but not to Titus Price) that the situation of that archway cost five pounds a year in horseflesh, and that five pounds was the interest on a hundred. The place was badly located, badly planned, and badly constructed. Its faults defied improvements. Titus Price remained in it only because he was chained there by arrears of rent; Tellwright hesitated to sell it only because the rent was a hundred a year, and the whole freehold would not have fetched eight hundred. He promised repairs in exchange for payment of arrears which he knew would never be paid, and his policy was to squeeze the last penny out of Price without forcing him into bankruptcy. Such was the predicament when Anna assumed ownership. As she surveyed the irregular and huddled frontage from the opposite side of the street, her first feeling was one of depression at the broken and dirty panes of the windows. A man in shirt-sleeves was standing on the weighing platform* under the archway; his back was towards her, but she could see the smoke issuing in puffs from his pipe. She crossed the road. Hearing her footfalls, the man turned round: it was Titus Price himself. He was wearing an apron, but no cap; the sleeves of his shirt were rolled up, exposing forearms covered with auburn hair. His puffed, heavy face, and general bigness and untidiness, gave the idea of a vast and torpid male slattern. Anna was astounded by the contrast between the Titus of Sunday and the Titus of Monday: a single glance compelled her to readjust all her notions of the man. She stammered a greeting, and he replied, and then they were both silent for a moment: in the pause Mr Price thrust his pipe between apron and waistcoat.

'Come inside, Miss Tellwright,' he said, with a sickly, conciliatory smile. 'Come into the office, will ye?'

She followed him without a word through the archway. To the right was an open door into the packing-house, where a man surrounded by straw was packing basins in a crate: with swift, precise movements, twisting straw between basin and basin, he forced piles of ware into a space inconceivably small. Mr Price lingered to watch him for a few seconds, and passed on. They were in the yard, a small quadrangle paved with black, greasy mud. In one corner a load of coal had been cast; in another lay a heap of broken saggars.* Decrepit doorways led to the various 'shops' on the ground floor; those on the upper floor were reached by narrow wooden stairs, which seemed to cling insecurely to the exterior walls. Up one of these stairways Mr Price climbed with heavy, elephantine movements: Anna prudently waited till he had reached the top before beginning to ascend. He pushed open a flimsy door, and with a nod bade her enter. The office was a long narrow room, the dirtiest that Anna had ever seen. If such was the condition of the master's quarters, she thought, what must the workshops be like? The ceiling, which bulged downwards, was as black as the floor, which sank away in the middle till it was hollow like a saucer. The revolution of an engine somewhere below shook everything with a periodic muffled thud. A greyish light came through one small window. By the window was a large double desk, with chairs facing each other. One of these chairs was occupied by Willie Price. The youth did not observe at first that another person had come in with his father. He was casting up figures in an account book, and murmuring numbers to himself. He wore an office coat, short at the wrists and torn at the elbows, and a battered felt hat was thrust far back over his head so that the brim rested on his dirty collar. He turned round at length, and, on seeing Anna, blushed brilliant crimson, and rose, scraping the legs of his chair horribly across the floor. Tall, thin, and ungainly in every motion, he had the look of a ninny: it was the fact that at school all the boys by a common instinct had combined to tease him, and that on the works the young paintresses* continually made private sport of him. Anna, however, had not the least impulse to mock him in her thoughts. For her there was nothing in his blue eyes but simplicity and good intentions. Beside him she felt old, sagacious, crafty: it seemed to her that some one ought to shield that transparent and confiding soul from his father and the intriguing world.

He spoke to her and lifted his hat, holding it afterwards in his great bony hand.

'Get down to th' entry, Will,' said his father, and Willie, with an apologetic sort of cough, slipped silently away through the door.

'Sit down, Miss Tellwright,' said old Price, and she took the windsor chair that had been occupied by Willie. Her tenant fell into the seat opposite – a leathern chair from which the stuffing had exuded, and with one of its arms broken. 'I hear as ye father is going into partnership with young Mynors – Henry Mynors.'

Anna started at this surprising item of news, which was entirely fresh to her. 'Father has said nothing to me about it,' she replied, coldly.

'Oh! Happen I've said too much. If so, you'll excuse me, Miss.

A smart fellow, Mynors. Now you should see *his* little works: not very much bigger than this, but there's everything you can think of there – all the latest machinery and dodges, and not over-rented, I'm told. The biggest fool i' Bursley couldn't help but make money there. This 'ere works 'ere, Miss Tellwright, wants mendin, with a new 'un.'

'It looks very dirty, I must say,' said Anna.

'Dirty!' he laughed – a short, acrid laugh – 'I suppose you've called about the rent.'

'Yes, Father asked me to call.'

'Let me see, this place belongs to you i' your own right, doesn't it, Miss?'

'Yes,' said Anna. 'It's mine – from my grandfather, you know.'

'Ah! Well, I'm sorry for to tell ye as I can't pay anything now – no, not a cent. But I'll pay twenty pounds in a week. Tell ye father I'll pay twenty pound in a week.'

'That's what you said last week,' Anna remarked, with more brusqueness than she had intended. At first she was fearful at her own temerity in thus addressing a superintendent of the Sunday-school; then, as nothing happened, she felt reassured, and strong in the justice of her position.

'Yes,' he admitted obsequiously. 'But I've been disappointed. One of our best customers put us off, to tell ye the truth. Money's tight, very tight. It's got to be give and take in these days, as ye father knows. And I may as well speak plain to ye, Miss Tellwright. We canna' stay here; we shall be compelled to give ye notice. What's amiss with this bank†* is that it wants pullin' down.' He went off into a rapid enumeration of ninety-and-nine alterations and repairs that must be done without the loss of a moment, and concluded: 'You tell ye father what I've told ye, and say as I'll send up twenty pounds next week. I can't pay anything now; I've nothing by me at all.'

'Father said particularly I was to be sure and get something on account.' There was a flinty hardness in her tone which astonished herself perhaps more than Titus Price. A long pause followed, and then Mr Price drew a breath, seeming to nerve himself to a tremendous sacrificial deed.

† Bank: manufactory.

'I tell ye what I'll do. I'll give ye ten pounds now, and I'll do what I can next week. I'll do what I can. There!'

'Thank you,' said Anna. She was amazed at her success.

He unlocked the desk, and his head disappeared under the lifted lid. Anna gazed through the window. Like many women, and not a few men, in the Five Towns, she was wholly ignorant of the staple manufacture. The interior of a works was almost as strange to her as it would have been to a farm-hand from Sussex. A girl came out of a door on the opposite side of the quadrangle: the creature was clothed in clayey rags, and carried on her right shoulder a board laden with biscuit† cups. She began to mount one of the wooden stairways, and as she did so the board, six feet in length, swayed alarmingly to and fro. Anna expected to see it fall with a destructive crash, but the girl went up in safety, and with a nonchalant jerk of the shoulder aimed the end of the board through another door and vanished from sight. To Anna it was a thrilling feat, but she noticed that a man who stood in the yard did not even turn his head to watch it. Mr Price recalled her to the business of her errand.

'Here's two fives,' he said, shutting down the desk with the sigh of a crocodile.

'Liar! You said you had nothing!' her unspoken thought ran, and at the same instant the Sunday-school and everything connected with it grievously sank in her estimation; she contrasted this scene with that on the previous day with the peccant schoolgirl: it was an hour of disillusion. Taking the notes, she gave a receipt and rose to go.

'Tell ye father' – it seemed to Anna that this phrase was always on his lips – 'tell ye father he must come down and look at the state this place is in,' said Mr Price, enheartened by the heroic payment of ten pounds. Anna said nothing; she thought a fire would do more good than anything else to the foul, squalid buildings: the passing fancy coincided with Mr Price's secret and most intense desire.

Outside she saw Willie Price superintending the lifting of a crate on to a railway lorry. After twirling in the air, the crate sank safely into the wagon. Young Price was perspiring.

'Warm afternoon, Miss Tellwright,' he called to her as she passed, with his pleasant bashful smile. She gave an affirmative.

† Biscuit: a term applied to ware which has been fired only once.

Then he came to her, still smiling, his face full of an intention to say something, however insignificant.

'I suppose you'll be at the Special Teachers' Meeting tomorrow night,' he remarked.

'I hope to be,' she said. That was all: William had achieved his small-talk: they parted.

'So Father and Mr Mynors are going into partnership,' she kept saying to herself on the way home.

CHAPTER FOUR

A Visit

The Special Teachers' Meeting to which Willie Price had referred was one of the final preliminaries to a Revival* – that is, a revival of godliness and Christian grace – about to be undertaken by the Wesleyan Methodist Society* in Bursley. Its object was to arrange for a personal visitation of the parents of Sunday-school scholars in their homes. Hitherto Anna had felt but little interest in the Revival: it had several times been brought indirectly before her notice, but she had regarded it as a phenomenon which recurred at intervals in the cycle of religious activity, and as not in any way affecting herself. The gradual centring of public interest, however – that mysterious movement which, defying analysis, gathers force as it proceeds, and ends by coercing the most indifferent – had already modified her attitude towards this forthcoming event. It got about that the preacher who had been engaged, a specialist in revivals, was a man of miraculous powers: the number of souls which he had snatched from eternal torment was precisely stated, and it amounted to tens of thousands. He played the cornet to the glory of God, and his cornet was of silver: his more distant past had been ineffably wicked, and the faint rumour of that dead wickedness clung to his name like a piquant odour. As Anna walked up Trafalgar Road from Price's she observed that the hoardings had been billed with great posters announcing the Revival and the revivalist, who was to commence his work on Friday night.

During tea Mr Tellwright interrupted his perusal of the evening *Signal* to give utterance to a rather remarkable speech.

'Bless us!' he said. 'Th' old trumpeter 'll turn the town upside down!'

'Do you mean the revivalist, Father?' Anna asked.

'Ay!'

'He's a beautiful man,' Agnes exclaimed with enthusiasm.

'Our teacher showed us his portrait after school this afternoon. I never saw such a beautiful man.'

Her father gazed hard at the child for an instant, cup in hand, and then turned to Anna with a slightly sardonic air.

'What are you doing i' this Revival, Anna?'

'Nothing,' she said. 'Only there's a teachers' meeting about it tomorrow night, and I have to go to that. Young Mr Price mentioned it to me specially today.'

A pause followed.

'Didst get anything out o' Price?' Tellwright asked.

'Yes; he gave me ten pounds. He wants you to go and look over the works – says they're falling to pieces.'

'Cheque, I reckon?'

She corrected the surmise.

'Better give me them notes, Anna,' he said after tea. 'I'm going to th' Bank i' th' morning, and I'll pay 'em in to your account.'

There was no reason why she should not have suggested the propriety of keeping at least one of the notes for her private use. But she dared not. She had never any money of her own, not a penny; and the effective possession of five pounds seemed far too audacious a dream. She hesitated to imagine her father's reply to such a request, even to frame the request to herself. The thing, viewed close, was utterly impossible. And when she relinquished the notes she also, without being asked, gave up her cheque-book, deposit-book, and pass-book. She did this while ardently desiring to refrain from doing it, as it were under the compulsion of an invincible instinct. Afterwards she felt more at ease, as though some disturbing question had been settled once and for all.

During the whole of that evening she timorously expected Mynors, saying to herself however that he certainly would not call before Thursday. On Tuesday evening she started early for the teachers' meeting. Her intention was to arrive among the first and to choose a seat in obscurity, since she knew well that every eye would be upon her. She was divided between the desire to see Mynors and the desire to avoid the ordeal of being seen by her colleagues in his presence. She trembled lest she should be incapable of commanding her mien so as to appear unconscious of this inspection by curious eyes.

The meeting was held in a large class-room, furnished with wooden seats, a chair, and a small table. On the grey distempered walls hung a few Biblical cartoons depicting scenes in the life of Joseph and his brethren – but without reference to Potiphar's wife.* From the whitewashed ceiling depended a T-shaped gas-fitting, one burner of which showed a glimmer, though the sun had not yet set. The evening was oppressively warm, and through the wide-open window came the faint effluvium of populous cottages and the distant but raucous cries of children at play. When Anna entered a group of young men were talking eagerly round the table; among these was Willie Price, who greeted her. No others had come: she sat down in a corner by the door, invisible except from within the room. Gradually the place began to fill. Then at last Mynors entered: Anna recognized his authoritative step before she saw him. He walked quickly to the chair in front of the table, and, including all in a friendly and generous smile, said that in the absence of Mr Titus Price it fell to him to take the chair: he was glad that so many had made a point of being present. Everyone sat down. He gave out a hymn, and led the singing himself, attacking the first note with an assurance born of practice. Then he prayed, and as he prayed Anna gazed at him intently. He was standing up, the ends of his fingers pressed against the top of the table. Very carefully dressed as usual, he wore a brilliant new red necktie, and a gardenia in his button-hole. He seemed happy, wholesome, earnest, and unaffected. He had the elasticity of youth with the firm wisdom of age. And it was as if he had never been younger and would never grow older, remaining always at just thirty and in his prime. Incomparable to the rest, he was clearly born to lead. He fulfilled his functions with tact, grace, and dignity. In such an affair as this present he disclosed the attributes of the skilled workman, whose easy and exact movements are a joy and wonder to the beholder. And behind all was the man, his excellent and strong nature, his kindliness, his sincerity. Yes, to Anna, Mynors was perfect that night; the reality of him exceeded her dreamy meditations. Fearful on the brink of an ecstatic bliss, she could scarcely believe that from the enticements of a thousand women this paragon had been preserved for her. Like most of us, she lacked the high courage to grasp happiness boldly and without apprehension; she had not learnt that nothing is too good to be true.

Mynors' prayer was a cogent appeal for the success of the Revival. He knew what he wanted, and confidently asked for it, approaching God with humility but with self-respect. The prayer was punctuated by Amens from various parts of the room. The atmosphere became suddenly fervent, emotional, and devout. Here was lofty endeavour, idealism, a burning spirituality; and not all the pettiness unavoidable in such an organization as a Sunday-school could hide the difference between this impassioned altruism and the ignoble selfishness of the worldly. Anna felt, as she had often felt before, but more acutely now, that she existed only on the fringe of the Methodist society. She had not been converted;* technically she was a lost creature: the converted knew it, and in some subtle way their bearing towards her, and others in her case, always showed that they knew it. Why did she teach? Not from the impulse of religious zeal. Why was she allowed to have charge of a class of immortal souls? The blind could not lead the blind, nor the lost save the lost. These considerations troubled her. Conscience pricked, accusing her of a continual pretence. The rôle of professing Christian, through false shame, had seemed distasteful to her: she had said that she could never stand up and say, 'I am for Christ,' without being uncomfortable. But now she was ashamed of her inability to profess Christ. She could conceive herself proud and happy in the very part which formerly she had despised. It was these believers, workers, exhorters, wrestlers with Satan, who had the right to disdain; not she. At that moment, as if divining her thoughts, Mynors prayed for those among them who were not converted. She blushed, and when the prayer was finished she feared lest every eye might seek hers in inquiry; but no one seemed to notice her.

Mynors sat down, and, seated, began to explain the arrangements for the Revival. He made it plain that prayers without industry would not achieve success. His remarks revealed the fact that underneath the broad religious structure of the enterprise, and supporting it, there was a basis of individual diplomacy and solicitation. The town had been mapped out into districts, and each of these was being importuned, as at an election: by the thoroughness and instancy of this canvass, quite as much as by the intensity of prayerful desire, would Christ conquer. The affair was a campaign before it was a prostration at the Throne of Grace. He spoke of the children, saying that in connexion with these they, the teachers, had at once the highest privilege and the most sacred responsibility. He told of a special service for the children, and the need of visiting them in their homes and inviting the parents also to this feast of God. He wished every teacher during tomorrow and the next day and the next day to go through the list of his or her scholars' names, and call if possible at every house. There must be no shirking. 'Will you ladies do that?' he exclaimed with an appealing, serious smile. 'Will you, Miss Dickinson? Will you, Miss Machin? Will you, Mrs Salt? Will you, Miss Sutton? Will you – ' Until at last it came: 'Will you, Miss Tellwright?' 'I will,' she answered, with averted eyes. 'Thank you. Thank you all.'

Some others spoke, hopefully, enthusiastically, and one or two prayed. Then Mynors rose: 'May the blessing of God the Father, the Son, and the Holy Ghost rest upon us now and for ever.' 'Amen,' someone ejaculated. The meeting was over.

Anna passed rapidly out of the door, down the Quadrangle, and into Trafalgar Road. She was the first to leave, daring not to stay in the room a moment. She had seen him; he had not altered since Sunday; there was no disillusion, but a deepening of the original impression. Caught up by the soaring of his spirit, her spirit lifted, and she was conscious of vague but intense longing skyward. She could not reason or think in that dizzying hour, but she made resolutions which had no verbal form, yielding eagerly to his influence and his appeal. Not till she had reached the bottom of Duck Bank and was breasting the first rise towards Bleakridge did her pace slacken. Then a voice called to her from behind. She recognized it, and turned sharply beneath the shock. Mynors raised his hat and greeted her.

'I'm coming to see your father,' he said.

'Yes?' she said, and gave him her hand.

'It was a very satisfactory meeting tonight,' he began, and in a moment they were talking seriously of the Revival. With the most oblique delicacy, the most perfect assumption of equality between them, he allowed her to perceive his genuine and profound anxiety for her spiritual welfare. The atmosphere of the meeting was still round about him, the divine fire still uncooled. 'I hope you will come to the first service on Friday night,' he pleaded.

'I must,' she replied. 'Oh, yes. I shall come.'

'That is good,' he said. 'I particularly wanted your promise.'

They were at the door of the house. Agnes, obviously expectant and excited, answered the bell. With an effort Anna and Mynors passed into a lighter mood.

'Father said you were coming, Mr Mynors,' said Agnes, and, turning to Anna, 'I've set supper all myself.'

'Have you?' Mynors laughed. 'Capital! You must let me give you a kiss for that.' He bent down and kissed her, she holding up her face to his with no reluctance. Anna looked on, smiling.

Mr Tellwright sat near the window of the back parlour, reading the paper. Twilight was at hand. He lowered his head as Mynors entered with Agnes in train, so as to see over his spectacles, which were half-way down his nose.

'How d'ye do, Mr Mynors? I was just going to begin my supper. I don't wait, you know,' and he glanced at the table.

'Quite right,' said Mynors, 'so long as you wouldn't eat it all. Would he have eaten it all, Agnes, do you think?' Agnes pressed her head against Mynors' arm and laughed shyly. The old man sardonically chuckled.

Anna, who was still in the passage, wondered what could be on the table. If it was only the usual morsel of cheese she felt that she should expire of mortification. She peeped: the cheese was at one end, and at the other a joint of beef, scarcely touched.

'Nay, nay,' said Tellwright, as if he had been engaged some seconds upon the joke, 'I'd have saved ye the bone.'

Anna went upstairs to take off her hat, and immediately Agnes flew after her. The child was breathless with news.

'Oh, Anna! As soon as you'd gone out Father told me that Mr Mynors was coming for supper. Did you know before?'

'Not till Mr Mynors told me, dear.' It was characteristic of her father to say nothing until the last moment.

'Yes, and he told me to put an extra plate, and I asked him if I had better put the beef on the table, and first he said "No," cross – you know – and then he said I could please myself, so I put it on. Why has Mr Mynors come, Anna?'

'How should I know? Some business between him and Father, I expect.'

'It's very *queer*,' said Agnes positively, with the child's aptitude for looking a fact squarely in the face.

'Why "queer"?'

'You know it is, Anna,' she frowned, and then breaking into a joyous smile. 'But isn't he nice? I think he's lovely.'

'Yes,' Anna assented coldly.

'But really?' Agnes persisted.

Anna brushed her hair and determined not to put on the apron which she usually wore in the house.

'Am I tidy, Anna?'

'Yes. Run downstairs now. I am coming directly.'

'I want to wait for you,' Agnes pouted.

'Very well, dear.'

They entered the parlour together, and Henry Mynors jumped up from his chair, and would not sit at table until they were seated. Then Mr Tellwright carved the beef, giving each of them a very small piece, and taking only cheese for himself. Agnes handed the water-jug and the bread. Mynors talked about nothing in especial, but he talked and laughed the whole time; he even made the old man laugh, by a comical phrase aimed at Agnes's mad passion for gillyflowers. He seemed not to have detected any shortcomings in the table appointments – the coarse cloth and plates, the chipped tumblers, the pewter cruet, and the stumpy knives – which caused anguish in the heart of the housewife. He might have sat at such a table every night of his life.

'May I trouble you for a little more beef?' he asked presently, and Anna fancied a shade of mischief in his tone as he thus forced the old man into a tardy hospitality. 'Thanks. *And* a morsel of fat.'

She wondered whether he guessed that she was worth fifty thousand pounds, and her father worth perhaps more.

But on the whole Anna enjoyed the meal. She was sorry when they had finished and Agnes had thanked God for the beef. It was not without considerable reluctance that she rose and left the side of the man whose arm she could have touched at any time during the previous twenty minutes. She had felt happy and perturbed in being so near to him, so intimate and free; already she knew his face by heart. The two girls carried the plates and dishes into the kitchen, Agnes making the last journey with the tablecloth, which Mynors had assisted her to fold.

'Shut the door, Agnes,' said the old man, getting up to light the gas. It was an order of dismissal to both his daughters. 'Let me light that,' Mynors exclaimed, and the gas was lighted before Mr Tellwright had struck a match. Mynors turned on the full force of gas. Then Mr Tellwright carefully lowered it. The summer quarter's gas-bill at that house did not exceed five shillings.

Through the open windows of the kitchen and parlour, Anna could hear the voices of the two men in conversation, Mynors' vivacious and changeful, her father's monotonous, curt, and heavy. Once she caught the old man's hard dry chuckle. The washing-up was done, Agnes had accomplished her home-lessons; the grandfather's clock chimed the half-hour after nine.

'You must go to bed, Agnes.'

'Mustn't I say good-night to him?'

'No, I will say good-night for you.'

'Don't forget to. I shall ask you in the morning.'

The regular sound of talk still came from the parlour. A full moon passed along the cloudless sky. By its light and that of a glimmer of gas, Anna sat cleaning silver, or rather nickel, at the kitchen table. The spoons and forks were already clean, but she felt compelled to busy herself with something. At length the talk stopped and she heard the scraping of chair-legs. Should she return to the parlour? Or should she – ? Even while she hesitated, the kitchen door opened.

'Excuse me coming in here,' said Mynors. 'I wanted to say good-night to you.'

She sprang up and he took her hand. Could he feel the agitation of that hand?

'Good-night.'

'Good-night.' He said it again.

'And Agnes wished me to say good-night to you for her.'

'Did she?' He smiled; till then his face had been serious.

'You won't forget Friday?'

'As if I could!' she murmured after he had gone.

CHAPTER FIVE

The Revival

Anna spent the two following afternoons in visiting the houses of her school-children. She had no talent for such work, which demands the vocal rather than the meditative temperament, and the apparent futility of her labours would have disgusted and disheartened her had she not been sustained and urged forward by the still active influence of Mynors and the teachers' meeting. There were fifteen names in her class-book, and she went to each house, except four whose tenants were impeccable Wesleyan families and would have considered themselves insulted by a quasi-didactic visit from an upstart like Anna. Of the eleven, some parents were rude to her; others begged, and she had nothing to give; others made perfunctory promises; only two seemed to regard her as anything but a somewhat tiresome impertinence. The fault was doubtless her own. Nevertheless she found joy in the uncongenial and ill-performed task – the cold, fierce joy of the nun in her penance. When it was done she said 'I have done it,' as one who has sworn to do it come what might, yet without quite expecting to succeed.

On the Friday afternoon, during tea, a boy brought up a large foolscap packet addressed to Mr Tellwright. 'From Mr Mynors,' the boy said. Tellwright opened it leisurely after the boy had gone, and took out some sheets covered with figures which he carefully examined. 'Anna,' he said, as she was clearing away the tea things, 'I understand thou'rt going to the Revival meeting tonight. I shall have a message as thou mun give to Mr Mynors.'

When she went upstairs to dress, she saw the Suttons' landau* standing outside their house on the opposite side of the road. Mrs Sutton came down the front steps and got into the carriage, and was followed by a little restless, nervous, alert man who carried in his hand a black case of peculiar form. 'The Revivalist!' Anna exclaimed, remembering that he was to stay with the Suttons during the Revival week. Then this was the renowned crusader, and the case held his renowned cornet! The carriage drove off down Trafalgar Road, and Anna could see that the little man was talking vehemently and incessantly to Mrs Sutton, who listened with evident interest; at the same time the man's eyes were everywhere, absorbing all details of the street and houses with unquenchable curiosity.

'What is the message for Mr Mynors, Father?' she asked in the parlour, putting on her cotton gloves.

'Oh!' he said, and then paused. 'Shut th' door, lass.'

She shut it, not knowing what this cautiousness foreshadowed. Agnes was in the kitchen.

'It's o' this'n,' Tellwright began. 'Young Mynors wants a partner wi' a couple o' thousand pounds, and he come to me. Ye understand; 'tis what they call a sleeping partner he's after. He'll give a third share in his concern for two thousand pound now. I've looked into it and there's money in it. He's no fool and he's gotten hold of a good thing. He sent me up his stock-taking and balance sheet today, and I've been o'er the place mysen.* I'm telling thee this, lass, because I have na' two thousand o' my own idle just now, and I thought as thou might happen like th' investment.'

'But Father – '

'Listen. I know as there's only four hundred o' thine in th' Bank now, but next week 'll see the beginning o' July and dividends coming in. I've reckoned as ye'll have nigh on fourteen hundred i' dividends and interests, and I can lend ye a couple o' hundred in case o' necessity. It's a rare chance; thou's best tak' it.'

'Of course, if you think it's all right, Father, that's enough,' she said without animation.

'Am' na I telling thee I think it's all right?' he remarked sharply. 'You mun tell Mynors as I say it's satisfactory. Tell him that, see? I say it's satisfactory. I shall want for to see him later on. He told me he couldna' come up any night next week, so ask him to make it the week after. There's no hurry. Dunna'* forget.'

What surprised Anna most in the affair was that Henry Mynors should have been able to tempt her father into a speculation. Ephraim Tellwright the investor was usually as shy as a well-fed trout, and this capture of him by a youngster only two years established in business might fairly be regarded as a prodigious feat. It was indeed the highest distinction of Mynors' commercial career. Henry was so prominently active in the Wesleyan Society that the members of that society, especially the women, were apt to ignore the other side of his individuality. They knew him supreme as a religious worker; they did not realize the likelihood of his becoming supreme in the staple manufacture. Left an orphan at seventeen, Mynors belonged to a family now otherwise extinct in the Five Towns – one of those families which by virtue of numbers, variety, and personal force seem to permeate a whole district, to be a calculable item of it, an essential part of its identity. The elders of the Mynors blood had once occupied the red house opposite Tellwright's, now used as a school, and had there reared many children: the school building was still known as Mynors's by old-fashioned people. Then the parents died in middle age: one daughter married in the North, another in the South; a third went to China as a missionary and died of fever; the eldest son died; the second had vanished into Canada and was reported a scapegrace; the third was a sea-captain. Henry (the youngest) alone was left, and of all the family Henry was the only one to be connected with the earthenware trade. There was no inherited money, and during ten years he had worked for a large firm in Turnhill, as clerk, as traveller, and last as manager, living always quietly in lodgings. In the fullness of time he gave notice to leave, was offered a partnership, and refused it. Taking a newly erected manufactory in Bursley near the canal, he started in business for himself, and it became known that, at the age of twenty-eight, he had saved fifteen hundred pounds. Equally expert in the labyrinths of manufacture and in the niceties of the markets (he was reckoned a peerless traveller), Mynors inevitably flourished. His order-books were filled and flowing over at remunerative prices, and insufficiency of capital was the sole peril to which he was exposed. By the raising of a finger he could have had a dozen working and moneyed partners, but he had no desire for a working partner. What he wanted was a capitalist who had confidence in him, Mynors. In Ephraim Tellwright he found the man. Whether it was by instinct, good luck, or skilful diplomacy that Mynors secured this invaluable prize no one could positively say, and perhaps even he himself could not have catalogued all the obscure motives that had guided him to the shrewd miser of Manor Terrace.

Anna had meant to reach chapel before the commencement

of the meeting, but the interview with her father threw her late. As she entered the porch an officer told her that the body of the chapel was quite full and that she should go into the gallery, where a few seats were left near the choir. She obeyed: pew-holders* had no rights at that service. The scene in the auditorium astonished her, effectually putting an end to the worldly preoccupation caused by her father's news. The historic chapel was crowded almost in every part, and the congregation – impressed, excited, eager – sang the opening hymn with unprecedented vigour and sincerity; above the rest could be heard the trained voices of a large choir, and even the choir, usually perfunctory, seemed to share the general fervour. In the vast mahogany pulpit the Reverend Reginald Banks, the superintendent minister, a stout pale-faced man with pendent cheeks and cold grey eyes, stood impassively regarding the assemblage, and by his side was the revivalist, a manikin in comparison with his colleague; on the broad balustrade of the pulpit lay the cornet. The fiery and inquisitive eyes of the revivalist probed into the furthest corners of the chapel; apparently no detail of any single face or of the florid decoration escaped him, and as Anna crept into a small empty pew next to the east wall she felt that she too had been separately observed. Mr Banks gave out the last verse of the hymn, and simultaneously with the leading chord from the organ the revivalist seized his cornet and joined the melody. Massive yet exultant, the tones rose clear over the mighty volume of vocal sound, an incitement to victorious effort. The effect was instant: an ecstatic tremor seemed to pass through the congregation, like wind through ripe corn, and at the close of the hymn it was not until the revivalist had put down his cornet that the people resumed their seats. Amid the *frou-frou** of dresses and subdued clearing of throats, Mr Banks retired softly to the back of the pulpit, and the revivalist, mounting a stool, suddenly dominated the congregation. His glance swept masterfully across the chapel and round the gallery. He raised one hand with the stilling action of a mesmerist, and the people, either kneeling or inclined against the front of the pews, hid their faces from those eyes. It was as though the man had in a moment measured their iniquities, and had courageously resolved to intercede for them with God, but was not very sanguine as to the result. Everyone except the organist, who was searching his tune-book for the next tune, seemed to feel humbled, bitterly ashamed, as it were caught in the act of sin. There was a solemn and terrible pause.

Then the revivalist began:

'Behold us, O dread God, suppliants for thy mercy – '

His voice was rich and full, but at the same time sharp and decisive. The burning eyes were shut tight, and Anna, who had a profile view of his face, saw that every muscle of it was drawn tense. The man possessed an extraordinary histrionic gift, and he used it with imagination. He had two audiences, God and the congregation. God was not more distant from him than the congregation, or less real to him, or less a heart to be influenced. Declamatory and full of effects carefully calculated – a work of art, in fact – his appeal showed no error of discretion in its approach to the Eternal. There was no minimizing of committed sin, nor yet an insincere and grovelling self-accusation. A tyrant could not have taken offence at its tone, which seemed to pacify God while rendering the human audience still more contrite. The conclusion of the catalogue of wickedness and swift confident turn to Christ's Cross was marvellously impressive. The congregation burst out into sighs, groans, blessings, and Amens; and the pillars of distant rural conventicles* who had travelled from the confines of the circuit to its centre in order to partake of this spiritual excitation began to feel that they would not be disappointed.

'Let the Holy Ghost descend upon us now,' the revivalist pleaded with restrained passion; and then, opening his eyes and looking at the clock in front of the gallery, he repeated, 'Now, now, at twenty-one minutes past seven.' Then his eyes, without shifting, seemed to ignore the clock, to gaze through it into some unworldly dimension, and he murmured in a soft dramatic whisper: 'I see the Divine Dove! – '*

The doors, closed during prayer, were opened, and more people entered. A youth came into Anna's pew.

The superintendent minister gave out another hymn, and when this was finished the revivalist, who had been resting in a chair, came forward again. 'Friends and fellow-sinners,' he said, 'a lot of you, fools that you are, have come here tonight to hear me play my cornet. Well, you have heard me. I have played the cornet, and I will play it again. I would play it on my head if by so doing I could bring sinners to Christ. I have been called a mountebank. I am one. I glory in it. I am God's mountebank, doing God's precious business in my own way. But God's precious business cannot be carried on, even by a mountebank, without money, and there will be a collection towards the expenses of the Revival. During the collection we will sing "Rock of Ages",* and you shall hear my cornet again. If you feel willing to give us your sixpences, give; but if you resent a collection,' here he adopted a tone of ferocious sarcasm, 'keep your miserable sixpences and get sixpenny-worth of miserable enjoyment out of them elsewhere.'

As the meeting proceeded, submitting itself more and more to the imperious hypnotism of the revivalist, Anna gradually became oppressed by a vague sensation which was partly sorrow and partly an inexplicable dull anger – anger at her own penitence. She felt as if everything was wrong and could never by any possibility be righted. After two exhortations, from the minister and the revivalist, and another hymn, the revivalist once more prayed, and as he did so Anna looked stealthily about in a sick, preoccupied way. The youth at her side stared glumly in front of him. In the orchestra Henry Mynors was whispering to the organist. Down in the body of the chapel the atmosphere was electric, perilous, over-charged with spiritual emotion. She was glad she was not down there. The voice of the revivalist ceased, but he kept the attitude of supplication. Sobs were heard in various quarters, and here and there an elder of the chapel could be seen talking quietly to some convicted sinner. The revivalist began softly to sing 'Jesu, lover of my soul',* and most of the congregation, standing up, joined him; but the sinners stricken of the Spirit remained abjectly bent, tortured by conscience, pulled this way by Christ and that by Satan. A few rose and went to the Communion rails, there to kneel in the sight of all. Mr Banks descended from the pulpit and opening the wicket which led to the Communion table spoke to these over the rails, reassuringly, as a nurse to a child. Other sinners, desirous of fuller and more intimate guidance, passed down the aisles and so into the preacher's vestry at the eastern end of the chapel, and were followed thither by class-leaders and other proved servants of God: among these last were Titus Price and Mr Sutton.

'The blood of Christ atones,' said the revivalist solemnly at the end of the hymn. 'The spirit of Christ is working among us.

Let us engage in private prayer. Let us drive the devil out of this chapel.'

More sighs and groans followed. Then some one cried out in sharp, shrill tones, 'Praise Him'; and another cried, 'Praise Him'; and an old woman's quavering voice sang the words, 'I know that my Redeemer liveth.'* Anna was in despair at her own predicament, and the sense of sin was not more strong than the sense of being confused and publicly shamed. A man opened the pew-door, and sitting down by the youth's side began to talk with him. It was Henry Mynors. Anna looked steadily away, at the wall, fearful lest he should address her too. Presently the youth got up with a frenzied gesture and walked out of the gallery, followed by Mynors. In a moment she saw the youth stepping awkwardly along the aisle beneath, towards the inquiry room, his head forward, and the lower lip hanging as though he were sulky.

Anna was now in the profoundest misery. The weight of her sins, of her ingratitude to God, lay on her like a physical and intolerable load, and she lost all feeling of shame, as a sea-sick voyager loses shame after an hour of nausea. She knew then that she could no longer go on living as aforetime. She shuddered at the thought of her tremendous responsibility to Agnes – Agnes who took her for perfection. She recollected all her sins individually – lies, sloth, envy, vanity, even theft in her infancy. She heaped up all the wickedness of a lifetime, hysterically augmented it, and found a horrid pleasure in the exaggeration. Her virtuous acts shrank into nothingness.

A man, and then another, emerged from the vestry door with beaming, happy face. These were saved; they had yielded to Christ's persuasive invitation. Anna tried to imagine herself converted, or in the process of being converted. She could not. She could only sit moveless, dull, and abject. She did not stir, even when the congregation rose for another hymn. In what did conversion consist? Was it to say the words, 'I believe'? She repeated to herself softly, 'I believe; I believe.' But nothing happened. Of course she believed. She had never doubted, nor dreamed of doubting, that Jesus died on the Cross to save her soul – *her* soul – from eternal damnation. She was probably unaware that any person in Christendom had doubted that fact so fundamental to her. What, then, was lacking? What was belief? What was faith?

A venerable class-leader came from the vestry, and, slowly climbing the pulpit stairs, whispered in the ear of the revivalist. The latter faced the congregation with a cry of joy. 'Lord,' he exclaimed, 'we bless Thee that seventeen souls have found Thee! Lord, let the full crop be gathered, for the fields are white unto harvest.' There was an exuberant chorus of praise to God.

The door of the pew was opened gently, and Anna started to see Mrs Sutton at her side. She at once guessed that Mynors had sent to her this angel of consolation.

'Are you near the light, dear Anna?' Mrs Sutton began.

Anna searched for an answer. She now sat huddled up in the corner of the pew, her face partially turned towards Mrs Sutton, who looked mildly into her eyes. 'I don't know,' Anna stammered, feeling like a naughty school-girl. A doubt whether the whole affair was not after all absurd flashed through her, and was gone.

'But it is quite simple,' said Mrs Sutton. 'I cannot tell you anything that you do not know. Cast out pride. Cast out pride – that is it. Nothing but earthly pride prevents you from realizing the saving power of Christ. You are afraid, Anna, afraid to be humble. Be brave. It is so simple, so easy. If one will but submit.'

Anna said nothing, had nothing to say, was conscious of nothing save excessive discomfort.

'Where do you feel your difficulty to be?' asked Mrs Sutton.

'I don't know,' she answered wearily.

'The happiness that awaits you is unspeakable. I have followed Christ for nearly fifty years and my happiness increases daily. Sometimes I do not know how to contain it all. It surges above all the trials and disappointments of this world. Oh Anna, if you will but believe!'

The ageing woman's thin distinguished face crowned with abundant grey hair glistened with love and compassion, and as Anna's eyes rested upon it Anna felt that here was something tangible, something to lay hold on.

'I think I do believe,' she said weakly.

'You "think"? Are you sure? Are you not deceiving yourself? Belief is not with the lips: it is with the heart.'

There was a pause. Mr Banks could be heard praying.

'I will go home,' Anna whispered at length, 'and think it out for myself.'

'Do, my dear girl, and God will help you.'

Mrs Sutton bent and kissed Anna affectionately and then hurried away to offer her ministrations elsewhere. As Anna left the chapel she encountered the chapel-keeper pacing regularly to and fro across the length of the broad steps. In the porch was a notice that cabinet photographs* of the revivalist could be purchased on application at one shilling each.

CHAPTER SIX

Willie

Anna closed the bedroom door softly; through the open window came the tones of Cauldon Church clock, famous for their sonority and richness, announcing eleven. Agnes lay asleep under the blue-and-white counterpane, on the side of the bed next the wall, the bed-clothes pushed down and disclosing the upper half of her nightgowned figure. She slept in absolute repose, with flushed cheek and every muscle lax, her hair by some chance drawn in a perfect straight line diagonally across the pillow. Anna glanced at her sister, the image of physical innocence and childish security, and then, depositing the candle, went to the window and looked out.

The bedroom was over the kitchen and faced south. The moon was hidden by clouds, but clear stretches of sky showed thick-studded clusters of stars brightly winking. To the far right across the fields the silhouette of Hillport Church could just be discerned on the ridge. In front, several miles away, the blast-furnaces of Cauldon Bar Ironworks shot up vast wreaths of yellow flame with canopies of tinted smoke. Still more distant were a thousand other lights crowning chimney and kiln, and nearer, on the waste lands west of Bleakridge, long fields of burning ironstone glowed with all the strange colours of decadence. The entire landscape was illuminated and transformed by these unique pyrotechnics of labour atoning for its grime, and dull, weird sounds, as of the breathings and sighings of gigantic nocturnal creatures, filled the enchanted air. It was a romantic scene, a romantic summer night, balmy, delicate, and wrapped in meditation. But Anna saw nothing there save the repulsive evidences of manufacture, had never seen anything else.

She was still horribly, acutely miserable, exhausted by the fruitless search for some solution of the enigma of sin – her sin in particular – and of redemption. She had cogitated in a vain circle until she was no longer capable of reasoned ideas. She gazed at the stars and into the illimitable spaces beyond them, and thought of life and its inconceivable littleness, as millions had done before in the presence of that same firmament. Then, after a time, her brain resumed its nightmarelike task. She began to probe herself anew. Would it have availed if she had walked publicly to the penitential form at the Communion rail, and, ranging herself with the working men and women, proved by that overt deed the sincerity of her contrition? She wished ardently that she had done so, yet knew well that such an act would always be impossible for her, even though the evasion of it meant eternal torture. Undoubtedly, as Mrs Sutton had implied, she was proud, stiff-necked, obstinate in iniquity.

Agnes stirred slightly in her sleep, and Anna, aroused, dropped the blind, turned towards the room and began to undress, slowly, with reflective pauses. Her melancholy became grim, sardonic; if she was doomed to destruction, so let it be. Suddenly, half-clad, she knelt down and prayed, prayed that pride might be cast out, burying her face in the coverlet and caging the passionate effusion in a whisper lest Agnes should be disturbed. Having prayed, she still knelt quiescent; her eyes were dry and burning. The last car thundered up the road, shaking the house, and she rose, finished undressing, blew out the candle, and slipped into bed by Agnes's side.

She could not sleep, did not attempt to sleep, but abandoned herself meekly to despair. Her thoughts covered again the interminable round, and again, and yet again. In the twilight of the brief summer night her accustomed eyes could distinguish every object in the room, all the bits of furniture which had been brought from Hanbridge and with which she had been familiar since her memory began: everything appeared mean, despicable, cheerless; there was nothing to inspire. She dreamed impossibly of a high spirituality which should metamorphose all, change her life, lend glamour to the most pitiful surroundings, ennoble the most ignominious burdens – a spirituality never to be hers.

At any rate she would tell her father in the morning that she was convicted of sin, and, however hopelessly, seeking salvation; she would tell both her father and Agnes at breakfast. The task would be difficult, but she swore to do it. She resolved, she endeavoured to sleep, and did sleep uneasily for a short period. When she woke the great business of the dawn had begun. She left the bed, and drawing up the blind looked forth. The furnace fires were paling; a few milky clouds sailed in the vast pallid blue. It was cool just then, and she shivered. She went to the glass, and examined her face carefully, but it gave no signs whatever of the inward warfare. She saw her plain and mended nightgown. Suppose she were married to Mynors! Suppose he lay asleep in the bed where Agnes lay asleep! Involuntarily she glanced at Agnes to certify that the child and none else was indeed there, and got into bed hurriedly and hid herself because she was ashamed to have had such a fancy. But she continued to think of Mynors. She envied him for his cheerfulness, his joy, his goodness, his dignity, his tact, his sex. She envied every man. Even in the sphere of religion, men were not fettered like women. No man, she thought, would acquiesce in the futility to which she had already half resigned; a man would either wring salvation from the heavenly powers or race gloriously to hell. Mynors – Mynors was a god!

She recollected her resolution to speak to her father and Agnes at breakfast, and shudderingly confirmed it, but less stoutly than before. Then an announcement made by Mr Banks in chapel on the previous evening presented itself, as though she was listening to it for the first time. It was the announcement of a prayer-meeting for workers in the Revival, to be held that (Saturday) morning at seven o'clock. She instantly decided to go to the meeting, and the decision seemed to give her new hope. Perhaps there she might find peace. On that faint expectancy she fell asleep again and did not wake till half-past six, after her usual hour. She heard noises in the yard; it was her father going towards the garden with a wheelbarrow. She dressed quickly, and when she had pinned on her hat she woke Agnes.

'Going out, Sis?' the child asked sleepily, seeing her attire.

'Yes, dear. I am going to the seven o'clock prayer-meeting. And you must get breakfast. You can – can't you?'

The child assented, glad of the chance.

'But what are you going to the prayer-meeting for?'

Anna hesitated. Why not confess? No. 'I must go,' she said quietly at length. 'I shall be back before eight.'

'Does Father know?' Agnes enquired apprehensively.

'No, dear.'

Anna shut the door quickly, went softly downstairs and along the passage, and crept into the street like a thief.

Men and women and boys and girls were on their way to work, with hurried clattering steps, some munching thick pieces of bread as they went, all self-centred, apparently morose, and not quite awake. The dust lay thick in the arid gutters, and in drifts across the pavement, as the night-wind had blown it. Vehicular traffic had not begun, and blinds were still drawn; and though the footpaths were busy the street had a deserted and forlorn aspect. Anna walked hastily down the road, avoiding the glances of such as looked at her, but peering furtively at the faces of those who ignored her. All seemed callous – hoggishly careless of the everlasting verities. At first it appeared strange to her that the potent revival in the Wesleyan chapel had produced no effect on these preoccupied people. Bursley, then, continued its dull and even course. She wondered whether any of them guessed that she was going to the prayer-meeting and secretly sneered at her therefore.

When she had climbed Duck Bank she found to her surprise that the doors of the chapel were fast closed, though it was ten minutes past seven. Was there to be no prayer-meeting? A momentary sensation of relief flashed through her, and then she saw that the gate of the school-yard was open. She should have known that early morning prayers were never offered up in the chapel, but in the lecture-hall. She crossed the quadrangle with beating heart, feeling now that she had embarked on a frightful enterprise. The door of the lecture-hall was ajar; she pushed it and went in. At the other end of the hall a meagre handful of worshippers were collected, and on the raised platform stood Mr Banks, vapid, perfunctory, and fatigued. He gave out a verse, and pitched the tune – too high, but the singers with a heroic effect accomplished the verse without breaking down. The singing was thin and feeble, and the eagerness of one or two voices seemed strained, as though with a determination to make the best of things. Mynors was not present, and Anna did not know whether to be sorry or glad at this. She recognized that save herself all present were old believers, tried warriors of the Lord. There was only one other woman, Miss Sarah Vodrey, an aged spinster who kept house for Titus Price and his son, and found her sole diversion in the variety of her religious experiences. Before the hymn was finished a young man joined the assembly, it was the youth who had sat near Anna on the previous night, an ecstatic and naïve bliss shone from his face. In his prayer the minister drew the attention of the Deity to the fact that although a score or more of souls had been ingathered at the first service, the Methodists of Bursley were by no means satisfied. They wanted more; they wanted the whole of Bursley; and they would be content with no less. He begged that their earnest work might not be shamed before the world by a partial success. In conclusion he sought the blessing of God on the revivalist and asked that this tireless enthusiast might be led to husband his strength: at which there was a fervent Amen.

Several men prayed, and a pause ensued, all still kneeling. Then the minister said in a tone of oily politeness:

'Will a sister pray?'

Another pause followed. 'Sister Tellwright?'

Anna would have welcomed death and damnation. She clasped her hands tightly, and longed for the endless moment to pass. At last Sarah Vodrey gave a preliminary cough. Miss Vodrey was always happy to pray aloud, and her invocations usually began with the same phrase: 'Lord, we thank Thee that this day finds us with our bodies out of the grave and our souls out of hell.'

Afterwards the minister gave out another hymn, and as soon as the singing commenced Anna slipped away. Once in the yard, she breathed a sigh of relief. Peace at the prayer-meeting? It was like coming out of prison. Peace was farther off than ever. Nay, she had actually forgotten her soul in the sensations of shame and discomfort. She had contrived only to make herself ridiculous, and perhaps the pious at their breakfast-tables would discuss her and her father, and their money, and the queer life they led.

If Mynors had but been present!

She walked out into the street. It was twenty minutes to eight by the town-hall clock. The last workmen's car of the morning was just leaving Bursley: it was packed inside and outside, and the conductor hung insecurely on the step. At the gates of the manufactory opposite the chapel, a man in a white smock stood placidly smoking a pipe. A prayer-meeting was a little thing, a trifle in the immense and regular activity of the town: this thought necessarily occurred to Anna. She hurried homewards, wondering what her father would say about that morning's unusual excursion. A couple of hundred yards distant from home she saw, to her astonishment, Agnes emerging from the front-door of the house. The child ran rapidly down the street, not observing Anna till they were close upon each other.

'Oh, Anna! You forgot to buy the bacon yesterday. There isn't a *scrap*, and Father's fearfully angry. He gave me sixpence, and I'm going down to Leal's to get some as quick as ever I can.'

It was a thunderbolt to Anna, this seemingly petty misadventure. As she entered the house she felt a tear on her cheek. She was ashamed to weep, but she wept. This, after the fiasco of the prayer-meeting, was a climax of woe; it overtopped and extinguished all the rest; her soul was nothing to her now. She quickly took off her hat and ran to the kitchen. Agnes had put the breakfast-things on the tray ready for setting; the bread was cut, the coffee portioned into the jug; the fire burned bright, and the kettle sang. Anna took the cloth from the drawer in the oak dresser, and went to the parlour to lay the table. Mr Tellwright was at the end of the garden, pointing the wall, his back to the house. The table set, Anna observed that the room was only partly dusted: there was a duster on the mantelpiece; she seized it to finish, and at that moment the kitchen clock struck eight. Simultaneously Mr Tellwright dropped his trowel, and came towards the house. She doggedly dusted one chair, and then, turning coward, flew away upstairs; the kitchen was barred to her since her father would enter by the kitchen door.

She had forgotten to buy bacon, and breakfast would be late: it was a calamity unique in her experience! She stood at the door of her bedroom, and waited, vehemently, for Agnes's return. At last the child raced breathlessly in; Anna flew to meet her. With incredible speed the bacon was whipped out of its wrapper, and Anna picked up the knife. At the first stroke she cut herself, and Agnes was obliged to bind the finger with rag. The clock struck the half-hour like a knell. It was twenty minutes to nine, forty minutes behind time, when the two girls hurried into the parlour, Anna bearing the bacon and hot plates, Agnes the bread and coffee. Mr Tellwright sat upright and ferocious in his chair, the image of offence and wrath. Instead of reading his letters he had fed full of this ineffable grievance. The meal began in a desolating silence. The male creature's terrible displeasure permeated the whole room like an ether, invisible but carrying vibrations to the heart. Then when he had eaten one piece of bacon, and cut his envelopes, the miser began to empty himself of some of his anger in stormy tones that might have uprooted trees. Anna ought to feel thoroughly ashamed. He could not imagine what she had been thinking of. Why didn't she tell him she was going to the prayer-meeting? Why did she go to the prayer-meeting? disarranging the whole household? How came she to forget the bacon? It was gross carelessness. A pretty example to her little sister! The fact was that *since her birthday* she had gotten above hersen.* She was careless and extravagant. Look how thick the bacon was cut. He should not stand it much longer. And her finger all red, and the blood dropping on the cloth: a nice sight at a meal! Go and tie it up again.

Without a word she left the room to obey. Of course she had no defence. Agnes, her tears falling, pecked her food timidly like a bird, not daring to stir from her chair, even to assist at the finger.

'What did Mr Mynors say?' Tellwright inquired fiercely when Anna had come back into the room.

'Mr Mynors?' she murmured, at a loss, but vaguely apprehending further trouble.

'Did ye see him?'

'Yes, Father.'

'Did ye give him my message?'

'I forgot it.' God in heaven! She had forgotten the message!

With a devastating grunt Mr Tellwright walked speechless out of the room. The girls cleared the table, exchanging sympathy with a single mute glance. Anna's one satisfaction was that, even if she had remembered the message, she could not possibly have delivered it.

Ephraim Tellwright stayed in the front parlour till half-past ten o'clock, unseen but felt, like an angry god behind a cloud. The consciousness that he was there, unappeased and dangerous, remained uppermost in the minds of the two girls during the morning. At half-past ten he opened the door.

'Agnes!' he commanded, and Agnes ran to him from the kitchen with the speed of propitiation.

'Yes, Father.'

'Take this note down to Price's, and don't wait for an answer.'

'Yes, Father.'

She was back in twenty minutes. Anna was sweeping the lobby.

'If Mr Mynors calls while I'm out, you mun tell him to wait,' Mr Tellwright said to Agnes, pointedly ignoring Anna's presence. Then, having brushed his greenish hat on his sleeve he went off towards town to buy meat and vegetables. He always did Saturday's marketing himself. At the butcher's and in the St Luke's covered market he was a familiar and redoubtable figure. Among the salespeople who stood in the market was a wrinkled, hardy old potato-woman from the other side of Moorthorne: every Saturday the miser bested* her in their higgling-match,* and nearly every Saturday she scornfully threw at him the same joke: 'Get thee along to th' post-office, Mester Terrick:† happen they'll give thee sixpenn'orth o' stamps for fivepence ha'penny.' He seldom failed to laugh heartily at this.

At dinner the girls could perceive that the shadow of his displeasure had slightly lifted, though he kept a frowning silence. Expert in all the symptoms of his moods, they knew that in a few hours he would begin to talk again, at first in monosyllables, and then in short detached sentences. An intimation of relief diffused itself through the house like a hint of spring in February.

These domestic upheavals followed always the same course, and Anna had learnt to suffer the later stages of them with calmness and even with impassivity. Henry Mynors had not called. She supposed that her father had expected him to call for the answer which she had forgotten to give him, and she had a hope that he would come in the afternoon: once again she had the idea that something definite and satisfactory might result if she could only see him – that she might, as it were, gather inspiration from the mere sight of his face. After dinner, while the girls were washing the dinner things in the scullery, Agnes's quick ear caught the sound of voices in the parlour. They listened. Mynors had come. Mr Tellwright must have seen him from the front window and opened the door to him before he could ring.

'It's him,' said Agnes, excited.

'Who?' Anna asked, self-consciously.

'Mr Mynors, of course,' said the child sharply, making it quite plain that this affectation could not impose on her for a single instant.

'Anna!' It was Mr Tellwright's summons, through the parlour window. She dried her hands, doffed her apron, and went to the parlour, animated by a thousand fears and expectations. Why was she to be included in the colloquy?

† *Terrick*: a corruption of Tellwright.

Mynors rose at her entrance and greeted her with conspicuous deference, a deference which made her feel ashamed.

'Hum!' the old man growled, but he was obviously content. 'I gave Anna a message for ye yesterday, Mr Mynors, but her forgot to deliver it, wench-like. Ye might ha' been saved th' trouble o' calling. Now as ye're here, I've summat for tell ye. It'll be Anna's money as 'll go into that concern o' yours. I've none by me; in fact, I'm a'most fast for brass,* but her'll have as near two thousand as makes no matter in a month's time, and her says her'll go in wi' you on th' strength o' my recommendation.'

This speech was evidently a perfect surprise for Henry Mynors. For a moment he seemed to be at a loss; then his face gave candid expression to a feeling of intense pleasure.

'You know all about this business then, Miss Tellwright?'

She blushed. 'Father has told me something about it.'

'And are you willing to be my partner?'

'Nay, I did na' say that,' Tellwright interrupted. 'It'll be Anna's money, but i' my name.'

'I see,' said Mynors gravely. 'But if it is Miss Anna's money, why should not she be the partner?' He offered one of his courtly diplomatic smiles.

'Oh – but – ' Anna began in deprecation.

Tellwright laughed. 'Ay!' he said, 'Why not? It 'll be experience for th' lass.'

'Just so,' said Mynors.

Anna stood silent, like a child who is being talked about. There was a pause.

'Would you care for that arrangement, Miss Tellwright?'

'Oh, yes,' she said.

'I shall try to justify your confidence. I needn't say that I think you and your father will have no reason to be disappointed. Two thousand pounds is of course only a trifle to you, but it is a great deal to me, and – and – ' He hesitated. Anna did not surmise that he was too much moved by the sight of her, and the situation, to continue, but this was the fact.

'There's nobbut one point, Mr Mynors,' Tellwright said bluntly, 'and that's the interest on th' capital, as must be deducted before reckoning profits. Us must have six per cent.'

'But I thought we had settled it at five,' said Mynors with sudden firmness.

'We 'n settled as you shall have five on your fifteen hundred,' the miser replied with imperturbable audacity, 'but us mun have our six.'

'I certainly thought we had thrashed that out fully, and agreed that the interest should be the same on each side.' Mynors was alert and defensive.

'Nay, young man. Us mun have our six. We're takkin' a risk.'

Mynors pressed his lips together. He was taken at a disadvantage. Mr Tellwright, with unscrupulous cleverness, had utilized the effect on Mynors of his daughter's presence to regain a position from which the younger man had definitely ousted him a few days before. Mynors was annoyed but he gave no sign of his annoyance.

'Very well,' he said at length, with a private smile at Anna to indicate that it was out of regard for her that he yielded.

Mr Tellwright made no pretence of concealing his satisfaction. He, too, smiled at Anna, sardonically: the last vestige of the morning's irritation vanished in a glow of triumph 'I'm afraid I must go,' said Mynors, looking at his watch 'There is a service at chapel at three. Our Revivalist came down with Mrs Sutton to look over the works this morning, and I told him I should be at the service. So I must. You coming, Mr Tellwright?'

'Nay, my lad. I'm owd enough to leave it to young uns.'

Anna forced her courage to the verge of rashness, moved by a swift impulse.

'Will you wait one minute?' she said to Mynors. 'I am going to the service. If I'm late back, Father, Agnes will see to the tea. Don't wait for me.' She looked him straight in the face. It was one of the bravest acts of her life. After the episode of breakfast, to suggest a procedure which might entail any risk upon another meal was absolutely heroic. Tellwright glanced away from his daughter, and at Mynors. Anna hurried upstairs.

'Who's thy lawyer, Mr Mynors?' Tellwright asked.

'Dane,' said Mynors.

'That 'll be convenient. Dane does my bit o' business, too. I'll see him, and make a bargain wi' him for th' partnership deed. He always works by contract for me. I've no patience wi' six-and-eightpences.'*

Mynors assented.

'You must come down some afternoon and look over the

works,' he said to Anna as they were walking down Trafalgar Road towards chapel.

'I should like to,' Anna replied. 'I've never been over a works in my life.'

'No? You are going to be a partner in the best works of its size in Bursley,' Mynors said enthusiastically.

'I'm glad of that,' she smiled, 'for I do believe I own the worst.'

'What – Price's do you mean?'

She nodded.

'Ah!' he exclaimed, and seemed to be thinking. 'I wasn't sure whether that belonged to you or your father. I'm afraid it isn't quite the best of properties. But perhaps I'd better say nothing about that. We had a grand meeting last night. Our little cornet-player quite lived up to his reputation, don't you think?'

'Quite,' she said faintly.

'You enjoyed the meeting?'

'No,' she blurted out, dismayed but resolute to be honest.

There was a silence.

'But you were at the early prayer-meeting this morning, I hear.'

She said nothing while they took a dozen paces, and then murmured, 'Yes.'

Their eyes met for a second, hers full of trouble.

'Perhaps,' he said at length, 'perhaps – excuse me saying this – but you may be expecting too much – '

'Well?' she encouraged him, prepared now to finish what had been begun.

'I mean,' he said, earnestly, 'that I – we – cannot promise you any sudden change of feeling, any sudden relief and certainty, such as some people experience. At least, I never had it. What is called conversion can happen in various ways. It is a question of living, of constant endeavour, with the example of Christ always before us. It need not always be a sudden wrench, you know, from the world. Perhaps you have been expecting too much,' he repeated, as though offering balm with that phrase.

She thanked him sincerely, but not with her lips, only with the heart. He had revealed to her an avenue of release from a situation which had seemed on all sides fatally closed. She sprang eagerly towards it. She realized afresh how frightful was the dilemma from which there was now a hope of escape, and she was grateful accordingly. Before, she had not dared steadily to face its terrors. She wondered that even her father's displeasure or the project of the partnership had been able to divert her from the plight of her soul. Putting these mundane things firmly behind her, she concentrated the activities of her brain on that idea of Christ-like living, day by day, hour by hour, of a gradual aspiration towards Christ and thereby an ultimate arrival at the state of being saved. This she thought she might accomplish; this gave opportunity of immediate effort, dispensing with the necessity of an impossible violent spiritual metamorphosis. They did not speak again until they had reached the gates of the chapel, when Mynors, who had to enter the choir from the back, bade her a quiet adieu. Anna enjoyed the service, which passed smoothly and uneventfully. At a Revival, night is the time of ecstasy and fervour and salvation; in the afternoon one must be content with preparatory praise and prayer.

That evening, while father and daughters sat in the parlour after supper, there was a ring at the door. Agnes ran to open, and found Willie Price. It had begun to rain, and the visitor, his jacket-collar turned up, was wet and draggled. Agnes left him on the mat and ran back to the parlour.

'Young Mr Price wants to see you, Father.'

Tellwright motioned to her to shut the door.

'You'd best see him, Anna,' he said. 'It's none my business.'

'But what has he come about, Father?'

'That note as I sent down this morning. I told owd Titus as he mun pay us twenty pun on Monday morning certain, or us should distrain. Them as can pay ten pun, especially in bank notes, can pay twenty pun, and thirty.'

'And suppose he says he can't?'

'Tell him he must. I've figured it out and changed my mind about that works. Owd Titus isna' done for yet, though he's getting on that road. Us can screw another fifty out o' him; that'll only leave six months rent owing; then us can turn him out. He'll go bankrupt; us can claim for our rent afore th' other creditors, and us 'll have a hundred or a hundred and twenty in hand towards doing the owd place up a bit for a new tenant.'

'Make him bankrupt, Father?' Anna exclaimed. It was the only part of the ingenious scheme which she had understood.

'Ay!' he said laconically.

'But – ' (Would Christ have driven Titus Price into the bankruptcy court?)

'If he pays, well and good.'

'Hadn't you better see Mr William, Father?'

'Whose property is it, mine or thine?' Tellwright growled. His good humour was still precarious, insecurely re-established, and Anna obediently left the room. After all, she said to herself, a debt is a debt, and honest people pay what they owe.

It was in an uncomplaisant tone that Anna invited Willie Price to the front parlour: nervousness always made her seem harsh, and moreover she had not the trick of hiding firmness under suavity.

'Will you come this way, Mr Price?'

'Yes,' he said with ingratiating, eager compliance. Dusk was falling, and the room in shadow. She forgot to ask him to take a chair, so they both stood up during the interview.

'A grand meeting we had last night,' he began, twisting his hat. 'I saw you there, Miss Tellwright.'

'Yes.'

'Yes. There was a splendid muster of teachers. I wanted to be at the prayer-meeting this morning, but couldn't get away. Did you happen to go, Miss Tellwright?'

She saw that he knew that she had been present, and gave him another curt monosyllable. She would have liked to be kind to him, to reassure him, to make him happy and comfortable, so ludicrous and touching were his efforts after a social urbanity which should appease; but, just as much as he, she was unskilled in the subtle arts of converse.

'Yes,' he continued, 'and I was anxious to be at tonight's meeting, but the Dad asked me to come up here. He said I'd better.' That term, 'the Dad', uttered in William's slow, drawling voice, seemed to show Titus Price in a new light to Anna, as a human creature loved, not as a mere gross physical organism: the effect was quite surprising. William went on: 'Can I see your father, Miss Tellwright?'

'Is it about the rent?'

'Yes,' he said.

'Well, if you will tell me – '

'Oh! I beg pardon,' he said quickly. 'Of course I know it's your property, but I thought Mr Tellwright always saw after it for you. It was he that wrote that letter this morning, wasn't it?'

'Yes,' Anna replied. She did not explain the situation.

'You insist on another twenty pounds on Monday?'

'Yes,' she said.

'We paid ten last Monday.'

'But there is still over a hundred owing.'

'I know, but – oh, Miss Tellwright, you mustn't be hard on us. Trade's bad.'

'It says in the *Signal* that trade is improving,' she interrupted sharply.

'Does it?' he said. 'But look at prices; they're cut till there's no profit left. I assure you, Miss Tellwright, my father and me are having a hard struggle. Everything's against us, and the works in particular, as *you* know.'

His tone was so earnest, so pathetic, that tears of compassion almost rose to her eyes as she looked at those simple naïve blue eyes of his. His lanky figure and clumsily-fitting clothes, his feeble placatory smile, the twitching movements of his long red hands, all contributed to the effect of his defencelessness. She thought of the text: 'Blessed are the meek',* and saw in a flash the deep truth of it. Here were she and her father, rich, powerful, autocratic; and there were Willie Price and his father, commercial hares hunted by hounds of creditors, hares that turned in plaintive appeal to those greedy jaws for mercy. And yet, she, a hound, envied at that moment the hares. Blessed are the meek, blessed are the failures, blessed are the stupid, for they, unknown to themselves, have a grace which is denied to the haughty, the successful, and the wise. The very repulsiveness of old Titus, his underhand methods, his insincerities, only served to increase her sympathy for the pair. How could Titus help being himself any more than Henry Mynors could help being himself? And that idea led her to think of the prospective partnership, destined by every favourable sign to brilliant success, and to contrast it with the ignoble and forlorn undertaking in Edward Street.

She tried to discover some method of soothing the young man's fears, of being considerate to him without injuring her father's scheme.

'If you will pay what you owe,' she said, 'we will spend it all, every penny, on improving the works.'

'Miss Tellwright,' he answered with fatal emphasis, 'we cannot pay.'

Ah! She wished to follow Christ day by day, hour by hour –

constantly to endeavour after saintliness. What was she to do now? Left to herself, she might have said in a burst of impulsive generosity, 'I forgive you all arrears. Start afresh.' But her father had to be reckoned with. . . .

'How much do you think you *can* pay on Monday?' she asked coldly.

At that moment her father entered the room. His first act was to light the gas. Willie Price's eyes blinked at the glare, as though he were trembling before the anticipated decree of this implacable old man. Anna's heart beat with sympathetic apprehension. Tellwright shook hands grimly with the youth, who re-stated hurriedly what he had said to Anna.

'It's o' this'n,'* the old man began with finality, and stopped. Anna caught a glance from him dismissing her. She went out in silence. On the Monday Titus Price paid another twenty pounds.

CHAPTER SEVEN

The Sewing Meeting

On an afternoon ten days later, Mr Sutton's coachman, Barrett by name, arrived at Ephraim Tellwright's back-door with a note. The Tellwrights were having tea. The note could be seen in his enormous hand, and Agnes went out.

'An answer, if you please, Miss,' he said to her, touching his hat, and giving a pull to the leathern belt which, surrounding his waist, alone seemed to hold his frame together. Agnes, much impressed, took the note. She had never before seen that resplendent automaton apart from the equipage which he directed. Always afterwards, Barrett formally saluted her in the streets, affording her thus, every time, a thrilling moment of delicious joy.

'A letter, and there's an answer, and he's waiting,' she cried, running into the parlour.

'Less row!' said her father. 'Here, give it me.'

'It's for Miss Tellwright – that's Anna, isn't it? Oh! Scent!' She put the grey envelope to her nose like a flower.

Anna, secretly as excited as her sister, opened the note and read: 'Lansdowne House, Wednesday. Dear Miss Tellwright, – Mother gives tea to the Sunday-school Sewing Meeting here *tomorrow*. Will you give us the pleasure of your company? I do not think you have been to any of the S.S.S. meetings yet, but we should all be glad to see you and have your assistance. Everyone is working very hard for the Autumn Bazaar,* and Mother has set her mind on the Sunday-school stall being the best. Do come, will you? Excuse this short notice. Yours sincerely, BEATRICE SUTTON. P.S. – We begin at 3.30.'

'They want me to go to their sewing meeting tomorrow,' she exclaimed timidly to her father, pushing the note towards him across the table. 'Must I go, Father?'

'What dost ask me for? Please thysen.* I've nowt do wi' it.'

'I don't want to go – '

'Oh! Sis, *do* go,' Agnes pleaded.

'Perhaps I'd better,' she agreed, but with the misgivings of diffidence. 'I haven't a rag to wear. I really must have a new dress, Father, at once.'

'Hast forgotten as that there coachman's waiting?' he remarked curtly.

'Shall I run and tell him you'll go?' Agnes suggested. 'It 'll be splendid for you.'

'Don't be silly, dear. I must write.'

'Well, write then,' said the child energetically, 'I'll get you the ink and paper.' She flew about and hovered over Anna while the answer to the invitation was being written. Anna made her reply as short and simple as possible, and then tendered it for her father's inspection. 'Will that do?'

He pretended to be nonchalant, but in fact he was somewhat interested.

'Thou's forgotten to put th' date in,' was all his comment, and he threw the note back.

'I've put Wednesday.'

'That's not the date.'

'Does it matter? Beatrice Sutton only puts Wednesday.'

His response was to walk out of the room.

'Is he vexed?' Agnes asked anxiously. There had been a whole week of almost perfect amenity.

The next day at half-past three Anna, having put on her best clothes, was ready to start. She had seen almost nothing of social life, and the prospect of taking part in this entertainment of the Suttons filled her with trepidation. Should she arrive early, in which case she would have to talk more, or late, in which case there would be the ordeal of entering a crowded room? She could not decide. She went into her father's bedroom, whose window overlooked Trafalgar Road, and saw from behind a curtain that small groups of ladies were continually passing up the street to disappear into Alderman Sutton's house. Most of the women she recognized; others she knew but vaguely by sight. Then the stream ceased, and suddenly she heard the kitchen clock strike four. She ran downstairs – Agnes, swollen by importance, was carrying her father's tea into the parlour – and hastened out the back way. In another moment she was at the Suttons' front-door. A servant in black alpaca, with white wristbands, cap, streamers, and embroidered apron (each article a *dernier cri** from Bostock's great shop at Hanbridge), asked her in a subdued and respectful tone to step within. Externally there had been no sign of the unusual, but once inside the house Anna found it a humming hive of activity. Women laden with stuffs and implements were crossing the picture-hung hall, their footsteps noiseless on the thick rugs which lay about in rich confusion. On either hand was an open door, and from each door came the sound of many eager voices. Beyond these doors a broad staircase rose majestically to unseen heights, closing the vista of the hall. As the servant was demanding Anna's name, Beatrice Sutton, radiant and gorgeous, came with a rush out of the room to the left, the dining-room, and, taking her by both hands, kissed her.

'My dear, we thought you were never coming. Everyone's here, except the men, of course. Come along upstairs and take your things off. I'm so glad you've kept your promise.'

'Did you think I should break it?' said Anna, as they ascended the easy gradient of the stairs.

'Oh, no, my dear. But you're such a shy little bird.'

The conception of herself as a shy little bird amused Anna. By a curious chain of ideas she came to wonder who could clean those stairs the better, she or this gay and flitting butterfly in a pale green teagown. Beatrice led the way to a large bedroom, crammed with furniture and knick-knacks. There were three mirrors in this spacious apartment – one in the wardrobe, a cheval-glass, and a third over the mantelpiece: the frame of the last was bordered with photographs.

'This is my room,' said Beatrice. 'Will you put your things on the bed?' The bed was already laden with hats, bonnets, jackets, and wraps.

'I hope your mother won't give me anything fancy to do,' Anna said. 'I'm no good at anything except plain sewing.'

'Oh, that's all right,' Beatrice answered carelessly. 'It's all plain sewing.' She drew a cardboard box from her pocket, and offered it to Anna. 'Here, have one.' They were chocolate creams.

'Thanks,' said Anna, taking one. 'Aren't they very expensive? I've never seen any like these before.'

'Oh! Just ordinary. Four shillings a pound. Papa buys them for me: I simply dote on them. I love to eat them in bed, if I can't sleep.' Beatrice made these statements with her mouth full. 'Don't you adore chocolates?' she added.

'I don't know,' Anna lamely replied. 'Yes, I like them.' She only adored her sister, and perhaps God; and this was the first time she had tasted chocolate.

'I couldn't *live* without them,' said Beatrice. 'Your hair is lovely. I never saw such a brown. What wash do you use?'

'Wash?' Anna repeated.

'Yes, don't you put anything on it?'

'No, never.'

'Well! Take care you don't lose it, that's all. Now, will you come and have just a peep at my studio – where I paint, you know? I'd like you to see it before we go down.'

They proceeded to a small room on the second floor, with a sloping ceiling and a dormer window.

'I'm obliged to have this room,' Beatrice explained, 'because it's the only one in the house with a north light, and of course you can't do without that. How do you like it?'

Anna said that she liked it very much.

The walls of the room were hung with various odd curtains of Eastern design. Attached somehow to these curtains some coloured plates, bits of pewter, and a few fans were hung high in apparently precarious suspense. Lower down on the walls were pictures and sketches, chiefly unframed, of flowers, fishes, loaves of bread, candlesticks, mugs, oranges, and tea-trays. On an immense easel in the middle of the room was an unfinished portrait of a man.

'Who's that?' Anna asked, ignorant of those rules of caution which are observed by the practised frequenter of studios.

'Don't you know?' Beatrice exclaimed, shocked. 'That's Papa; I'm doing his portrait; he sits in that chair there. The silly old master at the school won't let me draw from life yet – he keeps me to the antique – so I said to myself I would study the living model at home. I'm dreadfully in earnest about it, you know – I really am. Mother says I work far too long up here.'

Anna was unable to perceive that the picture bore any resemblance to Alderman Sutton, except in the matter of the aldermanic robe, which she could now trace beneath the portrait's neck. The studies on the walls pleased her much better. Their realism amazed her. One could make out not only that here, for instance, was a fish – there was no doubt that it was a halibut; the solid roundness of the oranges and the glitter on the tea-trays seemed miraculously achieved. 'Have you actually done all these?' she asked, in genuine admiration. 'I think they're splendid.'

'Oh, yes, they're all mine; they're only still-life studies,' Beatrice said contemptuously of them, but she was nevertheless flattered.

'I see now that that *is* Mr Sutton,' Anna said, pointing to the easel picture.

'Yes, it's Pa right enough. But I'm sure I'm boring you. Let's go down now, or perhaps we shall catch it from Mother.'

As Anna, in the wake of Beatrice, entered the drawing-room, a dozen or more women glanced at her with keen curiosity, and the even flow of conversation ceased for a moment, to be immediately resumed. In the centre of the room, with her back to the fireplace, Mrs Sutton was seated at a square table, cutting out. Although the afternoon was warm she had a white woollen wrap over her shoulders; for the rest she was attired in plain black silk, with a large stuff apron containing a pocket for scissors and chalk. She jumped up with the activity of which Beatrice had inherited a part, and greeted Anna, kissing her heartily.

'How are you, my dear? So pleased you have come.' The time-worn phrases came from her thin, nervous lips full of sincere and kindly welcome. Her wrinkled face broke into a warm, life-giving smile. 'Beatrice, find Miss Anna a chair.' There were two chairs in the bay of the window, and one of them was occupied by Miss Dickinson, whom Anna slightly knew. The other, being empty, was assigned to the late-comer.

'Now you want something to do, I suppose,' said Beatrice.

'Please.'

'Mother, let Miss Tellwright have something to get on with at once. She has a lot of time to make up.'

Mrs Sutton, who had sat down again, smiled across at Anna. 'Let me see, now, what can we give her?'

'There's several of those boys' nightgowns ready tacked,' said Miss Dickinson, who was stitching at a boy's nightgown. 'Here's one half-finished,' and she picked up an inchoate garment from the floor. 'Perhaps Miss Tellwright wouldn't mind finishing it.'

'Yes, I will do my best at it,' said Anna.

The thoughtless girl had arrived at the sewing meeting without needles or thimble or scissors, but one lady or another supplied these deficiencies, and soon she was at work. She stitched her best and her hardest, with head bent, and all her wits concentrated on the task. Most of the others seemed to be doing likewise, though not to the detriment of conversation. Beatrice sank down on a stool near her mother, and, threading a needle with coloured silk, took up a long piece of elaborate embroidery.

The general subjects of talk were the Revival, now over, with a superb record of seventy saved souls, the school-treat shortly to occur, the summer holidays, the fashions, and the change of ministers which would take place in August. The talkers were the wives and daughters of tradesmen and small manufacturers, together with a few girls of a somewhat lower status, employed in shops: it was for the sake of these latter that the sewing meeting was always fixed for the weekly half-holiday. The splendour of Mrs Sutton's drawing-room was a little dazzling to most of the guests, and Mrs Sutton herself seemed scarcely of a piece with it. The fact was that the luxury of the abode was mainly due to Alderman Sutton's inability to refuse anything to his daughter, whose tastes lay in the direction of rich draperies, large or quaint chairs, occasional tables, dwarf screens, hand-painted mirrors, and an opulence of bric-à-brac. The hand of Beatrice might be perceived everywhere, even in the position of the piano, whose back, adorned with carelessly-flung silks and photographs, was turned away from the wall. The pictures on the walls had been acquired gradually by Mr Sutton at auction sales: it was commonly held that he had an excellent taste in pictures, and that his daughter's aptitude for the arts came from him, and not from her mother. The gilt clock and side pieces on the mantelpiece were also peculiarly Mr Sutton's, having been publicly presented to him by the directors of a local building society of which he had been chairman for many years.

Less intimidated by all this unexampled luxury than she was reassured by the atmosphere of combined and homely effort, the lowliness of several of her companions, and the kind, simple face of Mrs Sutton, Anna quickly began to feel at ease. She paused in her work, and, glancing around her, happened to catch the eye of Miss Dickinson, who offered a remark about the weather. Miss Dickinson was head assistant at a draper's in St Luke's Square, and a pillar of the Sunday-school, which Sunday by Sunday and year by year had watched her develop from a rosy-checked girl into a confirmed spinster with sallow and warted face. Miss Dickinson supported her mother, and was a pattern to her sex. She was lovable, but had never been loved. She would have made an admirable wife and mother, but fate had decided that this material was to be wasted, Miss Dickinson found compensation for the rigour of destiny in gossip, as innocent as indiscreet. It was said that she had a tongue.

'I hear,' said Miss Dickinson, lowering her contralto voice to a confidential tone, 'that you are going into partnership with Mr Mynors, Miss Tellwright.'

The suddenness of the attack took Anna by surprise. Her first defensive impulse was boldly to deny the statement, or at the least to say that it was premature. A fortnight ago, under similar circumstances, she would not have hesitated to do so. But for more than a week Anna had been 'leading a new life', which chiefly meant a meticulous avoidance of the sins of speech. Never to deviate from the truth, never to utter an unkind or a thoughtless word, under whatever provocation: these were two of her self-imposed rules. 'Yes,' she answered Miss Dickinson, 'I am.'

'Rather a novelty, isn't it?' Miss Dickinson smiled amiably.

'I don't know,' said Anna. 'It's only a business arrangement; Father arranged it. Really I have nothing to do with it, and I had no idea that people were talking about it.'

'Oh! Of course *I* should never breathe a syllable,' Miss Dickinson said with emphasis. 'I make a practice of never talking about other people's affairs. I always find that best, don't you? But I happened to hear it mentioned in the shop.'

'It's very funny how things get abroad, isn't it?' said Anna.

'Yes, indeed,' Miss Dickinson concurred. 'Mr Mynors hasn't been to our sewing meetings for quite a long time, but I expect he'll turn up today.'

Anna took thought. 'Is this a sort of special meeting, then?'

'Oh, not at all. But we all of us said just now, while you were upstairs, that he would be sure to come.' Miss Dickinson's features, skilled in innuendo, conveyed that which was too delicate for utterance. Anna said nothing.

'You see a good deal of him at your house, don't you?' Miss Dickinson continued.

'He comes sometimes to see Father on business,' Anna replied sharply, breaking one of her rules.

'Oh! Of course I meant that. You didn't suppose I meant anything else, did you?' Miss Dickinson smiled pleasantly. She was thirty-five years of age. Twenty of those years she had passed in a desolating routine; she had existed in the midst of life and never lived; she knew no finer joy than that which she at that moment experienced.

Again Anna offered no reply. The door opened, and every eye was centred on the stately Mrs Clayton Vernon, who, with Mrs Banks, the minister's wife, was in charge of the other half of the sewing party in the dining-room. Mrs Clayton Vernon had heroic proportions, a nose which everyone admitted to be aristocratic, exquisite tact, and the calm consciousness of social superiority. In Bursley she was a great lady: her instincts were those of a great lady; and she would have been a great lady no matter to what sphere her God had called her. She had abundant white hair, and wore a flowered purple silk, in the antique taste.

'Beatrice, my dear,' she began, 'you have deserted us.'

'Have I, Mrs Vernon?' the girl answered with involuntary deference. 'I was just coming in.'

'Well, I am sent as a deputation from the outer room to ask you to sing something.'

'I'm very busy, Mrs Vernon. I shall never get this mantel-cloth* finished in time.'

'We shall all work better for a little music,' Mrs Clayton Vernon urged. 'Your voice is a precious gift, and should be used for the benefit of all. We entreat, my dear girl.'

Beatrice arose from the footstool and dropped her embroidery.

'Thank you,' said Mrs Clayton Vernon. 'If both doors are left open we shall hear nicely.'

'What would you like?' Beatrice asked.

'I once heard you sing "Nazareth",* and I shall never forget it. Sing that. It will do us all good.'

Mrs Clayton Vernon departed with the large movement of an argosy, and Beatrice sat down to the piano and removed her bracelets. 'The accompaniment is simply frightful towards the end,' she said, looking at Anna with a grimace. 'Excuse mistakes.'

During the song, Mrs Sutton beckoned with her finger to

Anna to come and occupy the stool vacated by Beatrice. Glad to leave the vicinity of Miss Dickinson, Anna obeyed, creeping on tiptoe across the intervening space. 'I thought I would like to have you near me, my dear,' she whispered maternally. When Beatrice had sung the song and somehow executed that accompaniment which has terrorized whole multitudes of drawing-room pianists, there was a great deal of applause from both rooms. Mrs Sutton bent down and whispered in Anna's ear: 'Her voice has been very well trained, has it not?' 'Yes, very,' Anna replied. But, though 'Nazareth' had seemed to her wonderful, she had neither understood it nor enjoyed it. She tried to like it, but the effect of it on her was bizarre rather than pleasing.

Shortly after half-past five the gong sounded for tea, and the ladies, bidden by Mrs Sutton, unanimously thronged into the hall and towards a room at the back of the house. Beatrice came and took Anna by the arm. As they were crossing the hall there was a ring at the door. 'There's Father – and Mr Banks, too,' Beatrice exclaimed, opening to them. Everyone in the vicinity, animated suddenly by this appearance of the male sex, turned with welcoming smiles. 'A greeting to you all,' the minister ejaculated with formal suavity as he removed his low hat. The Alderman beamed a rather absent-minded goodwill on the entire company, and said: 'Well! I see we're just in time for tea.' Then he kissed his daughter, and she accepted from him his hat and stick. 'Miss Tellwright, Pa,' Beatrice said, drawing Anna forward: he shook hands with her heartily, emerging for a moment from the benignant dream in which he seemed usually to exist.

That air of being rapt by some inward vision, common in very old men, probably signified nothing in the case of William Sutton: it was a habitual pose into which he had perhaps unconsciously fallen. But people connected it with his humble archaeological, geological, and zoological hobbies, which had sprung from his membership of the Five Towns Field Club, and which most of his acquaintances regarded with amiable secret disdain. At a school-treat once, held at a popular rural resort, he had taken some of the teachers to a cave, and pointing out the wave-like formation of its roof had told them that this peculiar phenomenon had actually been caused by waves of the sea. The discovery, valid enough and perfectly substantiated by an inquiry into the levels, was extremely creditable to the amateur geologist, but it seriously impaired his reputation among the Wesleyan community as a shrewd man of the world. Few believed the statement, or even tried to believe it, and nearly all thenceforth looked on him as a man who must be humoured in his harmless hallucinations and inexplicable curiosities. On the other hand, the collection of arrowheads, Roman pottery, fossils, and birds' eggs which he had given to the Museum in the Wedgwood Institution was always viewed with municipal pride.

The tea-room opened by a large French window into a conservatory, and a table was laid down the whole length of the room and the conservatory. Mr Sutton sat at one end and the minister at the other, but neither Mrs Sutton nor Beatrice occupied a distinctive place. The ancient clumsy custom of having tea-urns on the table itself had been abolished by Beatrice, who had read in a paper that carving was now never done at table, but by a neatly-dressed parlour-maid at the sideboard. Consequently the tea-urns were exiled to the sideboard, and the tea dispensed by a couple of maids. Thus, as Beatrice had explained to her mother, the hostess was left free to devote herself to the social arts. The board was richly spread with fancy breads and cakes, jams of Mrs Sutton's own celebrated preserving, diverse sandwiches compiled by Beatrice, and one or two large examples of the famous Bursley pork-pie.* Numerous as the company was, several chairs remained empty after everyone was seated. Anna found herself again next to Miss Dickinson; and five places from the minister, in the conservatory. Beatrice and her mother were higher up, in the room. Grace was sung, by request of Mrs Sutton. At first, silence prevailed among the guests, and the inquiries of the maids about milk and sugar were almost painfully audible. Then Mr Banks, glancing up the long vista of the table and pretending to descry some object in the distance, called out:

'Worthy host, I doubt not you are there, but I can only see you with the eye of faith.'

At this all laughed, and a natural ease was established. The minister and Mrs Clayton Vernon, who sat on his right, exchanged badinage on the merits and demerits of pork-pies, and their neighbours formed an appreciative audience. Then there was a sharp ring at the front door, and one of the maids went out.

'Didn't I tell you?' Miss Dickinson whispered to Anna.

'What?' asked Anna.

'That he would come today – Mr Mynors, I mean.'

'Who can that be?' Mrs Sutton's voice was heard from the room.

'I dare say it's Henry, Mother,' Beatrice answered.

Mynors entered, joyous and self-possessed, a white rose in his coat: he shook hands with Mr and Mrs Sutton, sent a greeting down the table to Mr Banks and Mrs Clayton Vernon, and offered a general apology for being late.

'Sit here,' said Beatrice to him, sharply, indicating a chair between Mrs Banks and herself. 'Mrs Banks has a word to say to you about the singing of that anthem* last Sunday.'

Mynors made some laughing rejoinder, and the voices sank so that Anna could not catch what was said.

'That's a new frock that Miss Sutton is wearing today,' Miss Dickinson remarked in an undertone.

'It looks new,' Anna agreed.

'Do you like it?'

'Yes. Don't you?'

'Hum! Yes. It was made at Brunt's at Hanbridge. It's quite the fashion to go there now,' said Miss Dickinson, and added, almost inaudibly, 'She's put it on for Mr Mynors. You saw how she saved that chair for him.'

Anna made no reply.

'Did you know they were engaged once?' Miss Dickinson resumed.

'No,' said Anna.

'At least people *said* they were. It was all over the town – oh! let me see, three years ago.'

'I had not heard,' said Anna.

During the rest of the meal she said little. On some natures Miss Dickinson's gossip had the effect of bringing them to silence. Anna had not seen Mynors since the previous Sunday, and now she was apparently unperceived by him. He talked gaily with Beatrice and Mrs Banks: that group was a centre of animation. Anna envied their ease of manner, their smooth and sparkling flow of conversation. She had the sensation of feeling vulgar, clumsy, tongue-tied; Mynors and Beatrice possessed something which she would never possess. So they had been engaged! But had they? Or was it an idle rumour, manufactured by one who spent her life in such creations? Anna was conscious of misgivings. She had despised Beatrice once, but now it seemed that after all Beatrice was the natural equal of Henry Mynors. Was it more likely that Mynors or she, Anna, should be mistaken in Beatrice? That Beatrice had generous instincts she was sure. Anna lost confidence in herself; she felt humbled, out-of-place, and shamed.

'If our hostess and the company will kindly excuse me,' said the minister with a pompous air, looking at his watch, 'I must go. I have an important appointment, or an appointment which some people think is important.'

He got up and made various adieux. The elaborate meal, complex with fifty dainties each of which had to be savoured, was not nearly over. The parson stopped in his course up the room to speak with Mrs Sutton. After he had shaken hands with her, he caught the admired violet eyes of his slim wife, a lady of independent fortune whom the wives of circuit stewards* found it difficult to please in the matter of furniture, and who despite her forty years still kept something of the pose of a spoiled beauty. As a minister's spouse this languishing but impeccable and invariably correct dame was unique even in the experience of Mrs Clayton Vernon.

'Shall you not be home early, Rex?' she asked in the tone of a young wife lounging amid the delicate odours of a boudoir.

'My love,' he replied with the stern fixity of a histrionic martyr, 'did you ever know me have a free evening?'

The Alderman accompanied his pastor to the door.

After tea, Mynors was one of the first to leave the room, and Anna one of the last, but he accosted her in the hall, on the way back to the drawing-room, and asked how she was, and how Agnes was, with such deference and sincerity of regard for herself and everything that was hers that she could not fail to be impressed. Her sense of humiliation and of uncertainty was effaced by a single word, a single glance. Uplifted by a delicious reassurance, she passed into the drawing-room, expecting him to follow: strange to say, he did not do so. Work was resumed, but with less ardour than before. It was in fact impossible to be strenuously diligent after one of Mrs Sutton's teas, and in every heart, save those which beat over the most perfect and vigorous digestive organs, there was a feeling of repentance. The building-society's clock on the mantelpiece intoned seven: all expressed surprise at the lateness of the hour, and Mrs Clayton Vernon, pleading fatigue after her recent indisposition, quietly departed.

As soon as she was gone, Anna said to Mrs Sutton that she too must go.

'Why, my dear?' Mrs Sutton asked.

'I shall be needed at home,' Anna replied.

'Ah! In that case – I will come upstairs with you, my dear,' said Mrs Sutton.

When they were in the bedroom, Mrs Sutton suddenly clasped her hand. 'How is it with you, dear Anna?' she said, gazing anxiously into the girl's eyes. Anna knew what she meant, but made no answer. 'Is it well?' the earnest old woman asked.

'I hope so,' said Anna, averting her eyes, 'I am trying.'

Mrs Sutton kissed her almost passionately. 'Ah my dear,' she exclaimed with an impulsive gesture, 'I am glad, so glad. I did so want to have a word with you. You must "lean hard", as Miss Havergal* says. "Lean hard" on Him. Do not be afraid.' And then, changing her tone: 'You are looking pale, Anna. You want a holiday. We shall be going to the Isle of Man* in August or September. Would your father let you come with us?'

'I don't know,' said Anna. She knew, however, that he would not. Nevertheless the suggestion gave her much pleasure.

'We must see about that later,' said Mrs Sutton, and they went downstairs.

'I must say goodbye to Beatrice. Where is she?' Anna said in the hall. One of the servants directed them to the dining-room. The Alderman and Henry Mynors were looking together at a large photogravure of Sant's *The Soul's Awakening*,* which Mr Sutton had recently bought, and Beatrice was exhibiting her embroidery to a group of ladies; sundry stitchers were scattered about, including Miss Dickinson.

'It is a great picture – a picture that makes you think,' Henry was saying, seriously, and the Alderman, feeling as the artist might have felt, was obviously flattered by this sagacious praise.

Anna said good-night to Miss Dickinson and then to Beatrice. Mynors, hearing the words, turned round. 'Well, I must go. Good evening,' he said suddenly to the astonished Alderman.

'What? Now?' the latter inquired, scarcely pleased to find that Mynors could tear himself away from the picture with so little difficulty.

'Yes.'

'Good-night, Mr Mynors,' said Anna.

'If I may I will walk down with you,' Mynors imperturbably answered.

It was one of those dramatic moments which arrive without the slightest warning. The gleam of joyous satisfaction in Miss Dickinson's eyes showed that she alone had foreseen this declaration. For a declaration it was, and a formal declaration. Mynors stood there calm, confident with masculine superiority, and his glance seemed to say to those swiftly alert women, whose faces could not disguise a thrilling excitation: 'Yes. Let all know that I, Henry Mynors, the desired of all, am honourably captive to this shy and perfect creature who is blushing because I have said what I have said.' Even the Alderman forgot his photogravure. Beatrice hurriedly resumed her explanation of the embroidery.

'How did you like the sewing meeting?' Mynors asked Anna when they were on the pavement.

Anna paused. 'I think Mrs Sutton is simply a splendid woman,' she said enthusiastically.

When, in a moment far too short, they reached Tellwright's house, Mynors, obeying a mutual wish to which neither had given expression, followed Anna up the side entry, and so into the yard, where they lingered for a few seconds. Old Tellwright could be seen at the extremity of the long narrow garden – a garden which consisted chiefly of a grass-plot sown with clothes-props and a narrow bordering of flower beds without flowers. Agnes was invisible. The kitchen-door stood ajar, and as this was the sole means of ingress from the yard Anna, humming an air, pushed it open and entered, Mynors in her wake. They stood on the threshold, happy, hesitating, confused, and looked at the kitchen as at something which they had not seen before. Anna's kitchen was the only satisfactory apartment in the house. Its furniture included a dresser of the simple and dignified kind which is now assiduously collected by amateurs of old oak. It had four long narrow shelves holding plates and saucers; the cups were hung in a row on small brass hooks screwed into the fronts of the shelves. Below the shelves were three drawers in a line, with brass handles, and below the drawers was a large recess which held stone jars, a copper preserving-saucepan,* and other receptacles. Seventy years of continuous polishing by a dynasty of priestesses of cleanliness had given to this dresser a rich ripe tone which the cleverest trade-trickster could not have imitated. In it was reflected the conscientious labour of generations. It had a soft and assuaged appearance, as though it had never been new and could never have been new. All its corners and edges had long lost the asperities of manufacture; and its smooth surfaces were marked by slight hollows similar in spirit to those worn by the naked feet of pilgrims into the marble steps of a shrine. The flat portion over the drawers was scarred with hundreds of scratches, and yet even all these seemed to be incredibly ancient, and in some distant past to have partaken of the mellowness of the whole. The dark woodwork formed an admirable background for the crockery on the shelves, and a few of the old plates, hand-painted according to some vanished secret in pigments which time could only improve, had the look of relationship by birth to the dresser. There must still be thousands of exactly similar dressers in the kitchens of the people, but they are gradually being transferred to the dining rooms of curiosity-hunters. To Anna this piece of furniture, which would have made the most taciturn collector vocal with joy, was merely 'the dresser.' She had always lamented that it contained no cupboard. In front of the fireless range was an old steel kitchen fender with heavy fire-irons.* It had in the middle of its flat top a circular lodgement for saucepans, but on this polished disc no saucepan was ever placed. The fender was perhaps as old as the dresser, and the profound depths of its polish served to mitigate somewhat the newness of the patent coal-economizing range which Tellwright had had put in when he took the house. On the high mantelpiece were four tall brass candlesticks which, like the dresser, were silently awaiting their apotheosis at the hands of some collector. Beside these were two or three common mustard tins,* polished to counterfeit silver, containing spices; also an abandoned coffee-mill and two flat-irons. A grandfather clock of oak to match the dresser stood to the left of the fireplace; it had a very large white dial with a grinning face in the centre. Though it would only run for twenty-four hours, its leisured movement seemed to have the certainty of a natural law, especially to Agnes, for Mr Tellwright never forgot to wind it before going to bed. Under the window was a plain deal table, with white top and stained legs. Two Windsor chairs* completed the catalogue of furniture. The glistening floor was of red and black tiles, and in front of the fender lay a list hearthrug* made by attaching innumerable bits of black cloth to a canvas base. On the painted walls were several grocers' almanacs,* depicting sailors in the arms of lovers, children crossing brooks, or monks swelling themselves with Gargantuan* repasts. Everything in this kitchen was absolutely bright and spotless, as clean as a cat in pattens,* except the ceiling, darkened by fumes of gas. Everything was in perfect order, and had the humanized air of use and occupation which nothing but use and occupation can impart to senseless objects. It was a kitchen where, in the housewife's phrase, you might eat off the floor, and to any Bursley matron it would have constituted the highest possible certificate of Anna's character, not only as housewife but as elder sister – for in her absence Agnes had washed the tea-things and put them away.

'This is the nicest room, I know,' said Mynors at length.

'Whatever do you mean?' Anna smiled, incapable of course of seeing the place with his eye.

'I mean there is nothing to beat a clean, straight kitchen,' Mynors replied, 'and there never will be. It wants only the mistress in a white apron to make it complete. Do you know, when I came in here the other night, and you were sitting at the table there, I thought the place was like a picture.'

'How funny!' said Anna, puzzled but well satisfied. 'But won't you come into the parlour?'

The Persian* with one ear met them in the lobby, his tail flying, but cautiously sidled upstairs at sight of Mynors. When Anna opened the door of the parlour she saw Agnes seated at the table over her lessons, frowning and preoccupied. Tears were in her eyes.

'Why, what's the matter, Agnes?' she exclaimed.

'Oh! Go away,' said the child crossly. 'Don't bother.'

'But what's the matter? You're crying.'

'No, I'm not. I'm doing my sums, and I can't get it – can't – ' The child burst into tears just as Mynors entered. His presence was a complete surprise to her. She hid her face in her pinafore, ashamed to be thus caught.

'Where is it?' said Mynors. 'Where is this sum that won't come right?' He picked up the slate and examined it while Agnes was finding herself again. 'Practice!'* he exclaimed. 'Has Agnes got as far as practice?' She gave him an instant's glance and murmured 'Yes.' Before she could shelter her face he had kissed her. Anna was enchanted by his manner, and as for Agnes, she surrendered happily to him at once. He worked the sum, and she copied the figures into her exercise-book. Anna sat and watched.

'Now I must go,' said Mynors.

'But surely you'll stay and see Father,' Anna urged.

'No. I really had not meant to call. Good-night, Agnes.' In a moment he was gone out of the room and the house. It was as if, in obedience to a sudden impulse, he had forcibly torn himself away.

'Was *he* at the sewing meeting?' Agnes asked, adding in parenthesis, 'I never dreamt he was here, and I was frightfully vexed. I felt such a baby.'

'Yes. At least, he came for tea.'

'Why did he call here like that?'

'How can I tell?' Anna said. The child looked at her.

'It's awfully queer, isn't it?' she said slowly. 'Tell me all about the sewing meeting. Did they have cakes or was it a plain tea? And did you go into Beatrice Sutton's bedroom?'

CHAPTER EIGHT

On the Bank

Anna began to receive her July interest and dividends. During a fortnight remittances, varying from a few pounds to a few hundreds of pounds, arrived by post almost daily. They were all addressed to her, since the securities now stood in her own name; and upon her, under the miser's superintendence, fell the new task of entering them in a book and paying them into the Bank. This mysterious begetting of money by money – a strange process continually going forward for her benefit, in various parts of the world, far and near, by means of activities of which she was completely ignorant and would always be completely ignorant – bewildered her and gave her a feeling of its unreality. The elaborate mechanism by which capital yields interest without suffering diminution from its original bulk is one of the commonest phenomena of modern life, and one of the least understood. Many capitalists never grasp it, nor experience the slightest curiosity about it until the mechanism through some defect ceases to revolve. Tellwright was of these; for him the interval between the outlay of capital and the receipt of interest was nothing but an efflux of time: he planted capital as a gardener plants rhubarb, tolerably certain of a particular result, but not dwelling even in thought on that which is hidden. The productivity of capital was to him the greatest achievement of social progress – indeed, the social organism justified its existence by that achievement; nothing could be more equitable than this productivity, nothing more natural. He would as soon have inquired into it as Agnes would have inquired into the ticking of the grandfather clock. But to Anna, who had some imagination, and whose imagination had been stirred by recent events, the arrival of moneys out of space, unearned, unasked, was a disturbing experience, affecting her as a conjuring trick affects a child, whose sensations hesitate between pleasure and apprehension. Practically, Anna could not believe that she was rich; and in fact she was not rich – she was merely a fixed point through which moneys that she was unable to arrest passed with the rapidity of trains. If money is a token, Anna was denied the satisfaction of fingering even the token: drafts and cheques were all that she touched (touched only to abandon) – the doubly tantalizing and insubstantial tokens of a token. She wanted to test the actuality of this apparent dream by handling coin and causing it to vanish over counters and into the palms of the necessitous. And moreover, quite apart from this curiosity, she really needed money for pressing requirements of Agnes and herself. They had yet had no new summer clothes, and Whitsuntide,* the time prescribed by custom for the refurnishing of wardrobes, was long since past. The intercourse with Henry Mynors, the visit to the Suttons, had revealed to her more plainly than ever the intolerable shortcomings of her wardrobe and similar imperfections. She was more painfully awake to these, and yet, by an unhappy paradox, she was even less in a position to remedy them, than in previous years. For now, she possessed her own fortune; to ask her father's bounty was therefore, she divined, a sure way of inviting a rebuff. But, even if she had dared, she might not use the income that was privately hers, for was not every penny of it already allocated to the partnership with Mynors! So it happened that she never once mentioned the matter to her father; she lacked the courage, since by whatever avenue she approached it circumstances would add an illogical and adventitious force to the brutal snubs which he invariably dealt out when petitioned for money. To demand his money, having fifty thousand of her own! To spend her own in the face of that agreement with Mynors! She could too easily guess his bitter and humiliating retorts to either proposition, and she kept silence, comforting herself with timid visions of a far distant future. The balance at the bank crept up to sixteen hundred pounds. The deed of partnership was drawn; her father pored over the blue draft,* and several times Mynors called and the two men discussed together. Then one morning her father summoned her into the front parlour, and handed to her a piece of parchment on which she dimly deciphered her own name coupled with that of Henry Mynors in large letters.

'You mun sign, seal, and deliver this,' he said, putting a pen in her hand.

She sat down obediently to write, but he stopped her with a scornful gesture.

'Thou'lt sign blind then, eh? Just like a woman!'

'I left it to you,' she said.

'Left it to me! Read it.'

She read through the deed, and after she had accomplished the feat one fact only stood clear in her mind, that the partnership was for seven years, a period extensible by consent of both parties to fourteen or twenty-one years. Then she affixed her signature, the pen moving awkwardly over the rough surface of the parchment.

'Now put thy finger on that bit o' wax, and say; "I deliver this as my act and deed."'

'I deliver this as my act and deed.'

The old man signed as witness. 'Soon as I give this to Lawyer Dane,' he remarked, 'thou'rt bound, willy-nilly. Law's law, and thou'rt bound.'

On the following day she had to sign a cheque which reduced her bank-balance to about three pounds. Perhaps it was the knowledge of this reduction that led Ephraim Tellwright to resume at once and with fresh rigour his new policy of 'squeezing the last penny' out of Titus Price (despite the fact that the latter had already achieved the incredible by paying thirty pounds in little more than a month), thus causing the catastrophe which soon afterwards befell. What methods her father was adopting Anna did not know, since he said no word to her about the matter: she only knew that Agnes had twice been dispatched with notes to Edward Street. One day, about noon, a clay-soiled urchin brought a letter addressed to herself: she guessed that it was some appeal for mercy from the Prices, and wished that her father had been at home. The old man was away for the whole day, attending a sale of property at Axe, the agricultural town in the north of the county, locally styled 'the metropolis of the moorlands.' Anna read: 'My dear Miss Tellwright, – Now that our partnership is an accomplished fact, will you not come and look over the works? I should much like you to do so. I shall be passing your house this afternoon about two, and will call on the chance of being able to take you down with me to the works. If you are unable to come no harm will be done, and some other day can be arranged; but of course I shall be disappointed. – Believe me, yours most sincerely, HY. MYNORS.'

She was charmed with the idea – to her so audacious – and

relieved that the note was not after all from Titus or Willie Price: but again she had to regret that her father was not at home. He would be capable of thinking and saying that the projected expedition was a truancy, contrived to occur in his absence. He might grumble at the house being left without a keeper. Moreover, according to a tacit law, she never departed from the fixed routine of her existence without first obtaining Ephraim's approval, or at least being sure that such a departure would not make him violently angry. She wondered whether Mynors knew that her father was away, and, if so, whether he had chosen that afternoon purposely. She did not care that Mynors should call for her – it made the visit seem so formal; and as in order to reach the works, down at Shawport by the canal-side, they would necessarily go through the middle of the town, she foresaw infinite gossip and rumour as one result. Already, she knew, the names of herself and Mynors were everywhere coupled, and she could not even enter a shop without being made aware, more or less delicately, that she was an object of piquant curiosity. A woman is profoundly interesting to women at two periods only – before she is betrothed and before she becomes the mother of her firstborn. Anna was in the first period; her life did not comprise the second.

When Agnes came home to dinner from school, Anna said nothing of Mynors' note until they had begun to wash up the dinner-things, when she suggested that Agnes should finish this operation alone.

'Yes,' said Agnes, ever compliant. 'But why?'

'I'm going out, and I must get ready.'

'Going out? And shall you leave the house all empty? What will Father say? Where are you going to?'

Agnes's tendency to anticipate the worst, and never to blink their father's tyranny, always annoyed Anna, and she answered rather curtly: 'I'm going to the works – Mr Mynors' works. He's sent word he wants me to.' She despised herself for wishing to hide anything, and added, 'He will call here for me about two o'clock.'

'Mr Mynors! How splendid!' And then Agnes's face fell somewhat. 'I suppose he won't call *before* two? If he doesn't, I shall be gone to school.'

'Do you want to see him?'

'Oh, no! I don't want to see him. But – I suppose you'll be out a long time, and he'll bring you back.'

'Of course he won't, you silly girl. And I shan't be out long. I shall be back for tea.'

Anna ran upstairs to dress. At ten minutes to two she was ready. Agnes usually left at a quarter to two, but the child had not yet gone. At five minutes to two, Anna called downstairs to her to ask her when she meant to depart.

'I'm just going now,' Agnes shouted back. She opened the front door and then returned to the foot of the stairs. 'Anna, if I meet him down the road shall I tell him you're ready waiting for him?'

'Certainly not. Whatever are you dreaming of?' the elder sister reproved. 'Besides, he isn't coming from the town.'

'Oh! All right. Goodbye.' And the child at last went.

It was something after two – every siren and hooter had long since finished the summons to work – when Mynors rang the bell. Anna was still upstairs. She examined herself in the glass, and then descended slowly.

'Good afternoon,' he said. 'I see you are ready to come. I'm very glad. I hope I haven't inconvenienced you, but just this afternoon seemed to be a good opportunity for you to see the works, and, you know, you ought to see it. Father in?'

'No,' she said. 'I shall leave the house to take care of itself. Do you want to see him?'

'Not specially,' he replied. 'I think we have settled everything.'

She banged the door behind her, and they started. As he held open the gate for her exit, she could not ignore the look of passionate admiration on his face. It was a look disconcerting by its mere intensity. The man could control his tongue, but not his eyes. His demeanour, as she viewed it, aggravated her self-consciousness as they braved the streets. But she was happy in her perturbation. When they reached Duck Bank, Mynors asked her whether they should go through the market-place or along King Street, by the bottom of St Luke's Square. 'By the market-place,' she said. The shop where Miss Dickinson was employed was at the bottom of St Luke's Square, and all the eyes of the market-place were preferable to the chance of those eyes.

Probably no one in the Five Towns takes a conscious pride in the antiquity of the potter's craft, nor in its unique and intimate relation to human life, alike civilized and uncivilized. Man hardened clay into a bowl before he spun flax and made a garment, and the last lone man will want an earthen vessel after he has abandoned his ruined house for a cave, and his woven rags for an animal's skin. This supremacy of the most ancient of crafts is in the secret nature of things, and cannot be explained. History begins long after the period when Bursley was first the central seat of that honoured manufacture: it is the central seat still – 'the mother of the Five Towns', in our local phrase – and though the townsmen, absorbed in a strenuous daily struggle, may forget their heirship to an unbroken tradition of countless centuries, the seal of their venerable calling is upon their foreheads. If no other relic of immemorial past is to be seen in these modernized sordid streets, there is at least the living legacy of that extraordinary kinship between workman and work, that instinctive mastery of clay which the past has bestowed upon the present. The horse is less to the Arab than clay is to the Bursley man. He exists in it and by it; it fills his lungs and blanches his cheek; it keeps him alive and it kills him. His fingers close round it as round the hand of a friend. He knows all its tricks and aptitudes; when to coax and when to force it, when to rely on it and when to distrust it. The weavers of Lancashire have dubbed him with an obscene epithet* on account of it, an epithet whose hasty use has led to many a fight, but nothing could be more illuminatively descriptive than that epithet, which names his vocation in terms of another vocation. A dozen decades of applied science have of course resulted in the interposition of elaborate machinery between the clay and the man; but no great vulgar handicraft has lost less of the human than potting. Clay is always clay, and the steam-driven contrivance that will mould a basin while a man sits and watches has yet to be invented. Moreover, if in some coarser process the hands are superseded, the number of processes has been multiplied ten-fold: the ware in which six men formerly collaborated is now produced by sixty; and thus, in one sense, the touch of finger on clay is more pervasive than ever before.

Mynors' works was acknowledged to be one of the best, of its size, in the district – a model three-oven bank, and it must be remembered that of the hundreds of banks in the Five Towns the vast majority are small, like this: the large manufactory with its corps of jacket-men,† one of whom is detached to show visitors round so much of the works as is deemed advisable for them to see, is the exception. Mynors paid three hundred pounds a year in rent, and produced nearly three hundred pounds worth of work a week. He was his own manager, and there was only one jacket-man on the place, a clerk at eighteen shillings. He employed about a hundred hands, and devoted all his ingenuity to prevent that wastage which is at once the easiest to overlook and the most difficult to check, the wastage of labour. No pains were spared to keep all departments in full and regular activity, and owing to his judicious firmness the feast of St Monday,* that canker eternally eating at the root of the prosperity of the Five Towns, was less religiously observed on his bank than perhaps anywhere else in Bursley. He had realized that when a workshop stands empty the employer has not only ceased to make money, but has begun to lose it. The architect of 'Providence* Works' (Providence stands godfather to many commercial enterprises in the Five Towns) knew his business and the business of the potter, and he had designed the works with a view to the strictest economy of labour. The various shops were so arranged that in the course of its metamorphosis the clay travelled naturally in a circle from the slip house by the canal to the packing-house by the canal: there was no carrying to and fro. The steam installation was complete: steam once generated had no respite; after it had exhausted itself in vitalizing fifty machines, it was killed by inches in order to dry the unfired ware and warm the dinners of the workpeople.

Henry took Anna to the canal-entrance, because the buildings looked best from that side.

'Now how much is a crate worth?' she asked, pointing to a crate which was being swung on a crane direct from the packing-house into a boat.

'That?' Mynors answered. 'A crateful of ware may be worth anything. At Minton's* I have seen a crate worth three hundred pounds. But that one there is only worth eight or nine pounds. You see you and I make cheap stuff.'

But don't you make any really good pots – are they all cheap?'

† *Jacket-man*: the artisan's satiric term for anyone who does not work in shirt-sleeves, who is not actually a producer, such as a clerk or a pretentious foreman.

'All cheap,' he said.

'I suppose that's business?' He detected a note of regret in her voice.

'I don't know,' he said, with the slightest impatient warmth. 'We make the stuff as good as we can for the money. We supply what everyone wants. Don't you think it's better to please a thousand folks than to please ten? I like to feel that my ware is used all over the country and the colonies. I would sooner do as I do than make swagger ware* for a handful of rich people.'

'Oh, yes,' she exclaimed, eagerly accepting the point of view, 'I quite agree with you.' She had never heard him in that vein before, and was struck by his enthusiasm. And Mynors was in fact always very enthusiastic concerning the virtues of the general markets. He had no sympathy with specialities, artistic or otherwise. He found his satisfaction in honestly meeting the public taste. He was born to be a manufacturer of cheap goods on a colossal scale. He could dream of fifty ovens, and his ambition blinded him to the present absurdity of talking about a three-oven bank spreading its productions all over the country and the colonies; it did not occur to him that there were yet scarcely enough plates to go round.

'I suppose we had better start at the start,' he said, leading the way to the slip-house. He did not need to be told that Anna was perfectly ignorant of the craft of pottery, and that every detail of it, so stale to him, would acquire freshness under her naïve and inquiring gaze.

In the slip-house begins the long manipulation which transforms raw porous friable clay into the moulded, decorated, and glazed vessel. The large whitewashed place was occupied by ungainly machines and receptacles through which the four sorts of clay used in the common 'body' – ball clay, China clay, flint clay, and stone clay – were compelled to pass before they became a white putty-like mixture meet for shaping by human hands. The blunger crushed the clay, the sifter extracted the iron from it by means of a magnet, the press expelled the water, and the pug-mill expelled the air. From the last reluctant mouth slowly emerged a solid stream neatly a foot in diameter, like a huge white snake. Already the clay had acquired the uniformity characteristic of a manufactured product.

Anna moved to touch the bolts of the enormous twenty-four-chambered press.

'Don't stand there,' said Mynors. 'The pressure is tremendous, and if the thing were to burst – '

She fled hastily. 'But isn't it dangerous for the workmen?' she asked.

Eli Machin, the engineman, the oldest employee on the works, a moneyed man, and the pattern of reliability, allowed a vague smile to flit across his face at this remark. He had ascended from the engine-house below in order to exhibit the tricks of the various machines, and that done he disappeared. Anna was awed by the sensation of being surrounded by terrific forces always straining for release and held in check by the power of a single wall.

'Come and see a plate made: that is one of the simplest things, and the batting-machine* is worth looking at,' said Mynors, and they went into the nearest shop, a hot interior in the shape of four corridors round a solid square middle. Here men and women were working side by side, the women subordinate to the men. All were preoccupied, wrapped up in their respective operations, and there was the sound of irregular whirring movements from every part of the big room. The air was laden with whitish dust, and clay was omnipresent – on the floor, the walls, the benches, the windows, on clothes, hands, and faces. It was in this shop, where both hollow-ware pressers and flat pressers* were busy as only craftsmen on piece-work* can be busy, that more than anywhere else clay was to be seen 'in the hand of the potter'.* Near the door a stout man with a good-humoured face flung some clay on to a revolving disc, and even as Anna passed a jar sprang into existence. One instant the clay was an amorphous mass, the next it was a vessel perfectly circular, of a prescribed width and a prescribed depth; the flat and apparently clumsy fingers of the craftsman had seemed to lose themselves in the clay for a fraction of time, and the miracle was accomplished. The man threw these vessels with the rapidity of a Roman candle* throwing off coloured stars, and one woman was kept busy in supplying him with material and relieving his bench of the finished articles. Mynors drew Anna along to the batting-machines for plate makers, at that period rather a novelty and the latest invention of the dead genius* whose brain has reconstituted a whole industry on new lines. Confronted with a piece of clay, the batting-machine descended upon it with the ferocity of a wild animal, worried it, stretched it, smoothed it into the width and thickness of a plate, and then desisted of itself and waited inactive for the flat presser to remove its victim to his more exact shaping machine. Several men were producing plates, but their rapid labours seemed less astonishing than the preliminary feat of the batting-machine. All the ware as it was moulded disappeared into the vast cupboards occupying the centre of the shop, where Mynors showed Anna innumerable rows of shelves full of pots in process of steam-drying. Neither time nor space nor material was wasted in this antheap of industry. In order to move to and fro, the women were compelled to insinuate themselves past the stationary bodies of the men. Anna marvelled at the careless accuracy with which they fed the batting-machines with lumps precisely calculated to form a plate of a given diameter. Everyone exerted himself as though the salvation of the world hung on the production of so much stuff by a certain hour; dust, heat, and the presence of a stranger were alike unheeded in the mad creative passion.

'Now,' said Mynors the cicerone, opening another door which gave into the yard, 'when all that stuff is dried and fettled – smoothed, you know – it goes into the biscuit oven: that's the first firing. There's the biscuit oven, but we can't inspect it because it's just being drawn.'

He pointed to the oven nearby, in whose dark interior the forms of men, naked to the waist, could dimly be seen struggling with the weight of saggars† full of ware. It seemed like some release of martyrs, this unpacking of the immense oven, which, after being flooded with a sea of flame for fifty-four hours, had cooled for two days, and was yet hotter than the Equator. The inertness and pallor of the saggars seemed to be the physical result of their fiery trial, and one wondered that they should have survived the trial. Mynors went into the place adjoining the oven, and brought back a plate out of an open saggar; it was still quite warm. It had the matt surface of a biscuit, and adhered slightly to the fingers: it was now a 'crook'; it had exchanged malleability for brittleness, and nothing mortal could undo what the fire had done. Mynors took the plate with him to the biscuit-warehouse, a long room where one was forced to keep to narrow alleys amid parterres of pots. A solitary biscuit-ware-

† *Saggars*: large oval receptacles of coarse clay, in which the ware is placed for firing.

houseman was examining the ware in order to determine the remuneration of the pressers.

They climbed a flight of steps to the printing-shop, where, by means of copper-plates, printing-presses, mineral colours, and transfer-papers, most of the decoration was done. The room was filled by a little crowd of people – oldish men, women, and girls, divided into printers, cutters, transferrers, and apprentices. Each interminably repeated some trifling process, and every article passed through a succession of hands until at length it was washed in a tank and rose dripping therefrom with its ornament of flowers and scrolls fully revealed. The room smelt of oil and flannel and humanity; the atmosphere was more languid, more like that of a family party, than in the pressers' shop: the old women looked stern and shrewish, the pretty young women pert and defiant, the younger girls meek. The few men seemed out of place. By what trick had they crept into the very centre of that mass of femininity? It seemed wrong, scandalous that they should remain. Contiguous with the printing-shop was the painting-shop, in which the labours of the former were taken to a finish by the brush of the paintress, who filled in outlines with flat colour, and thus converted mechanical printing into handiwork. The paintresses form the *noblesse** of the banks. Their task is a light one, demanding deftness first of all; they have delicate fingers, and enjoy a general reputation for beauty: the wages they earn may be estimated from their finery on Sundays. They come to business in cloth jackets, carry dinner in little satchels; in the shop they wear white aprons, and look startlingly neat and tidy. Across the benches over which they bend their coquettish heads gossip flies and returns like a shuttle; they are the source of a thousand intrigues, and one or other of them is continually getting married or omitting to get married. On the bank they constitute 'the sex'. An infinitesimal proportion of them, from among the branch known as ground-layers, die of lead-poisoning* – a fact which adds pathos to their frivolous charm. In a subsidiary room off the painting-shop a single girl was seated at a revolving table actuated by a treadle. She was doing the 'band-and-line' on the rims of saucers. Mynors and Anna watched her as with her left hand she flicked saucer after saucer into the exact centre of the table, moved the treadle, and, holding a brush firmly against the rim of the piece, produced with infallible exactitude the band and the line. She was a brunette, about twenty-eight: she had a calm, vacuously contemplative face; but God alone knew whether she thought. Her work represented the summit of monotony; the regularity of it hypnotized the observer, and Mynors himself was impressed by this stupendous phenomenon of absolute sameness, involuntarily assuming towards it the attitude of a showman.

'She earns as much as eighteen shillings a week* sometimes,' he whispered.

'May I try?' Anna timidly asked of a sudden, curious to experience what the trick was like.

'Certainly,' said Mynors, in eager assent. 'Priscilla, let this lady have your seat a moment, please.'

The girl got up, smiling politely. Anna took her place.

'Here, try on this,' said Mynors, putting on the table the plate which he still carried.

'Take a full brush,' the paintress suggested, not attempting to hide her amusement at Anna's unaccustomed efforts. 'Now push the treadle. There! It isn't in the middle yet. Now!'

Anna produced a most creditable band, and a trembling but passable line, and rose flushed with the small triumph.

'You have the gift,' said Mynors; and the paintress respectfully applauded.

'I felt I could do it,' Anna responded. 'My mother's mother was a paintress, and it must be in the blood.'

Mynors smiled indulgently. They descended again to the ground floor, and following the course of manufacture came to the 'hardening-on' kiln, a minor oven where for twelve hours the oil is burnt out of the colour in decorated ware. A huge, jolly man in shirt and trousers, with an enormous apron, was in the act of drawing the kiln, assisted by two thin boys. He nodded a greeting to Mynors and exclaimed, 'Warm!' The kiln was nearly emptied. As Anna stopped at the door, the man addressed her.

'Step inside, miss, and try it.'

'No, thanks!' she laughed.

'Come now,' he insisted, as if despising this hesitation. 'An ounce of experience – ' The two boys grinned and wiped their foreheads with their bare skeleton-like arms. Anna, challenged by the man's look, walked quickly into the kiln. A blasting heat seemed to assault her on every side, driving her back; it was incredible that any human being could support such a temperature.

'There!' said the jovial man, apparently summing her up with his bright, quizzical eyes. 'You know summat as you didn't know afore, miss. Come along, lads,' he added with brisk heartiness to the boys, and the drawing of the kiln proceeded.

Next came the dipping-house, where a middle-aged woman, enveloped in a protective garment from head to foot, was dipping jugs into a vat of lead-glaze, a boy assisting her. The woman's hands were covered with the grey, slimy glaze. She alone of all the employees appeared to be cool.

'That is the last stage but one,' said Mynors. 'There is only the glost-firing,'* and they passed out into the yard once more. One of the glost-ovens was empty; they entered it and peered into the lofty inner chamber, which seemed like the cold crater of an exhausted volcano, or like a vault, or like the ruined seat of some forgotten activity. The other oven was firing, and Anna could only look at its exterior, catching glimpses of the red glow at its twelve mouths, and guess at the Tophet,* within, where the lead was being fused into glass.

'Now for the glost-warehouse, and you will have seen all,' said Mynors, 'except the mould-shop,* and that doesn't matter.'

The warehouse was the largest place on the works, a room sixty feet long and twenty broad, low, whitewashed, bare, and clean. Piles of ware occupied the whole of the walls and of the immense floor-space, but there was no trace here of the soilure and untidiness incident to manufacture; all processes were at an end, clay had vanished into crock: and the calmness and the whiteness atoned for the disorder, noise, and squalor which had preceded. Here was a sample of the total and final achievement towards which the thousands of small, disjointed efforts that Anna had witnessed, were directed. And it seemed a miraculous, almost impossible, result; so definite, precise, and regular after a series of acts apparently variable, inexact, and casual; so unhuman after all that intensely human labour;* so vast in comparison with the minuteness of the separate endeavours. As Anna looked, for instance, at a pile of tea-sets, she found it difficult even to conceive that, a fortnight or so before, they had been nothing but lumps of dirty clay. No stage of the manufacture was incredible by itself, but the result was incredible. It was the result that appealed to the imagination, authenticating the adage that fools and children should never see anything till it is done.

Anna pondered over the organizing power, the forethought, the wide vision, and the sheer ingenuity and cleverness which were implied by the contents of this warehouse. 'What brains!' she thought, of Mynors; 'what quantities of all sorts of things he must know!' It was a humble and deeply-felt admiration.

Her spoken words gave no clue to her thoughts. 'You seem to make a fine lot of tea-sets,' she remarked.

'Oh, no,' he said carelessly. 'These few that you see here are a special order. I don't go in much for tea-sets: they don't pay; we lose fifteen per cent of the pieces in making. It's toilet-ware that pays, and that is our leading line.' He waved an arm vaguely towards rows and rows of ewers and basins in the distance. They walked to the end of the warehouse, glancing at everything.

'See here,' said Mynors, 'isn't that pretty?' He pointed through the last window to a view of the canal, which could be seen thence in perspective, finishing in a curve. On one side, close to the water's edge, was a ruined and fragmentary building, its rich browns reflected in the smooth surface of the canal. On the other side were a few grim, grey trees bordering the towpath. Down the vista moved a boat steered by a woman in a large mob-cap. 'Isn't that picturesque?' he said.

'Very,' Anna assented willingly. 'It's really quite strange, such a scene right in the middle of Bursley.'

'Oh! There are others,' he said. 'But I always take a peep at that whenever I come into the warehouse.'

'I wonder you find time to notice it – with all this place to see after,' she said. 'It's a splendid works.'

'It will do – to be going on with,' he answered, satisfied. 'I'm very glad you've been down. You must come again. I can see you would be interested in it, and there are plenty of things you haven't looked at yet, you know.'

He smiled at her. They were alone in the warehouse. 'Yes,' she said; 'I expect so. Well, I must go, at once; I'm afraid it's very late now. Thank you for showing me round, and explaining, and – I'm frightfully stupid and ignorant. Goodbye.'

Vapid and trite phrases: what unimaginable messages the hearer heard in you!

Anna held out her hand, and he seized it almost convulsively, his incendiary eyes fastened on her face.

'I must see you out,' he said, dropping that ungloved hand.

It was ten o'clock that night before Ephraim Tellwright returned home from Axe. He appeared to be in a bad temper. Agnes had gone to bed. His supper of bread-and-cheese and water was waiting for him, and Anna sat at the table while he consumed it. He ate in silence, somewhat hungrily, and she did not deem the moment propitious for telling him about her visit to Mynors' works.

'Has Titus Price sent up?' he asked at length, gulping down the last of the water.

'Sent up?'

'Yes. Art fond, lass? I told him as he mun send up some more o' thy rent today – twenty-five pun. He's not sent?'

'I don't know,' she said timidly. 'I was out this afternoon.'

'Out, wast?'

'Mr Mynors sent word to ask me to go down and look over the works; so I went. I thought it would be all right.'

'Well, it was'na all right. And I'd like to know what business thou hast gadding out,* as soon as my back's turned. How can I tell whether Price sent up or not? And what's more, thou knows as th' house hadn't ought to be left.'

'I'm sorry,' she said pleasantly, with a determination to be meek and dutiful.

He grunted. 'Happen he didna' send. And if he did, and found th' house locked up, he should ha' sent again. Bring me th' inkpot, and I'll write a note as Agnes must take when her goes to school tomorrow morning.'

Anna obeyed. 'They'll never be able to pay twenty-five pounds, Father,' she ventured. 'They've paid thirty already, you know.'

'Less gab,' he said shortly, taking up the pen. 'Here – write it thysen.' He threw the pen towards her. 'Tell Titus if he doesn't pay five-and-twenty this wik, us'll put bailiffs in.'

'Won't it come better from you, Father?' she pleaded.

'Whose property is it?' The laconic question was final. She knew she must obey, and began to write. But, realizing that she would perforce meet both Titus Price and Willie on Sunday, she merely demanded the money, omitting the threat. Her hand trembled as she passed the note to him to read.

'Will that do?'

His reply was to tear the paper across. 'Put down what I tell ye,' he ordered, 'and don't let's have any more paper wasted.' Then he dictated a letter which was an ultimatum in three lines. 'Sign it,' he said.

She signed it, weeping. She could see the wistful reproach in Willie Price's eyes.

'I suppose,' her father said, when she bade him 'Good-night', 'I suppose if I hadn't asked, I should ha' heard nowt o' this gadding-about wi' Mynors?'

'I was going to tell you I had been to the works, Father,' she said.

'Going to!' That was his final blow, and having delivered it, he loosed the victim. 'Go to bed,' he said.

She went upstairs, resolutely read her Bible, and resolutely prayed.

CHAPTER NINE

The Treat

This surly and terrorizing ferocity of Tellwright's was as instinctive as the growl and spring of a beast of prey. He never considered his attitude towards the women of his household as an unusual phenomenon which needed justification, or as being in the least abnormal. The women of a household were the natural victims of their master; in his experience it had always been so. In his experience the master had always, by universal consent, possessed certain rights over the self-respect, the happiness, and the peace of the defenceless souls set under him – rights as unquestioned as those exercised by Ivan the Terrible.* Such rights were rooted in the secret nature of things. It was futile to discuss them, because their necessity and their propriety were equally obvious. Tellwright would not have been angry with any man who impugned them: he would merely have regarded the fellow as a crank and a born fool, on whom logic or indignation would be entirely wasted. He did as his father and uncles had done. He still thought of his father as a grim customer, infinitely more redoubtable than himself. He really believed that parents spoiled their children nowadays: to be knocked down by a single blow was one of the punishments of his own generation. He could recall the fearful timidity of his mother's eyes without a trace of compassion. His treatment of his daughters was no part of a system, nor obedient to any defined principles, nor the expression of a brutal disposition, nor the result of gradually-acquired habit. It came to him like eating, and like parsimony. He belonged to the great and powerful class of house-tyrants, the backbone of the British nation, whose views on income-tax* cause ministries to tremble. If you had talked to him of the domestic graces of life, your words would have conveyed to him no meaning. If you had indicted him for simple unprovoked rudeness, he would have grinned, well knowing that, as the King can do no wrong,* so a man cannot be rude in his own house. If you had told him that he inflicted purposeless misery not only on others but on himself, he would have grinned again, vaguely aware that he had not tried to be happy, and rather despising happiness as a sort of childish gewgaw. He had, in fact, never been happy at home: he had never known that expansion of the spirit which is called joy; he existed continually under a grievance. The atmosphere of Manor Terrace afflicted him, too, with a melancholy gloom – him, who had created it. Had he been capable of self-analysis, he would have discovered that his heart lightened whenever he left the house, and grew dark whenever he returned; but he was incapable of the feat. His case, like every similar case, was irremediable.

The next morning his preposterous displeasure lay like a curse on the house: Anna was silent, and Agnes moved on timid feet. In the afternoon Willie Price called in answer to the note. The miser was in the garden, and Agnes at school. Willie's craven and fawning humility was inexpressibly touching and shameful to Anna. She longed to say to him, as he stood hesitant and confused in the parlour: 'Go in peace. Forget this despicable rent. It sickens me to see you so.' She foresaw, as the effect of her father's vindictive pursuit of her tenants, an interminable succession of these mortifying interviews.

'You're rather hard on us,' Willie Price began, using the old phrases, but in a tone of forced and propitiatory cheerfulness, as though he feared to bring down a storm of anger which should ruin all. 'You'll not deny that we've been doing our best.'

'The rent is due, you know, Mr William,' she replied blushing.

'Oh, yes,' he said quickly. 'I don't deny that. I admit that. I – did you happen to see Mr Tellwright's postscript to your letter?

'No,' she answered, without thinking.

He drew the letter, soiled and creased, from his pocket, and displayed it to her. At the foot of the page she read, in Ephraim's thick and clumsy characters: 'P.S. This is final.'

'My Father,' said Willie, 'was a little put about. He said he'd never received such a letter before in the whole of his business career. It isn't as if – '

'I needn't tell you,' she interrupted, with a sudden determination to get to the worst without more suspense, 'that of course I am in Father's hands.'

'Oh! Of course, Miss Tellwright; we quite understand that – quite. It's just a matter of business. We owe a debt and we must pay it. All we want is time.' He smiled piteously at her, his blue eyes full of appeal. She was obliged to gaze at the floor.

'Yes,' she said, tapping her foot on the rug. 'But Father means what he says.' She looked up at him again, trying to soften her words by means of something more subtle than a smile.

'He means what he says,' Willie agreed; 'and I admire him for it.'

The obsequious, truckling* lie was odious to her.

'Perhaps I could see him,' he ventured.

'I wish you would,' Anna said, sincerely. 'Father, you're wanted,' she called curtly through the window.

'I've got a proposal to make to him,' Price continued, while they awaited the presence of the miser, 'and I can't hardly think he'll refuse it.'

'Well, young sir,' Tellwright said blandly, with an air almost insinuating, as he entered. Willie Price, the simpleton, was deceived by it, and, taking courage, adopted another line of defence. He thought the miser was a little ashamed of his postscript.

'About your note, Mr Tellwright; I was just telling Miss Tellwright that my Father said he had never received such a letter in the whole of his business career.' The youth assumed a discreet indignation.

'Thy feyther's had dozens o' such letters, lad,' the miser said with cold emphasis, 'or my name's not Tellwright. Dunna tell me as* Titus Price's never heard of a bumbailiff* afore.'

Willie was crushed at a blow, and obliged to retreat. He smiled painfully. 'Come, Mr Tellwright. Don't talk like that. All we want is time.'

'Time is money,' said Tellwright, 'and if us give you time us give you money. 'Stead o' that, it's you as mun give us money. That's right reason.'

Willie laughed with difficulty. 'See here, Mr Tellwright. To cut a long story short, it's like this. You ask for twenty-five pounds. I've got in my pocket a bill of exchange* drawn by us on Mr Sutton and endorsed by him, for thirty pounds, payable in three months. Will you take that? Remember it's for thirty, and you only ask for twenty-five.'

'So Mr Sutton has dealings with ye, eh?' Tellwright remarked.

'Oh, yes,' Willie answered proudly. 'He buys off us regularly. We've done business for years.'

'And pays i' bills at three months, eh?' The miser grinned.

'Sometimes,' said Willie.

'Let's see it,' said the miser.

'What – the bill?'

'Ay!'

'Oh! The bill's all right.' Willie took it from his pocket, and opening out the blue paper, gave it to old Tellwright; Anna perceived the anxiety on the youth's face. He flushed and his hand trembled. She dared not speak, but she wished to tell him to be at ease. She knew from infallible signs that her father would take the bill. Ephraim gazed at the stamped paper as at something strange and unprecedented in his experience.

'Father would want you not to negotiate that bill,' said Willie. 'The fact is, we promised Mr Sutton that that particular bill should not leave our hands – unless it was absolutely necessary. So Father would like you not to discount it, and he will redeem it before it matures. You quite understand – we don't care to offend an old customer like Mr Sutton.'

'Then this bit o' paper's worth nowt for welly†* three months?' the old man said, with an affectation of bewildered simplicity.

Happily inspired for once, Willie made no answer, but put the question: 'Will you take it?'

'Ay! Us'll tak' it,' said Tellwright, 'though it is but a promise.' He was well pleased.

Young Price's face showed his relief. It was now evident that he had been passing through an ordeal. Anna guessed that perhaps everything had depended on the acceptance by Tellwright of that bill. Had he refused it, Price's, she thought, might have come to sudden disaster. She felt glad and disburdened for the moment; but immediately it occurred to her that her father would not be satisfied for long; a few weeks, and he would give another turn to the screw.

The Tellwrights were destined to have other visitors that afternoon. Agnes, coming from school, was accompanied by a lady. Anna, who was setting the tea-table, saw a double shadow pass the window, and heard voices. She ran into the kitchen, and found Mrs Sutton seated on a chair, breathing quickly.

'You'll excuse me coming in so unceremoniously, Anna,' she

† *Welly*: nearly.

said, after having kissed her heartily. 'But Agnes said that *she* always came in by the back way, so I came that way too. Now I'm resting a minute. I've had a walk today. Our horse has gone lame.'

This kind heart radiated a heavenly goodwill, even in the most ordinary phrases. Anna began to expand at once.

'Now do come into the parlour,' she said, 'and let me make you comfortable.'

'Just a minute, my dear,' Mrs Sutton begged, fanning herself with her handkerchief. 'Agnes's legs are so long.'

'Oh, Mrs Sutton,' Agnes protested, laughing, 'how can you? I could scarcely keep up with you!'

'Well, my dear, I never could walk slowly. I'm one of them that go till they drop. It's very silly.' She smiled, and the two girls smiled happily in return.

'Agnes,' said the housewife, 'set another cup and saucer and plate.' Agnes threw down her hat and satchel of books, eager to show hospitality.

'It still keeps very warm,' Anna remarked, as Mrs Sutton was silent.

'It's beautifully cool here,' said Mrs Sutton. 'I see you've got your kitchen like a new pin, Anna, if you'll excuse me saying so. Henry was very enthusiastic about this kitchen the other night, at our house.'

'What! Mr Mynors?' Anna reddened to the eyes.

'Yes, my dear; and he's a very particular young man, you know.'

The kettle conveniently boiled at that moment, and Anna went to the range to make the tea.

'Tea is all ready, Mrs Sutton,' she said at length. 'I'm sure you could do with a cup.'

'That I could,' said Mrs Sutton. 'It's what I've come for.'

'We have tea at four. Father will be glad to see you.' The clock struck, and they went into the parlour, Anna carrying the tea-pot and the hot-water jug. Agnes had preceded them. The old man was sitting expectant in his chair.

'Well, Mr Tellwright,' said the visitor, 'you see I've called to see you, and to beg a cup of tea. I overtook Agnes coming home from school – overtook her, mind – me, at my age!' Ephraim rose slowly and shook hands.

'You're welcome,' he said curtly, but with a kindliness that amazed Anna. She was unaware that in past days he had known Mrs Sutton as a young and charming girl, a vision that had stirred poetic ideas in hundreds of prosaic breasts, Tellwright's included. There was scarcely a middle-aged male Wesleyan in Bursley and Hanbridge who had not a peculiar regard for Mrs Sutton, and who did not think that he alone truly appreciated her.

'What an' you bin tiring yourself with this afternoon?' he asked, when they had begun tea, and Mrs Sutton had refused a second piece of bread-and-butter.

'What have I been doing? I've been seeing to some inside repairs to the superintendent's house. Be thankful you aren't a circuit steward's wife, Anna.'

'Why, does she have to see to the repairs of the minister's house?' Anna asked, surprised.

'I should just think she does. She has to stand between the minister's wife and the funds of the society. And Mrs Reginald Banks has been used to the very best of everything. She's just a bit exacting, though I must say she's willing enough to spend her own money too. She wants a new boiler in the scullery now, and I'm sure her boiler is a great deal better than ours. But we must try to please her. She isn't used to us rough folks and our ways. Mr Banks said to me this afternoon that he tried always to shield her from the worries of this world.' She smiled almost imperceptibly.

There was a ring at the bell, and Agnes, much perturbed by the august arrival, let in Mr Banks himself.

'Shall I enter, my little dear?' said Mr Banks. 'Your father, your sister, in?'

'It ne'er rains but it pours,' said Tellwright, who had caught the minister's voice.

'Speak of angels* – ' said Mrs Sutton, laughing quietly.

The minister came grandly into the parlour. 'Ah! How do you do, Brother Tellwright, and you, Miss Tellwright? Mrs Sutton, we two seem happily fated to meet this afternoon. Don't let me disturb you, I beg – I cannot stay. My time is very limited. I wish I could call oftener, Brother Tellwright; but really the new regime leaves no time for pastoral visits. I was saying to my wife only this morning that I haven't had a free afternoon for a month.' He accepted a cup of tea.

'Us'n have a tea-party this afternoon,' said Tellwright quasi-privately to Mrs Sutton.

'And now,' the minister resumed, 'I've come to beg. The special fund, you know, Mr Tellwright, to clear off the debt on the new school-buildings. I referred to it from the pulpit last Sabbath. It's not in my province to go round begging, but someone must do it.'

'Well, for me, I'm beforehand with you, Mr Banks,' said Mrs Sutton, 'for it's on that very errand I've called to see Mr Tellwright this afternoon. His name is on my list.'

'Ah! Then I leave our brother to your superior persuasions.'

'Come, Mr Tellwright,' said Mrs Sutton, 'you're between two fires, and you'll get no mercy. What will you give?'

The miser foresaw a probable discomfiture, and sought for some means of escape.

'What are others giving?' he asked.

'My husband is giving fifty pounds, and you could buy him up, lock, stock, and barrel.'

'Nay, nay!' said Tellwright, aghast at this sum. He had underrated the importance of the Building Fund.

'And I,' said the parson solemnly, 'I have but fifty pounds in the world, but I am giving twenty to this fund.'

'Then you're giving too much,' said Tellwright with quick brusqueness. 'You canna' afford it.'

'The Lord will provide,' said the parson.

'Happen He will, happen not. It's as well you've gotten a rich wife, Mr Banks.'

The parson's dignity was obviously wounded, and Anna wondered timidly what would occur next. Mrs Sutton interposed. 'Come now, Mr Tellwright,' she said again, 'to the point: what will you give?'

'I'll think it over and let you hear,' said Ephraim.

'Oh, no! That won't do at all, will it, Mr Banks? I, at any rate, am not going away without a definite promise. As an old and good Wesleyan, of course you will feel it your duty to be generous with us.'

'You used to be a pillar of the Hanbridge circuit – was it not so?' said Mr Banks to the miser, recovering himself.

'So they used to say,' Tellwright replied grimly. 'That was because I cleared 'em of debt in ten years. But they've slipped into th' ditch again sin' I left 'em.'

'But if I am right, you do not meet† with us,' the minister pursued imperturbably.

'No.'

'My own class is at three on Saturdays,' said the minister. 'I should be glad to see you.'

'I tell you what I'll do,' said the miser to Mrs Sutton. 'Titus Price is a big man at th' Sunday-school. I'll give as much as he gives to th' school buildings. That's fair.'

'Do you know what Mr Price is giving?' Mrs Sutton asked the minister.

'I saw Mr Price yesterday. He is giving twenty-five pounds.'

'Very well, that's a bargain,' said Mrs Sutton, who had succeeded beyond her expectations.

Ephraim was the dupe of his own scheming. He had made sure that Price's contribution would be a small one. This ostentatious munificence on the part of the beggared Titus filled him with secret anger. He determined to demand more rent at a very early date.

'I'll put you down for twenty-five pounds as a first subscription,' said the minister, taking out a pocket-book. 'Perhaps you will give Mrs Sutton or myself the cheque today?'

'Has Mr Price paid?' the miser asked, warily.

'Not yet.'

'Then come to me when he has.' Ephraim perceived the way of escape.

When the minister was gone, as Mrs Sutton seemed in no hurry to depart, Anna and Agnes cleared the table.

'I've just been telling your father, Anna,' said Mrs Sutton, when Anna returned to the room, 'that Mr Sutton and myself and Beatrice are going to the Isle of Man soon for a fortnight or so, and we should very much like you to come with us.'

Anna's heart began to beat violently, though she knew there was no hope for her. This, then, doubtless, was the main object of Mrs Sutton's visit! 'Oh! But I couldn't, really!' said Anna, scarcely aware what she did say.

'Why not?' asked Mrs Sutton.

'Well – the house.'

† *Meet*: meet in class – a gathering for the exchange of religious counsel and experience.

'The house? Agnes could see to what little housekeeping your father would want. The schools will break up next week.'

'What do these young folks want holidays for?' Tellwright inquired with philosophic gruffness. 'I never had one. And what's more, I wouldn't thank ye for one. I'll pig on at Bursley. When ye've gotten a roof of your own, where's the sense o' going elsewhere and pigging?'

'But we really want Anna to go,' Mrs Sutton went on. 'Beatrice is very anxious about it. Beatrice is very short of suitable friends.'

'I should na' ha' thought it,' said Tellwright. 'Her seems to know everyone.'

'But she is,' Mrs Sutton insisted.

'I think as you'd better leave Anna out this year,' said the miser stubbornly.

Anna wished profoundly that Mrs Sutton would abandon the futile attempt. Then she perceived that the visitor was signalling to her to leave the room. Anna obeyed, going into the kitchen to give an eye to Agnes, who was washing up.

'It's all right,' said Mrs Sutton contentedly, when Anna returned to the parlour. 'Your father has consented to your going with us. It is very kind of him, for I'm sure he'll miss you.'

Anna sat down, limp, speechless. She could not believe the news.

'You are awfully good,' she said to Mrs Sutton in the lobby, as the latter was leaving the house. 'I'm ever so grateful – you can't think.' And she threw her arms round Mrs Sutton's neck.

Agnes ran up to say goodbye.

Mrs Sutton kissed the child. 'Agnes will be the little housekeeper, eh?' The little housekeeper was almost as pleased at the prospect of housekeeping as if she too had been going to the Isle of Man. 'You'll both be at the school-treat next Tuesday, I suppose,' Mrs Sutton said, holding Agnes by the hand. Agnes glanced at her sister in inquiry.

'I don't know,' Anna replied. 'We shall see.'

The truth was, that not caring to ask her father for the money for the tickets, she had given no thought to the school-treat.

'Did I tell you that Henry Mynors will most likely come with us to the Isle of Man?' said Mrs Sutton from the gate.

Anna retired to her bedroom to savour an astounding happiness in quietude. At supper the miser was in a mood not unbenevolent. She expected a reaction the next morning, but Ephraim, strange to say, remained innocuous. She ventured to ask him for the money for the treat tickets, two shillings. He made no immediate reply. Half an hour afterwards, he ejaculated: 'What i' th' name o' fortune dost thee want wi' school-treats?'

'It's Agnes,' she answered; 'of course Agnes can't go alone.'

In the end he threw down a florin.* He became perilous for the rest of the day, but the florin was an indisputable fact in Anna's pocket.

The school-treat was held in a twelve-acre field near Sneyd, the seat of a marquis, and a Saturday afternoon resort very popular in the Five Towns. The children were formed at noon on Duck Bank into a procession, which marched to the railway station to the singing of 'Shall we gather at the river?'* Thence a special train carried them, in seething compartments, excited and strident, to Sneyd, where the procession was reformed along a country road. There had been two sharp showers in the morning, and the vacillating sky threatened more rain; but because the sun had shone dazzlingly at eleven o'clock all the women and girls, too easily tempted by the glory of the moment, blossomed forth in pale blouses and parasols. The chattering crowd, bright and defenceless as flowers, made at Sneyd a picture at once gay and pathetic. It had rained there at half-past twelve; the roads were wet; and among the two hundred and fifty children and thirty teachers there were less than a score umbrellas. The excursion was theoretically in charge of Titus Price, the Senior Superintendent, but this dignitary had failed to arrive on Duck Bank, and Mynors had taken his place. In the train Anna heard that some one had seen Mr Price, wearing a large grey wideawake, leap into the guard's van at the very instant of departure. He had not been at school on the previous Sunday, and Anna was somewhat perturbed at the prospect of meeting the man who had defined her letter to him as unique in the whole of his business career. She caught a glimpse of the grey wideawake on the platform at Sneyd, and steered her own scholars so as to avoid its vicinity. But on the march to the field Titus reviewed the procession, and she was obliged to meet his eyes and return his salutation. The look of the man was a shock to her. He seemed thinner, nervous, restless, preoccupied, and terribly careworn; except the new brilliant hat, all his summer clothes were soiled and shabby. It was as though he had forced himself, out of regard for appearances, to attend the fête, but had left his thoughts in Edward Street. His uneasy and hollow cheerfulness was painful to watch. Anna realized the intensity of the crisis through which Mr Price was passing. She perceived in a single glance, more clearly than she could have done after a hundred interviews with the young and unresponsible William – however distressing these might be – that Titus must for weeks have been engaged in a truly frightful struggle. His face was a proof of the tragic sincerity of William's appeals to herself and her father. That Price should have contrived to pay seventy pounds of rent in a little more than a month seemed to her, imperfectly acquainted alike with Ephraim's ruthless compulsions and with the financial jugglery often practised by hard-pressed debtors, to be an almost miraculous effort after honesty. Her conscience smote her for conniving at what she now saw to be a persecution. She felt as sorry for Titus as she had felt for his son. The obese man, with his reputation in rags about him, was acutely wistful in her eyes, as a child might have been.

A carriage rolled by, raising the dust in places where the strong sun had already dried the road. It was Mr Sutton's landau, driven by Barrett. Beatrice, in white, sat solitary amid cushions, while two large hampers occupied most of the coachman's box. The carriage seemed to move with lordly ease and rapidity, and the teachers, already weary and fretted by the endless pranks of the children, bitterly envied the enthroned maid who nodded and smiled to them with such charming condescension. It was a social triumph for Beatrice. She disappeared ahead like a goddess in a cloud, and scarcely a woman who saw her from the humble level of the roadway but would have married a satyr to be able to do as Beatrice did. Later, when the field was reached, and the children bursting through the gate had spread like a flood over the daisied grass, the landau was to be seen drawn up near the refreshment tent; Barrett was unpacking the hampers, which contained delicate creamy confectionery for the teachers' tea; Beatrice explained that these were her mother's gift, and that she had driven down in order to preserve the fragile pasties from the risks of a railway journey. Gratitude became vocal, and Beatrice's success was perfected.

Then the more conscientious teachers set themselves seriously to the task of amusing the smaller children, and the smaller children consented to be amused according to the recipes appointed by long custom for school-treats. Many round-games, which invariably comprised singing or kissing, being thus annually resuscitated by elderly people from the deeps of memory, were preserved for a posterity which otherwise would never have known them. Among these was Bobby-Bingo.* For twenty-five years Titus Price had played at Bobby-Bingo with the infant classes at the school-treat, and this year he was bound by the expectations of all to continue the practice. Another diversion which he always took care to organize was the three-legged race for boys. Also, he usually joined in the tut-ball,* a quaint game which owes its surprising longevity to the fact that it is equally proper for both sexes. Within half an hour the treat was in full career; football, cricket, rounders, tick,* leap-frog,* prison-bars,* and round-games, transformed the field into a vast arena of complicated struggles and emulations. All were occupied, except a few of the women and older girls, who strolled languidly about in the rôle of spectators. The sun shone generously on scores of vivid and frail toilettes, and parasols made slowly-moving hemispheres of glowing colour against the rich green of the grass. All around were yellow cornfields, and meadows where cows of a burnished brown indolently meditated upon the phenomena of a school-treat. Every hedge and ditch and gate and stile was in that ideal condition of plenary correctness which denotes that a great landowner is exhibiting the beauties of scientific farming for the behoof of his villagers. The sky, of an intense blue, was a sea in which large white clouds sailed gently but capriciously; on the northern horizon a low range of smoke marked the sinister region of the Five Towns.

'Will you come and help with the bags and cups?' Henry Mynors asked Anna. She was standing by herself, watching Agnes at play with some other girls. Mynors had evidently walked across to her from the refreshment tent, which was at the opposite extremity of the field. In her eyes he was once more the exemplar of style. His suit of grey flannel, his white straw hat, became him to admiration. He stood at ease with his hands in his coat-pockets, and smiled contentedly.

'After all,' he said, 'the tea is the principal thing, and, although it wants two hours to tea-time yet, it's as well to be beforehand.'

'I should like something to do,' Anna replied.

'How are you?' he said familiarly, after this abrupt opening, and then shook hands. They traversed the field together, with many deviations to avoid trespassing upon areas of play.

The flapping refreshment tent seemed to be full of piles of baskets and piles of bags and piles of cups, which the contractor had brought in a wagon. Some teachers were already beginning to put the paper bags into the baskets; each bag contained bread-and-butter, currant cake, an Eccles-cake,* and a Bath bun.* At the far end of the tent Beatrice Sutton was arranging her dainties on a small trestle-table.

'Come along quick, Anna,' she exclaimed, 'and taste my tarts, and tell me what you think of them. I do hope the good people will enjoy them.' And then, turning to Mynors, 'Hello! Are you seeing after the bags and things? I thought that was always Willie Price's favourite job!'

'So it is,' said Mynors. 'But, unfortunately, he isn't here today.'

'How's that, pray? I never knew *him* miss a school-treat before.'

'Mr Price told me they couldn't both be away from the works just now. Very busy, I suppose.'

'Well, William would have been more use than his father, anyhow.'

'Hush, hush!' Mynors murmured with a subdued laugh.

Beatrice was in one of her 'downright' moods, as she herself called them.

Mynors' arrangements for the prompt distribution of tea at the appointed hour were very minute, and involved a considerable amount of back-bending and manual labour. But, though they were enlivened by frequent intervals of gossip, and by excursions into the field to observe this and that amusing sight, all was finished half an hour before time.

'I will go and warn Mr Price,' said Mynors. 'He is quite capable of forgetting the clock.' Mynors left the tent, and proceeded to the scene of an athletic meeting, at which Titus Price, in shirt-sleeves, was distributing prizes of sixpences and pennies. The famous three-legged race had just been run. Anna followed at a saunter, and shortly afterwards Beatrice overtook her.

'The great Titus looks better than he did when he came on

the field,' Beatrice remarked. And indeed the superintendent had put on quite a merry appearance – flushed, excited, and jocular in his elephantine way – it seemed as if he had not a care in the world. The boys crowded appreciatively round him. But this was his last hour of joy.

'Why! Willie Price *is* here,' Anna exclaimed, perceiving William in the fringe of the crowd. The lanky fellow stood hesitatingly, his left hand busy with his moustache.

'So he is,' said Beatrice. 'I wonder what that means.'

Titus had not observed the newcomer, but Henry Mynors saw William, and exchanged a few words with him. Then Mr Mynors advanced into the crowd and spoke to Mr Price, who glanced quickly round at his son. The girls, at a distance of forty yards, could discern the swift change in the man's demeanour. In a second he had reverted to the deplorable Titus of three hours ago. He elbowed his way roughly to William, getting into his coat as he went. The pair talked, William glanced at his watch, and in another moment they were leaving the field. Henry Mynors had to finish the prize distribution. So much Anna and Beatrice plainly saw. Others, too, had not been blind to this sudden and dramatic departure. It aroused universal comment among the teachers.

'Something must be wrong at Price's works,' Beatrice said, 'and Willie has had to fetch his papa.' This was the conclusion of all the gossips. Beatrice added: 'Dad has mentioned Price's several times lately, now I think of it.'

Anna grew extremely self-conscious and uncomfortable. She felt as though all were saying of her: 'There goes the oppressor of the poor!' She was fairly sure, however, that her father was not responsible for this particular incident. There must, then, be other implacable creditors. She had been thoroughly enjoying the afternoon, but now her pleasure ceased.

The treat ended disastrously. In the middle of the children's meal, while yet the enormous double-handled tea-cans were being carried up and down the thirsty rows, and the boys were causing their bags to explode with appalling detonations, it began to rain sharply. The fickle sun withdrew his splendour from the toilettes, and was seen no more for a week afterwards. 'It's come at last,' ejaculated Mynors, who had watched the sky with anxiety for an hour previously. He mobilized the children and ranked them under a row of elms. The teachers, running to the tent for their own tea, said to one another that the shower could only be a brief one. The wish was father to the thought, for they were a little ashamed to be under cover while their charges precariously sheltered beneath dripping trees – yet there was nothing else to be done; the men took turns in the rain to keep the children in their places. The sky was completely overcast. 'It's set in for a wet evening, and so we may as well make the best of it,' Beatrice said grimly, and she sent the landau home empty. She was right. A forlorn and disgusted snake of a procession crawled through puddles to the station. The platform resounded with sneezes. None but a dressmaker could have discovered a silver lining to the black and all-pervading cloud which had ruined so many dozens of fair costumes. Anna, melancholy and taciturn, exerted herself to minimize the discomfort of her scholars. A word from Mynors would have been balm to her; but Mynors, the general of a routed army, was parleying by telephone* with the traffic-manager of the railway for the expediting of the special train.

CHAPTER TEN

The Isle

About this time Anna was not seeing very much of Henry Mynors. At twenty a man is rash in love, and again, perhaps, at fifty; a man of middle-age enamoured of a young girl is capable of sublime follies. But the man of thirty who loves for the first time is usually the embodiment of cautious discretion. He does not fall in love with a violent descent, but rather lets himself gently down, continually testing the rope. His social value, especially if he have achieved worldly success, is at its highest, and, without conceit, he is aware of it. He has lost many illusions concerning women; he has seen more than one friend wrecked in the sea of foolish marriage; he knows the joys of a bachelor's freedom, without having wearied of them; he perceives risks where the youth perceives only ecstasy, and the oldster only a blissful release from solitude. Instead of searching, he is sought for; accordingly he is selfish and exacting. All these things combine to tranquillize passion at thirty. Mynors was in love with Anna, and his love had its ardent moments; but in the main it was a temperate affection, an affection that walked circumspectly, with its eyes open, careful of its dignity, too proud to seem in a hurry; if, by impulse, it chanced now and then to leap forward, the involuntary movement was mastered and checked. Mynors called at Manor Terrace once a week, never on the same day of the week, nor without discussing business with the miser. Occasionally he accompanied Anna from school or chapel. Such methods were precisely to Anna's taste. Like him, she loved prudence and decorum, preferring to make haste slowly. Since the Revival, they had only once talked together intimately; on that sole occasion Henry had suggested to her that she might care to join Mrs Sutton's class, which met on Monday nights; she accepted the hint with pleasure, and found a well of spiritual inspiration in Mrs Sutton's modest and simple yet fervent homilies. Mynors was not guilty of blowing both hot and cold. She was sure of him. She waited calmly for events, existing, as her habit was, in the future.

The future, then, meant the Isle of Man. Anna dreamed of an enchanted isle and hours of unimaginable rapture. For a whole week after Mrs Sutton had won Ephraim's consent, her vision never stooped to practical details. Then Beatrice called to see her; it was the morning after the treat, and Anna was brushing her muddy frock; she wore a large white apron, and held a clothes-brush in her hand as she opened the door.

'You're busy?' said Beatrice.

'Yes,' said Anna, 'but come in. Come into the kitchen – do you mind?'

Beatrice was covered from neck to heel with a long mackintosh, which she threw off when entering the kitchen.

'Anyone else in the house?' she asked.

'No,' said Anna, smiling, as Beatrice seated herself, with a sigh of content, on the table.

'Well, let's talk, then.' Beatrice drew from her pocket the indispensable chocolates and offered them to Anna. 'I say, wasn't last night perfectly awful? Henry got wet through in the end, and mother made him stop at our house, as he was at the trouble to take me home. Did you see him go down this morning?'

'No; why?' said Anna, stiffly.

'Oh – no reason. Only I thought perhaps you did. I simply can't tell you how glad I am that you're coming with us to the Isle of Man; we shall have rare fun. We go every year, you know – to Port Erin,* a lovely little fishing village. All the fishermen know us there. Last year Henry hired a yacht for the fortnight, and we all went mackerel-fishing, every day; except sometimes Pa. Now and then Pa had a tendency to go fiddling in caves and things. I do hope it will be fine weather again by then, don't you?'

'I'm looking forward to it, I can tell you,' Anna said. 'What day are we supposed to start?'

'Saturday week.'

'So soon?' Anna was surprised at the proximity of the event.

'Yes; and quite late enough, too. We should start earlier, only the Dad always makes out he can't. Men always pretend to be so frightfully busy, and I believe it's all put on.' Beatrice continued to chat about the holiday, and then of a sudden she asked: 'What are you going to wear?'

'Wear!' Anna repeated; and added with hesitation: 'I suppose one will want some new clothes?'

'Well, just a few! Now let me advise you. Take a blue serge skirt. Sea-water won't harm it, and if it's dark enough it will look well to any mortal blouse. Secondly, you can't have too many blouses; they're always useful at the seaside. Plain straw-hats are my tip. A coat for nights, and thick boots. There! Of course no one ever *dresses* at Port Erin. It isn't like Llandudno, and all that sort of thing.* You don't have to meet your young man on the pier, because there isn't a pier.'

There was a pause. Anna did not know what to say. At length she ventured: 'I'm not much for clothes, as I dare say you've noticed.'

'I think you always look nice, my dear,' Beatrice responded. Nothing was said as to Anna's wealth, no reference made as to the discrepancy between that and the style of her garments. By a fiction, there was supposed to be no discrepancy.

'Do you make your own frocks?' Beatrice asked, later.

'Yes.'

'Do you know I thought you did. But they do you great credit. There's few people can make a plain frock look decent.'

This conversation brought Anna with a shock to the level of earth. She perceived – only too well – a point which she had not hitherto fairly faced in her idyllic meditations: that her father was still a factor in the case. Since Mrs Sutton's visit both Anna and the miser avoided the subject of the holiday.

'You can't have too many blouses.' Did Beatrice, then, have blouses by the dozen? A coat, a serge skirt, straw hats (how many?) – the catalogue frightened her. She began to suspect that she would not be able to go to the Isle of Man.

'About me going with Suttons to the Isle of Man?' she accosted her father, in the afternoon, outwardly calm, but with secret trembling.

'Well?' he exclaimed savagely.

'I shall want some money – a little.' She would have given much not to have added that 'little', but it came out of itself.

'It's a waste o' time and money – that's what I call it. I can't think why Suttons asked ye. Ye aren't ill, are ye?' His savagery changed to sullenness.

'No, father; but as it's arranged, I suppose I shall have to go.'

'Well, I'm none so set up with the idea mysen'.'

'Shan't you be all right with Agnes?'

'Oh, yes. I shall be all right. *I* don't want much. *I*'ve no fads and fal-lals. How long art going to be away?'

'I don't know. Didn't Mrs Sutton tell you? You arranged it.'

'That I didna'. Her said nowt to me.'

'Well, anyhow I shall want some clothes.'

'What for? Art naked?'

'I must have some money.' Her voice shook. She was getting near tears.

'Well, thou's gotten thy own money, hast na'?'

'All I want is that you shall let me have some of my own money. There's forty odd pounds now in the bank.'

'Oh!' he repeated, sneering, 'all ye want is as I shall let thee have some o' thy own money. And there's forty odd pound i' the bank. Oh!'

'Will you give me my cheque-book out of the bureau? And I'll draw a cheque; I know how to.' She had conquered the instinct to cry, and unwillingly her tones became somewhat peremptory. Ephraim seized the chance.

'No, I won't give ye the cheque-book out o' th' bureau,' he said flatly. 'And I'll thank ye for less sauce.'*

That finished the episode. Proudly she took an oath with herself not to re-open the question, and resolved to write a note to Mrs Sutton saying that on consideration she found it impossible to go to the Isle of Man.

The next morning there came to Anna a letter from the secretary of a limited company enclosing a post-office order for ten pounds. Some weeks previously her father had discovered an error of that amount in the deduction of income-tax from the dividend paid by this company, and had instructed Anna to demand the sum. She had obeyed, and then forgotten the affair. Here was the answer. Desperate at the thought of missing the holiday, she cashed the order, bought and made her clothes in secret, and then, two days before the arranged date of departure told her father what she had done. He was enraged; but since his anger was too illogical to be rendered effectively coherent in words, he had the wit to keep silence. With bitterness Anna reflected that she owed her holiday to the merest accident – for if the remittance had arrived a little earlier or a little later, or in the form of a cheque, she could not have utilized it.

It was an incredible day, the following Saturday, a warm and benign day of earliest autumn. The Suttons, in a hired cab, called for Anna at half-past eight, on the way to the main line station at Shawport. Anna's tin box was flung on to the roof of the cab amid the trunks and portmanteaux already there.

'Why should not Agnes ride with us to the station?' Beatrice suggested.

'Nay, nay; there's no room,' said Tellwright, who stood at the door impelled by an unacknowledged awe of Mrs Sutton thus to give official sanction to Anna's departure.

'Yes, yes,' Mrs Sutton exclaimed. 'Let the little thing come, Mr Tellwright.'

Agnes, far more excited than any of the rest, seized her straw hat, and slipping the elastic under her small chin, sprang into the cab, and found a haven between Mr Sutton's short, fat legs. The driver drew his whip smartly across the aged neck of the cream mare. They were off. What a rumbling, jolting, delicious journey, down the first hill, up Duck Bank, through the market-place, and down the steep declivity of Oldcastle Street! Silent and shy, Agnes smiled ecstatically at the others. Anna answered remarks in a dream. She was conscious only of present happiness and happy expectation. All bitterness had disappeared. At least thirty thousand Bursley folk were not going to the Isle of Man that day – their preoccupied and cheerless faces swam in a continuous stream past the cab window – and Anna sympathized with every unit of them. Her spirit overflowed with universal compassion. What haste and exquisite confusion at the station! The train was signalled, and the porter, crossing the line with the luggage, ran his truck perilously under the very buffers of the incoming engine. Mynors was awaiting them admirably attired as a tourist. He had got the tickets, and secured a private compartment in the through-coach for Liverpool; and he found time to arrange with the cabman to drive Agnes home on the box-seat. Certainly there was none like Mynors. From the footboard of the carriage Anna bent down to kiss Agnes. The child had been laughing and chattering. Suddenly, as Anna's lips touched hers, she burst into tears, sobbed passionately as though overtaken by some terrible and unexpected misfortune. Tears stood also in Anna's eyes. The sisters had never been parted before.

'Poor little thing!' Mrs Sutton murmured; and Beatrice told her father to give Agnes a shilling to buy chocolates at Stephenson's in St Luke's Square, that being the best shop. The shilling fell between the footboard and the platform. A scream from Beatrice! The attendant porter promised to rescue the shilling in due course. The engine whistled, the silver-mounted guard asserted his authority, Mynors leaped in, and amid laughter and tears the brief and unique joy of Anna's life began.

In a moment, so it seemed, the train was thundering through the mile of solid rock which ends at Lime Street Station, Liverpool.* Thenceforward, till she fell asleep that night, Anna existed in a state of blissful bewilderment, stupefied by an overdose of novel and wondrous sensations. They lunched in amazing magnificence at the Bear's Paw,* and then walked through the crowded and prodigious streets to Prince's landing-stage.* The luggage had disappeared by some mysterious agency – Mynors said that they would find it safe at Douglas;* but Anna could not banish the fear that her tin box had gone for ever.

The great, wavy river, churned by thousands of keels; the monstrous steamer – the 'Mona's Isle'* – whose side rose like solid wall out of the water; the vistas of its decks; its vast saloons, storey under storey, solid and palatial (could all this float?); its high bridge; its hawsers as thick as trees; its funnels like sloping towers; the multitudes of passengers; the whistles, hoots, cries; the far-stretching panorama of wharves and docks; the squat ferry-craft carrying horses and carts, and no one looking twice at the feat – it was all too much, too astonishing, too lovely. She had not guessed at this.

'They call Liverpool the slum of Europe,' said Mynors.

'How can you!' she exclaimed, shocked.

Beatrice, seeing her radiant and rapt face, walked to and fro with Anna, proud of the effect produced on her friend's inexperience by these sights. One might have thought that Beatrice had built Liverpool and created its trade by her own efforts.

Suddenly the landing-stage and all the people on it moved away bodily from the ship; there was green water between; a tremor like that of an earthquake ran along the deck; handkerchiefs were waved. The voyage had commenced. Mynors found chairs for all the Suttons, and tucked them up on the lee-side of a deck-house; but Anna did not stir. They passed New Brighton, Seaforth, and the Crosby and Formby light-ships.*

'Come and view the ship,' said Mynors, at her side. 'Suppose we go round and inspect things a bit?'

'It's a very big one, isn't it?' she asked.

'Pretty big,' he said; 'of course not as big as the Atlantic liners – I wonder we didn't meet one in the river – but still pretty big. Three hundred and twenty feet over all. I sailed on her last year on her maiden voyage. She was packed, and the weather very bad.'

'Will it be rough today?' Anna inquired timidly.

'Not if it keeps like this,' he laughed. 'You don't feel queer, do you?'

'Oh, no. It's as firm as a house. No one could be ill with this?'

'Couldn't they?' he exclaimed. 'Beatrice could be.'

They descended into the ship, and he explained all its internal economy, with a knowledge that seemed to her encyclopaedic. They stayed a long time watching the engines, so Titanic,* ruthless, and deliberate; even the smell of the oil was pleasant to Anna. When they came on deck again the ship was at sea. For the first time Anna beheld the ocean. A strong breeze blew from prow to stern, yet the sea was absolutely calm, the unruffled mirror of effulgent sunlight. The steamer moved alone on the waters, exultantly, leaving behind it an endless track of white froth in the green, and the shadow of its smoke. The sun, the salt breeze, the living water, the proud gaiety of the ship, produced a feeling of intense, inexplicable joy, a profound satisfaction with the present, and a negligence of past and future. To exist was enough, then. As Anna and Henry leaned over the starboard quarter and watched the torrent of foam rush madly and ceaselessly from under the paddle-box to be swallowed up in the white wake, the spectacle of the wild torrent almost hypnotized them, destroying thought and reason, and all sense of their relation to other things. With difficulty Anna raised her eyes, and perceived the dim receding line of the Lancashire coast.

'Shall we get quite out of sight of land?' she asked.

'Yes, for a little while, about half an hour or so. Just as much out of sight of land as if we were in the middle of the Atlantic.'

'I can scarcely believe it.'

'Believe what?'

'Oh! The idea of that – of being out of sight of land – nothing but sea.'

When at last it occurred to them to reconnoitre the Suttons, they found all three still in their deck-chairs, enwrapped and languid. Mr Sutton and Beatrice were apparently dozing. This part of the deck was occupied by somnolent, basking figures.

'Don't wake them,' Mrs Sutton enjoined, whispering out of her hood. Anna glanced curiously at Beatrice's yellow face.

'Go away, do,' Beatrice exclaimed, opening her eyes and shutting them again, wearily.

So they went away, and discovered two empty deck-chairs on the fore-deck. Anna was innocently vain of her immunity from *malaise*.* Mynors appeared to appoint himself little errands about the deck, returning frequently to his chair. 'Look over there. Can you see anything?'

Anna ran to the rail, with the infantile idea of getting nearer, and Mynors followed, laughing. What looked like a small slate-coloured cloud lay on the horizon.

'I seem to see something,' she said.

'That is the Isle of Man.'

By insensible gradations the contours of the land grew clearer in the afternoon haze.

'How far are we off now?'

'Perhaps twenty miles.'

Twenty miles of uninterrupted flatness, and the ship steadily invading that separating solitude, yard by yard, furlong by furlong! The conception awed her. There, a morsel in the waste of the deep, a speck under the infinite sunlight, lay the island, mysterious, enticing, enchanted, a glinting jewel on the sea's bosom, a remote entity fraught with strange secrets. It was all unspeakable.

'Anna, you have covered yourself with glory,' said Mrs Sutton, when they were in the diminutive and absurd train* which by breathless plunges annihilates the sixteen miles between Douglas and Port Erin in sixty-five minutes.

'Have I?' she answered. 'How?'

'By not being ill.'

'That's always the beginner's luck,' said Beatrice, pale and dishevelled. They all relapsed into the silence of fatigue. It was growing dusk when the train stopped at the tiny terminus. The station was a hive of bustling activity, the arrival of this train being the daily event at that end of the world. Mynors and the Suttons were greeted familiarly by several sailors, and one of these, Tom Kelly,* a tall, middle-aged man, with grey beard, small grey eyes, a wrinkled skin of red mahogany, and an enormous fist, was introduced to Anna. He raised his cap, and shook hands. She was touched by the sad, kind look on his face, the melancholy impress of the sea. Then they drove to their lodging,* and here again the party was welcomed as being old and tried friends. A fire was burning in the parlour. Throwing herself down in front of it, Mrs Sutton breathed, 'At last! Oh, for some tea.' Through the window, Anna had a glimpse of a deeply indented bay at the foot of cliffs below them, with a bold headland to the right. Fishing vessels with flat red sails seemed to hang undecided just outside the bay. From cottage chimneys beneath the road blue smoke softly ascended.

All went early to bed, for the weariness of Mr and Mrs Sutton seemed to communicate itself to the three young people, who might otherwise have gone forth into the village in search of adventures. Anna and Beatrice shared a room. Each inspected the other's clothes, and Beatrice made Anna try on the new serge skirt. Through the thin wall came the sound of Mr and Mrs Sutton talking, a high voice, then a bass reply, in continual alternation. Beatrice said that these two always discussed the day's doings in such manner. In a few moments Beatrice was snoring; she had the subdued but steady and serious snore characteristic of some muscular men. Anna felt no inclination to sleep. She lived again hour by hour through the day, and beneath Beatrice's snore her ear caught the undertone of the sea.

The next morning was as lovely as the last. It was Sunday, and every activity of the village was stilled. Sea and land were equally folded in a sunlit calm. During breakfast – a meal abundant in fresh herrings, fresh eggs, and fresh rolls, eaten with the windows wide open – Anna was puzzled by the singular amenity of her friends to one another and to her. They were as polite as though they had been strangers; they chatted amiably, were full of goodwill, and as anxious to give happiness as to enjoy it. She thought at first, so unusual was it to her as a feature of domestic privacy, that this demeanour was affected, or at any rate a somewhat exaggerated punctilio due to her presence; but she soon came to see that she was mistaken. After breakfast Mr Sutton suggested that they should attend the Wesleyan Chapel on the hill leading to the Chasms.* Here they met the sailors of the night before, arrayed now in marvellous blue Melton coats* with velveteen collars. Tom Kelly walked back with them to the beach, and showed them the yacht *Fay* which Mynors had arranged to hire for mackerel-fishing; it lay on the sands speckless in new white paint. All the afternoon they dozed on the cliffs, doing nothing whatever, for this Sunday was tacitly regarded, not as part of the holiday, but as a preparation for the holiday; all felt that the holiday, with its proper exertions and appointed delights, would really begin on Monday morning.

'Let us go for a walk,' said Mynors, after tea, to Beatrice and Anna. They stood at the gate of the lodging-house. The old people were resting within.

'You two go,' Beatrice replied, looking at Anna. 'You know I hate walking, Henry. I'll stop with Mother and Dad.'

Throughout the day Anna had been conscious of the fact that all the Suttons showed a tendency, slight but perceptible, to treat Henry and herself as a pair desirous of opportunities for being alone together. She did not like it. She flushed under the passing glance with which Beatrice accompanied the words: 'You two go.' Nevertheless, when Mynors placidly remarked: 'Very well?' and his eyes sought hers for a consent, she could not refuse it. One part of her nature would have preferred to find an excuse for staying at home; but another, and a stronger, part insisted on seizing this offered joy.

They walked straight up out of the village towards the high coast-range which stretches peak after peak from Port Erin to Peel.* The stony and devious lanes wound about the bleak hillside, passing here and there small solitary cottages of white-washed stone, with children, fowls, and dogs at the doors, all embowered in huge fuchsia trees. Presently they had surmounted the limit of habitation and were on the naked flank of Bradda,* following a narrow track which crept upwards amid short mossy turf of the most vivid green. Nothing seemed to flourish on this exposed height except bracken, sheep, and boulders that, from a distance, resembled sheep; there was no tree, scarcely a shrub; the immense contours, stark, grim, and unrelieved, rose in melancholy and defiant majesty against the sky; the hand of man could coax no harvest from these smooth but obdurate slopes; they had never relented, and they would never relent. The spirit was braced by the thought that here, to the furthest eternity of civilization more and more intricate, simple, and strong souls would always find solace and repose.

Mynors bore to the left for a while, striking across the moor in the direction of the sea. Then he said:

'Look down, now.'

The little bay* lay like an oblong swimming-bath five hundred feet below them. The surface of the water was like glass; the strand, with its phalanx of boats drawn up in Sabbath tidiness, glittered like marble in the living light, and over this marble black dots moved slowly to and fro; behind the boats were the houses – doll's houses – each with a curling wisp of smoke; further away the railway and the high road ran out in a black and white line to Port St Mary;* the sea, a pale grey, encompassed all; the southern sky had a faint sapphire tinge, rising to delicate azure. The sight of this haven at rest, shut in by the restful sea and by great moveless hills, a calm within a calm, aroused profound emotion.

'It's lovely,' said Anna, as they stood gazing. Tears came to her eyes and hung there. She wondered that scenery should cause tears, felt ashamed, and turned her face so that Mynors should not see. But he had seen.

'Shall we go on to the top?' he suggested, and they set their faces northwards to climb still higher. At length they stood on the rocky summit of Bradda, seven hundred feet from the sea. The Hill of the Night Watch* lifted above them to the north, but on east, south, and west, the prospect was bounded only by the ocean. The coast-line was revealed for thirty miles, from Peel to Castletown.* Far to the east was Castletown Bay, large, shallow, and inhospitable, its floor strewn with a thousand unseen wrecks; the lighthouse at Scarlet Point* flashed dimly in the dusk; thence the beach curved nearer in an immense arc, without a sign of life, to the little cove of Port St Mary, and jutted out again into a tongue of land at the end of which lay the Calf of Man with its single white cottage and cart-track. The dangerous Calf Sound, where the vexed tide is forced to run nine hours one way and three the other, seemed like a grey ribbon, and the Chicken Rock* like a tiny pencil on a vast slate. Port Erin was hidden under their feet. They looked westward.

The darkening sky was a labyrinth of purple and crimson scarves drawn pellucid, as though by the finger of God, across a sheet of pure saffron. These decadent tints of the sunset faded in every direction to the same soft azure which filled the south, and one star twinkled in the illimitable field. Thirty miles off, on the horizon, could be discerned the Mourne Mountains of Ireland.*

'See!' Mynors exclaimed, touching her arm.

The huge disc of the moon was rising in the east, and as this mild lamp passed up the sky, the sense of universal quiescence increased. Lovely, Anna had said. It was the loveliest sight her eyes had ever beheld, a panorama of pure beauty transcending all imagined visions. It overwhelmed her, thrilled her to the heart, this revelation of the loveliness of the world. Her thoughts went back to Hanbridge and Bursley and her life there; and all the remembered scenes, bathed in the glow of a new ideal, seemed to lose their pain. It was as if she had never been really unhappy, as if there was no real unhappiness on the whole earth. She perceived that the monotony, the austerity, the melancholy of her existence had been sweet and beautiful of its kind, and she recalled, with a sort of rapture, hours of companionship with the beloved Agnes, when her father was equable and pacific. Nothing was ugly nor mean. Beauty was everywhere, in everything.

In silence they began to descend, perforce walking quickly because of the steep gradient. At the first cottage they saw a little girl in a mob-cap playing with two kittens.

'How like Agnes!' Mynors said.

'Yes. I was just thinking so,' Anna answered.

'I thought of her up on the hill,' he continued. 'She will miss you, won't she?'

'I know she cried herself to sleep last night. You mightn't guess it, but she is extremely sensitive.'

'Not guess it? Why not? I am sure she is. Do you know – I am very fond of your sister. She's a simply delightful child. And there's a lot in her, too. She's so quick and bright, and somehow like a little woman.'

'She's exactly like a woman sometimes,' Anna agreed. 'Sometimes I fancy she's a great deal older than I am.'

'Older than any of us,' he corrected.

'I'm glad you like her,' Anna said, content. 'She thinks all the world of you.' And she added: 'My word, wouldn't she be vexed if she knew I had told you that!'

This appreciation of Agnes brought them into closer intimacy, and they talked the more easily of other things.

'It will freeze tonight,' Mynors said; and then, suddenly looking at her in the twilight: 'You are feeling chill.'

'Oh, no!' she protested.

'But you are. Put this muffler round your neck.' He took a muffler from his pocket.

'Oh, no, really! You will need it yourself.' She drew a little away from him, as if to avoid the muffler.

'Please take it.'

She did so, and thanked him, tying it loosely and untidily round her throat. That feeling of the untidiness of the muffler, of its being something strange to her skin, something with the rough virtue of masculinity, which no one could detect in the gloom, was in itself pleasant.

'I wager Mrs Sutton has a good fire burning when we get in,' he said.

She thought with joyous anticipation of the warm, bright, sitting-room, the supper, and the vivacious good-natured conversation. Though the walk was nearly at an end, other delights were in store. Of the holiday, thirteen complete days yet remained, each to be as happy as the one now closing. It was an age! At last they entered the human cosiness of the village. As they walked up the steps of their lodging and he opened the door for her, she quickly drew off the muffler and returned it to him with a word of thanks.

On Monday morning, when Beatrice and Anna came downstairs, they found the breakfast odorously cooling on the table, and nobody in the room.

'Where are they all, I wonder. Any letters?' Beatrice said.

'There's your mother, out on the front – and Mr Mynors too.'

Beatrice threw up the window, and called: 'Come along, Henry; come along, Mother. Everything's going cold.'

'Is it?' Mynors cheerfully replied. 'Come out here, both of you, and begin the day properly with a dose of ozone.'

'I loathe cold bacon,' said Beatrice, glancing at the table, and they went out into the road, where Mrs Sutton kissed them with as much fervour as if they had arrived from a long journey.

'You look pale, Anna,' she remarked.

'Do I?' said Anna, 'I don't feel pale.'

'It's that long walk last night,' Beatrice put in. 'Henry always goes too far.'

'I don't – ' Anna began; but at that moment Mr Sutton, lumbering and ponderous, joined the party.

'Henry,' he said, without greeting anyone, 'hast noticed those half-finished houses down the road yonder by the "Falcon"?* I've been having a chat with Kelly, and he tells me the fellow that was building them has gone bankrupt, and they're at a standstill. The Receiver wants to sell 'em. In fact Kelly says they're going cheap. I believe they'd be a good spec.'

'Eh, dear!' Mrs Sutton interrupted him. 'Father, I wish you would leave your specs alone when you're on your holiday.'

'Now, missis!' he affectionately protested, and continued: 'They're fairly well built, seemingly, and the rafters are on the roof. Anna,' he turned to her quickly, as if counting on her sympathy, 'you must come with me and look at 'em after breakfast. Happen they might suit your father – or you. I know your father's fond of a good spec.'

She assented with a ready smile. This was the beginning of a fancy which the Alderman always afterwards showed for Anna.

After breakfast Mrs Sutton, Beatrice, and Anna arranged to go shopping.

'Father – brass,' Mrs Sutton ejaculated in two monosyllables to her husband.

'How much will content ye?' he asked mildly.

'Give me five or ten pounds to go on with.'

He opened the left-hand front pocket of his trousers – a pocket which fastened with a button; and leaning back in his chair drew out a fat purse, and passed it to his wife with a preoccupied air. She helped herself, and then Beatrice intercepted the purse and lightened it of half a sovereign.

'Pocket-money,' Beatrice said; 'I'm ruined.'

The Alderman's eyes requested Anna to observe how he was robbed. At last the purse was safely buttoned up again.

Mrs Sutton's purchases of food at the three principal shops of the village seemed startlingly profuse to Anna, but gradually she became accustomed to the scale, and to the amazing habit of always buying the very best of everything, from beefsteak to grapes. Anna calculated that the housekeeping could not cost less than six pounds a week for the five. At Manor Terrace three people existed on a pound. With her half-sovereign Beatrice bought a belt and a pair of sand-shoes, and some cigarettes for Henry. Mrs Sutton bought a pipe with a nickel cap, such as is used by sailors. When they returned to the house, Mr Sutton and Henry were smoking on the front. All five walked in a row down to the harbour, the Alderman giving an arm each to Beatrice and Anna. Near the 'Falcon' the procession had to be stopped in order to view the unfinished houses. Tom Kelly had a cabin partly excavated out of the rock* behind the little quay. Here they found him entangled amid nets, sails, and oars. All crowded into the cabin and shook hands with its owner, who remarked with severity on their pallid faces, and insisted that a change of complexion must be brought about. Mynors offered him his tobacco-pouch, but on seeing the light colour of the tobacco he shook his head and refused it, at the same time taking from within his jersey a lump of something that resembled leather.

'Give him this, Henry,' Mrs Sutton whispered, handing Mynors the pipe which she had bought.

'Mrs Sutton wishes you to accept this,' said Mynors.

'Eh, thank ye,' he exclaimed. 'There's a leddy that knows my taste.' He cut some shreds from his plug with a clasp knife and charged and lighted the pipe, filling the cabin with asphyxiating fumes.

'I don't know how you can smoke such horrid, nasty stuff,' said Beatrice, coughing.

He laughed condescendingly at Beatrice's petulant manner. 'That stuff of Henry's is boy's tobacco,' he said shortly.

It was decided that they should go fishing in the *Fay*. There was a light southerly breeze, a cloudy sky, and smooth water. Under charge of young Tom Kelly, a sheepish lad of sixteen, with his father's smile, they all got into an inconceivably small dinghy, loading it down till it was almost awash. Old Tom himself helped Anna to embark, told her where to tread, and forced her gently into a seat at the stern. No one else seemed to be disturbed, but Anna was in a state of desperate fear. She had never committed herself to a boat before, and the little waves spat up against the sides in a most alarming way as young Tom jerked the dinghy along with the short sculls. She went white, and clung in silence fiercely to the gunwale. In a few moments they were tied up to the *Fay*, which seemed very big and safe in comparison with the dinghy. They clambered on board, and in the deep well of the two-ton yacht Anna contrived to collect her wits. She was reassured by the painted legend in the well, 'Licensed to carry eleven.' Young Tom and Henry busied themselves with ropes, and suddenly a huge white sail began to ascend the mast; it flapped like thunder in the gentle breeze. Tom pulled up the anchor, curling the chain round and round on the forward deck, and then Anna noticed that, although the wind was scarcely perceptible, they were gliding quickly past the embankment. Henry was at the tiller. The next minute Tom had set the jib, and by this time the *Fay* was approaching the breakwater at a great pace. There was no rolling or pitching, but simply a smooth, swift progression over the calm surface. Anna thought it the ideal of locomotion. As soon as they were beyond the breakwater and the sails caught the breeze from the Sound, the *Fay* lay over as if shot, and a little column of green water flung itself on the lee coaming of the well.* Anna screamed as she saw the water and felt the angle of the floor suddenly change, but when everyone laughed, she laughed too. Henry, noticing the whiteness of her knuckles as she gripped the coaming, explained the disconcerting phenomena. Anna tried to be at ease, but she was not. She could not for a long time dismiss the suspicion that all these people were foolishly blind to a peril which she alone had the sagacity to perceive.

They cruised about while Tom prepared the lines. The short waves chopped cheerfully against the carvel* sides of the yacht; the clouds were breaking at a hundred points; the sea grew lighter in tone; gaiety was in the air; no one could possibly be indisposed in that innocuous weather. At length the lines were ready, but Tom said the yacht was making at least a knot too much for serious fishing, so Henry took a reef in the mainsail, showing Anna how to tie the short strings. The Alderman, lying on the fore-deck, was placidly smoking. The lines were thrown out astern, and Mrs Sutton and Beatrice each took one. But they had no success; young Tom said it was because the sun had appeared.

'Caught anything?' Mr Sutton inquired at intervals. After a time he said:

'Suppose Anna and I have a try?'

It was agreed.

'What must I do?' asked Anna, brave now.

'You just hold the line – so. And if you feel a little jerk-jerk, that's a mackerel.' These were the instructions of Beatrice. Anna was becoming excited. She had not held the line ten seconds before she cried out:

'I've got one.'

'Nonsense,' said Beatrice. 'Everyone thinks at first that the motion of the waves against the line is a fish.'

'Well,' said Henry, giving the tiller to young Tom. 'Let's haul in and see, anyway.' Before doing so he held the line for a moment, testing it, and winked at Anna. While Anna and Henry were hauling in, the Alderman, dropping his pipe, began also to haul in his own line with great fury.

'Got one, Father?' Mrs Sutton asked.

'Ay!'

Both lines came in together, and on each was a pounder. Anna saw her fish gleam and flash like silver in the clear water as it neared the surface. Henry held the line short, letting the mackerel plunge and jerk, and then seized and unhooked the catch.

'How cruel!' Anna cried, startled at the nearness of the two fish as they sprang about in an old sugar box at her feet. Young Tom laughed loud at her exclamation. 'They cairn't feel, miss,' he sniggered. Anna wondered that a mouth so soft and kind could utter such heartless words.

In an hour the united efforts of the party had caught nine mackerel; it was not a multitude, but the sun, in perfecting the weather, had spoilt the sport. Anna had ceased to commiserate the captured fish. She was obliged, however, to avert her head when Tom cut some skin from the side of one of the mackerel to provide fresh bait; this device seemed to her the extremest refinement of cruelty. Beatrice grew ominously silent and inert, and Mrs Sutton glanced first at her daughter and then at her husband; the latter nodded.

'We'd happen better be getting back, Henry,' said the Alderman.

The *Fay* swept home like a bird. They were at the quay, and Kelly was dragging them one by one from the black dinghy on to what the Alderman called *terra-firma*. Henry had the fish on a string.

'How many did ye catch, Miss Tellwright?' Kelly asked benevolently.

'I caught four,' Anna replied. Never before had she felt so proud, elated, and boisterous. Never had the blood so wildly danced in her veins. She looked at her short blue skirt which showed three inches of ankle, put forward her brown-shod foot like a vain coquette, and darted a covert look at Henry. When he caught it she laughed instead of blushing.

'Ye're doing well,' Tom Kelly approved. 'Ye'll make a famous mackerel-fisher.'

Five of the mackerel were given to young Tom, the other four preceded a fowl in the menu for dinner. They were called Anna's mackerel, and all the diners agreed that better mackerel had never been lured out of the Irish Sea.

In the afternoon the Alderman and his wife slept as usual, Mr Sutton with a bandanna handkerchief over his face. The rest went out immediately; the invitation of the sun and the sea was far too persuasive to be resisted.

'I'm going to paint,' said Beatrice, with a resolute mien. 'I want to paint Bradda Head frightfully. I tried last year, but I got it too dark, somehow. I've improved since then. What are you going to do?'

'We'll come and watch you,' said Henry.

'Oh, no, you won't. At least *you* won't; you're such a critic. Anna can if she likes.'

'What! And me be left all afternoon by myself?'

'Well, suppose you go with him, Anna, just to keep him from being bored?'

Anna hesitated. Once more she had the uncomfortable suspicion that Mynors and herself were being manoeuvred.

'Look here,' said Mynors to Beatrice. 'Have you decided absolutely to paint?'

'Absolutely.' The finality of the answer seemed to have a touch of resentment.

'Then' – he turned to Anna – 'let's go and get that dinghy and row about the bay. Eh?'

She could offer no rational objection, and they were soon putting off from the jetty, impelled seaward by a mighty push from Kelly's arm. It was very hot. Mynors wore white flannels. He removed his coat, and turned up his sleeves, showing thick, hairy arms. He sculled in a manner almost dramatic, and the dinghy shot about like a water-spider on a brook. Anna had nothing to do except to sit still and enjoy. Everything was drowned in dazzling sunlight, and both Henry and Anna could feel the process of tanning on their faces. The bay shimmered with a million diamond points; it was impossible to keep the eyes open without frowning, and soon Anna could see the beads of sweat on Henry's crimson brow.

'Warm?' she said. This was the first word of conversation. He merely smiled in reply. Presently they were at the other side of the bay, in a cave whose sandy and rock-strewn floor trembled clear under a fathom of blue water. They landed on a jutting rock; Henry pushed his straw hat back, and wiped his forehead. 'Glorious! glorious!' he exclaimed. 'Do you swim? No? You should get Beatrice to teach you. I swam out here this morning at seven o'clock. It was chilly enough then. Oh! I forgot, I told you at breakfast.'

She could see him in the translucent water, swimming with long, powerful strokes. Dozens of boats were moving lazily in the bay, each with a cargo of parasols.

'There's a good deal of the sunshade afloat,' he remarked. 'Why haven't you got one? You'll get as brown as Tom Kelly.'

'That's what I want,' she said.

'Look at yourself in the water there,' he said, pointing to a little pool left on the top of the rock by the tide. She did so, and saw two fiery cheeks, and a forehead divided by a horizontal line into halves of white and crimson; the tip of the nose was blistered.

'Isn't it disgraceful?' he suggested.

'Why,' she exclaimed, 'they'll never know me when I get home!'

It was in such wise that they talked, endlessly exchanging trifles of comment. Anna thought to herself: 'Is this love-making?' It could not be, she decided; but she infinitely preferred it so. She was content. She wished for nothing better than this apparently frivolous and irresponsible dalliance. She felt that if Mynors were to be tender, sentimental, and serious, she would become wretchedly self-conscious.

They re-embarked, and, skirting the shore, gradually came round to the beach. Up above them, on the cliffs, they could discern the industrious figure of Beatrice, with easel and sketching-umbrella, and all the panoply of the earnest amateur.

'Do you sketch?' she asked him.

'Not I!' he said scornfully.

'Don't you believe in that sort of thing, then?'

'It's all right for professional artists,' he said; 'people who *can* paint. But – Well, I suppose it's harmless for the amateurs – finds them something to do.'

'I wish I could paint, anyway,' she retorted.

'I'm glad you can't,' he insisted.

When they got back to the cliffs, towards tea-time, Beatrice was still painting, but in a new spot. She seemed entirely absorbed in her work, and did not hear their approach.

'Let's creep up and surprise her,' Mynors whispered. 'You go first, and put your hands over her eyes.'

'Oh!' exclaimed Beatrice, blindfolded; 'how horrid you are, Henry! I know who it is – I know who it is.'

'You just don't, then,' said Henry, now in front of her. Anna removed her hands.

'Well, you told her to do it, I'm sure of that. And I was getting on so splendidly! I shan't do another stroke now.'

'That's right,' said Henry. 'You've wasted quite enough time as it is.'

Beatrice pouted. She was evidently annoyed with both of them. She looked from one to the other, jealous of their mutual understanding and agreement. Mr and Mrs Sutton issued from the house, and the five stood chatting till tea was ready; but the shadow remained on Beatrice's face. Mynors made several attempts to laugh it away, and at dusk these two went for a stroll to Port St Mary. They returned in a state of deep intimacy. During supper Beatrice was consciously and elaborately angelic, and there was that in her voice and eyes, when sometimes she addressed Mynors, which almost persuaded Anna that he might once have loved his cousin. At night, in the bedroom, Anna imagined that she could detect in Beatrice's attitude the least shade of condescension. She felt hurt, and despised herself for feeling hurt.

So the days passed, without much variety, for the Suttons were not addicted to excursions. Anna was profoundly happy; she had forgotten care. She agreed to every suggestion for amusement; each moment had its pleasure, and this pleasure was quite independent of the thing done; it sprang from all activities and idlenesses. She was at special pains to fraternize with Mr Sutton. He made an interesting companion, full of facts about strata, outcrops, and breaks, his sole weakness being the habit of quoting extremely sentimental scraps of verse when walking by the seashore. He frankly enjoyed Anna's attention to him, and took pride in her society. Mrs Sutton, that simple heart, devoted herself to the attainment of absolute quiescence. She had come for a rest, and she achieved her purpose. Her kindliness became for the time passive instead of active. Beatrice was a changing quantity in the domestic equation. Plainly her parents had spoiled their only child, and she had frequent fits of petulance, particularly with Mynors; but her energy and spirits atoned well for these. As for Mynors, he behaved exactly as on the first Monday. He spent many hours alone with Anna – (Beatrice appeared to insist on leaving them together, even while showing a faint resentment at the loneliness thus entailed on herself) – and his attitude was such as Anna, ignorant of the ways of brothers, deemed a brother might adopt.

On the second Monday an incident occurred. In the afternoon Mr Sutton had asked Beatrice to go with him to Port St Mary, and she had refused on the plea that the light was of a suitable grey for painting. Mr Sutton had slipped off alone, unseen by Anna and Henry, who had meant to accompany him in place of Beatrice. Before tea, while Anna, Beatrice, and Henry were awaiting the meal in the parlour, Mynors referred to the matter.

'I hope you've done some decent work this afternoon,' he said to Beatrice.

'I haven't,' she replied shortly; 'I haven't done a stroke.'

'But you said you were going to paint hard!'

'Well, I didn't.'

'Then why couldn't you have gone to Port St Mary, instead of breaking your fond father's heart by a refusal?'

'He didn't want me, really.'

Anna interjected: 'I think he did, Bee.'

'You know you're very self-willed, not to say selfish,' Mynors said.

'No, I'm not,' Beatrice protested seriously. 'Am I, Anna?'

'Well – ' Anna tried to think of a diplomatic pronouncement. Beatrice took offence at the hesitation.

'Oh! You two are bound to agree, of course. You're as thick as thieves.'

She gazed steadily out of the window, and there was a silence. Mynors' lip curled.

'Oh! There's the loveliest yacht just coming into the bay,'

Beatrice cried suddenly, in a tone of affected enthusiasm. 'I'm going out to sketch it.' She snatched up her hat and sketching-block, and ran hastily from the room. The other two saw her sitting on the grass, sharpening a pencil. The yacht, a large and luxurious craft, had evidently come to anchor for the night.

Mrs Sutton arrived from her bedroom, and then Mr Sutton also came in. Tea was served. Mynors called to Beatrice through the window and received no reply. Then Mrs Sutton summoned her.

'Go on with your tea,' Beatrice shouted, without turning her head. 'Don't wait for me. I'm bound to finish this now.'

'Fetch her, Anna dear,' said Mrs Sutton after another interval. Anna rose to obey, half-fearful.

'Aren't you coming in, Bee?' She stood by the sketcher's side, and observed nothing but a few meaningless lines on the block.

'Didn't you hear what I said to Mother?'

Anna retired in discomfiture.

Tea was finished. They went out, but kept at a discreet distance from the artist, who continued to use her pencil until dusk had fallen. Then they returned to the sitting-room, where a fire had been lighted, and Beatrice at length followed. As the others sat in a circle round the fire, Beatrice, who occupied the sofa in solitude, gave a shiver.

'Beatrice, you've taken cold,' said her mother, 'sitting out there like that.'

'Oh, nonsense, Mother – what a fidget you are!'

'A fidget I certainly am not, my darling, and that you know very well. As you've had no tea, you shall have some gruel at once, and go to bed and get warm.'

'Oh no, Mother!' But Mrs Sutton was resolved, and in half an hour she had taken Beatrice to bed and tucked her up.

When Anna went to the bedroom Beatrice was awake.

'Can't you sleep?' she inquired kindly.

'No,' said Beatrice, in a feeble voice, 'I'm restless, somehow.'

'I wonder if it's influenza,'* said Mrs Sutton, on the following morning, when she learnt from Anna that Beatrice had had a bad night, and would take breakfast in bed. She carried the invalid's food upstairs herself. 'I hope it isn't influenza,' she said later. 'The girl is very hot.'

'You haven't a clinical thermometer?' Mynors suggested.

'Go, see if you can buy one at the little chemist's,' she replied eagerly. In a few minutes he came back with the instrument.

'She's at over a hundred,' Mrs Sutton reported, having used the thermometer. 'What do you say, Father? Shall we send for a doctor? I'm not so set up with doctors as a general rule,' she added, as if in defence, to Anna. 'I brought Beatrice through measles and scarlet fever without a doctor – we never used to think of having a doctor in those days for ordinary ailments; but influenza – that's different. Eh, I dread it; you never know how it will end. And poor Beatrice had such a bad attack last Martinmas.'*

'If you like, I'll run for a doctor now,' said Mynors.

'Let be till tomorrow,' the Alderman decided. 'We'll see how she goes on. Happen it's nothing but a cold.'

'Yes,' assented Mrs Sutton; 'it's no use crying out before you're hurt.'

Anna was struck by the placidity with which they covered their apprehension. Towards noon, Beatrice, who said that she felt better, insisted on rising. A fire was lighted at once in the parlour, and she sat in front of it till tea-time, when she was obliged to go to bed again. On the Wednesday morning, after a night which had been almost sleepless for both girls, her temperature stood at 103°, and Henry fetched the doctor, who pronounced it a case of influenza, severe, demanding very careful treatment. Instantly the normal movement of the household was changed. The sickroom became a mysterious centre round which everything revolved, and the parlour, without the alteration of a single chair, took on a deserted, forlorn appearance. Meals were eaten like the passover, with loins girded for any sudden summons. Mrs Sutton and Anna, as nurses, grew important in the eyes of the men, who instinctively effaced themselves, existing only like messenger-boys whose business it is to await a call. Yet there was no alarm, flurry, or excitement. In the evening the doctor returned. The patient's temperature had not fallen. It was part of the treatment that a medicine should be administered every two hours with absolute regularity, and Mrs Sutton said that she should sit up through the night.

'I shall do that,' said Anna.

'Nay, I won't hear of it,' Mrs Sutton replied, smiling.

But the three men (the doctor had remained to chat in the parlour), recognizing Anna's capacity and reliability, and perhaps impressed also by her businesslike appearance as, arrayed in a white apron, she stood with firm lips before them, gave a unanimous decision against Mrs Sutton.

'We'st have you ill next, lass,' said the Alderman to his wife; 'and that'll never do.'

'Well,' Mrs Sutton surrendered, 'if I can leave her to anyone, it's Anna.'

Mynors smiled appreciatively.

On the Thursday morning there was still no sign of recovery. The temperature was 104°, and the patient slightly delirious. Anna left the sickroom at eight o'clock to preside at breakfast, and Mrs Sutton took her place.

'You look tired, my dear,' said the Alderman affectionately.

'I feel perfectly well,' she replied with cheerfulness.

'And you aren't afraid of catching it?' Mynors asked.

'Afraid?' she said; 'there's no fear of me catching it.'

'How do you know?'

'I know, that's all. I'm never ill.'

'That's the right way to keep well,' the Alderman remarked.

The quiet admiration of these two men was very pleasant to her. She felt that she had established herself for ever in their esteem. After breakfast, in obedience to them, she slept for several hours on Mrs Sutton's bed. In the afternoon Beatrice was worse. The doctor called, and found her temperature at 105°.

'This can't last,' he remarked briefly.

'Well, Doctor,' Mr Sutton said, 'it's i' your hands.'

'Nay,' Mrs Sutton murmured with a smile, 'I've left it with God. It's with Him.'

This was the first and only word of religion, except grace at table, that Anna heard from the Suttons during her stay in the Isle of Man. She had feared lest vocal piety might form a prominent feature of their daily life, but her fear had proved groundless. She, too, from reason rather than instinct, had tried to pray for Beatrice's recovery. She had, however, found much more satisfaction in the activity of nursing.

Again that night she sat up, and on the Friday morning Beatrice was better. At noon all immediate danger was past; the patient slept; her temperature was almost correct. Anna went to bed in the afternoon and slept soundly till supper-time, when she awoke very hungry. For the first time in three days Beatrice could be left alone. The other four had supper together, cheerful and relieved after the tension.

'She'll be as right as a trivet in a few days,' said the Alderman.

'A few weeks,' said Mrs Sutton.

'Of course,' said Mynors, 'you'll stay on here, now?'

'We shall stay until Beatrice is quite fit to travel,' Mr Sutton answered. 'I might have to run over to th' Five Towns for a day or two middle of next week, but I can come back immediately.'

'Well, I must go tomorrow,' Mynors sighed.

'Surely you can stay over Sunday, Henry?'

'No; I've no one to take my place at school.'

'And I must go tomorrow, too,' said Anna suddenly.

'Fiddle-de-dee, Anna!' the Alderman protested.

'I must,' she insisted. 'Father will expect me. You know I came for a fortnight. Besides, there's Agnes.'

'Agnes will be all right.'

'I must go.' They saw that she was fixed.

'Won't a short walk do you good?' Mynors suggested to her, with singular gravity, after supper. 'You've not been outside for two days.'

She looked inquiringly at Mrs Sutton.

'Yes, take her, Henry; she'll sleep better for it. Eh, Anna, but it's a shame to send you home with those rings round your eyes.'

She went upstairs for a jacket. Beatrice was awake. 'Anna,' she exclaimed in a weak voice, without any preface, 'I was awfully silly and cross the other afternoon, before all this business. Just now, when you came into the room, I was feeling quite ashamed.'

'Oh Bee!' she answered, bending over her, 'what nonsense! Now go off to sleep at once.' She was very happy. Beatrice, victim of a temperament which had the childishness and the impulsiveness of the artist without his higher and sterner traits, sank back in facile content.

The night was still and very dark. When Anna and Mynors got outside they could distinguish neither the sky nor the sea; but the faint, restless murmur of the sea came up the cliffs. Only the lights of the houses disclosed the direction of the road.

'Suppose we go down to the jetty, and then along as far as the breakwater?'* he said, and she concurred. 'Won't you take my muffler – again?' he added, pulling this ever-present article from his pocket.

'No, thanks,' she said, almost coldly, 'it's really quite warm.' She regarded the offer of the muffler as an indiscretion – his sole indiscretion during their acquaintance. As they walked down the hill to the shore she thought how Beatrice's illness had sharply interrupted their relations. If she had come to the Isle of Man with a vague idea that he would possibly propose to her, the expectation was disappointed; but she felt no disappointment. She felt that events had lifted her to a higher plane than that of love-making. She was filled with the proud satisfaction of a duty accomplished. She did not seek to minimize to herself the fact that she had been of real value to her friends in the last few days, had probably saved Mrs Sutton from illness, had certainly laid them all under an obligation. Their gratitude, unexpressed, but patent on each face, gave her infinite pleasure. She had won their respect by the manner in which she had risen to the height of an emergency that demanded more than devotion. She had proved, not merely to them but to herself, that she could be calm under stress, and could exert moral force when occasion needed. Such were the joyous and exultant reflections which passed through her brain – unnaturally active in the factitious wakefulness caused by excessive fatigue. She was in an extremely nervous and excitable condition – and never guessed it, fancying indeed that her emotions were exceptionally tranquil that night. She had not begun to realize the crisis through which she had just lived.

The uneven road to the ruined breakwater was quite deserted. Having reached the limit of the path, they stood side by side, solitary, silent, gazing at the black and gently heaving surface of the sea. The eye was foiled by the intense gloom; the ear could make nothing of the strange night-noises of the bay and the ocean beyond; but the imagination was stimulated by the appeal of all this mystery and darkness. Never had the water seemed so wonderful, terrible, and austere.

'We are going away tomorrow,' he said at length.

Anna started and shook with apprehension at the tremor in his voice. She had read that a woman was always well warned by her instincts when a man meant to propose to her. But here was the proposal imminent, and she had not suspected. In a flash of insight she perceived that the very event which had separated them for three days had also impelled the lover forward in his course. It was the thought of her vigils, her fortitude, her compassion, that had fanned the flame. She was not surprised, only made uncomfortable, when he took her hand.

'Anna,' he said, 'it's no use making a long story of it. I'm tremendously in love with you; you know I am.'

He stepped back, still holding her hand. She could say nothing.

'Well?' he ventured. 'Didn't you know?'

'I thought – I thought,' she murmured stupidly, 'I thought you liked me.'

'I can't tell you how I admire you. I'm not going to praise you to your face, but I simply never met anyone like you. From the very first moment I saw you, it was the same. It's something in your face, Anna – Anna, will you be my wife?'

The actual question was put in a precise, polite, somewhat conventional tone. To Anna he was never more himself than at that moment.

She could not speak; she could not analyse her feelings; she could not even think. She was adrift. At last she stammered: 'We've only known each other – '

'Oh, dear,' he exclaimed masterfully, 'what does that matter? If it had been a dozen years instead of one, that would have made no difference.' She drew her hand timidly away, but he took it again. She felt that he dominated her and would decide for her. 'Say yes.'

'Yes,' she said.

She saw pictures of her career as his wife, and resolved that one of the first acts of her freedom should be to release Agnes from the more ignominious of her father's tyrannies.

They walked home almost in silence. She was engaged, then. Yet she experienced no new sensation. She felt as she had felt on the way down, except that she was sorely perturbed. There was no ineffable rapture, no ecstatic bliss. Suddenly the prospect of happiness swept over her like a flood.

At the gate she wished to make a request to him, but hesitated, because she could not bring herself to use his Christian name. It was proper for her to use his Christian name, however, and she would do so, or perish.

'Henry,' she said, 'don't tell anyone here.' He merely kissed her once more. She went straight upstairs.

CHAPTER ELEVEN

The Downfall

In order to catch the Liverpool steamer at Douglas it was necessary to leave Port Erin at half-past six in the morning. The freshness of the morning, and the smiles of the Alderman and his wife as they waved God-speed from the doorstep, filled Anna with a serene content which she certainly had not felt during the wakeful night. She forgot, then, the hours passed with her conscience in realizing how serious and solemn a thing was this engagement, made in an instant on the previous evening. All that remained in her mind, as she and Henry walked quickly down the road, was the tonic sensation of high resolves to be a worthy wife. The duties, rather than the joys, of her condition, had lain nearest her heart until that moment of setting out, giving her an anxious and almost worried mien which at breakfast neither Henry nor the Suttons could quite understand. But now the idea of duty ceased for a time to be paramount, and she loosed herself to the pleasures of the day in store. The harbour was full of low wandering mists, through which the brown sails of the fishing-smacks played at hide-and-seek. High above them the round forms of immense clouds were still carrying the colours of sunrise. The gentle salt wind on the cheek was like the touch of a life-giver. It was impossible, on such a morning, not to exult in life, not to laugh childishly from irrational glee, not to dismiss the memory of grief and the apprehension of grief as morbid hallucinations. Mynors' face expressed the double happiness of present and anticipated pleasure. He had once again succeeded, he who had never failed; and the voyage back to England was for him a triumphal progress. Anna responded eagerly to his mood. The day was an ecstasy, a bright expanse unstained. To Anna in particular it was a unique day, marking the apogee of her existence. In the years that followed she could always return to it and say to herself: 'That day I was happy, foolishly, ignorantly, but utterly. And all that I have since learnt cannot alter it – I was happy.'

When they reached Shawport Station a cab was waiting for Anna. Unknown to her, Henry had ordered it by telegraph. This considerateness was of a piece, she thought, with his masterly conduct of the entire journey – on the steamer, at Liverpool, in the train; nothing that an experienced traveller could devise had been lacking to her comfort. She got into the cab alone, while Mynors, followed by a boy and his bag, walked to his rooms in Mount Street. It had been arranged, at Anna's wish, that he should not appear at Manor Terrace till suppertime. Ephraim opened for her the door of her home. It seemed to her that he was pleased.

'Well, Father, here I am again, you see.'

'Ay, lass.' They shook hands, and she indicated to the cabman where to deposit her tin box. She was glad and relieved to be back. Nothing had changed, except herself, and this absolute sameness was at once pleasant and pathetic to her.

'Where's Agnes?' she asked, smiling at her father. In the glow of arrival she had a vague notion that her relations with him had been permanently softened by absence.

'I see thou's gotten into th' habit o' flitting about* in cabs,' he said, without answering her question.

'Well, Father,' she said, smiling yet, 'there was the box. I couldn't carry the box.'

'I reckon thou couldst ha' hired a lad to carry it for sixpence.'

She did not reply. The cabman had gone to his vehicle.

'Art'na going to pay th' cabby?'

'I've paid him, Father.'

'How much?'

She paused. 'Eighteen-pence, Father.' It was a lie; she had paid two shillings.

She went eagerly into the kitchen, and then into the parlour, where tea was set for one. Agnes was not there. 'Her's upstairs,' Ephraim said, meeting Anna as she came into the lobby again. She ran softly upstairs, and into the bedroom. Agnes was replacing ornaments on the mantelpiece with mathematical exactitude; under her arm was a duster. The child turned, startled, and gave a little shriek.

'Eh, I didn't know you'd come. How early you are!'

They rushed towards each other, embraced, and kissed. Anna was overcome by the pathos of her sister's loneliness in that grim house for fourteen days, while she, the elder, had been absorbed in selfish gaiety. The pale face, large, melancholy eyes, and long, thin arms, were a silent accusation. She wondered that she could ever have brought herself to leave Agnes even for a day. Sitting down on the bed, she drew the child on her knee in a fury of love, and kissed her again, weeping. Agnes cried too, for sympathy.

'Oh, my dear, dear Anna, I'm so glad you've come back!' She dried her eyes, and in quite a different tone of voice asked: 'Has Mr Mynors proposed to you?'

Anna could not avoid a blush at this simple and astounding query. She said: 'Yes.' It was the one word of which she was capable, under the circumstances. That was not the moment to tax Agnes with too much precocity and abruptness.

'You're engaged, then? Oh, Anna, does it feel nice? It must. I knew you would be!'

'How did you know, Agnes?'

'I mean I knew he would ask you, some time. All the girls at school knew too.'

'I hope you didn't talk about it,' said the elder sister.

'Oh, *no*! But they did; they were always talking about it.'

'You never told me that.'

'I – I didn't like to. Anna, shall I have to call him Henry now?'

'Yes, of course. When we're married he will be your brother-in-law.'

'Shall you be married soon, Anna?'

'Not for a very long time.'

'When you are – shall I keep house alone? I can, you know – I shall never dare to call him Henry. But he's awfully nice; isn't he, Anna? Yes, when you are married, I shall keep house here, but I shall come to see you every day. Father will *have* to let me do that. Does Father know you're engaged?'

'Not yet. And you mustn't say anything. Henry is coming for supper. And then Father will be told.'

'Did he kiss you, Anna?'

'Who – Father?'

'No, silly! Henry, of course – I mean when he'd asked you?'

'I think you are asking all the questions. Suppose I ask you some now. How have you managed with Father? Has he been nice?'

'Some days – yes,' said Agnes, after thinking a moment. 'We have had some new cups and saucers up from Mr Mynors' works. And Father has swept the kitchen chimney. And, oh Anna! I asked him today if I'd kept house well, and he said "Pretty well," and he gave me a penny. Look! it's the first money I've ever had, you know. I wanted you at nights, Anna – and all the time, too. I've been frightfully busy. I cleaned silvers all afternoon. Anna, I *have* tried – And I've got some tea for you. I'll go down and make it. Now you mustn't come into the kitchen. I'll bring it to you in the parlour.'

'I had my tea at Crewe,'* Anna was about to say, but refrained, in due course drinking the cup prepared by Agnes. She felt passionately sorry for Agnes, too young to feel the shadow which overhung her future. Anna would marry into freedom, but Agnes would remain the serf. Would Agnes marry? Could she? Would her father allow it? Anna had noticed that in families the youngest, petted in childhood, was often sacrificed in maturity. It was the last maid who must keep her maidenhood, and, vicariously filial, pay out of her own life the debt of all the rest.

'Mr Mynors is coming up for supper tonight. He wants to see you,' Anna said to her father, as calmly as she could. The miser grunted. But at eight o'clock, the hour immutably fixed for supper, Henry had not arrived. The meal proceeded, of course, without him. To Anna his absence was unaccountable and disturbing, for none could be more punctilious than he in the matter of appointments. She expected him every moment, but he did not appear. Agnes, filled full of the great secret confided to her, was more openly impatient than her sister. Neither of them could talk, and a heavy silence fell upon the family group, a silence which her father, on that particular evening of Anna's return, resented.

'You dunna' tell us much,' he remarked, when the supper was finished.

She felt that the complaint was a just one. Even before supper, when nothing had occurred to preoccupy her, she had spoken little. There had seemed so much to tell – at Port Erin, and now there seemed nothing to tell. She ventured into a flaccid, perfunctory account of Beatrice's illness, of the fishing, of the unfinished houses which had caught the fancy of Mr Sutton; she said the sea had been smooth, that they had had something to eat at Liverpool, that the train for Crewe was very prompt; and then she could think of no more. Silence fell again. The supper-things were cleared away and washed up. At a quarter-past nine, Agnes, vainly begging permission to stay up in order to see Mr Mynors, was sent to bed, only partially comforted by a clothes-brush, long desired, which Anna had brought for her as a present from the Isle of Man.

'Shall you tell Father yourself, now Henry hasn't come?' the child asked Anna, who had gone upstairs to unpack her box.

'Yes,' said Anna briefly.

'I wonder what he'll say,' Agnes reflected, with that habit, always annoying to Anna, of meeting trouble half-way.

At a quarter to ten Anna ceased to expect Mynors, and finally braced herself to the ordeal of a solemn interview with her father, well knowing that she dared not leave him any longer in ignorance of her engagement. Already the old man was locking and bolting the door; he had wound up the kitchen clock. When he came back to the parlour to extinguish the gas she was standing by the mantelpiece.

'Father,' she began, 'I've something I must tell you.'

'Eh, what's that ye say?' his hand was on the gas-tap. He dropped it, examining her face curiously.

'Mr Mynors has asked me to marry him; he asked me last night. We settled he should come up tonight to see you – I can't think why he hasn't. It must be something very unexpected and important, or he'd have come.' She trembled, her heart beat violently; but the words were out, and she thanked God.

'Asked ye to marry him, did he?' The miser gazed at her quizzically out of his small blue eyes.

'Yes, Father.'

'And what didst say?'

'I said I would.'

'Oh! Thou saidst thou wouldst! I reckon it was for thatten as thou must go gadding off to the seaside, eh?'

'Father, I never dreamt of such a thing when Suttons asked me to go. I do wish Henry' – the cost of that Christian name! – 'had come. He quite meant to come tonight.' She could not help insisting on the propriety of Henry's intentions.

'Then I am for be consulted, eh?'

'Of course, Father.'

'Ye've soon made it up, between ye.'

His tone was, at the best, brusque; but she breathed more easily, divining instantly from his manner that he meant to offer no violent objection to the engagement. She knew that only tact was needed now. The miser had, indeed, foreseen the possibility of this marriage for months past, and had long since decided in his own mind that Henry would make a satisfactory son-in-law. Ephraim had no social ambitions – with all his meanness, he was above them; he had nothing but contempt for rank, style, luxury, and 'the theory of what it is to be a lady and a gentleman.' Yet, by a curious contradiction, Henry's smartness of appearance – the smartness of an unrivalled commercial traveller – pleased him. He saw in Henry a young and sedate man of remarkable shrewdness, a man who had saved money, had made money for others, and was now making it for himself; a man who could be trusted absolutely to perform that feat of 'getting on'; a 'safe' and profoundly respectable man, at the same time audacious and imperturbable. He was well aware that Henry had really fallen in love with Anna, but nothing would have convinced him that Anna's money was not the primal cause of Henry's genuine passion for Anna's self.

'You like Henry, don't you, Father?' Anna said. It was a failure in the desired tact, for Ephraim had never been known to admit that he liked anyone or anything. Such natures are capable of nothing more positive than toleration.

'He's a hardy-headed* chap, and he knows the value o' money. Ay! that he does; he knows which side his bread's buttered on.' A sinister emphasis marked the last sentence.

Instead of remaining silent, Anna, in her nervousness, committed another imprudence. 'What do you mean, Father?' she asked, pretending that she thought it impossible he could mean what he obviously did mean.

'Thou knows what I'm at, lass. Dost think he isna' marrying thee for thy brass? Dost think as he canna' make a fine guess what thou'rt worth? But that wunna' bother thee as long as thou'st hooked a good-looking chap.'

'Father!'

'Ay! thou mayst bridle; but it's true. Dunna' tell me.'

Securely conscious of the perfect purity of Mynors' affection, she was not in the least hurt. She even thought that her father's attitude was not quite sincere, an attitude partially due to mere wilful churlishness. 'Henry has never even mentioned money to me,' she said mildly.

'Happen not; he isna' such a fool as that.' He paused, and

continued: 'Thou'rt free to wed, for me. Lasses will do it, I reckon, and thee among th' rest.' She smiled, and on that smile he suddenly turned out the gas. Anna was glad that the colloquy had ended so well. Congratulations, endearments, loving regard for her welfare: she had not expected these things, and was in no wise grieved by their absence. Groping her way towards the lobby, she considered herself lucky, and only wished that nothing had happened to keep Mynors away. She wanted to tell him at once that her father had proved tractable.

The next morning, Tellwright, whose attendance at chapel was losing the strictness of its old regularity, announced that he should stay at home. Sunday's dinner was to be a cold repast, and so Anna and Agnes went to chapel. Anna's thoughts were wholly occupied with the prospect of seeing Mynors, and hearing the explanation of his absence on Saturday night.

'There he is!' Agnes exclaimed loudly, as they were approaching the chapel.

'Agnes,' said Anna, 'when will you learn to behave in the street?'

Mynors stood at the chapel-gates; he was evidently awaiting them. He looked grave, almost sad. He raised his hat and shook hands, with a particular friendliness for Agnes, who was speculating whether he would kiss Anna, as his betrothed, or herself, as being only a little girl, or both or neither of them. Her eyes already expressed a sort of ownership in him.

'I should like to speak to you a moment,' Henry said. 'Will you come into the school-yard?'

'Agnes, you had better go straight into chapel,' said Anna. It was an ignominious disaster to the child, but she obeyed.

'I didn't give you up last night till nearly ten o'clock,' Anna remarked as they passed into the school-yard. She was astonished to discover in herself an inclination to pout, to play the offended fair one, because Mynors had failed in his appointment. Contemptuously she crushed it.

'Have you heard about Mr Price?' Mynors began.

'No. What about him? Has anything happened?'

'A very sad thing has happened. Yes – ' He stopped, from emotion. 'Our superintendent has committed suicide!'

'Killed himself?' Anna gasped.

'He hanged himself yesterday afternoon at Edward Street, in

the slip-house, after the works were closed. Willie had gone home, but he came back, when his father didn't turn up for dinner, and found him. Mr Price was quite dead. He ran in to my place to fetch me just as I was getting my tea. That was why I never came last night.'

Anna was speechless.

'I thought I would tell you myself,' Henry resumed. 'It's an awful thing for the Sunday-school, and the whole society, too. He, a prominent Wesleyan, a worker among us! An awful thing!' he repeated, dominated by the idea of the blow thus dealt to the Methodist connexion by the man now dead.

'Why did he do it?' Anne demanded, curtly.

Mynors shrugged his shoulders, and ejaculated: 'Business troubles, I suppose; it couldn't be anything else. At school this morning I simply announced that he was dead.' Henry's voice broke, but he added, after a pause: 'Young Price bore himself splendidly last night.'

Anna turned away in silence. 'I shall come up for tea, if I may,' Henry said, and then they parted, he to the singing-seat, she to the portico of the chapel. People were talking in groups on the broad steps and in the vestibule. All knew of the calamity, and had received from it a new interest in life. The town was aroused as if from a lethargy. Consternation and eager curiosity were on every face. Those who arrived in ignorance of the event were informed of it in impressive tones, and with intense satisfaction to the informer; nothing of equal importance had happened in the society for decades. Anna walked up the aisle to her pew, filled with one thought:

'We drove him to it, Father and I.'

Her fear was that the miser had renewed his terrible insistence during the previous fortnight. She forgot that she had disliked the dead man, that he had always seemed to her mean, pietistic, and two-faced. She forgot that in pressing him for rent many months overdue she and his father had acted within their just rights – acted as Price himself would have acted in their place. She could think only of the strain, the agony, the despair that must have preceded the miserable tragedy. Old Price had atoned for all in one sublime sin, the sole deed that could lend dignity and repose to such a figure as his. Anna's feverish imagination reconstituted the scene in the slip-house: she saw it as something grand, accusing, and unanswerable; and she could not dismiss a feeling of acute remorse that she should have been engaged in pleasure at that very hour of death. Surely some instinct should have warned her that the hare which she had helped to hunt was at its last gasp!

Mr Sargent, the newly-appointed second minister, was in the pulpit – a little, earnest bachelor, who emphasized every sentence with a continual tremor of the voice. 'Brethren,' he said, after the second hymn – and his tones vibrated with a singular effect through the half-empty building: 'Before I proceed to my sermon I have one word to say in reference to the awful event which is doubtless uppermost in the minds of all of you. It is not for us to judge the man who is now gone from us, ushered into the dread presence of his Maker with the crime of self-murder upon his soul. I say it is not for us to judge him. The ways of the Almighty are past finding out. Therefore at such a moment we may fitly humble ourselves before the Throne, and while prostrate there let us intercede for the poor young man who is left behind, bereft, and full of grief and shame. We will engage in silent prayer.' He lifted his hand, and closed his eyes, and the congregation leaned forward against the fronts of the pews. The appealing face of Willie presented itself vividly to Anna.

'Who is it?' Agnes asked, in a whisper of appalling distinctness. Anna frowned angrily, and gave no reply.

While the last hymn was being sung, Anna signed to Agnes that she wished to leave the chapel. Everyone would be aware that she was among Price's creditors, and she feared that if she stayed till the end of the service some chatterer might draw her into a distressing conversation. The sisters went out, and Agnes's burning curiosity was at length relieved.

'Mr Price has hanged himself,' Anna said to her father when they reached home.

The miser looked through the window for a moment. 'I am na' surprised,' he said. 'Suicide's i' that blood. Titus's uncle 'Lijah tried to kill himself twice afore he died o' gravel.* Us'n have to do summat wi' Edward Street at last.'

She wanted to ask Ephraim if he had been demanding more rent lately, but she could not find courage to do so.

Agnes had to go to Sunday-school alone that afternoon. Without saying anything to her father, Anna decided to stay at home. She spent the time in her bedroom, idle, preoccupied; and did not come downstairs till half-past three. Ephraim had gone out. Agnes presently returned, and then Henry came in with Mr Tellwright. They were conversing amicably, and Anna knew that her engagement was finally and satisfactorily settled. During tea no reference was made to it, nor to the suicide. Mynors' demeanour was quiet but cheerful. He had partly recovered from the morning's agitation, and gave Ephraim and Agnes a vivacious account of the attractions of Port Erin. Anna noticed the amusement in his eye when Agnes, reddening, said to him: 'Will you have some more bread-and-butter, Henry?' It seemed to be tacitly understood afterwards that Agnes and her father would attend chapel, while Henry and Anna kept house. No one was ingenious enough to detect an impropriety in the arrangement. For some obscure reason, immediately upon the departure of the chapelgoers, Anna went into the kitchen, rattled some plates, stroked her hair mechanically, and then stole back again to the parlour. It was a chilly evening, and instead of walking up and down the strip of garden the betrothed lovers sat together under the window. Anna wondered whether or not she was happy. The presence of Mynors was, at any rate, marvellously soothing.

'Did your father say anything about the Price affair?' he began, yielding at once to the powerful hypnotism of the subject which fascinated the whole town that night, and which Anna could bear neither to discuss nor to ignore.

'Not much,' she said, and repeated to him her father's remark.

Mynors told her all he knew; how Willie had discovered his father with his toes actually touching the floor, leaning slightly forward, quite dead; how he had then cut the rope and fetched Mynors, who went with him to the police-station; how they had tied up the head of the corpse, and then waited till night to wheel the body on a hand-cart from Edward Street to the mortuary chamber at the police-station; how the police had telephoned to the coroner,* and settled at once that the inquest should be held on Tuesday in the court-room at the town-hall; and how quiet, self-contained, and dignified Willie had been, surprising everyone by this new-found manliness. It all seemed hideously real to Anna, as Henry added detail to detail.

'I think I ought to tell you,' she said very calmly, when he had finished the recital, 'that I – I'm dreadfully upset over it. I can't help thinking that I – that Father and I, I mean – are somehow partly responsible for this.'

'For Price's death? How?'

'We have been so hard on him for his rent lately, you know.'

'My dearest girl! What next?' He took her hand in his. 'I assure you the idea is absurd. You've only got it because you're so sensitive and high-strung. I undertake to say Price was stuck fast everywhere – everywhere – hadn't a chance.'

'Me high-strung!' she exclaimed. He kissed her lovingly. But, beneath the feeling of reassurance, which by superior force he had imposed on her, there lay a feeling that she was treated like a frightened child who must be tranquillized in the night. Nevertheless, she was grateful for his kindness, and when she went to bed she obtained relief from the returning obsession of the suicide by making anew her vows to him.

As a theatrical effect the death of Titus Price could scarcely have been surpassed. The town was profoundly moved by the spectacle of this abject yet heroic surrender of all those pretences by which society contrives to tolerate itself. Here was a man whom no one respected, but everyone pretended to respect – who knew that he was respected by none, but pretended that he was respected by all; whose whole career was made up of dissimulations: religious, moral, and social. If any man could have been trusted to continue the decent sham to the end, and so preserve the general self-esteem, surely it was this man. But no! Suddenly abandoning all imposture, he transgresses openly, brazenly; and, snatching a bit of hemp, cries: 'Behold me; this is real human nature. This is the truth; the rest was lies. I lied; you lied. I confess it, and you shall confess it.' Such a thunderclap shakes the very base of the microcosm. The young folk in particular could with difficulty believe their ears. It seemed incredible to them that Titus Price, the Methodist, the Sunday-school superintendent, the loud champion of the highest virtues, should commit the sin of all sins – murder. They were dazed. The remembrance of his insincerity did nothing to mitigate the blow. In their view it was perhaps even worse that he had played false to his own falsity. The elders were a little less disturbed. The event was not unique in their experience. They had lived longer and felt these seismic shocks before. They could go back into the past and find other cases where a swift impulse had shattered the edifice of a lifetime. They knew that the history of families and of communities is crowded with disillusion. They had discovered that character is changeless, irrepressible, incurable. They were aware of the astonishing fact, which takes at least thirty years to learn, that a Sunday-school superintendent is a man. And the suicide of Titus Price, when they had realized it, served but to confirm their most secret and honest estimate of humanity, that estimate which they never confided to a soul. The young folk thought the Methodist Society shamed and branded by the tragic incident, and imagined that years must elapse before it could again hold up its head in the town. The old folk were wiser, foreseeing with certainty that in only a few days this all-engrossing phenomenon would lose its significance, and be as though it had never been.

Even in two days, time had already begun its work, for by Tuesday morning the interest of the affair – on Sunday at the highest pitch – had waned so much that the thought of the inquest was capable of reviving it. Although everyone knew that the case presented no unusual features, and that the coroner's inquiry would be nothing more than a formal ceremony, the almost greedy curiosity of Methodist circles lifted it to the level of a *cause célèbre.** The court was filled with irreproachable respectability when the coroner drove into the town, and each animated face said to its fellow: 'So you're here, are you?' Late comers of the official world – councillors,* guardians of the poor,* members of the school board,* and one or two of their ladies, were forced to intrigue for room with the police and the town-hall keeper, and, having succeeded, sank into their narrow seats with a sigh of expectancy and triumph. Late comers with less influence had to retire, and by a kind of sinister fascination were kept wandering about the corridor before they could decide to go home. The market-place was occupied by hundreds of loafers, who seemed to find a mystic satisfaction in beholding the coroner's dogcart and the exterior of the building which now held the corpse.

It was by accident that Anna was in the town. She knew that the inquest was to occur that morning, but had not dreamed of attending it. When, however, she saw the stir of excitement in the market-place, and the police guarding the entrances of the town-hall, she walked directly across the road, past the two officers at the east door, and into the dark main corridor of the building, which was dotted with small groups idly conversing. She was conscious of two things: a vehement curiosity, and the existence somewhere in the precincts of a dead body, unsightly, monstrous, calm, silent, careless – the insensible origin of all this simmering ferment which disgusted her even while she shared in it. At a small door, half hidden by a curtain, she was startled to see Mynors.

'You here!' he exclaimed, as if painfully surprised, and shook hands with a preoccupied air. 'They are examining Willie. I came outside while he was in the witness-box.'

'Is the inquest going on in there?' she asked, pointing to the door. Each appeared to be concealing a certain resentment against the other; but this appearance was due only to nervous agitation.

A policeman down the corridor called: 'Mr Mynors, a moment.' Henry hurried away, answering Anna's question as he went: 'Yes, in there. That's the witnesses' and jurors' door; but please don't go in. I don't like you to, and it is sure to upset you.'

She opened the door and went in. None said nay, and she found a few inches of standing-room behind the jury-box. A terrible stench nauseated her; the chamber was crammed, and not a window open. There was silence in the court – no one seemed to be doing anything; but at last she perceived that the coroner, enthroned on the bench of justice, was writing in a book with blue leaves. In the witness-box stood William Price, dressed in black, with kid gloves, not lounging in an ungainly attitude, as might have been expected, but perfectly erect; he kept his eyes fixed on the coroner's head. Sarah Vodrey, Price's aged housekeeper, sat on a chair near the witness-box, weeping into a black-bordered handkerchief; at intervals she raised her small, wrinkled, red face, with its glistening, inflamed eyes, and then buried it again in the handkerchief. The members of the jury, whom Anna could see only in profile, shuffled to and fro on their long, pew-like seats – they were mostly working men, shabbily clothed; but the foreman was Mr Leal, the provision dealer, a freemason, and a sidesman* at the parish church. The general public sat intent and vacuous; their minds gaped, if not their mouths; occasionally one whispered inaudibly to another; the jury, conscious of an official status, exchanged remarks in a whisper courageously loud. Several tall policemen, helmet in hand, stood in various corners of the room, and the coroner's officer sat near the witness-box to administer the oath. At length the coroner lifted his head. He was rather a young man, with a large, intelligent face; he wore eyeglasses, and his chin was covered with a short, wavy beard. His manner showed that, while secretly proud of his supreme position in that assemblage, he was deliberately trying to make it appear that this exercise of judicial authority was nothing to him, that in truth these eternal inquiries, which interested others so deeply, were to him a weariness conscientiously endured.

'Now, Mr Price,' the coroner said blandly, and it was plain that he was being ceremoniously polite to an inferior, in obedience to the rules of good form, 'I must ask you some more questions. They may be inconvenient, even painful; but I am here simply as the instrument of the law, and I must do my duty. And these gentlemen here,' he waved a hand in the direction of the jury, 'must be told the whole facts of the case. We know, of course, that the deceased committed suicide – that has been proved beyond doubt; but, as I say, we have the right to know more.' He paused, well satisfied with the sound of his voice, and evidently thinking that he had said something very weighty and impressive.

'What do you want to know?' Willie Price demanded, his broad Five Towns speech contrasting with the Kensingtonian* accents of the coroner. The latter, who came originally from Manchester, was irritated by the brusque interruption; but he controlled his annoyance, at the same time glancing at the public as if to signify to them that he had learnt not to take too seriously the unintentional rudeness characteristic of their district.

'You say it was probably business troubles that caused your late father to commit the rash act?'

'Yes.'

'You are sure there was nothing else?'

'What else could there be?'

'Your late father was a widower?'

'Yes.'

'Now as to these business troubles – what were they?'

'We were being pressed by creditors.'

'Were you a partner with your late father?'

'Yes.'

'Oh! You were a partner with him!'

The jury seemed surprised, and the coroner wrote again: 'What was your share in the business?'

'I don't know.'

'You don't know? Surely that is rather singular?'

'My father took me in Co. not long since. We signed a deed, but I forget what was in it. My place was principally on the bank, not in the office.'

'And so you were being pressed by creditors?'

'Yes. And we were behind with the rent.'

'Was the landlord pressing you, too?'

Anna lowered her eyes, fearful lest every head had turned towards her.

'Not then; he had been – she, I mean.'

'The landlord is a lady?' Here the coroner faintly smiled. 'Then, as regards the landlord, the pressure was less than it had been?'

'Yes; we had paid some rent, and settled some other claims.'

'Does it not seem strange – ?' the coroner began, with a suave air of suggesting an idea.

'If you must know,' Willie surprisingly burst out, 'I believe it was the failure of a firm in London that owed us money that caused Father to hang himself.'

'Ah!' exclaimed the coroner. 'When did you hear of that failure?'

'By second post on Friday. Eleven in the morning.'

'I think we have heard enough, Mr Coroner,' said Leal, standing up in the jury-box. 'We have decided on our verdict.'

'Thank you, Mr Price,' said the coroner, dismissing Willie. He added, in a tone of icy severity to the foreman: 'I had concluded my examination of the witness.' Then he wrote further in his book.

'Now, gentlemen of the jury,' the coroner resumed, having first cleared his throat; 'I think you will agree with me that this is a peculiarly painful case. Yet at the same time – '

Anna hastened from the court as impulsively as she had entered it. She could think of nothing but the quiet, silent, pitiful corpse; and all this vapid mouthing exasperated her beyond sufferance.

On the Thursday afternoon, Anna was sitting alone in the house, with the Persian cat and a pile of stockings on her knee, darning. Agnes had with sorrow returned to school; Ephraim was out. The bell sounded violently, and Anna, thinking that perhaps for some reason her father had chosen to enter by the front door, ran to open it. The visitor was Willie Price; he wore the new black suit which had figured in the coroner's court. She invited him to the parlour and they both sat down, tongue-tied. Now that she had learnt from his evidence given at the inquest that Ephraim had not been pressing for rent during her absence in the Isle of Man, she felt less like a criminal before Willie than she would have felt without that assurance. But at the best she was nervous, self-conscious, and shamed. She supposed that he had called to make some arrangement with reference to the tenure of the works, or, more probably, to announce a bankruptcy and stoppage.

'Well, Miss Tellwright,' Willie began, 'I've buried him. He's gone.'

The simple and profound grief, and the restrained bitterness against all the world, which were expressed in these words – the sole epitaph of Titus Price – nearly made Anna cry. She would have cried, if the cat had not opportunely jumped on her knee again; she controlled herself by dint of stroking it. She sympathized with him more intensely in that first moment of his loneliness than she had ever sympathized with anyone, even Agnes. She wished passionately to shield, shelter, and comfort him, to do something, however small, to diminish his sorrow and humiliation; and this despite his size, his ungainliness, his coarse features, his rough voice, his lack of all the conventional refinements. A single look from his guileless and timid eyes atoned for every shortcoming. Yet she could scarcely open her mouth. She knew not what to say. She had no phrases to soften the frightful blow which Providence had dealt him.

'I'm very sorry,' she said. 'You must be relieved it's all over.'

If she could have been Mrs Sutton for half an hour! But she was Anna, and her feelings could only find outlet in her eyes. Happily young Price was of those meek ones who know by instinct the language of the eyes.

'You've come about the works, I suppose?' she went on.

'Yes,' he said. 'Is your father in? I want to see him very particular.'

'He isn't in now,' she replied: 'but he will be back by four o'clock.'

'That's an hour. You don't know where he is?' She shook her head. 'Well,' he continued, 'I must tell you then. I've come up to do it, and do it I must. I can't come up again; neither can I wait. You remember that bill of exchange as we gave you some weeks back towards rent?'

'Yes,' she said. There was a pause. He stood up, and moved to the mantelpiece. Her gaze followed him intently, but she had no idea what he was about to say.

'It's forged, Miss Tellwright.' He sat down again, and seemed calmer, braver, ready to meet any conceivable set of consequences.

'Forged!' she repeated, not immediately grasping the significance of the avowal.

'Mr Sutton's name is forged on it. So I came to tell your father; but you'll do as well. I feel as if I should like to tell you all about it,' he said, smiling sadly. 'Mr Sutton had really given us a bill for thirty pounds, but we'd paid that away when Mr Tellwright sent word down – you remember – that he should put bailiffs in if he didn't have twenty-five pounds next day. We were just turning the corner then, Father said to me. There was a goodish sum due to us from a London firm in a month's time, and if we could only hold out till then, Father said he could see daylight for us. But he knew as there'd be no getting round Mr Tellwright. So he had the idea of using Mr Sutton's name – just temporary like. He sent me to the post-office to buy a bill stamp, and he wrote out the bill all but the name. "You take this up to Tellwright's," he says, "and ask 'em to take it and hold it, and we'll redeem it, and that'll be all right. No harm done there, Will!" he says. Then he tries Sutton's name on the back of an envelope. It's an easy signature, as you know; but he couldn't do it. "Here, Will," he says, "my old hand shakes; you have a go," and he gives me a letter of Sutton's to copy from. I did it easy enough after a try or two. "That'll be all right, Will," he says, and I put my hat on and brought the bill up here. That's the truth, Miss Tellwright. It was the smash of that London firm that finished my poor old father off.'

Her one feeling was the sense of being herself a culprit. After all, it was her father's action, more than anything else, that had led to the suicide, and he was her agent.

'Oh, Mr Price,' she said foolishly, 'whatever shall you do?'

'There's nothing to be done,' he replied. 'It was bound to be. It's our luck. We'd no thought but what we should bring you thirty pound in cash and get that bit of paper back, and rip it up, and no one the worse. But we were always unlucky, me and him. All you've got to do is just to tell your father, and say I'm ready to go to the police-station when he gives the word. It's a bad business, but I'm ready for it.'

'Can't we do something?' she naïvely inquired, with a vision of a trial and sentence, and years of prison.

'Your father keeps the bill, doesn't he? Not you?'

'I could ask him to destroy it.'

'He wouldn't,' said Willie. 'You'll excuse me saying that, Miss Tellwright, but he wouldn't.'

He rose as if to go, bitterly. As for Anna, she knew well that her father would never permit the bill to be destroyed. But at any cost she meant to comfort him then, to ease his lot, to send him away less grievous than he came.

'Listen!' she said, standing up, and abandoning the cat, 'I will see what can be done. Yes. Something *shall* be done – something or other. I will come and see you at the works tomorrow afternoon. You may rely on me.'

She saw hope brighten his eyes at the earnestness and resolution of her tone, and she felt richly rewarded. He never said another word, but gripped her hand with such force that she flinched in pain. When he had gone, she perceived clearly the dire dilemma; but cared nothing, in the first bliss of having reassured him.

During tea it occurred to her that as soon as Agnes had gone to bed she would put the situation plainly before her father, and, for the first and last time in her life, assert herself. She would tell him that the affair was, after all, entirely her own, she would firmly demand possession of the bill of exchange, and she would insist on it being destroyed. She would point out to the old man that, her promise having been given to Willie Price, no other course than this was possible. In planning this night-surprise on her father's obstinacy, she found argument after argument auspicious of its success. The formidable tyrant was at last to meet his equal, in force, in resolution, and in pugnacity. The swiftness of her onrush would sweep him, for once, off his feet. At whatever cost, she was bound to win, even though victory resulted in eternal enmity between father and daughter. She saw herself towering over him, morally, with blazing eye and scornful nostril. And, thus meditating on the grandeur of her adventure, she fed her courage with indignation. By the act of death, Titus Price had put her father for ever in the wrong. His corpse accused the miser, and Anna, incapable now of seeing aught save the pathos of suicide, acquiesced in the accusation with all the strength of her remorse. She did not reason – she felt; reason was shrivelled up in the fire of emotion. She almost trembled with the urgency of her desire to protect from further shame the figure of Willie Price, so frank, simple, innocent, and big; and to protect also the lifeless and dishonoured body of his parent. She reviewed the whole circumstances again and again, each time finding less excuse for her father's implacable and fatal cruelty.

So her thoughts ran until the appointed hour of Agnes's bedtime. It was always necessary to remind Agnes of that hour; left to herself, the child would have stayed up till the very Day of Judgement. The clock struck, but Anna kept silence. To utter the word 'bedtime' to Agnes was to open the attack on her father, and she felt as the conductor of an opera feels before setting in motion a complicated activity which may end in either triumph or an unspeakable fiasco. The child was reading; Anna looked and looked at her, and at length her lips were set for the phrase, 'Now, Agnes,' when, suddenly, the old man forestalled her:

'Is that wench going to sit here all night?' he asked of Anna, menacingly.

Agnes shut her book and crept away.

This accident was the ruin of Anna's scheme. Her father, always the favourite of circumstance, had by chance struck the first blow; ignorant of the battle that awaited him, he had unwittingly won it by putting her in the wrong, as Titus Price had put him in the wrong. She knew in a flash that her enterprise was hopeless; she knew that her father's position in regard to her was impregnable, that no moral force, no consciousness of right, would avail to overthrow that authority which she had herself made absolute by a life-long submission; she knew that face to face with her father she was, and always would be, a coward. And now, instead of finding arguments for success, she found arguments for failure. She divined all the retorts that he would fling at her. What about Mr Sutton – in a sense the victim of this fraud? It was not merely a matter of thirty pounds. A man's name had been used. Was he, Ephraim Tellwright, and she, his daughter, to connive at a felony? The felony was done, and could not be undone. Were they to render themselves liable, even in theory, to a criminal prosecution? If Titus Price had killed himself, what of that? If Willie Price was threatened with ruin, what of that? Them as made the bed must lie on it. At the best, and apart from any forgery, the Prices had swindled their creditors; even in dying, old Price had been guilty of a commercial swindle. And was the fact that father and son between them had committed a direct and flagrant crime to serve as an excuse for sympathizing with the survivor? Why was Anna so anxious to shield the forger? What claim had he? A forger was a forger, and that was the end of it.

She went to bed without opening her mouth. Irresolute, shamed, and despairing, she tried to pray for guidance, but she could bring no sincerity of appeal into this prayer; it seemed an empty form. Where, indeed, was her religion? She was obliged to acknowledge that the fervour of her aspirations had been steadily cooling for weeks. She was not a whit more a true Christian now than she had been before the Revival; it appeared that she was incapable of real religion, possibly one of those souls foreordained to damnation.* This admission added to the general sense of futility, and increased her misery. She lay awake for hours, confronting her deliberate promise to Willie Price. *Something shall be done. Rely on me.* He was relying on her, then. But on whom could she rely? To whom could she turn? It is significant that the idea of confiding in Henry Mynors did not present itself for a single moment as practical. Mynors had been kind to Willie in his trouble, but Anna almost resented this kindness on account of the condescending superiority with which she had overheard Mynors saying to himself: 'Here is this poor, crushed worm. It is my duty as a Christian to pity and succour him. I will do so. I am a righteous man.' The thought of anyone stooping to Willie was hateful to her. She felt equal with him, as a mother feels equal with her child when it cries and she soothes it. And she felt, in another way, that he was equal with her, as she thought of his sturdy and simple confession, and of the loyal love in his voice when he spoke of his father. She liked him for hurting her hand, and for refusing to snatch at the slender chance of her father's clemency. She could never reveal Willie's sin, if it was a sin, to Henry Mynors – that symbol of correctness and of success. She had fraternized with sinners, like Christ; and, with amazing injustice, she was capable of deeming

Mynors a Pharisee because she could not find fault with him, because he lived and loved so impeccably and so triumphantly. There was only one person from whom she could have asked advice and help, and that wise and consoling heart was far away in the Isle of Man.

'Why won't Father give up the bill?' she demanded, half aloud, in sullen wrath. She could not frame the answer in words, but nevertheless she knew it and felt it. Such an act of grace would have been impossible to her father's nature – that was all.

Suddenly the expression of her face changed from utter disgust into a bitter and proud smile. Without thinking further, without daring to think, she rose out of bed and, night-gowned and barefooted, crept with infinite precaution downstairs. The oil-cloth on the stairs froze her feet; a cold, grey light issuing through the glass square over the front door showed that dawn was beginning. The door of the front-parlour was shut; she opened it gently, and went within. Every object in the room was faintly visible, the bureau, the chair, the files of papers, the pictures, the books on the mantelshelf, and the safe in the corner. The bureau, she knew, was never locked; fear of her father had always kept its privacy inviolate from Anna and Agnes, without the aid of a key. As Anna stood in front of it, a shaking figure with hair hanging loose, she dimly remembered having one day seen a blue paper among white in the pigeon-holes. But if the bill was not there she vowed that she would steal her father's keys while he slept, and force the safe. She opened the bureau, and at once saw the edge of a blue paper corresponding with her recollection. She pulled it forth and scanned it. 'Three months after date pay to our order . . . Accepted payable, *William Sutton*.' So here was the forgery, here the two words for which Willie Price might have gone to prison! What a trifle! She tore the flimsy document to bits, and crumpled the bits into a little ball. How should she dispose of the ball? After a moment's reflection she went into the kitchen, stretched on tiptoe to reach the match-box from the high mantelpiece, struck a match, and burnt the ball in the grate. Then, with a restrained and sinister laugh, she ran softly upstairs.

'What's the matter, Anna?' Agnes was sitting up in bed, wide awake.

'Nothing; go to sleep, and don't bother,' Anna angrily whispered.

Had she closed the lid of the bureau? She was compelled to return in order to make sure. Yes, it was closed. When at length she lay in bed, breathless, her heart violently beating, her feet felt like icicles, she realized what she had done. She had saved Willie Price, but she had ruined herself with her father. She knew well that he would never forgive her.

On the following afternoon she planned to hurry to Edward Street and back while Ephraim and Agnes were both out of the house. But for some reason her father sat persistently after dinner, conning a sale catalogue. At a quarter to three he had not moved. She decided to go at any risks. She put on her hat and jacket, and opened the front door. He heard her.

'Anna!' he called sharply. She obeyed the summons in terror. 'Art going out?'

'Yes, Father.'

'Where to?'

'Down town to buy some things.'

'Seems thou'rt always buying.'

That was all; he let her free. In an unworthy attempt to appease her conscience she did in fact go first into the town; she bought some wool; the trick was despicable. Then she hastened to Edward Street. The decrepit works seemed to have undergone no change. She had expected the business would be suspended, and Willie Price alone on the bank; but manufacture was proceeding as usual. She went direct to the office, fancying, as she climbed the stairs, that every window of all the workshops was full of eyes to discern her purpose. Without knocking, she pushed against the unlatched door and entered. Willie was lolling in his father's chair, gloomy, meditative, apparently idle. He was coatless, and wore a dirty apron; a battered hat was at the back of his head, and his great hands which lay on the desk in front of him, were soiled. He sprang up, flushing red, and she shut the door; they were alone together.

'I'm all in my dirt,' he murmured apologetically. Simple and silly creature, to imagine that she cared for his dirt!

'It's all right,' she said; 'you needn't worry any more. It's all right.' They were glorious words for her, and her face shone.

'What do you mean?' he asked gruffly.

'Why,' she smiled, full of happiness, 'I got that paper and burnt it!'

He looked at her exactly as if he had not understood. 'Does your father know?'

She still smiled at him happily. 'No; but I shall tell him this afternoon. It's all right. I've burnt it.'

He sank down in the chair, and, laying his head on the desk, burst into sobbing tears. She stood over him, and put a hand on the sleeve of his shirt. At that touch he sobbed more violently.

'Mr Price, what is it?' She asked the question in a calm, soothing tone.

He glanced up at her, his face wet, yet apparently not shamed by the tears. She could not meet his gaze without herself crying, and so she turned her head. 'I was only thinking,' he stammered, 'only thinking – what an angel you are.'

Only the meek, the timid, the silent, can, in moments of deep feeling, use this language of hyperbole without seeming ridiculous.

He was her great child, and she knew that he worshipped her. Oh, ineffable power, that out of misfortune canst create divine happiness!

Later, he remarked in his ordinary tone: 'I was expecting your father here this afternoon about the lease. There is to be a deed of arrangement with the creditors.'

'My father!' she exclaimed, and she bade him goodbye.

As she passed under the archway she heard a familiar voice: 'I reckon I shall find young Mester Price in th' office?' Ephraim, who had wandered into the packing-house, turned and saw her through the doorway; a second's delay, and she would have escaped. She stood waiting the storm, and then they walked out into the road together.

'Anna, what art doing here?'

She did not know what to say.

'What art doing here?' he repeated coldly.

'Father, I – was just going back home.'

He hesitated an instant. 'I'll go with thee,' he said. They walked back to Manor Terrace in silence. They had tea in silence; except that Agnes with dreadful inopportuneness, continually worried her father for a definite promise that she might leave school at Christmas. The idea was preposterous; but Agnes, fired by her recent success as a housekeeper, clung to it.

Ignorant of her imminent danger, and misinterpreting the signs of his face, she at last pushed her insistence too far.

'Get to bed, this minute,' he said, in a voice suddenly terrible. She perceived her error then, but it was too late. Looking wistfully at Anna, the child fled.

'I was told this morning, miss,' Ephraim began, as soon as Agnes was gone, 'that young Price had bin seen coming to this house 'ere yesterday afternoon. I thought as it was strange as thoud'st said nowt about it to thy feyther; but I never suspected as a daughter o' mine was up to any tricks. There was a hang-dog look on thy face this afternoon when I asked where thou wast going, but I didna' think thou wast lying to me.'

'I wasn't,' she began, and stopped.

'Thou wast! Now, what is it? What's this carrying-on between thee and Will Price? I'll have it out of thee.'

'There is no carrying-on, Father.'

'Then why hast thou gotten secrets? Why dost go sneaking about to see him – sneaking, creeping, like any brazen moll?'*

The miser was wounded in the one spot where there remained to him any sentiment capable of being wounded; his faith in the irreproachable, absolute chastity, in thought and deed, of his woman-kind.

'Willie Price came in here yesterday,' Anna began, white and calm, 'to see you. But you weren't in. So he saw me. He told me that bill of exchange, that blue paper, for thirty pounds was forged. He said he had forged Mr Sutton's name on it.' She stopped, expecting the thunder.

'Get on with thy tale,' said Ephraim, breathing loudly.

'He said he was ready to go to prison as soon as you gave the word. But I told him, "No such thing!" I said it must be settled quietly. I told him to leave it to me. He was driven to the forgery, and I thought – '

'Dost mean to say,' the miser shouted, 'as that blasted scoundrel came here and told thee he'd forged a bill, and thou told him to leave it to thee to settle?' Without waiting for an answer, he jumped up and strode to the door, evidently with the intention of examining the forged document for himself.

'It isn't there – it isn't there!' Anna called to him wildly.

'What isna' there?'

'The paper. I may as well tell you, Father. I got up early this morning and burnt it.'

The man was staggered at this audacious and astounding impiety.

'It was mine, really,' she continued; 'and I thought – '

'Thou thought!'

Agnes, upstairs, heard that passionate and consuming roar. 'Shame on thee, Anna Tellwright! Shame on thee for a shameless hussy! A daughter o' mine, and just promised to another man! Thou'rt an accomplice in forgery. Thou sees the scamp on the sly!* Thou – ' He paused, and then added, with furious scorn: 'Shalt speak o' this to Henry Mynors?'

'I will tell him if you like,' she said proudly.

'Look thee here!' he hissed, 'if thou breathes a word o' this to Henry Mynors, or any other man, I'll cut thy tongue out. A daughter o' mine! If thou breathes a word – '

'I shall not, Father.'

It was finished; grey with frightful anger, Ephraim left the room.

CHAPTER TWELVE

At the Priory

She was not to be pardoned: the offence was too monstrous, daring, and final. At the same time, the unappeasable ire of the old man tended to weaken his power over her. All her life she had been terrorized by the fear of a wrath which had never reached the superlative degree until that day. Now that she had seen and felt the limit of his anger, she became aware that she could endure it; the curse was heavy, and perhaps more irksome than heavy, but she survived; she continued to breathe, eat, drink, and sleep; her father's power stopped short of annihilation. Here, too, was a satisfaction: that things could not be worse. And still greater comfort lay in the fact that she had not only accomplished the deliverance of Willie Price, but had secured absolute secrecy concerning the episode.

The next day was Saturday, when, after breakfast, it was Ephraim's custom to give Anna the weekly sovereign for housekeeping.

'Here, Agnes,' he said, turning in his armchair to face the child, and drawing a sovereign from his waistcoat-pocket, 'take charge o' this, and mind ye make it go as far as ye can.' His tone conveyed a subsidiary message: 'I am terribly angry, but I am not angry with you. However, behave yourself.'

The child mechanically took the coin, scared by this proof of an unprecedented domestic convulsion. Anna, with a tightening of the lips, rose and went into the kitchen. Agnes followed, after a discreet interval, and in silence gave up the sovereign.

'What is it all about, Anna?' she ventured to ask that night.

'Never mind,' said Anna curtly.

The question had needed some courage, for, at certain times, Agnes would as easily have trifled with her father as with Anna. From that moment, with the passive fatalism characteristic of her years, Agnes's spirits began to rise again to the normal level. She accepted the new situation, and fitted herself into it with a child's adaptability. If Anna naturally felt a slight resentment against this too impartial and apparently callous attitude on the part of the child, she never showed it.

Nearly a week later, Anna received a postcard from Beatrice announcing her complete recovery, and the immediate return of her parents and herself to Bursley. That same afternoon, a cab encumbered with much luggage passed up the street as Anna was fixing clean curtains in her father's bedroom. Beatrice, on the look-out, waved a hand and smiled, and Anna responded to the signals. She was glad now that the Suttons had come back, though for several days she had almost forgotten their existence. On the Saturday afternoon, Mynors called. Anna was in the kitchen; she heard him scuffling with Agnes in the lobby, and then talking to her father. Three times she had seen him since her disgrace, and each time the secret bitterness of her soul, despite conscientious effort to repress it, had marred the meeting – it had been plain, indeed, that she was profoundly disturbed; he had affected at first not to observe the change in her, and she, anticipating his questions, hinted briefly that the trouble was with her father, and had no reference to himself, and that she preferred not to discuss it at all; reassured, and too young in courtship yet to presume on a lover's rights, he respected her wish, and endeavoured by every art to restore her to equanimity. This time, as she went to greet him in the parlour, she resolved that he should see no more of the shadow. He noticed instantly the difference in her face.

'I've come to take you into Sutton's for tea – and for the evening,' he said eagerly. 'You must come. They are very anxious to see you. I've told your father,' he added. Ephraim had vanished into his office.

'What did he say, Henry?' she asked timidly.

'He said you must please yourself, of course. Come along, love. Mustn't she, Agnes?'

Agnes concurred, and said that she would get her father's tea, and his supper too.

'You will come,' he urged. She nodded, smiling thoughtfully, and he kissed her, for the first time in front of Agnes, who was filled with pride at this proof of their confidence in her.

'I'm ready, Henry,' Anna said, a quarter of an hour later, and they went across to Sutton's.

'Anna, tell me all about it,' Beatrice burst out when she and Anna had fled to her bedroom. 'I'm so glad. Do you love him really – truly? He's dreadfully fond of you. He told me so this morning; we had quite a long chat in the market. I think you're both very lucky, you know.' She kissed Anna effusively for the third time. Anna looked at her smiling but silent.

'Well?' Beatrice said.

'What do you want me to say?'

'Oh! You are the funniest girl, Anna, I ever met. "What do you want me to say," indeed!' Beatrice added in a different tone: 'Don't imagine this affair was the least bit of a surprise to us. It wasn't. The fact is, Henry had – oh! well, never mind. Do you know, Mother and Dad used to think there was something between Henry and me. But there wasn't, you know – not really. I tell you that, so that you won't be able to say you were kept in the dark. When shall you be married, Anna?'

'I haven't the least idea,' Anna replied, and began to question Beatrice about her convalescence.

'I'm perfectly well,' Beatrice said. 'It's always the same. If I catch anything I catch it bad and get it over quickly.'

'Now, how long are you two chatterboxes going to stay here?' It was Mrs Sutton who came into the room. 'Bee, you've got those sewing-meeting letters to write. Eh, Anna, but I'm glad of this. You'll make him a good wife. You two'll just suit each other.'

Anna could not but be impressed by this unaffected joy of her friends in the engagement. Her spirits rose, and once more she saw visions of future happiness. At tea, Alderman Sutton added his felicitations to the rest, with that flattering air of intimate sympathy and comprehension which some middle-aged men can adopt towards young girls. The tea, made specially magnificent in honour of the betrothal, was such a meal as could only have been compassed in Staffordshire or Yorkshire – a high tea of the last richness and excellence, exquisitely gracious to the palate, but ruthless in its demands on the stomach. At one end of the table, which glittered with silver, glass, and Longshaw china,* was a fowl which had been boiled for four hours; at the other, a hot pork-pie, islanded in liquor, which might have satisfied a regiment. Between these two dishes were all the delicacies which differentiate high tea from tea, and on the quality of which the success of the meal really depends; hot pikelets, hot crumpets, hot toast, sardines with tomatoes, raisin-bread, currant-bread, seed-cake, lettuce, home-made marmalade, and home-made hams. The repast occupied over an hour, and even then not a quarter of the food was consumed. Surrounded by all that good fare and good-will, with the Alderman on her left, Henry on her right, and a bright fire in front of her, Anna quickly caught the gaiety of the others. She forgot everything but the gladness of reunion, the joy of the moment, the luxurious comfort of the house. Conversation was busy with the doings of the Suttons at Port Erin after Anna and Henry had left. A listener would have caught fragments like this: 'You know such-and-such a point. . . . No, not there, over the hill. Well, we hired a carriage and drove. . . . The weather was simply. . . . Tom Kelly said he'd never. . . . And that little guard on the railway came all the way down to the steamer. . . . Did you see anything in the *Signal* about the actress being drowned? Oh! It was awfully sad. We saw the corpse just after. . . . Beatrice, will you hush?'

'Wasn't it terrible about Titus Price?' Beatrice exclaimed.

'Eh, my!' sighed Mrs Sutton, glancing at Anna. 'You can never tell what's going to happen next. I'm always afraid to go away for fear of something happening.'

A silence followed. When tea was finished Beatrice was taken away by her mother to write the letters concerning the immediate resumption of sewing-meetings, and for a little time Anna was left in the drawing-room alone with the two men, who began to talk about the affairs of the Prices. It appeared that Mr Sutton had been asked to become trustee for the creditors under a deed of arrangement, and that he had hopes of being able to sell the business as a going concern. In the meantime it would need careful management.

'Will Willie Price manage it?' Anna inquired. The question seemed to divert Henry and the Alderman, to afford them a contemptuous and somewhat inimical amusement at the expense of Willie.

'No,' said the Alderman, quietly, but emphatically.

'Master William is fairly good on the works,' said Henry; 'but in the office, I imagine, he is worse than useless.'

Grieved and confused, Anna bent down and moved a hassock in order to hide her face. The attitude of these men to Willie Price, that victim of circumstances and of his own simplicity, wounded Anna inexpressibly. She perceived that they could see in him only a defaulting debtor, that his misfortune made no appeal to their charity. She wondered that men so warm-hearted and kind in some relations could be so hard in others.

'I had a talk with your father at the creditors' meeting yesterday,' said the Alderman. '*You* won't lose much. Of course you've got a preferential claim for six months' rent.' He said this reassuringly, as though it would give satisfaction. Anna did not know what a preferential claim might be, nor was she aware of any creditors' meeting. She wished ardently that she might lose as much as possible – hundreds of pounds. She was relieved when Beatrice swept in, her mother following.

'Now, your worship,' said Beatrice to her father, 'seven stamps for these letters, please.' Anna glanced up inquiringly on hearing the form of address. 'You don't mean to say that you didn't know that Father is going to be mayor this year?' Beatrice asked, as if shocked at this ignorance of affairs. 'Yes, it was all settled rather late, wasn't it, Dad? And the mayor-elect pretends not to care much, but actually he is filled with pride, isn't he, Dad? As for the mayoress – ?'

'Eh, Bee!' Mrs Sutton stopped her, smiling; 'you'll tumble over that tongue of yours some day.'

'Mother said I wasn't to mention it,' said Beatrice, 'lest you should think we were putting on airs.'

'Nay, not I!' Mrs Sutton protested. 'I said no such thing. Anna knows us too well for that. But I'm not so set up with this mayor business as some people will think I am.'

'Or as Beatrice is,' Mynors added.

At half-past eight, and again at nine, Anna said that she must go home; but the Suttons, now frankly absorbed in the topic of the mayoralty, their secret preoccupation, would not spoil the confidential talk which had ensued by letting the lovers depart. It was nearly half-past nine before Anna and Henry stood on the pavement outside, and Beatrice, after facetious farewells, had shut the door.

'Let us just walk round by the Manor Farm,' Henry pleaded. 'It won't take more than a quarter of an hour or so.'

She agreed dutifully. The footpath ran at right angles to Trafalgar Road, past a colliery whose engine-fires glowed in the dark, moonless, autumn night, and then across a field. They stood on a knoll near the old farmstead, that extraordinary and pathetic survival of a vanished agriculture. Immediately in front of them stretched acres of burning ironstone – a vast tremulous carpet of flame woven in red, purple, and strange greens. Beyond were the skeleton-like silhouettes of pit-heads, and the solid forms of furnace and chimney-shaft. In the distance a canal reflected the gigantic illuminations of Cauldon Bar Ironworks. It was a scene mysterious and romantic enough to kindle the raptures of love, but Anna felt cold, melancholy, and apprehensive of vague sorrows. 'Why am I so?' she asked herself, and tried in vain to shake off the mood.

'What will Willie Price do if the business is sold?' she questioned Mynors suddenly.

'Surely,' he said to soothe her, 'you aren't still worrying about that misfortune. I wish you had never gone near the inquest; the thing seems to have got on your mind.'

'Oh, no!' she protested, with an air of cheerfulness. 'But I was just wondering.'

'Well, Willie will have to do the best he can. Get a place somewhere, I suppose. It won't be much, at the best.'

Had he guessed what perhaps hung on that answer, Mynors might have given it in a tone less callous and perfunctory. Could he have seen the tightening of her lips, he might even afterwards have repaired his error by some voluntary assurance that Willie Price should be watched over with a benevolent eye and protected with a strong arm. But how was he to know that in misprizing Willie Price before her, he was misprizing a child to its mother? He had done something for Willie Price, and considered that he had done enough. His thoughts, moreover, were on other matters.

'Do you remember that day we went up to the park?' he murmured fondly; 'that Sunday? I have never told you that that evening I came out of chapel after the first hymn, when I noticed you weren't there, and walked up past your house. I couldn't help it. Something drew me. I nearly called in to see you. Then I thought I had better not.'

'I saw you,' she said calmly. His warmth made her feel sad. 'I saw you stop at the gate.'

'You did? But you weren't at the window?'

'I saw you through the glass of the front-door.' Her voice grew fainter, more reluctant.

'Then you were watching?' In the dark he seized her with such violence, and kissed her so vehemently, that she was startled out of herself.

'Oh! Henry!' she exclaimed.

'Call me Harry,' he entreated, his arm still round her waist; 'I want you to call me Harry. No one else does or ever has done, and no one shall, now.'

'Harry,' she said deliberately, bracing her mind to a positive determination. She must please him, and she said it again: 'Harry; yes, it has a nice sound.'

Ephraim sat reading the *Signal* in the parlour when she arrived home at five minutes to ten. Imbued then with ideas of duty, submission, and systematic kindliness, she had an impulse to attempt a reconciliation with her father.

'Good-night, Father,' she said, 'I hope I've not kept you up.'

He was deaf.

She went to bed resigned; sad, but not gloomy. It was not for nothing that during her life she had been accustomed to infelicity. Experience had taught her this: to be the mistress of herself. She knew that she could face any fact – even the fact of her dispassionate frigidity under Mynors' caresses. It was on the firm, almost rapturous resolve to succour Willie Price, if need be, that she fell asleep.

The engagement, which had hitherto been kept private, became the theme of universal gossip immediately upon the return of the Suttons from the Isle of Man. Two words let fall by Beatrice in the St Luke's covered market on Saturday morning had increased and multiplied till the whole town echoed with the news. Anna's private fortune rose as high as a quarter of a million. As for Henry Mynors, it was said that Henry Mynors knew what he was about. After all, he was like the rest. Money, money! Of course it was inconceivable that a fine, prosperous figure of a man, such as Mynors, would have made up to *her*, if she had not been simply rolling in money. Well, there was one thing to be said for young Mynors, he would put money to good use; you might rely he would not hoard it up same as it had been hoarded up. However, the more saved, the more for young Mynors, so *he* needn't grumble. It was to be hoped he would make her dress herself a bit better – though indeed it hadn't been her fault she went about so shabby; the old skinflint would never allow her a penny of her own. So tongues wagged.

The first Sunday was a tiresome ordeal for Anna, both at school and at chapel. 'Well, I never!' seemed to be written like a note of exclamation on every brow; the monotony of the congratulations fatigued her as much as her involuntary efforts to grasp what each speaker had left unsaid of innuendo, malice, envy, or sycophancy. Even the people in the shops, during the next few days, could not serve her without direct and curious reference to her private affairs. The general opinion that she was a cold and bloodless creature was strengthened by her attitude at this period. But the apathy which she displayed was neither affected nor due to an excessive diffidence. As she seemed, so she felt. She often wondered what would have happened to her if that vague 'something' between Henry and Beatrice, to which Beatrice had confessed, had ever taken definite shape.

'Hancock came back from Lancashire last night,' said Mynors, when he arrived at Manor Terrace on the next Saturday afternoon. Ephraim was in the room, and Henry, evidently joyous and triumphant, addressed both him and Anna.

'Is Hancock the commercial traveller?' Anna asked. She knew that Hancock was the commercial traveller, but she experienced a nervous compulsion to make idle remarks in order to hide the breach of intercourse between her father and herself.

'How much?' asked the miser.

Henry named the amount of orders taken in a fortnight's journey.

'Humph!' the miser ejaculated. 'That's better than a bat in the eye with a burnt stick.'* From him, this was the superlative of praise. 'You're making good money at any rate?'

'We are,' said Mynors.

'That reminds me,' Ephraim remarked gruffly. 'When dost think o' getting wed? I'm not much for long engagements, and so I tell ye.' He threw a cold glance sideways at Anna. The idea penetrated her heart like a stab: 'He wants to get me out of the house!'

'Well,' said Mynors, surprised at the question and the tone, and, looking at Anna as if for an explanation: 'I had scarcely thought of that. What does Anna say?'

'I don't know,' she murmured; and then, more bravely, in a louder voice, and with a smile: 'The sooner the better.' She thought, in her bitter and painful resentment: 'If he wants me to go, go I will.'

Henry tactfully passed on to another phase of the subject: 'I met Mr Sutton yesterday, and he was telling me of Price's house up at Toft End. It belonged to Mr Price, but of course it was mortgaged up to the hilt. The mortgagees have taken possession, and Mr Sutton said it would be to let cheap at Christmas. Of course Willie and old Sarah Vodrey, the housekeeper, will clear out. I was thinking it might do for us. It's not a bad sort of house, or, rather, it won't be when it's repaired.'

'What will they ask for it?' Ephraim inquired.

'Twenty-five or twenty-eight. It's a nice large house – four bedrooms, and a very good garden.'

'Four bedrooms!' the miser exclaimed. 'What dost want wi' four bedrooms? You'd have for keep a servant.'

'Naturally we should keep a servant,' Mynors said, with calm politeness.

'You could get one o' them new houses up by th' park for fifteen pounds as would do you well enough,' the miser protested against these dreams of extravagance.

'I don't care for that part of the town,' said Mynors. 'It's too new for my taste.'

After tea, when Henry and Anna went out for the Saturday evening stroll, Mynors suddenly suggested: 'Why not go up and look through that house of Price's?'

'Won't it seem like turning them out if we happen to take it?' she asked.

'Turning them out! Willie is bound to leave it. What use is it to him? Besides, it's in the hands of the mortgagees now. Why shouldn't we take it just as well as anybody else, if it suits us?'

Anna had no reply, and she surrendered herself placidly enough to his will; nevertheless she could not entirely banish a misgiving that Willie Price was again to be victimized. Infinitely more disturbing than this illogical sensation, however, was the instinctive and sure knowledge, revealed in a flash, that her father wished to be rid of her. So implacable, then, was his animosity against her! Never, never had she been so deeply hurt. The wound, in fact, was so severe that at first she felt only a numbness that reduced everything to unimportance, robbing her of volition. She walked up to Toft End as if walking in her sleep.

Price's house, sometimes called Priory House, in accordance with a legend that a priory had once occupied the site, stood in the middle of the mean and struggling suburb of Toft End, which was flung up the hillside like a ragged scarf. Built of red brick, towards the end of the eighteenth century, double-fronted, with small, evenly disposed windows, and a chimney stack at either side, it looked westward over the town smoke towards a horizon of hills. It had a long, narrow garden, which ran parallel with the road. Behind it, adjoining, was a small, disused potworks, already advanced in decay. On the north side, and enclosed by a brick wall which surrounded also the garden, was a small orchard of sterile and withered fruit trees. In parts the wall had crumpled under the assaults of generations of boys, and from the orchard, through the gaps, could be seen an expanse of grey-green field, with a few abandoned pit-shafts scattered over it. These shafts, imperfectly protected by ruinous masonry, presented an appearance strangely sinister and forlorn, raising visions in the mind of dark and mysterious depths peopled with miserable ghosts of those who had toiled there in the days when to be a miner was to be a slave. The whole place, house and garden, looked ashamed and sad, with a shabby mournfulness acquired gradually from its inmates during many years. But, nevertheless, the house was substantial, and the air on that height fresh and pure.

Mynors rang in vain at the front door, and then they walked round the house to the orchard, and discovered Sarah Vodrey taking in clothes from a line – a diminutive and wasted figure, with scanty, grey hair, a tiny face permanently soured, and bony hands contorted by rheumatism.

'My rheumatism's that bad,' she said in response to greetings, 'I can scarce move about, and this house is a regular barracks to keep clean. No; Willie's not in. He's at th' works, as usual – Saturday like any other day. I'm by myself here all day and every day. But I reckon us'n be flitting soon, and me lived here eight-and-twenty year! Praise God, there's a mansion up there for me at last. And not sorry shall I be when He calls.'

'It must be very lonely for you, Miss Vodrey,' said Mynors. He knew exactly how to speak to this dame who lived her life like a fly between two panes of glass, and who could find room in her head for only three ideas, namely: that God and herself were on terms of intimacy; that she was, and had always been, indispensable to the Price family; and that her social status was far above that of a servant. 'It's a pity you never married,' Mynors added.

'Me, marry! What would *they* ha' done without me? No, I'm none for marriage and never was. I'd be shamed to be like some o' them spinsters down at chapel, always hanging round chapel-yard on the off-chance of a service, to catch that there young Mr Sargent, the new minister. It's a sign of a hard winter, Miss Terrick, when the hay runs after the horse,* that's what I say.'

'Miss Tellwright and myself are in search of a house,' Mynors gently interrupted the flow, and gave her a peculiar glance which she appreciated. 'We heard you and Willie were going to leave here, and so we came up just to look over the place, if it's quite convenient to you.'

'Eh, I understand ye,' she said; 'come in. But ye mun tak' things as ye find 'em, Miss Terrick.'

Dismal and unkempt, the interior of the house matched the exterior. The carpets were threadbare, the discoloured wall-papers hung loose on the walls, the ceilings were almost black, the paint had nearly been rubbed away from the woodwork; the exhausted furniture looked as if it would fall to pieces in despair if compelled to face the threatened ordeal of an auction-sale. But to Anna the rooms were surprisingly large, and there seemed so many of them! It was as if she were exploring an immense abode, like a castle, with odd chambers continually showing themselves in unexpected places. The upper storey was even less inviting than the ground-floor – barer, more chill, utterly comfortless.

'This is the best bedroom,' said Miss Vodrey. 'And a rare big room too! It's not used now. *He* slept here. Willie sleeps at back.'

'A very nice room,' Mynors agreed blandly, and measured it, as he had done all the others, with a two-foot* entering the figures in his pocket-book.

Anna's eye wandered uneasily across the room, with its dismantled bed and decrepit mahogany suite.

'I'm glad he hanged himself at the works, and not here,' she thought. Then she looked out at the window. 'What a splendid view!' she remarked to Mynors.

She saw that he had taken a fancy to the house. The sagacious fellow esteemed it, not as it was, but as it would be, re-papered, re-painted, re-furnished, the outer walls pointed, the garden stocked; everything cleansed, brightened, renewed. And there was indeed much to be said for his fancy. The house was large, with plenty of ground; the boundary wall secured that privacy which young husbands and young wives instinctively demand; the outlook was unlimited, the air the purest in the Five Towns.

And the rent was low, because the great majority of those who could afford such a house would never deign to exist in a quarter so poverty-stricken and unfashionable.

After leaving the house they continued their walk up the hill, and then turned off to the left on the high road from Hanbridge to Moorthorne. The venerable but not dignified town lay below them, a huddled medley of brown brick under a thick black cloud of smoke. The gold angel of the town-hall gleamed in the evening light, and the dark, squat tower of the parish church, sole relic of the past, stood out grim and obdurate amid the featureless buildings which surrounded it. To the north and east miles of moorland, defaced by collieries and murky hamlets, ran to the horizon. Across the great field at their feet a figure slouched along, past the abandoned pitshafts. They both recognized the man.

'There's Willie Price going home!' said Mynors.

'He looks tired,' she said. She was relieved that they had not met him at the house.

'I say,' Mynors began earnestly, after a pause, 'why shouldn't we get married soon, since the old gentleman seems rather to expect it? He's been rather awkward lately, hasn't he?'

This was the only reference made by Mynors to her father's temper. She nodded. 'How soon?' she asked.

'Well, I was just thinking. Suppose, for the sake of argument, this house turns out all right. I couldn't get it thoroughly done up much before the middle of January – couldn't begin till these people had moved. Suppose we said early in February?'

'Yes!'

'Could you be ready by that time?'

'Oh, yes,' she answered, 'I could be ready.'

'Well, why shouldn't we fix February, then?'

'There's the question of Agnes,' she said.

'Yes; and there will always be the question of Agnes. Your father will have to get a housekeeper. You and I will be able to see after little Agnes, never fear.' So, with tenderness in his voice, he reassured her on that point.

'Why not February?' she reflected. 'Why not tomorrow, as Father wants me out of the house?'

It was agreed.

'I've taken the Priory, subject to your approval,' Henry said, less than a fortnight later. From that time he invariably referred to the place as the Priory.

It was on the very night after this eager announcement that the approaching tragedy came one step nearer. Beatrice, in a modest evening-dress, with a white cloak – excited, hurried, and important – ran in to speak to Anna. The carriage was waiting outside. She and her father and mother had to attend a very important dinner at the mayor's house at Hillport, in connexion with Mr Sutton's impending mayoralty. Old Sarah Vodrey had just sent down a girl to say that she was unwell, and would be grateful if Mrs Sutton or Beatrice would visit her. It was a most unreasonable time for such a summons, but Sarah was a fidgety old crotchet, and knew how frightfully good-natured Mrs Sutton was. Would Anna mind going up to Toft End? And would Anna come out to the carriage and personally assure Mrs Sutton that old Sarah should be attended to? If not, Beatrice was afraid her mother would take it into her head to do something stupid.

'It's very good of you, Anna,' said Mrs Sutton, when Anna went outside with Beatrice. 'But I think I'd better go myself. The poor old thing may feel slighted if I don't, and Beatrice can well take my place at this affair at Hillport, which I've no mind for.' She was already half out of the carriage.

'Nothing of the kind,' said Anna firmly, pushing her back. 'I shall be delighted to go and do what I can.'

'That's right, Anna,' said the Alderman from the darkness of the carriage, where his shirt-front gleamed; 'Bee said you'd go, and we're much obliged to ye.'

'I expect it will be nothing,' said Beatrice, as the vehicle drove off; 'Sarah has served Mother this trick before now.'

As Anna opened the garden-gate of the Priory she discerned a figure amid the rank bushes, which had been allowed to grow till they almost met across the narrow path leading to the front door of the house. It was a thick and mysterious night – such a night as death chooses; and Anna jumped in vague terror at the apparition.

'Who's there?' said a voice sharply.

'It's me,' said Anna. 'Miss Vodrey sent down to ask Mrs Sutton to come up and see her, but Mrs Sutton had an engagement, so I came instead.'

The figure moved forward; it was Willie Price. He peered into her face, and she could see the mortal pallor of his cheeks.

'Oh!' he exclaimed, 'it's Miss Tellwright, is it? Will ye come in, Miss Tellwright?'

She followed him with beating heart, alarmed, apprehensive. The front door stood wide open, and at the far end of the gloomy passage a faint light shone from the open door of the kitchen. 'This way,' he said. In the large, bare, stone-floored kitchen Sarah Vodrey sat limp and with closed eyes in an old rocking-chair close to the fireless range. The window, which gave on to the street, was open; through that window Sarah, in her extremity, had called the child who ran down to Mrs Sutton's. On the deal table were a dirty cup and saucer, a teapot, bread, butter, and a lighted candle – sole illumination of the chamber.

'I come home, and I find this,' he said.

Daunted for a moment by the scene of misery, Anna could say nothing.

'I find this,' he repeated, as if accusing God of spitefulness; and he lifted the candle to show the apparently insensible form of the woman. Sarah's wrinkled and seamed face had the flush of fever, and the features were drawn into the expression of a terrible anxiety; her hands hung loose; she breathed like a dog after a run.

'I wanted her to have the doctor yesterday,' he said, 'but she wouldn't. Ever since you and Mr Mynors called she's been cleaning the house down. She said you'd happen be coming again soon, and the place wasn't fit to be seen. No use me arguing with her.'

'You had better run for a doctor,' Anna said.

'I was just going off when you came. She's been complaining more of her rheumatism, and pain in her hips, lately.'

'Go now; fetch Mr Macpherson, and call at our house and say I shall stay here all night. Wait a moment.' Seeing that he was exhausted from lack of food, she cut a thick piece of bread-and-butter. 'Eat this as you go,' she said.

'I can't eat; it'll choke me.'

'Let it choke you,' she said. 'You've got to swallow it.'

Child of a hundred sorrows, he must be treated as a child. As soon as Willie was gone she took off her hat and jacket, and lit a lamp; there was no gas in the kitchen.

'What's that light?' the old woman asked peevishly, rousing herself and sitting up. 'I doubt* I'll be late with Willie's tea. Eh, Miss Terrick, what's amiss?'

'You're not quite well, Miss Vodrey,' Anna answered. 'If you'll show me your room, I'll see you into bed.' Without giving her a moment for hesitation, Anna seized the feeble creature under the arms, and so, coaxing, supporting, carrying, got her to bed. At length she lay on the narrow mattress, panting, exhausted. It was Sarah's final effort.

Anna lit fires in the kitchen and in the bedroom, and when Willie returned with Dr Macpherson, water was boiling and tea made.

'You'd better get a woman in,' said the doctor curtly, in the kitchen, when he had finished his examination of Sarah. 'Some neighbour for tonight, and I'll send a nurse up from the cottage-hospital early tomorrow morning. Not that it will be the least use. She must have been dying for the last two days at least. She's got pericarditis and pleurisy. She's breathing I don't know how many to the minute, and her temperature is just about as high as it can be. It all follows from rheumatism, and then taking cold. Gross carelessness and neglect all through! I've no patience with such work.' He turned angrily to Willie. 'I don't know what on earth you were thinking of, Mr Price, not to send for me earlier.'

Willie, abashed and guilty, found nothing to say. His eye had the meek wistfulness of Holman Hunt's *Scapegoat*.*

'Mr Price wanted her to have the doctor,' said Anna, defending him with warmth; 'but she wouldn't. He is out at the works all day till late at night. How was he to know how she was? She could walk about.'

The tall doctor glanced at Anna in surprise, and at once modified his tone. 'Yes,' he said, 'that's the curious thing. It passes me how she managed to get about. But there is no knowing what an obstinate woman won't force herself to do. I'll send the medicine up tonight, and come along myself with the nurse early tomorrow. Meantime, keep carefully to my instructions.'

That night remains for ever fixed in Anna's memory: the grim rooms, echoing and shadowy; the countless journeys up and down dark stairs and passages; Willie sitting always immovable in the kitchen, idle because there was nothing for him to do;

Sarah incessantly panting on the truckle-bed; the hired woman from up the street, buxom, kindly, useful, but fatuous in the endless monotony of her commiserations.

Towards morning, Sarah Vodrey gave sign of a desire to talk.

'I've fought the fight,' she murmured to Anna, who alone was in the bedroom with her, 'I've fought the fight; I've kept the faith. In that box there ye'll see a purse. There's seventeen pound six in it. That will pay for the funeral, and Willie must have what's over. There would ha' been more for the lad, but *he* never paid me no wages this two years past. I never troubled him.'

'Don't tell Willie that,' Anna said impetuously.

'Eh, bless ye, no!' said the dying drudge, and then seemed to doze.

Anna went to the kitchen, and sent the woman upstairs.

'How is she?' asked Willie, without stirring. Anna shook her head. 'Neither her nor me will be here much longer, I'm thinking,' he said, smiling wearily.

'What?' she exclaimed, startled.

'Mr Sutton has arranged to sell our business as a going-concern – some people at Turnhill are buying it. I shall go to Australia; there's no room for me here. The creditors have promised to allow me twenty-five pounds, and I can get an assisted passage.* Bursley'll know me no more. But – but – I shall always remember you and what you've done.'

She longed to kneel at his feet, and to comfort him, and to cry: 'It is I who have ruined you – driven your father to cheating his servant, to crime, to suicide; driven you to forgery, and turned you out of your house which your old servant killed herself in making clean for me. I have wronged you, and I love you like a mother because I have wronged you and because I saved you from prison.'

But she said nothing except: 'Some of us will miss you.'

The next day Sarah Vodrey died – she who had never lived save in the fetters of slavery and fanaticism. After fifty years of ceaseless labour, she had gained the affection of one person, and enough money to pay for her own funeral. Willie Price took a cheap lodging with the woman who had been called in on the night of Sarah's collapse. Before Christmas he was to sail for Melbourne.* The Priory, deserted, gave up its rickety furniture to a van from Hanbridge, where in an auction-room, the frail sticks lost their identity in a medley of other sticks, and ceased to be. Then the bricklayer, the plasterer, the painter, and the paper-hanger came to the Priory, and whistled and sang in it.

CHAPTER THIRTEEN

The Bazaar

The Wesleyan Bazaar, the greatest undertaking of its kind ever known in Bursley, gradually became a cloud which filled the entire social horizon. Mrs Sutton, organizer of the Sunday-school stall, pressed all her friends into the service, and a fortnight after the death of Sarah Vodrey, Anna and even Agnes gave much of their spare time to the work, which was carried on under pressure increasing daily as the final moments approached. This was well for Anna, in that it diverted her thoughts by keeping her energies fully engaged. One morning, however, it occurred to Mrs Sutton to reflect that Anna, at such a period of life, should be otherwise employed. Anna had called at the Suttons' to deliver some finished garments.

'My dear,' she said, 'I am very much obliged to you for all this industry. But I've been thinking that as you are to be married in February you ought to be preparing your things.'

'My things!' Anna repeated idly; and then she remembered Mynors' phrase, on the hill, 'Can you be ready by that time?'

'Yes,' said Mrs Sutton; 'but possibly you've been getting forward with them on the quiet.'

'Tell me,' said Anna, with an air of interest; 'I've meant to ask you before: Is it the bride's place to provide all the house-linen, and that sort of thing?'

'It was in my day; but those things alter so. The bride took all the house-linen to her husband, and as many clothes for herself as would last a year; that was the rule. We used to stitch everything at home in those days – everything; and we had what we called a "bottom drawer" to store them in. As soon as a girl passed her fifteenth birthday, she began to sew for the "bottom drawer". But all those things change so, I dare say it's different now.'

'How much will it cost to buy everything, do you think?' Anna asked.

Just then Beatrice entered the room.

'Beatrice, Anna is inquiring how much it will cost to buy her trousseau, and the house-linen. What do you say?'

'Oh!' Beatrice replied, without any hesitation, 'a couple of hundred at least.'

Mrs Sutton, reading Anna's face, smiled reassuringly. 'Nonsense, Bee! I dare say you could do it on a hundred with care, Anna.'

'Why should Anna want to do it with care?' Beatrice asked curtly.

Anna went straight across the road to her father, and asked him for a hundred pounds of her own money. She had not spoken to him, save under necessity, since the evening spent at the Suttons'.

'What's afoot now?' he questioned savagely.

'I must buy things for the wedding – clothes and things, Father.'

'Ay! clothes! clothes! What clothes dost want? A few pounds will cover them.'

'There'll be all the linen for the house.'

'Linen for – It's none thy place for buy that.'

'Yes, Father, it is.'

'I say it isna',' he shouted.

'But I've asked Mrs Sutton, and she says it is.'

'What business an' ye for go blabbing thy affairs all over Bosley?* I say it isna' thy place for buy linen, and let that be sufficient. Go and get dinner. It's nigh on twelve now.'

That evening, when Agnes had gone to bed, she resumed the struggle.

'Father, I must have that hundred pounds. I really must. I mean it.'

'*Thou means it!* What?'

'I mean I must have a hundred pounds.'

'I'd advise thee to tak' care o' thy tongue, my lass. *Thou means it!*'

'But you needn't give it me all at once,' she pursued.

He gazed at her, glowering.

'I shanna' give it thee. It's Henry's place for buy th' house linen.'

'Father, it isn't.' Her voice broke, but only for an instant. 'I'm asking you for my own money. You seem to want to make me miserable just before my wedding.'

'I wish to God thou'dst never seen Henry Mynors. It's given thee pride and made thee undutiful.'

'I'm only asking you for my own money.'

Her calm insistence maddened him. Jumping up from his chair, he stamped out of the room, and she heard him strike a match in his office. Presently he returned, and threw angrily on to the table in front of her a cheque-book and pass-book. The deposit-book she had always kept herself for convenience of paying into the bank.

'Here,' he said scornfully, 'tak' thy traps and ne'er speak to me again. I wash my hands of ye. Tak' 'em and do what ye'n a mind. Chuck thy money into th' cut† for aught I care.'

The next evening Henry came up. She observed that his face had a grave look, but intent on her own difficulties she did not remark on it, and proceeded at once to do what she resolved to do. It was a cold night in November, yet the miser, wrathfully sullen, chose to sit in his office without a fire. Agnes was working sums in the kitchen.

'Henry,' Anna began, 'I've had a difficulty with Father, and I must tell you.'

'Not about the wedding, I hope,' he said.

'It was about money. Of course, Henry, I can't get married without a lot of money.'

'Why not?' he inquired.

'I've my own things to get,' she said, 'and I've all the house-linen to buy.'

'Oh! You buy the house-linen, do you?' She saw that he was relieved by that information.

'Of course. Well, I told Father I must have a hundred pounds, and he wouldn't give it me. And when I stuck to him he got angry – you know he can't bear to see money spent – and at last he got a little savage and gave me my bank-books, and said he'd have nothing more to do with my money.'

Henry's face broke into a laugh, and Anna was obliged to smile. 'Capital!' he said. 'Couldn't be better.'

'I want you to tell me how much I've got in the bank,' she said. 'I only know I'm always paying in odd cheques.'

He examined the three books. 'A very tidy bit,' he said;

† *Cut*: canal.

'something over two hundred and fifty pounds. So you can draw cheques at your ease.'

'Draw me a cheque for twenty pounds,' she said; and then, while he wrote: 'Henry, after we're married, I shall want you to take charge of all this.'

'Yes, of course; I will do that, dear. But your money will be yours. There ought to be a settlement on you. Still, if your father says nothing, it is not for me to say anything.'

'Father will say nothing – now,' she said. 'You've never shown any interest in it, Henry; but as we're talking of money, I may as well tell you that Father says I'm worth fifty thousand pounds.'

The man of business was astonished and enraptured beyond measure. His countenance shone with delight.

'Surely not!' he protested formally.

'That's what Father told me, and he made me read a list of shares, and so on.'

'We will go slow, to begin with,' said Mynors solemnly. He had not expected more than fifteen or twenty thousand pounds, and even this sum had dazzled his imagination. He was glad that he had taken over the house at Toft End on a yearly tenancy. He now saw himself the dominant figure in all the Five Towns.

Later in the evening he disclosed, perfunctorily, the matter which had been a serious weight on his mind when he entered the house, but which this revelation of vast wealth had diminished to a trifle. Titus Price had been the treasurer of the building fund which the bazaar was designed to assist. Mynors had assumed the position of the dead man, and that day, in going through the accounts, he had discovered that a sum of fifty pounds was missing.

'It's a dreadful thing for Willie, if it gets about,' he said; 'a tale of that sort would follow him to Australia.'

'Oh, Henry, it is!' she exclaimed, sorrow-stricken; 'but we mustn't let it get about. Let us pay the money ourselves. You must enter it in the books and say nothing.'

'That is impossible,' he said firmly. 'I can't alter the accounts. At least I can't alter the bank-book and the vouchers. The auditor would detect it in a minute. Besides, I should not be doing my duty if I kept a thing like this from the Superintendent-minister. He, at any rate, must know, and perhaps the stewards.'

'But you can urge them to say nothing. Tell them that you will make it good. I will write a cheque at once.'

'I had meant to find the fifty myself,' he said. It was a peddling* sum to him now.

'Let me pay half, then,' she asked.

'If you like,' he urged, smiling faintly at her eagerness. 'The thing is bound to be kept quiet – it would create such a frightful scandal. Poor old chap!' he added, carelessly, 'I suppose he was hard run, and meant to put it back – as they all do mean.'

But it was useless for Mynors to affect depression of spirits, or mournful sympathy with the errors of a dead sinner. The fifty thousand danced a jig in his brain that night.

Anna was absorbed in contemplating the misfortune of Willie Price. She prayed wildly that he might never learn the full depth of his father's fall. The miserable robbery of Sarah's wages was buried for evermore, and this new delinquency, which all would regard as flagrant sacrilege, must be buried also. A soul less loyal than Anna's might have feared that Willie, a self-convicted forger, had been a party to the embezzlement; but Anna knew that it could not be so.

It was characteristic of Mynors' cautious prudence that, the first intoxication having passed, he made no further reference of any kind to Anna's fortune. The arrangements for their married life were planned on a scale which ignored the fifty thousand pounds. For both their sakes he wished to avoid all friction with the miser, at any rate until his status as Anna's husband would enable him to enforce her rights, if that should be necessary, with dignity and effectiveness. He did not precisely anticipate trouble, but the fact had not escaped him that Ephraim still held the whole of Anna's securities. He was in no hurry to enlarge his borders. He knew that there were twenty-four hours in every day, three hundred and sixty-five days in every year, and thirty good years in life still left to him; and therefore that there would be ample time, after the wedding, for the execution of his purposes in regard to that fifty thousand pounds. Meanwhile, he told Anna that he had set aside two hundred pounds for the purchase of furniture for the Priory – a modest sum; but he judged it sufficient. His method was to buy a piece at a time, always second-hand, but always good. The bargain-hunt was up, and Anna soon yielded to its mild satisfactions. In the matter of her trousseau and the house-linen, Anna having obtained the needed money – at so dear a cost – found yet another obstacle in the imminent bazaar, which occupied Mrs Sutton and Beatrice so completely that they could not contrive any opportunity to assist her in shopping. It was decided between them that every article should be bought ready-made and seamed, and that the first week of the New Year, if indeed Mrs Sutton survived the bazaar, should be entirely and absolutely devoted to Anna's business.

At nights, when she had leisure to think, Anna was astonished how during the day she had forgotten her preoccupations in the activities precedent to the bazaar, or in choosing furniture with Mynors. But she never slept without thinking of Willie Price, and hoping that no further disaster might overtake him. The incident of the embezzled fifty pounds had been closed, and she had given a cheque for twenty-five pounds to Mynors. He had acquainted the minister with the facts, and Mr Banks had decided that the two circuit stewards must be informed. Beyond these the scandalous secret was not to go. But Anna wondered whether a secret shared by five persons could long remain a secret.

The bazaar was a triumphant and unparalleled success, and, of the seven stalls, the Sunday-school stall stood first each night in the nightly returns. The scene in the town-hall, on the fourth and final night, a Saturday, was as delirious and gay as a carnival. Four hundred and twenty pounds had been raised up to tea-time, and it was the impassioned desire of everyone to achieve five hundred. The price of admission had been reduced to threepence, in order that the artisan might enter and spend his wages in an excellent cause. The seven stalls, ranged round the room like so many bowers of beauty, draped and frilled and floriated, and still laden with countless articles of use and ornament, were continually reinforced with purchasers by emissaries canvassing the crowd which filled the middle of the paper-strewn floor. The horse was not only taken to the water, but compelled to drink; and many a man who, outside, would have laughed at the risk of being robbed, was robbed openly, shamelessly, under the gaze of ministers and class-leaders. Bouquets were sold at a shilling each, and at the refreshment stall a glass of milk cost sixpence. The noise rivalled that of a fair; there was no quiet anywhere, save in the farthest recess of each stall, where the lady in supreme charge of it, like a spider in the middle of its web, watched customers and cash-box with equal cupidity.

Mrs Sutton, at seven o'clock, had not returned from tea, and Anna and Beatrice, who managed the Sunday-school stall in her absence, feared that she had at last succumbed under the strain. But shortly afterwards she hurried back breathless to her place.

'See that, Anna? It will be reckoned in our returns,' she said, exhibiting a piece of paper. It was Ephraim's cheque for twenty-five pounds promised months ago, but on a condition which had not been fulfilled.

'She has the secret of persuading him,' thought Anna. 'Why have I never found it?'

Then Agnes, in a new white frock, came up with three shillings, proceeds of bouquets.

'But you must take that to the flower-stall, my pet,' said Mrs Sutton.

'Can't I give it to you?' the child pleaded. 'I want your stall to be the best.'

Mynors arrived next, with something concealed in tissue-paper. He removed the paper, and showed, in a frame of crimson plush, a common white plate decorated with a simple band and line, and a monogram in the centre – 'A.T.' Anna blushed, recognizing the plate which she had painted that afternoon in July at Mynors' works.

'Can you sell this?' Mynors asked Mrs Sutton.

'I'll try to,' said Mrs Sutton doubtfully – not in the secret 'What's it meant for?'

'Try to sell it to me,' said Mynors.

'Well,' she laughed, 'what will you give?'

'A couple of sovereigns.'

'Make it guineas.'

He paid the money, and requested Anna to keep the plate for him.

At nine o'clock it was announced that, though raffling was forbidden, the bazaar would be enlivened by an auction. A licensed auctioneer was brought, and the sale commenced. The auctioneer, however, failed to attune himself to the wild spirit of the hour, and his professional efforts would have resulted in a fiasco had not Mynors, perceiving the danger, leaped to the platform and masterfully assumed the hammer. Mynors surpassed himself in the kind of wit that amuses an excited crowd, and the auction soon monopolized the attention of the room, it was always afterwards remembered as the crowning success of the bazaar. The incredible man took ten pounds in twenty minutes. During this episode Anna, who had been left alone in the stall, first noticed Willie Price in the room. His ship sailed on the Monday, but steerage* passengers had to be aboard on Sunday, and he was saying goodbye to a few acquaintances. He seemed quite cheerful, as he walked about with his hands in his pockets, chatting with this one and that; it was the false and hysterical gaiety that precedes a final separation. As soon as he saw Anna he came towards her.

'Well, goodbye, Miss Tellwright,' he said jauntily. 'I leave for Liverpool tomorrow morning. Wish me luck.'

Nothing more; no word, no accent, to recall the terrible but sublime past.

'I do,' she answered. They shook hands. Others approaching, he drifted away. Her glance followed him like a beneficent influence.

For three days she had carried in her pocket an envelope containing a bank-note for a hundred pounds, intending by some device to force it on him as a parting gift. Now the last chance was lost, and she had not even attempted this difficult feat of charity. Such futility, she reflected, self-scorning, was of a piece with her life. 'He hasn't really gone. He hasn't really gone,' she kept repeating, and yet knew well that he had gone.

'Do you know what they are saying, Anna?' said Beatrice, when, after eleven o'clock, the bazaar was closed to the public, and the stall-holders and their assistants were preparing to depart, their movements hastened by the stern aspect of the town-hall keeper.

'No. What?' said Anna; and in the same moment guessed.

'They say old Titus Price embezzled fifty pounds from the building fund, and Henry made it up, privately, so that there shouldn't be a scandal. Just fancy! Do you believe it?'

The secret was abroad. She looked round the room, and saw it in every face.

'Who says?' Anna demanded fiercely.

'It's all over the place. Miss Dickinson told me.'

'You will be glad to know, ladies,' Mynors' voice sang out from the platform, 'that the total proceeds, so far as we can calculate them now, exceed five hundred and twenty-five pounds.'

There was clapping of hands, which died out suddenly.

'Now, Agnes,' Anna called, 'come along, quick; you're as white as a sheet. Good-night, Mrs Sutton; good-night, Bee.'

Mynors was still occupied on the platform.

The town-hall keeper extinguished some of the lights. The bazaar was over.

CHAPTER FOURTEEN

End of a Simple Soul

The next morning, at half-past seven Anna was standing in the garden-doorway of the Priory. The sun had just risen, the air was cold; roof and pavement were damp; rain had fallen, and more was to fall. A door opened higher up the street, and Willie Price came out, carrying a small bag. He turned to speak to some person within the house, and then stepped forward. As he passed Anna she sprang forth.

'Oh!' she cried, 'I had just come up here to see if the workmen had locked up properly. We have some of our new furniture in the house, you know.' She was as red as the sun over Hillport.

He glanced at her. 'Have *you* heard?' he asked simply.

'About what?' she whispered.

'About my poor old father.'

'Yes. I was hoping – hoping you would never know.'

By a common impulse they went into the garden of the Priory, and he shut the door.

'Never know?' he repeated. 'Oh! they took care to tell me.'

A silence followed.

'Is that your luggage?' she inquired. He lifted up the handbag, and nodded.

'All of it?'

'Yes,' he said. 'I'm only an emigrant.'

'I've got a note here for you,' she said. 'I should have posted it to the steamer; but now you can take it yourself. I want you not to read it till you get to Melbourne.'

'Very well,' he said, and crumpled the proffered envelope into his pocket. He was not thinking of the note at all. Presently he asked: 'Why didn't you tell me about my father? If I had to hear it, I'd sooner have heard it from you.'

'You must try to forget it,' she urged him. 'You are not your father.'

'I wish I had never been born,' he said. 'I wish I'd gone to prison.'

Now was the moment when, if ever, the mother's influence should be exerted.

'Be a man,' she said softly. 'I did the best I could for you. I shall always think of you, in Australia, getting on.'

She put a hand on his shoulder. 'Yes,' she said again, passionately: 'I shall always remember you – always.'

The hand with which he touched her arm shook like an old man's hand. As their eyes met in an intense and painful gaze, to her, at least, it was revealed that they were lovers. What he had learnt in that instant can only be guessed from his next action. . . .

Anna ran out of the garden into the street, and so home, never looking behind to see if he pursued his way to the station.

Some may argue that Anna, knowing she loved another man, ought not to have married Mynors. But she did not reason thus; such a notion never even occurred to her. She had promised to marry Mynors, and she married him. Nothing else was possible. She who had never failed in duty did not fail then. She who had always submitted and bowed the head, submitted and bowed the head then. She had sucked in with her mother's milk the profound truth that a woman's life is always a renunciation, greater or less. Hers by chance was greater. Facing the future calmly and genially, she took oath with herself to be a good wife to the man whom, with all his excellences, she had never loved. Her thoughts often dwelt lovingly on Willie Price, whom she deemed to be pursuing in Australia an honourable and successful career, quickened at the outset by her hundred pounds. This vision of him was her stay. But neither she nor anyone in the Five Towns or elsewhere ever heard of Willie Price again. And well might none hear! The abandoned pitshaft does not deliver up its secret. And so – the Bank of England is the richer by a hundred pounds unclaimed, and the world the poorer by a simple and meek soul stung to revolt only in its last hour.

THE POTTERIES: A SKETCH

North of a line drawn from the Wash to the beak of Carnarvon,* and due south of the Trent's source,* lies a tract of country some seven miles long by four at its widest, bearing in shape a rough similarity to the contour of England, less Cornwall and Devon. Its face is an unbroken alternation of hillock and valley, the highest hills scarcely reaching 300 feet, and in the whole of it there is no river broader than a brook.

This is the home of pottery. Five contiguous towns, whose red-brown bricks have inundated the moorland like a succession of great lakes strung together by some St Lawrence* of a main road, devote themselves, with several smaller townships, to the manufacture from their own and other clays of every sort of earthenware, china and porcelain. In these parts the sound of the shattering of an earthen vessel, elsewhere unpleasing to the housewife's ear, is music; for upon the frequency of such fractures all the world over the welfare, almost the very existence, of the inhabitants chiefly depends. The towns are mean and ugly in appearance – sombre, shapeless, hard-featured, uncouth; and the vaporous poison of their ovens and chimneys has soiled and shrivelled the surrounding greenness of Nature till there is no country lane within miles but what presents a gaunt travesty of rural charms. Nothing could be more prosaic than the aspect of the huddled streets; nothing more seemingly remote from romance. Yet romance dwells even here, though unsuspected by its very makers – the romance which always attends the alchemic processes of skilled, transmuting labour. The infrequent poet may yield himself to its influence as, wandering on the scarred heights above the densest of the smoke-wrack, he suddenly comprehends the secret significance of the vast, effective Doing which here continually goes forward; the stranger who is being conducted through some 'works' may vaguely divine a miracle while he watches the slow transformations of the tortured clay from the pug-mill to the long room, where, amid chatter and clatter, young girls smooth the finished ware with knives; the dreaming native may get a nameless thrill when in an unfamiliar street the low thunder of subterranean machinery or a glimpse of the creative craftsman through a dark window startles his sleepy senses. But these appreciations are exceptional enough to prove the main fact that the nimbus of romance beautifying the squalor, softening the coarseness of all this indispensable work, shines unperceived.

Because they seldom think, the townsmen take shame when indicted for having disfigured half a county in order to live. They do not see that this disfigurement is just an incident in the unending warfare of man and Nature, and calls for no contrition. Here, indeed, is Nature repaid for some of her notorious cruelties. She imperiously bids man sustain and reproduce himself, and this is one of the places where in the act itself of obedience he insults and horribly maltreats her. To go out beyond the municipal confines where, in the thick of the altercation, the subsidiary industries of coal and iron prosper amid a wreck of verdure, ought surely to raise one's estimate not only of man but of Nature: so thorough and ruthless is his havoc of her, and so indomitable her ceaseless recuperation. The struggle is grim, tremendous, heroic; on the one side a wresting from Nature's own bowels of the means to waste her; on the other an undismayed, enduring fortitude, with now and then a smart return blow in the shape of a mine-explosion or a famine. And if here man has made of the very daylight an infamy, he can boast that he adds to the darkest night the weird beauty of fire, and flame-tinted cloud. From roof and hill you may see on every side furnace calling to furnace with fiery tongues and wreathing messages of smoke across the blue-red glow of acres of burning ironstone. The unique pyrotechnics of labour atoning for its grime!

This race of contemners of Nature bears the inevitable characteristics of its environment. It is harsh in dialect, religion, and sport; indifferent to visible loveliness, but delighting in the beauty of sound, especially the sound of brass bands and human song, and singing naturally – like the Elizabethans; cunning ('No people whatever are esteemed more subtle,' said Plott,* in the seventeenth century); striving and scornful of the languid South; thriving in spite of those deep-rooted intestinal jealousies which for a thousand years hindered any advance upon a system of local government invented by Alfred. But what stands out most saliently is the ancient instinctive sympathy – at once the fruit and the one monument of immemorial tradition – which the people have for their craft. Even in the mother-town, whose borders have yielded clay to the potter since before the beginning of history, there is no palpable trace of an unrivalled antiquity, unless it be a squat church tower, black and grey with eight centuries of smoke. The past lives solely, and lives perhaps sufficiently, in that exquisite accord between workman and work which everywhere manifests itself and which only the longest use could have so perfected.

CLAY IN THE HANDS OF THE POTTER*

Although the world, when it takes any interest at all in the Five Towns, identifies the district with clay, I do not think that I have ever seen Five Towns children playing at being potters. At the period when local history begins, earthen vessels were being made in the Five Towns, and certainly there is an unbroken record of at least twelve hundred years of pottery manufacture down there; it is equally certain that I myself have the clay in my blood, for my grandfather had the reputation of unsurpassed skill as a 'turner', and scores of my forbears must, like him, have earned a living by the actual handling of clay. Yet I never felt any curiosity concerning the great staple industry – surely one of the oldest of man's crafts – until I was twenty-nine or thirty, when I wanted some information about it for a novel. The fact is that half the people of the Five Towns have no knowledge of the industry, and are quite content in their ignorance. The industry goes on behind the long, many-windowed mysterious walls of innumerable manufactories, and the ignorant half pass up and down the façades of those buildings, and let the matter go at that. They see neither the raw clay, which is brought by sea and canals from afar off, nor the finished articles, which leave the works hidden in straw-stuffed crates. And if you want to buy a plate or a cup and saucer, there is positively no worse equipped place in the civilized world. This is, no doubt, human.

But when at last I did put myself to the trouble of visiting and comprehending a modern earthenware manufactory – it belonged to one of my uncles,* and he was very proud of his new machinery – the gateway of romance was opened to me. I saw, as it were, in a sudden revelation, what a wonderful, ticklish, sensitive, capricious, baffling, unreasonable substance is clay. I could appreciate why its behaviour under handling had puzzled a whole province for a dozen centuries and more, and still puzzles.

In my uncle's manufactory some two hundred individuals

spend their lives in trying to get the better of clay, with or without the aid of machinery. The machinery, in my opinion, despite my relative's pride in it, was not essentially very important; it only bullied the clay by physical force, or divided it into mathematically equal quantities, or shaped it into certain simple forms. The machinery was pretentious and blustering; it never helped in a real difficulty.

In an earthenware manufactory they have, after twelve centuries, thoroughly learnt one lesson, namely, that clay is a living thing, and therefore enigmatic. Indeed, it presents so many enigmas that the potters have had to divide their forces and attack the creature by instalments. A plate may appear to you to be a ridiculously simple article; and you think that if you had to make it, you would just dig up the right sort of clay, fashion it, and then burn it. But the right sort of clay does not naturally exist. The basis of every earthenware manufactory is a workshop where bearded and reverend men thoughtfully examine several different natural sorts of clay, and cause them to be mixed together by the brute force of machines, in the hope that the produce will be white and serviceable. These men are grey – they have grown grey in the vain study of bits of their mother-earth, which still not seldom play them tricks – and they are the descendants of similar men. And by their side you will see a youth or two, watching them and helping, and picking up notions of the exceeding 'plaguiness' of clay. And the hair of these youths, too, will turn, and the clay will still be inventing new problems for them.

These men have naught to do with the shaping of clay. They would be capable of looking at a plate and saying: 'What is this? I have never seen such a thing!' Their affair is only with clay in the shapeless mass.

Another set of men take up the attack when the time comes for persuading clay to assume definitive forms. And these men and their boys and their women-helpers correspond better than the first group with your conventional idea of the potter. Their fingers really are manipulating a pale malleable substance which you would at once recognize as clay. Machinery helps them, but merely as a brainless servant. In many manufactures the man is the servant of the machine; it will probably never be so in pottery. The fingers of these men and boys are finer tools than any wood or metal could be. See the boy pull off a piece of clay from the big lump and roll it; watch his fingers – that boy's fingers might be twelve hundred years old in skill. Look away and then look back, and lo! what was a hunch of clay is a little plate, and there is no clay left over. The boy had pulled off precisely the right quantity of clay for a vessel of which the dimensions had to conform precisely to a pattern.

See the man gazing at the plate, caressing it with a healing touch, and pushing it aside. See the man near by making a mug with his fingers over a revolving table. The mug grows like a flower; the man seems to be drawing it upwards by magic out of the table. The table comes to a standstill – and there the mug is, perfect! See the minor workers carrying off these soft and fragile vessels with apparent casualness. If you or I touched one of them, the result would be ruin. These people, however, understand clay – as well as clay can be understood – in that particular stage of its career. Their sympathy with clay shaped but unfired is the slow result of all those centuries. But their sympathy goes no farther than that. The idiosyncrasies of clay under fire are beyond their ken.

And we come back to yet another set of students of clay, the men who imprison the clay – now in the form of vessels, but entirely useless as such – in a vast fiery inferno, the men who victimize clay, who change clay so effectually that it can by no chemical process ever be changed back again to its original state. These men are more mystically priest-like than the others. They often work at night. Once a job is begun, they never under any consideration leave it till it is finished. A single indiscretion, and thousands of pounds' worth of moulded clay may be rendered futile and valueless. And they themselves do not know what is going on in the inferno which they have created. They can only hope that the clay under the ordeal of fire is not behaving too obstreperously, for it is obvious that they may not enter their own inferno to see how affairs are moving. They have to guess. They are very good guessers. They have been guessing since before the Norman Conquest of England. But a guess remains a guess. And when they let the fire die down, their pessimism or their optimism asserts itself, and during the cooling period torments or enheartens them. The cooling period is long – nearly a couple of days – and even then the ovens are too hot that you or I could not enter them without fainting. But the potter, stripped to the waist, enters nonchalantly the ghostly interior, lined and piled with pale martyred vessels, and carries them out in parcels, and at last, in the light of day, the experts can regard the clay and decide whether it has beaten them again. It always does beat them to a certain extent. What is this yellow stain on this teapot? Nobody can tell. A caprice of the clay, the clay's freakish protest against fire. Sometimes a whole ovenful of stuff is damaged, sometimes only a small percentage; but never, never does the entire consignment of clay behave as it was expected to behave and as it ought to behave.

And even now your simple, easy-looking plate is far from achieved. It looks rather more like whitewashed dog-biscuit than a plate. It generally has to be decorated – at any rate, it has to be glazed – and it has to go through the ordeal of fire at least once more – perhaps twice more. And each further process is a new opportunity for the clay to prove its intractableness and its unforseeableness. And each further process is presided over by lifelong students of just that particular part of the clay's evolution. Even the packer, sitting among straw and wrapping up each piece separately and protecting the clay from itself, has to know quite a lot about the wilfulness of earthenware when subjected to certain strains. Earthenware will often maintain itself intact in a railroad smash, only to shatter in the delicate touch of a general servant aged nineteen. Have you not heard her say: 'Please'm, the handle came off in my hand.' To the very last, clay is incalculable.

Decoration plays a more and more important part in the staple industry of the Five Towns. Housewives want gayer and more gilded crockery, and they also want to pay less for it. Hence the invention of cheaper methods of more gorgeous decoration. Now, clay is not so restive under decoration as might be imagined. But the antics played by fire on the colour-substances cause difficulties which rival the original difficulties due to the natural perverseness of the clay itself. And all this part of the manufacture is less interesting to the workman than the handling of the clay. It is an affair of the mechanical transfer of patterns designed elsewhere, and the mechanical application of pigments for which distant and unknown chemists are alone responsible. Nevertheless, the simpler and better forms of decoration remain, and with them the unspoilt human interest that is inseparable from them. For instance, round the edge of that plate there may be a couple of rings of colour, one broad and the other narrow. In the Five Towns this is called 'band-and-line' decoration. It seems, on the plate, to be too miraculously perfect for human accomplishment. And yet it was done by hand, and by a young woman's hand, and will probably always be so done.

In the manufactories, the painting-shops, where the band-and-line goes forward, are the quietest and, as a rule, the cleanest of all the shops – often very noticeably more spick-and-span than the den in which the head of the enterprise conducts his wholesale schemes. For these painting-shops are under the dominion of young women who have an enormous idea of themselves as factors in the universe. You may see them, if you arise soon enough, on the early tram-cars and trains, or walking primly down the streets. They are very neat. They wear gloves – the supreme insignia of rank in these worlds within the world. Nay, I have seen them wearing kid gloves. They carry a small covered wicker-basket, which basket contains their dinner. They arrive at the 'pot-bank' – as an earthenware manufactory is called in the Five Towns – and, lifting their skirts over the impurities that disfigure most parts of it, they reach their own sacred fastness, and put away their street things and don a large white apron – and when I say white I mean white. They then attend to their brushes and their colours, and they sit down, each of them, to a tiny revolving table, with a pile of plates or saucers or cups or mugs at one hand.

See them take a vessel and with one unerring gesture plant it exactly in the centre of the table. See them take a broad brush and hold it firmly and gently against the edge of the now spinning vessel. The 'band' is made; it is made in a second! A thinner brush, and with equal precision the line is made. And that vessel is pushed off the table, and another pushed on. And then another, and then another. Dozens! Scores! Hundreds! And then a bell rings, or a hooter hoots, for one o'clock. And the young woman rises, goes elsewhere, primly eats her dinner, perhaps goes for a little walk. And when the next bell rings, or the next hooter hoots, she sits down again, and the table begins to revolve again. More dozens! More scores! More hundreds! At six o'clock she departs, gloved and hatted and mantled, and primly takes her tram-car or train, or perhaps walks home.

The next morning she starts afresh on exactly the same task. For you must remember that there are in existence millions upon millions of vessels decorated with band-and-line, and that they have all of them been painted separately by young women seated at revolving tables. It is a wondrous and a dreadful thought, but it is part of the singular romance of clay. The skill for the task is soon learnt. The task is monotonous in the highest degree. It is endless. You might suppose that its monotony and its endlessness would drive these young women into some form of lunacy or melancholia. But no! The vocation merely endows them with a sort of benignant placidity. Their faces are like no other faces, their movements like no other movements. Such intellect as they have may not be highly developed, but they possess qualities of calm, of patience, even of mild spiritual dignity which are – well, nun-like! They are among the most curious products of industrialism, and among the most curious by-products of the Odyssey of clay.

No person of imagination who has taken the trouble to follow with intelligence the Odyssey of clay, from its stratum in the earth to its apotheosis on the domestic table, can pick up a simple plate without a certain emotion. The clay of it is indeed dead, but what adventures led up to its fiery demise, and what human associations are imbedded in its everlasting rigidity! Strange, that Five Towns children do not play at being potters!

MY RELIGIOUS EXPERIENCE

In my native town there were four principal churches of the Church of England and five principal chapels of Nonconformity.* We Nonconformists had a double attitude towards the churches. Socially we admired and envied them. So much so that we often preferred to go to them for the religious ceremony of marriage, whereas we might have been just as securely married elsewhere. Religiously we despised Church of Englanders. They were not in our eyes so ineffably wicked or inexcusably misguided as Roman Catholics; but they were pretty far gone in error, wilful or stupid. Indeed, it was impossible to trust certain Nonconformist preachers, and especially lay preachers, without being convinced that all Church of Englanders were on the sure way to everlasting damnation.

For Nonconformists of whatever sect were generally agreed on this: that to keep out of hell it was absolutely necessary to be 'converted'. Good morals, good works, were futile without conversion. It was no use being born in the belief that Christ died on the cross for sinners; you had to be 'born again', you had suddenly to see a mystic light, under the influence of which you believed with a new and immeasurably intenser belief. Church of Englanders condemned this experience as being allied to hysteria. Nonconformists pitied them for their blindness.

The double attitude of Nonconformity towards the Established Church puzzled, and offended, such unsubtle minds as my own. Further, considering that comparatively few persons were converted, it followed that the vast majority of the citizens were damned. And whenever as a child I thought about the matter at all I smiled malevolently to think that at least 90 per cent of the wayfarers on pavements and in tram-cars would in due course join me in Hades, in spite of the fact that all of them had some religion. For in the seventies and eighties of the last century there were almost no 'atheists' in our town. And if anybody did by chance ostentatiously deny the God of the Bible, sure enough he – I say 'he' because female atheists were utterly unknown – he would one day, and soon rather than late, get himself converted in a manner equally ostentatious.

I will not say that I flouted the dogma of the Wesleyan Methodist sect. I suppose that I passively accepted it. But my acceptance of it had no emotional quality. The notion of being converted was very repugnant to me. I preferred damnation to conversion, as being less humiliating. The arguments in favour of the dogma did not make much appeal to me; nor was I impressed by the mentality of the individuals who marshalled those arguments before my attention. My counter-arguments (brought forward only in strictly private boy-to-boy debates) were painfully crude but rather effective. As for example: 'If God is omniscient He knows whether I am going to heaven or hell. If He knows, the question is already decided. If it is already decided, what does it matter what I do?' Although the answer to this argument is quite simple and plausible, nobody ever suggested it to me. True, I did not dare to submit the point to the mighty.

Nothing happened in my childhood to foster in me any religious faith. And there were many things calculated to destroy faith. One of these was the fact that some of the pillars of the chapel had a rather dubious reputation for commercial integrity. Dishonest myself, and unsaved, I was cruelly uncompromising in my verdicts on the conduct of the saved. But one thing that most damaged in me the chances of a secure religious belief was the religious misbehaviour of my father. So far as I can remember I never had any religious instruction at home. My father compelled us to go to chapel and Sunday school, but for many years he did not go to Sunday school himself, and he very seldom went to chapel. On the rare occasions when he did decide to go to evening chapel the avowed word ran round the house: 'Pa is going to chapel.' And it was as though chapel ought to be grateful for his condescension.

Such a state of affairs was bound to give unreality to all professions of religious faith. We children felt that religious observance was imposed upon us, not for religious but for disciplinary reasons. And this suspicion, or certainty, made Sunday all the more odious to us. Sunday was the worst day of the week, anticipated with horror, and finished with an exquisite relief. Two attendances at Sunday school and two religious services in a day! About six hours in durance, while my father either lay in bed or read magazines in the bow window! It was inevitable that religion should come to be unalterably connected in my mind with the ideas of boredom, injustice, and insincerity.

And sometimes the offence was outrageous. As when a minister had the monstrous and callous effrontery to institute a Bible class for boys on the Saturday half-holiday. The resentment which I felt at this innovation, and at my father's upholding of it, burns in my mind today. It was surpassed only by my resentment against a sudden capricious paternal command that we children should say our prayers at our mother's knee. There was, for me, something revolting in the sentimentality, the story-bookishness, of this injunction! Anyhow we loathed the act, which filled us with shame. Nobody could possibly in the history of the world have been in a mood more fatal to prayer than I was in the moments when I obeyed the command. I used to say bitterly to myself: 'He likes to see us doing it.' This did not, however, affect my general attitude towards prayer. Neither before nor since did I ever say a prayer with the slightest hope of it being answered.

When at the age of twenty-one I left home for London, one of the leading thoughts in my head was that I should be free of chapels and Sunday schools, and the desolation of Sabbaths. Such was the main result of my father's education of me in ceremonial religion, acting on my mocking and sceptical temperament. I had no religious beliefs and I was profoundly inimical to all manifestations of religion. In various other ways my father's influence on me was admirable, and I owe a great deal to it. I regret that I should have to lay stress on that part of his training in which he failed.

[illegible] with the stamp of [illegible] and [illegible].

[illegible]

[illegible]

[illegible]

NOTES

These notes explain words, phrases, quotations and allusions whose meaning or source are not immediately clear from their context. Words and phrases (including dialect terms) that can be found in *Chambers Dictionary* (1993 edn) are not annotated unless Bennett uses them in special ways. Information on known or putative originals of the Staffordshire locations and people mentioned in the novel can be found in Appendix 1. Technical terms related to the pottery industry are only annotated if their meaning is not explained in the text or in Bennett's own footnotes. References to Methodist history, practices and organizations are explained in these notes, but further background information is given in Appendix 2.

The volumes of Bennett's letters and journals are abbreviated as *L* and *J* (see Suggestions for Further Reading for publication details). Bennett is referred to as AB. The *Oxford English Dictionary* (2nd edn, 1989) is referred to as *OED*. For other books mentioned, the place of publication is London unless otherwise stated.

Dedication

Herbert Sharpe: (1861–1925), pianist, teacher and composer and from 1884 Professor at the Royal College of Music, was a close friend of AB, who met him through Frederick Marriott, in whose Chelsea house he was a lodger from 1891–8.

Epigraph

Therefore . . . hearts: William Wordsworth (1775–1850), 'Michael' (1800), ll. 34–6. AB was reading the poem in June 1901, just after finishing *Anna* and described it as 'one of the great English poems' (*L*ii 158).

Chapter 1

p. 5 prize-books bound in vivid tints: Sunday school prize-books, many of them published for the purpose by Methodist and other religious organizations, often had brightly coloured covers.

p. 5 Connexional buildings: John Wesley (1703–91), the founder of

Methodism, used the word 'connexion' to describe those associated with him in his religious work; among his followers it came to have the sense of 'religious society' or 'denomination'.

p. 5 chapel-keeper: caretaker of the chapel.

p. 6 men's Bible-class: the class, meeting regularly for prayer, bible-study or religious discussion, was a key feature of Methodism from its earliest days. Separate classes were held for men and women. See also AB's note, p. 112 and Appendix 2.

p. 7 sewing-meeting: group meetings for sewing (and gossip) became an important element in the social life of Methodism in the late nineteenth century. See Appendix 2.

p. 7 'Where *two or three* are gathered together': Matthew 18:21.

p. 8 potter's valuer and commission agent: Alderman Sutton transacts business on commission for pottery manufacturers, acting as a middleman between factory and retail outlet.

p. 10 *Janey's Sacrifice or the Spool of Cotton*: I have not been able to trace a book with this title, which is characteristic of its type.

p. 12 'Money'll do owt'; that was the proverb: the *Oxford Dictionary of English Proverbs* (3rd edn, 1970) cites a number of versions of this proverb, including W. Gamage, *Linsey-Woolsey* (1613): 'The prouerbe is, Dame Mony can do All' (p. 540).

p. 12 *The Emperor's Hymn*: composed in 1797 by Joseph Haydn (1732–1809) in honour of Francis of Austria (1768–1835), who as Francis II reigned as Holy Roman Emperor 1892–1806, and as Francis I was Emperor of Austria 1804–35. It was used as the national hymn of Austria until 1918 and thereafter as the German national anthem with the words 'Deutschland über alles'. In England it is usually sung to the words 'Glorious things of thee are spoken'.

p. 13 Alfred's England: Alfred reigned as King of Wessex 871–900.

p. 14 gillyflowers: flowers with the scent of cloves.

p. 15 Hanbridge circuit: at the Methodist conference in 1756 the country was first divided into circuits, each served by a group of itinerant preachers. Circuits grew into a major organizational element within Methodism, appointing their own ministers and having a Superintendent and other officers, in which capacity Tellwright serves.

Chapter 2

p. 18 **the rent £30:** in spite of his wealth Tellwright chooses to live in one of the cheaper houses on Trafalgar Road.

p. 19 **Free Library:** the Public Libraries Act of 1850 empowered borough councils with populations of over 10,000 to levy a halfpenny rate in order to provide a free library service. In 1855 the rate was increased to 1d and the population limit lowered to 5,000, before being removed altogether in 1866. Burslem adopted the Act in 1863, and the Free Library (which was housed in the Wedgwood Institute) opened in 1870, with a stock of 1,500 books. There were at that time 25,000 people in Burslem and there were 15,000 issues in the first year.

p. 20 **erysipelas:** an inflammatory skin disease, also called St Anthony's Fire.

p. 20 **the Old Guard of Methodism ... Primitive Methodist Secession of 1808 ... Warren affrays of '28 ... Fly-Sheets in '49:** See Appendix 2.

p. 20 **Atonement:** the doctrine relating to Christ's redemptive power and the expiation of sins.

p. 20 **Bethesda:** Bethesda was a healing pool in Jerusalem (see John 5: 2–4); it was a name frequently used for Nonconformist chapels. See Appendix 1.

p. 21 **puerperal fever:** a fever following childbirth, often caused by insanitary conditions attending the birth; a major cause of maternal death in the nineteenth century.

p. 23 **eleemosynary:** charitable.

p. 23 **orchestra ... singing-seat:** the part of the chapel, sometimes a gallery, where the choir sits. AB's use of 'singing-seat' is cited as an example in the *OED*.

Chapter 3

p. 26 **encaustic tiles:** tiles on which inlaid patterns of different coloured clays have been burnt in.

p. 26 **an:** have.

p. 27 **Brussels carpet:** a carpet similar to Wilton, but with a backing made of cheaper materials. It was introduced into England from Belgium in the 1740s and was manufactured in this country from the 1830s.

p. 27 **'The Light of the World':** a painting (1851–3) by William Holman

Hunt (1827–1910), exhibited at the Royal Academy in 1854 and now in Keble College, Oxford. (A later version is in St Paul's Cathedral.) Its frame carries the words: 'Behold, I stand at the door, and knock; if any man hear my voice and open the door, I will come in to him, and will sup with him, and he with me' (Revelations 3:20). It depicts Christ holding a lantern and knocking at a door. An engraving by W. H. Simmonds was published in 1858, but many other reproductions were available and were common in households throughout England.

p. 27 a patent gas-saving mantle: gas lighting was installed in the Potteries in the 1820s. It is typical of Tellwright that he should install a device to lower the cost of gas.

p. 28 Woodfall's *Landlord and Tenant*, Jordan's *Guide to Company Law*, *Whitaker's Almanack* and a Gazetteer of the Five Towns: William Woodfall's *The Law of Landlord and Tenant* was first published in 1802; by 1889 it had reached its 14th edition. The guide to company law published by Jordan and Co. first appeared in 1867. *Whitaker's Almanack*, published annually since 1868, gives general information about the governments, finance and population of the world. *Keates's Gazetteer and Directory of the Staffordshire Potteries, Newcastle and District* was published in Hanley under various titles by Keates and Co. from 1865 to 1893. It was the *Gazetteer* from 1876.

p. 28 what-not: a small piece of furniture with shelves for displaying ornaments.

p. 28 Government stock . . . Toft End Colliery and Brickworks Ltd . . . North Staffordshire Railway Company . . . Five Towns Waterworks Company Limited: Government stock, paying a steady and reliable but comparatively low return, is clearly less attractive to Tellwright than his shrewd investments in key utilities serving the expanding economy of the Potteries.

p. 29 pun: pounds.

p. 29 till: than.

p. 29 shardrucks: heaps of shards, or pieces of broken pottery.

p. 30 learn: teach; this was formerly a standard meaning, but is now regarded as incorrect.

p. 32 specs: speculations.

p. 35 weighing platform: a wide, low platform for weighing heavy loads of pottery.

p. 35 **saggars:** a fire-proof clay box or vessel in which pottery is packed before firing in a kiln.

p. 36 **paintresses:** see notes to pp. 99–100.

p. 37 **bank:** see AB's note; short for 'potbank', a pottery. AB's use of the word in this sense is cited as an example in *OED*.

Chapter 4

p. 40 **Revival:** a campaign to reaffirm or reawaken religious feeling in a chapel or community.

p. 40 **Wesleyan Methodist Society:** 'Society' was a term used by Wesley himself for local groups (congregations or chapels) of Methodists.

p. 42 **Joseph . . . Potiphar's wife:** Genesis 39: 7–23; the wife of Joseph's Egyptian employer attempts to seduce him and has him imprisoned when he rejects her advances. This part of Joseph's story would clearly make an unsuitable picture for a chapel building.

p. 43 **She had not been converted:** see the discussion of Anna's religious position in Appendix 2.

Chapter 5

p. 48 **landau:** a carriage with a folding top; compare AB's comment on the Suttons' carriage, p. 7.

p. 49 **mysen:** myself.

p. 49 **dunna':** do not.

p. 51 **pew-holders:** people who pay rent for the exclusive use of a pew in a church or chapel.

p. 51 ***frou-frou*:** (French) a rustling, as of silk.

p. 52 **conventicles:** a conventicle has the sense of a secret or illegal religious meeting, such as those held by English dissenters or Scottish Presbyterians in the seventeenth century. Rural Methodism had its own character and clung to the original system of itinerant preachers as opposed to the fixed ministers of urban chapels. Perhaps AB uses the word here to suggest that they are less amenable to circuit control: though they are clearly willing enough to attend an urban revival service, perhaps because of their continuing adherence to the pure Methodist doctrine, which would include a strong emphasis on conversion.

p. 52 **Divine Dove:** the dove is a common image for the Holy Spirit; see

Matthew 3:16: 'and, lo, the heavens were opened unto him, and he saw the Spirit of God descending like a Dove.'

p. 53 **'Rock of Ages'**: a popular hymn with words by Augustus Montague Toplady (1740–78), an Anglican divine who engaged in controversy with John Wesley on the issue of Calvinism.

p. 53 **'Jesu, lover of my soul'**: a popular hymn with words by John Wesley's brother Charles (1707–88).

p. 54 **'I know that my Redeemer liveth'**: Job 19:25; an aria from *The Messiah* (1741), by George Frediric Handel (1685–1759).

p. 56 **cabinet photographs:** a photograph of a suitable size for displaying in a cabinet or frame, hence larger than the standard visiting-card size.

Chapter 6

p. 63 **hersen:** herself.

p. 64 **bested:** outwitted.

p. 64 **higgling-match:** bargaining.

p. 65 **a'most fast for brass:** almost out of ready money.

p. 66 **six-and-eightpences:** this sum – one-third of £1 – was a standard lawyer's fee in the nineteenth century.

p. 70 **'Blessed are the meek'**: Matthew 5:3.

p. 71 **It's o' this'n:** this is the situation *or* it's like this.

Chapter 7

p. 72 **Autumn Bazaar:** bazaars as a means of fund-raising and as social occasions were a popular feature of English Nonconformist life from the late nineteenth century. See Appendix 2.

p. 72 **thysen:** thyself.

p. 74 ***dernier cri***: (French) the last word; i.e., the latest fashion.

p. 79 **mantel-cloth:** a decorated or embroidered cloth, often with a fringe or tassels, to be draped over the mantelpiece of a fireplace.

p. 79 **'Nazareth'**: 'Jésus de Nazareth. Chant évangélique', by Charles Gounod (1818–93), with words by A. Porte, published in Paris in 1856. 'Nazareth. Sacred song' with words by H. F. Chorley ('Tho' poor be the chamber') for solo voice and piano accompaniment was published in London in 1862; another English version, by M.X. Hayes, was published in London in 1882. It was available in settings for a wide variety of forces, from solo piano to brass band. Gounod's sentimental religious songs were immensely popular in England in the late nineteenth century, and included a setting of 'There is a green hill far away' (1871). See Derek B. Scott, *The Singing Bourgeois: Songs of the Victorian Drawing Room and Parlour* (Milton Keynes: Open University Press, 1988), pp. 110–11.

p. 81 **Bursley pork-pie:** pork pies, made with short-crust pastry, are a speciality of many towns in the midlands and north of England.

p. 82 **anthem:** a musical piece written to be sung by the choir of a church or chapel rather than the whole congregation. Mynors has a good voice (p. 23) and may have taken a solo part.

p. 83 **circuit-stewards:** officers appointed annually by the Superintendent of the circuit to assist with organization and management.

p. 84 **lean hard . . . Miss Havergal:** Frances Ridley Havergal (1836–79) was a popular and prolific writer of hymns and religious poetry. In *Clayhanger* (Book I, Chapter 7) there is a reference to her 'little book *Lean Hard*'. Although I have not been able to trace this book or her specific use of the phrase, it may be one of the 'many small devotional tracts and narratives in prose' mentioned in her *Dictionary of National Biography* entry. Her works contain frequent references to the idea of leaning on Christ, as in the second verse of her hymn 'Another year is dawning': 'Another year of leaning / Upon thy loving breast'.

p. 84 **Isle of Man:** an increasingly popular holiday resort in the late nineteenth century, especially with visitors from the industrial areas of north England. By the end of the century the annual number of holidaymakers had risen to over 350,000. From 1883 onwards the Bennett family spent a few weeks there in July or August. It lies in the Irish Sea about thirty miles off the north-west coast of England and is approximately 220 square miles in area.

p. 84 **Sant's *The Soul's Awakening*:** James Sant (1820–1916) was an extremely prolific painter of portraits, allegorical female figures and genre subjects. He was created ARA in 1861 and RA in 1869; in 1872 he became portrait painter to the Queen, and her Principal Painter in Ordinary in 1878. He exhibited at the Royal Academy from 1840 to 1914, and the painting referred to here was shown in 1888. In Sant's *Times* obituary (13 July 1916, p. 11) *The Soul's Awakening* was described as a 'picture by which Sant is still known in hundreds of homes . . . a picture of which the sentimentality delighted the public'.

Alderman Sutton's enthusiasm for the painting is an implicit comment on his taste.

p. 85 a copper preserving-saucepan: for use in making jams, chutneys, etc.

p. 86 fire-irons: i.e., poker, tongs and shovel.

p. 86 common mustard tins: mustard in powder form is sold in small rectangular tins with rounded corners.

p. 86 Windsor chairs: a wooden chair of which the back is formed of upright rods held in place by a crosspiece.

p. 86 a list hearthrug: as described in text, 'list' is selvage or a piece of cloth.

p. 87 grocers' almanacs: calendars given to regular customers as a form of advertising.

p. 87 Gargantuan: from the giant with a huge appetite in *Gargantua* (1534) by François Rabelais (c. 1494–c. 1553).

p. 87 pattens: wooden clogs or shoes, sometimes with iron heels to raise the wearer above the ground.

p. 87 Persian: a breed of cat.

p. 87 Practice: a complex kind of multiplication using different denominations, as in the calculation of price per weight or length.

Chapter 8

p. 90 Whitsuntide: it was common for children and young people to have new clothes for the Whitsuntide (Pentecost) holiday in late May. Sunday-school outings and other treats often coincided with this holiday.

p. 90 the blue draft: at this time the drafts of legal documents were written on blue paper.

p. 94 obscene epithet: in spite of exhaustive research and the exercise of much imagination I have been unable to identify this expression.

p. 95 feast of St Monday: pottery workers frequently took an unofficial holiday on Monday either to recover from or continue with the indulgences of the weekend. Charles Shaw discusses the practice in *When I Was a Child* (1903; Seaford, Sussex: Caliban Books, 1977), pp. 185ff., where he relates it to the special nature of working conditions and industrial relations in the Potteries. Mynors' firmness about this practice is another feature marking him out as a modern employer.

p. 95 Providence: in the sense of God's care or intervention; an appropriate name given the precarious nature of the pottery industry, where it was possible for the owner of a small potbank to lose everything if a single firing went wrong.

p. 95 Minton's: Thomas Minton (1765–1836) was born in Shropshire and worked in London as an engraver for Josiah Spode. He moved to Stoke-on-Trent in 1789, and in 1793 he set up his own pottery business, which traded under a variety of names; it was known as 'Mintons' from 1858 to 1883 and 'Mintons Ltd' thereafter.

p. 96 swagger ware: high-quality pottery.

p. 97 batting-machine: a machine for stretching and pressing raw clay to the requisite thickness and diameter.

p. 97 hollow-ware pressers . . . flat pressers: hollow-ware is the term for bowls or tube-shaped pottery; flat-ware is plates and dishes. Steam-powered throwing and pressing machines (called 'jiggers' and 'jollies') were introduced early in the nineteenth century, often in the teeth of opposition from workers. Their use became more general after 1870 and, as a modern manufacturer, Mynors would certainly wish to have them in his factory.

p. 97 piece-work: work undertaken and paid for by the piece.

p. 97 clay . . . 'in the hands of the potter': see Bennett's essay with this title, reprinted in this volume; cf. Jeremiah 18:6: 'O house of Israel, cannot I do with you as this potter? saith the Lord. Behold, as the clay is in the potter's hand, so are ye in mine, O house of Israel.'

p. 97 Roman candle: a kind of firework.

p. 97 the dead genius: this is presumably Josiah Wedgwood (1730–95). His epitaph in St Peter's Church, Stoke-on-Trent describes how he 'converted a rude and inconsiderable manufactory into an elegant art, and an important part of national commerce'. His Etruria Works (now demolished), begun in 1767 on the banks of the Trent and Mersey Canal, set a pattern for a new kind of works design, which enabled him to apply the principle of division of labour. He was interested in scientific and technical experiment, and associated with Priestley, Boulton, Watt and Erasmus Darwin through the Birmingham Lunar Society. Steam engines by Boulton and Watt – the forerunners of Mynors' batting machine – were installed at the works between 1782 and 1800.

p. 99 *noblesse*: aristocracy.

p. 99 die of lead poisoning: AB's comment plays down a major health hazard. The lead in glazes might be absorbed through the skin in the dipping process; lead fumes or dust might be inhaled; and glaze or paint from paintresses' hands might find its way into their mouths or eyes. Blindness, epilepsy, paralysis and still births were among the recorded symptoms of lead-poisoning. The Factory Act of 1891 stipulated precautionary measures, but employers opposed the Act and the dispute was only resolved by arbitration in 1894 and further government intervention in 1898. In the years 1896–8, 1,085 cases of lead poisoning were notified in the Potteries, 607 of the victims being girls and women. By 1906, however, only seventy-six cases were notified in eight months.

p. 100 eighteen shillings a week: if she earns this every week (excluding holidays) Priscilla would have an annual income of between £40 and £50. In 1891 a cup- and saucer-maker earned between 25s and 27s a week, a hollow-ware presser between 28s and 35s and a thrower between 40s and 42s. See Harold Owen, *The Staffordshire Potter* (1901; Bath: Kingsmead Reprints, 1970). Compare Anna's recently acquired income of £3,300 per annum, although she continues to keep house for three on £1 per week.

p. 101 glost-firing: 'glost' is a dialect form of 'gloss', the lead-glaze used for pottery.

p. 101 Tophet: Hell; a site of human sacrifice near Jerusalem: see Jeremiah 19:6.

p. 101 mould-shop: in which the moulds for various shapes of vessels were made.

p. 101 so unhuman . . . human labour: this is the reading of the first edition; in subsequent impressions this was corrupted to 'so inhuman . . . inhuman labour'.

p. 103 gadding out: going out for pleasure.

Chapter 9

p. 105 Ivan the Terrible: the cruel and tyrannical Ivan IV (1530–84), the first Russian ruler to adopt the title of Tsar.

p. 105 income-tax: during the nineteenth century, direct taxation (as opposed to taxes on goods and services) was an increasing source of government revenue. Middle-class male householders, among those most likely to be liable for income tax, formed an influential part of the electorate, and any government wishing to stay in power would need to respect their views.

p. 105 the King can do no wrong: 'That the King can do no wrong, is a necessary and fundamental principle of the English constitution', Sir William Blackstone (1723–80), *Commentaries on the Lawes of England* (1765), Book 3, Chapter 17.

p. 107 truckling: behaving in a servile manner.

p. 107 as: that.

p. 107 bumbailiff: a sheriff's officer who made arrests, especially of debtors.

p. 107 bill of exchange: 'A written order by the writer or "drawer" to the "drawee" (the person to whom it is addressed) to pay a certain sum on a given date to the "drawer" or to a third person named in the bill, known as the payee' (*OED*).

p. 108 welly: see AB's footnote: a contraction of 'well nigh'.

p. 110 speak of angels: a euphemism for the proverbial 'Talk of the devil, and he is sure to appear'.

p. 114 florin: a silver coin worth two shillings.

p. 114 Shall we gather at the river?: Hymn by R. Lowry (1826–99), collected in *Sacred Songs and Solos* (1873 et seq.), usually regarded as the joint work of the prominent American evangelists Dwight L. Moody (1837–99) and Ira D. Sankey (1840–1908), but now known to be the work of Sankey alone. They had an extremely successful mission in England, Scotland and Ireland, which included a visit to the Staffordshire pottery towns during 1873–5.

p. 116 Bobby-Bingo: this children's game is known in several versions, some from Staffordshire, played to the following song: 'There *was* a farmer *had* a dog. / His name was Bobby Bingo. / B-i-n-g-o, B-i-n-g-o, B-i-n-g-o, / His name was Bobby Bingo.' The children stand in a ring, with one in the middle. 'In the Tean [Staffs] version, the one in the centre points, standing still, to some in the ring to say the letters B.I.N.G; the letter O has to be sung; if not, the one who says it goes in the ring, and repeats it all again until the game is given up. In the other Staffordshire version, when they stop, the one in the middle points to five of the others in turn, who have to say the letters forming "Bingo", while the one to whom O comes has to sing it on the note on which the others left off. Anyone who says the wrong letter, or fails to sing the O right, takes the place of the middle one' (Alice B. Gomme, *The Traditional Games of England, Scotland and Ireland*, vol. 1 (David Nutt, 1894), pp. 31–2).

p. 116 tut-ball: similar to rounders using a ball and no bat. Players hit the ball with their hands and have to run round a ring of 'tuts' or pieces of brick.

p. 116 tick: the game of tig or catch.

p. 116 leap-frog: a game in which one player bends over so that others can vault over his or her back.

p. 116 prison-bars: a game for two teams, each with its own base, the aim being to take prisoners by touching members of the opposing team when they leave their base.

p. 117 Eccles-cake: a sugared cake of short-crust pastry filled with currants and candied peel.

p. 117 Bath bun: a sweet bun containing candied peel and sultanas and sprinkled with sugar and peel.

p. 119 telephone: the first telephones were installed in the Potteries in 1862 and by 1863 there were offices in Stoke, Hanley, Burslem, Longton and Tunstall. By 1890 there were 211 private subscribers as well as widely distributed public call offices. As in his business, Mynors takes advantage of up-to-date technology.

Chapter 10

p. 121 Port Erin: a fishing village on the south-west coast of the island which grew rapidly in the late nineteenth century into a popular holiday resort.

p. 122 Llandudno, and all that sort of thing: Llandudno was a popular seaside resort on the North Wales coast; the Bennetts went there every year from 1878 to 1882.

p. 123 sauce: impudence.

p. 125 Lime Street Station, Liverpool: Liverpool's main station, built in 1868–71 to a design by Alfred Waterhouse.

p. 125 Bear's Paw: a restaurant, established in 1883, in the busy thoroughfare of Lord Street, on the route between Lime Street Station and the docks.

p. 125 Prince's landing-stage: after it was opened in 1857 passengers no longer had to be rowed out to steamers at low tide.

p. 125 Douglas: capital of the Isle of Man (replacing Castletown) from 1869. It was a popular seaside resort, particularly after improvements to its harbour and other services in the 1860s.

p. 122 the 'Mona's Isle': there are three candidates for the original of this ship: *Mona's Isle III* (330 feet, 1,563 tons, launched in 1882); *Mona's Queen II* (320 feet, 1,595 tons, 1885); and *Mona III* (324 feet, 1,212 tons, 1889). All three were paddle-steamers, as is the vessel described in the novel. Of the first two, A.W. Moore comments, 'Not only were these vessels some three-quarters of an hour faster than any of their predecessors – the "Mona's Isle" accomplished the passage between Liverpool and Douglas in three hours and thirty-five minutes – but they were much larger, and had more luxurious accommodation for passengers' (*An Historical Account of the Isle of Man Steam Packet Co. Limited, 1830–1904*, Douglas, Isle of Man, 1904, p. 32).

p. 126 New Brighton, Seaforth, and the Crosby and Formby light-ships: the first of these would lie on the port side as the ship leaves the Mersey for the Irish Sea; the other three would be on the starboard side, the light-ships marking dangerous sands north of Liverpool.

p. 126 Titanic: gigantic; the Titans were the older generations of gods whom Zeus supplanted.

p. 127 *malaise*: sea-sickness.

p. 127 the diminutive and absurd train: the steam train system operated by the Isle of Man Railway Company was completed in 1879. The south line, which ran through a mountainous area from Douglas via Ballasalla, Castletown and Colby to Port Erin, a journey of about sixteen miles, was opened to public traffic in August 1874.

p. 128 Tom Kelly: Kelly is one of the commonest surnames on the Isle of Man.

p. 128 their lodging: the party are probably staying in one of the recently erected guest houses above the cliff, high above the bay and with Bradda Head (see note p. 129) visible to the north.

p. 129 the Wesleyan Chapel on the hill leading to the Chasms: the party is probably going to the Howe Chapel on the Port Erin–Cregneish road. The Chasms are gigantic fissures, ranging in width from a few inches to several feet, running vertically down the face of the cliffs just below the village of Cregneish.

p. 129 Melton coats: a coat made out of strong woollen cloth manufactured in Melton Mowbray in Leicestershire.

p. 129 the high coast-range . . . Peel: Peel lies about ten miles north of Port Erin.

p. 129 Bradda: the southern terminal point of the range of peaks that runs north-east to south-west across the island. It rises to 766 feet above sea level.

p. 130 the little bay: one of the bays on the coast north of Port Erin; they soon turn northwards to climb Bradda.

p. 130 Port St Mary: on the eastern side of the island's south-west peninsula, opposite Port Erin.

p. 130 The Hill of the Night Watch: AB is presumably referring to Cronk ny Arrey Laa (Hill of the Morning, not Night, Watch) which is about three miles north of Bradda and rises to 1,449 feet.

p. 130 Castletown: second largest town on the island, and formerly the capital; about five miles north-east of the peak of Bradda.

p. 130 the lighthouse at Scarlet Point: south of Castletown and about five miles from where Anna and Henry are standing.

p. 130 Calf of Man . . . Calf Sound . . . Chicken Rock: an island of only 600 acres half a mile off the south-west tip of the Isle of Man, the Calf of Man is approached by the treacherous Calf Sound. Chicken Rock lies one mile south of the Calf of Man; its lighthouse, built in 1875, is 122 feet high and marks a dangerous tidal reef.

p. 131 the Mourne Mountains of Ireland: fifty miles due west of Port Erin.

p. 133 the 'Falcon': there is still a Falcon's Nest Hotel in Port Erin.

p. 134 a cabin partly excavated out of the rock: a cavity cut out of the cliff face, with wooden doors and used by Manx fishermen for storing their gear.

p. 135 coaming of the well: the raised edge of a shaft protecting the boat's pumps.

p. 135 carvel: a carvel-built boat has the planks laid flush to one another, as opposed to clinker-built, where they overlap.

p. 141 influenza: Mrs Sutton would have some causes to fear influenza, which at that time was often fatal. There was a serious epidemic in 1889, which spread from Russia over continental Europe to England and then the east coast of America. There were recurrences in 1891 (when the English midlands were especially badly affected) and 1892, when the outbreak in England was particularly severe.

p. 142 **Martinmas:** the feast of St Martin of Tours is celebrated on 11 November and was a day on which hiring fairs were often held. Traditionally, wages in the Potteries were negotiated at this time, a practice which in the nineteenth century led to a number of industrial disputes.

p. 144 **the jetty . . . the breakwater:** the breakwater was begun in 1864, with the intention of providing safe harbour at Port Erin. It was completely washed away during a severe storm in 1884, hence the reference on p. 145 to 'the ruined breakwater'.

Chapter 11

p. 148 **flitting about:** moving quickly from place to place (*OED*).

p. 150 **Crewe:** a major railway junction, about fifteen miles from Stoke-on-Trent.

p. 152 **hardy-headed:** usually 'hard-headed'; sensible, practical.

p. 155 **gravel:** gravel or stones in the kidneys or bladder.

p. 156 **coroner:** officer (usually a doctor or a lawyer) appointed by the court to preside over inquests into cases of sudden or suspicious death.

p. 158 ***cause célèbre*:** (French) famous case.

p. 158 **councillors:** the 1888 Local Government Act replaced the previous patchwork of local administration with over a hundred counties and county boroughs, each with an elected body of representative councillors.

p. 158 **guardians of the poor:** under the terms of the Poor Law Amendment Act of 1834, the administration of relief was entrusted to an elected Board of Guardians, assisted by salaried officials. Boards varied in the strictness with which they applied the terms of the 1834 Act and its successors. 'Guardians of the poor' could therefore be an ironical description.

p. 158 **members of the school board:** the 1870 Education Act stipulated that elementary schools, run by elected Boards, should be provided for every child in the country.

p. 159 **foreman . . . freemason . . . sidesman:** the foreman is the person elected by the members of the jury to address the court on their behalf. In this case the choice falls on a respectable tradesman, who is a member of a semi-secret society and a deputy churchwarden in the Anglican Church.

p. 160 Kensingtonian: Kensington was (and is) a fashionable area of west London. AB often uses this adjective, usually in a satirical manner.

p. 166 foreordained to damnation: see the discussion of Anna's religious position in Appendix 2.

p. 170 brazen moll: shameless; 'moll' is often 'prostitute', but here is presumably used in its general sense of 'girl' or 'woman'.

p. 171 sees the scamp on the sly: meets the rascal in secret.

Chapter 12

p. 174 Longshaw china: fine bone china made in Longton.

p. 179 a bat in the eye with a burnt stick: this saying was used by Bennett's father: see 'The Making of Me' in *Sketches for Autobiography*, ed. James Hepburn (Allen & Unwin, 1979), p. 4.

p. 182 It's a sign of a hard winter . . . when the hay runs after the horse: see AB's journal entry for 10 August 1899: 'I have just remembered a saying of Mrs Dunmer, our new housekeeper at Witley. She said to me: "There's a lot of old maids in this village, sir, as wants men. There was three of 'em after a curate as we had here, a very nice young gentleman he was, sir. No matter how often the church was opened those women would be there, sir, even if it was five times a day. It's a sign of a hard winter, sir, when the hay begins to run after the horse"' (*Ji* 93). No similar saying is listed in the *Oxford Dictionary of English Proverbs*.

p. 182 a two-foot: a rule measuring two feet.

p. 186 doubt: fear (*OED*).

p. 186 Holman Hunt's *Scapegoat*: see note p. 27; Hunt's painting exists in several versions, all dating from the mid to late 1850s. It depicts the biblical scapegoat as a symbol of expiation as described in Leviticus 16: 10, 22, and is appropriate to the situation of Willie Price, who is similarly about to be cast into the wilderness and perform an act of atonement.

p. 187 an assisted passage: by 1878 government-assisted passages for emigration to the colonies, available since the 1820s, had been withdrawn; it is possible that Willie receives assistance from a charitable (Methodist) source.

p. 187 Melbourne: the state capital of Victoria in Australia.

Chapter 13

p. 190 Bosley: dialect form of 'Bursley', indicating Tellwright's pronunciation.

p. 193 peddling: petty, of little consequence.

p. 196 steerage: the cheapest class of passenger on a ship, accommodated on a lower deck.

The Potteries: A Sketch

On 29 August 1897 Willie Boulton, who was engaged to AB's younger sister Tertia, drowned in a bathing accident. AB received the news in France on 2 September and immediately travelled to Burslem. His journal entry for 10 September reads as follows:

> During this week, when I have been taking early morning walks with Tertia, and when I have been traversing the district after dark, the grim and original beauty of certain aspects of the Potteries, to which I have referred in the introduction to "Anna Tellwright", has fully revealed itself for the first time. Before breakfast, on the heights of Sneyd Green, where the air blows as fresh and pure (seemingly) as at the seaside, one gets glimpses of Burslem and of the lands between Burslem and Norton, which have the very strangest charm. The stretch of road on which one stands, used by men and young women on their way to work, is sufficiently rural and untouched to be intrinsically attractive. It winds through pretty curves and undulations; it is of a good earthy colour and its borders are green and bushy. Down below is Burslem, nestled in the hollow between several hills, and showing a vague picturesque mass of bricks through its heavy pall of smoke. If it were an old Flemish town, beautiful in detail and antiquely interesting, one would say its situation was ideal. It is *not* beautiful in detail, but the smoke transforms its ugliness into a beauty transcending the work of architects and of time. Though a very old town, it bears no sign of great age – the eye is never reminded of its romance and history – but instead it thrills and reverberates with the romance of machinery and manufacture, the romance of our fight against nature, of the gradual taming of the earth's secret forces. And surrounding the town on every side are the long straight smoke and steam wreaths, the dull red flames, and all the visible evidence of the immense secular struggle for

> existence, the continual striving towards a higher standard of comfort.
>
> This romance, this feeling which permeates the district, is quite as wonderfully inspiring as any historic memory could be.
>
> And if the effects of morning are impressive, what shall be said of the night-scenes – of the flame-lit expanses bearing witness to a never-ceasing activity; the sky-effects of fire and cloud; and the huge dark ring of hills surrounding this tremendous arena. (*J*i 46–7)

These walks, perhaps because of the melancholy circumstances in which they were taken, had a great effect on AB, and form an important element in his 'discovery' of the Potteries as a literary subject. On 10 October 1897 he wrote to H.G. Wells:

> I am very glad to have your letter, & very glad to find that the Potteries made such an impression on you. I lived there till I was 21, & have been away from it 9 years, & only during the last few years have I begun to see its possibilities. Particularly this year I have [been] deeply impressed by it. It seems to me that there are immense possibilities in the very romance of manufacture – not wonders of machinery & that sort of stuff – but in the tremendous altercation with nature that is continually going on – & in various other matters. Anyhow I am trying to shove the notions into my next novel. Only it wants doing on a Zolaesque scale. I would send you a rough sketch of my somewhat vague ideas in this direction, but fear to bore you. To my mind it is just your field. As for the people, I know 'em inside out, & if you are a Northern man you would grasp them instinctively.
>
> I am quite sure there is an aspect of these industrial districts which is really *grandiose*, full of dark splendours, & which has been absolutely missed by all novelists up to date. . . .
>
> I trouble you with all this because you are the first man I have come across whom the Potteries has impressed, emotionally. There are a number of good men in the Potteries, but I have never yet met one who could be got to see what I saw; they were all inclined to scoff (*L*ii 90–91).

This essay clearly contributed to AB's vision of the Five Towns in *Anna*. Its relation to the corresponding passage in the novel is discussed in the Introduction (pp. xxxvi–xxxvii).

p. 200 **the Wash to the Beak of Carnarvon:** the Wash lies on the east coast of England, surrounded by the coasts of Lincolnshire and Norfolk. The beak of Carnarvon is the Lleyn Peninsula, due west of the Wash on the south side of Carnarfon Bay.

p. 200 the Trent's source: the Trent rises on Biddulph Manor, a few miles to the east of Stoke-on-Trent.

p. 200 the great lakes . . . St Lawrence: the Great Lakes on the St Lawrence River in Canada.

p. 201 Plott: Robert Plot (1640–96), an antiquary whose *The Natural History of Staffordshire* was published in 1686.

Clay in the Hands of the Potter

Although it postdates the publication of *Anna* by some years, this essay is included here because it is one of AB's few sustained pieces of writing about the pottery industry, and because it refers to some of the research he undertook when writing the novel.

p. 203 Title: see note on p. 97 above.

p. 203 modern earthenware manufactory . . . one of my uncles: AB's maternal aunt Frances was married to Ezra Bourne, a pottery manufacturer.

My Religious Experience

This essay postdates *Anna* by over twenty years, but the extract printed here (about a quarter of the full text) throws light on AB's early life in the Wesleyan Methodist community and provides interesting background to Anna's religious position (see Appendix 2).

p. 209 four principal churches . . . chapels of Nonconformity: the five Nonconformist chapels AB refers to are probably those of the Baptists, Congregationalists, Wesleyan Methodists, Primitive Methodists and the Methodist New Connexion. In the 1870s and 1880s, when AB was growing up, there were about twenty Nonconformist places of worship in and around Burslem, an indication of the extent to which Nonconformity dominated the area.

APPENDIX 1: PLACES AND PEOPLE IN *ANNA OF THE FIVE TOWNS*

(*Note*: In this appendix, references are discussed largely but not exclusively in the order in which they appear in the novel. The names of the places, people, etc. on which Bennett bases his fictional recreations are given in brackets. It may be assumed that, if a character or location is not mentioned here, I have not been able to identify an original with any certainty. The work of Louis Tillier and E. J. D. Warrillow has been particularly helpful, and full details of their books are given in Suggestions for Further Reading.)

Most of the action of the novel takes place in and around Bursley, Bennett's fictional recreation of Burslem. *Anna* opens in the yard of the Wesleyan Methodist Chapel at Duck Bank. This is based on Swan Bank, where the Bennett family worshipped and where Bennett himself attended Sunday school (see also Appendix 2). The 'Connexional buildings' (p. 5) surrounding this yard include the Sunday school and lecture-hall, settings for a number of later scenes in the novel (see pp. 60 and 111).

Anna, Agnes and Mynors soon move on to the 'latest outcome of municipal enterprise in Bursley' (p. 10), its new park on Moor Road (Moorland Road) which runs out to Moorthorne (Smallthorne). Burslem Park was opened to the public in August 1894, and Bennett's descriptions (see pp. 12–13) conform closely to its layout. It rises steeply east–west from 'the railway cutting' (p. 12) which served the now demolished Burslem Station to the 'street of small villas almost on the ridge of the hill' (p. 12), which is presumably Park Road. This street would no doubt be among the "new houses up by the park" (p. 214) where Ephraim thinks Anna and Henry should live after they are married. Since Tellwright owns most of the land on which this new development is taking place – and may indeed himself be one of the developers (p. 18) – he stands to make a considerable profit from the area. Laid out in a series of terraces, the Park still has many of the features mentioned in the novel: lodge, lake, waterfall, balustrades, shelters, bandstand. The scene Bennett is describing obviously takes place soon after the park has opened, because the crowds are inspecting these and other features they have read about in recent newspaper reports describing the new civic amenity.

From the highest terrace of the park Anna and her companions can see below them the whole expanse of what Bennett calls the Five Towns – Turnhill, Bursley, Hanbridge, Knype and Longshaw (Tunstall, Burslem, Hanley, Stoke and Longton). He omitted Fenton, the sixth town in the Potteries, because 'the sound of the phrase "Six Towns" is not so good as the phrase "Five Towns"' (quoted by Warrillow, *Arnold Bennett and Stoke-on-Trent*, p. 52). The six towns were federated in 1910 as the County Borough of Stoke-on-Trent, an event that forms part of the action of *The Old Wives' Tale*. Burslem itself became a chartered borough in 1878, and was governed from its town hall (formally opened in 1857), on whose spire a gold-covered copper angel representing civic victory can still be seen (p. 13).

The Tellwrights live on Trafalgar Road (Waterloo Road), a section of the spinal thoroughfare that connects all six towns. Waterloo Road runs from Burslem to Hanley, and was opened in 1817. It was laid out to commemorate the battle after which it is named and much of the construction work was undertaken by discharged soldiers. The Tellwrights live on the part of the road that runs through Bleakridge (Cobridge), which in the 1880s was developing into a middle-class suburb between Burslem and Hanley, much favoured by the professional classes, like the Tellwrights' neighbours, 'the Wesleyan Superintendent minister, the vicar of St Luke's (St John's) Church, an alderman and a doctor' (p. 19). The Tellwrights live in Manor Terrace, which is probably based on Grange Terrace (nos 196–200), named after the large Grange Farm, once a Roman Catholic chapel, which lay downhill on the western side of the Waterloo Road. Certainly elsewhere in his fiction Bennett calls the Grange 'the Manor'. The Bennett family lived at no. 198 (then 224) from c. 1878–80). The houses on Grange Terrace are not of yellow brick, like the Tellwrights', but a few houses along lies Clifton Terrace (nos 220–4) where the houses are of yellow brick. Perhaps Bennett changed these details to make precise identification impossible.

It is even harder to identify precisely the 'antique red mansion ... home of the Mynors family for two generations' (p. 18). The 1898 Ordnance Survey map shows a large building in roughly the right position opposite the Tellwrights' house, but I can find no reference to its ever having been used as a school. By contrast, the 'imposing row of four new houses' (pp. 18–19) further south on Waterloo Road is readily identified as the short terrace including no. 205, where the Bennett family lived from 1880. The land cost £200 and Enoch Bennett raised a further £900 on mortgage to build the house. The house next door, no. 207, called Lansdowne House in the novel (p. 72), is the home of the Suttons. Further south along the road is 'the Roman Catholic chapel' (p. 19), which is St Peter's chapel, now replaced by a modern building.

The steam-cars from Burslem to Hanley (see p. 5) ran along Waterloo Road, having replaced horse-drawn trams in 1882 and being in turn replaced by electric trams in 1899. Bennett's first known publication, in the *Staffordshire Sentinel* for 30 April 1887, was on the subject. In Hanley itself on Albion Street, stands 'the big Bethesda chapel' (p. 20), built in 1819, with an imposing Italianate front added in 1859. While a stalwart of the Hanbridge circuit, Ephraim has been living at Pireford (p. 20), Bennett's name for Basford, which lies west of Hanley on the way to Newcastle.

Bennett also refers to a number of other places in the centre of Burslem whose originals are not difficult to identify. St Luke's Square (p. 32) is St John's Square, although the church of that name (p. 19) stands further south, on a spacious site bounded by Enoch Street to the north and Wood Street (now Card Street) to the south. At the north end of St John's Square was the Manchester and Liverpool District Bank, the original for the Birmingham, Sheffield and District Bank (p. 32). I have not been able to identify 'the Quadrangle' (p. 44), but the context suggests that it is another name for Swan Bank.

The Wedgwood Institution (p. 81) is Bennett's recreation of the Wedgwood Institute in Queen Street, undoubtedly the most striking building in the centre of Burslem. Built between 1863 and 1869 in the Italian style, it is elaborately decorated with a varied use of terracotta, reliefs of months of the year, mosaics of the signs of the zodiac, panels illustrating processes in the potting industry and a statue of Josiah Wedgwood over the main entrance. Until 1906, it housed the School of Art, which is perhaps the school attended by Beatrice Sutton (see p. 75). From 1870 it also housed the Free Library, where Anna borrows her books (see p. 19 and note). From 1877 to 1880 Bennett was a pupil at the Endowed School on the premises and also attended night school there from 1883 to 1885. William Clowes Street, formerly Church Street and the original of Bennett's King Street (p. 93), runs south from Queen Street. Although it is impossible to determine the exact whereabouts of Mynors' works, we know that they are conveniently placed 'by the canal' (p. 95); this is the Trent and Mersey, which runs to the west of Burlsem.

A number of locations in the area around Burslem also feature in the novel. Hillport, an 'aristocratic suburb' (p. 7), is Bennett's name for Porthill, which lies to the west of Burslem, on the Newcastle-under-Lyme road, an area to which successful pottery manufacturers aspired as it placed them above and beyond the grime of the industrial areas. Warrillow identifies this as the area at the top of Porthill bank, while Hillport House (p. 22), home of the recently deceased William Wilbraham JP, is Porthill House, demolished in the 1950s, which then stood at the top of the hill on the Newcastle Road. Hillport Church is also mentioned (p. 73).

Toft End is Bennett's name for Sneyd Green, and the colliery and brickworks (p. 29) lie to the east of Burslem town centre. Edward Street, where Titus Price rents his works from Anna, is impossible to locate with any certainty. It is on the same side of the town as Sneyd Green, so that the Edward Street (now Leonora Street) shown west of Waterloo Road on the 1898 Ordnance Survey map is in entirely the wrong place. Its location is symbolic as much as geographical, in 'a miserable quarter – two rows of blackened infinitesimal cottages and her manufactory at the end – a frontier post of the town' (p. 34). Bennett perhaps has in mind one of the streets, shown but unnamed on the 1898 map, just north of the colliery and brick-works, which at that time were at the eastern limit of Burslem. There are in the vicinity a number of footpaths which might qualify as the 'rough road across unoccupied land dotted with the mouths of abandoned pits' (p. 34) that lay between this area of Burslem and the village of Sneyd Green, where the Prices have their house. The general location of Priory House (p. 180), on the road now called Sneyd Street, is readily determined, but I can find no reference to a house associated with a priory. After viewing the house, Anna and Henry walk along 'the high road from Hanbridge to Moorthorne' (p. 183); this is Hanley Road, which runs north–south on the east side of Sneyd Green. From here, they can survey the tract of wasteland referred to earlier, where Willie Price is soon to meet his end.

South of Sneyd Green, and really part of Hanley, is Shelton, which Bennett calls Cauldon, evoking both the 'sonority and richness' of the church clock and the 'vast wreaths of yellow flame with canopies of tinted smoke' from Cauldon Bar (Shelton Bar) Ironworks (p. 57). Ephraim Tellwright attends a sale of property at 'Axe . . . "the metropolis of the moorlands"' (p. 91); this is Bennett's name for Leek, about nine miles north-east of Stoke-on-Trent on the Derbyshire border.

One of the novel's great set-pieces occurs in Chapter 9, 'The Treat', which takes many of the characters on a Sunday school outing to a field 'near Sneyd, the seat of a marquis' (p. 114). Sneyd Hall, which appears in other works by Bennett, notably *The Card* (see Chapter 6, III, pp. 83ff.), is his name for Trentham Hall, which stood in Trentham Park, a few miles south of Stoke-on-Trent. Trentham was one of the seats of the Dukes of Sutherland. The second Duke rebuilt the house between 1833 and 1842, employing Charles Barry, architect of the Houses of Parliament; it was demolished in 1911. From 1856 there was an annual exodus of people from the Potteries for a 'Trentham Day' and it was also a popular destination for family days out and treats such as the one described here. The party sets out by train from Burslem station on the Potteries Loop Line (p. 114) and presumably travels to Trentham station, where the station building was also designed by Barry.

Bennett describes the setting for the school treat as being 'in that ideal condition of plenary correctness which denotes that a great landowner is exhibiting the beauties of scientific farming for the behoof of his villagers' (p. 116). He is probably being ironical here. It is true that the Dukes of Sutherland were noted for their interest in farming and their benevolent if paternalistic attitude towards the inhabitants of Trentham, which was developed as a model village. At the same time, however, they were shrewd businessmen, who invested wisely in new industrial developments, playing a part in the building of workers' houses in Stoke-on-Trent. Although by the time the novel is set (the fourth Duke succeeded to the title in 1892) they had retired to a largely rentier function, the 'low range of smoke' marking 'the sinister region of the Five Towns' (p. 116) is a reminder of the source of much of their wealth.

Tillier identifies real-life originals for a number of the main characters. Of Henry Mynors he says that 'many of the local readers recognized in [him] the powerful personality and organizing abilities of J. W. Dean, one of the most remarkable teachers that Swan Square Sunday School had in the eighties' (Tillier, p. 30). Mrs Sutton (p. 7 and passim), who appears elsewhere in Bennett's work, seems to be based on Mrs Spencer Lawton, whose husband was an alderman and thrice mayor of Burslem. The Lawtons lived at 207 Waterloo Road, next door to the Bennetts. Mrs Clayton Vernon (p. 7), whose name is composed of the surnames of Bennett's maternal and paternal grandmothers, is based on a prominent Methodist, Mrs Maxwell Edge. 'As to the cornet-playing revivalist', writes Tillier, 'his musical talent, rather uncommon among preachers, enables us to identify him with the Rev. Mr Middleton, who often visited Burslem on "missions"' (Tillier, p. 30). The other characters appear to be either composites or imaginative creations. *Kelly's Directory* for 1880 lists a Samuel Tellwright, living at 272 Waterloo Road, but as Bennett's footnote makes clear, Tellwright was a common surname in the Potteries and there is no reason to suppose that he has any real original in mind for Ephraim (p. 19).

Titus Price seems also to be an imaginative creation, but his suicide may have been influenced by Bennett's memories of three deaths. Henry Wilkinson, headmaster of the Swan Bank Wesleyan Day School, who committed suicide in 1878, had a similar status to Titus in chapel life. Bennett's cousin Samson, who in 1889 hanged himself in one of his pottery shops, killed himself in similar circumstances to Titus. Henry Wilkinson's cousin, Councillor A. J. Wilkinson, another prominent citizen, took his own life in Montreux in 1891.

Most of the shops Bennett mentions can also be identified. 'Bostock's great shop at Hanbridge' (p. 74) and 'Brunt's at Hanbridge' (p. 82), both patronized by the Suttons, are based on two well-known shops in Hanley: McIlroys on the corner of Lamb Street and Miles Bank and Huntbach's, which by 1899 occupied premises in four shops in Lamb Street. Both shops play a central part in Bennett's short story 'A Feud' (*Tales of the Five Towns*). The draper's where Miss Dickinson is head assistant is 'at the bottom of St Luke's Square' (pp. 77 and 93) and is no doubt based on the shop kept in St John's Square by Robert Longson, Bennett's maternal grandfather; it is also the original of Baines's in *The Old Wives' Tale*. Agnes nearly loses the shilling Alderman Sutton gives her to buy chocolate at 'Stephenson's in St Luke's Square' (p. 125). Bennett perhaps has in mind Mrs Harriett Stephenson, listed in the *Kelly's Directory* for 1880 as a confectioner at 13 Market Place, Burslem. Ephraim Tellwright pursues bargains in St Luke's covered market; St John's covered market, which stood in Burslem market place, was opened in 1879 and has since been demolished.

Anna's valuable investments, carefully managed by her father, are in leading and for the most part easily identified companies. The Toft End (Sneyd Green) Colliery Brickworks Ltd would offer vital raw materials to the main pottery industry (p. 29). The North Staffordshire Railway Company and Five Towns Waterworks Company Ltd (p. 29) are Bennett's names for the North Staffordshire Railway and Canal Company Ltd and the Staffordshire Potteries Waterworks Company. The former was authorized to operate by Acts of Parliament in 1846; in the same year it merged with the Trent & Mersey Canal company, and ran its first trains in 1848. It built the main Potteries line from Stafford via Stoke-on-Trent to Macclesfield. The Staffordshire Potteries Waterworks Co. was founded in 1845, and began to supply water in 1849. In the case of Norris's Brewery Ltd (p. 29), Bennett probably had no particular original in mind, but Staffordshire is a notable brewing county, and Burton-on-Trent is one of Britain's leading beer-making towns.

The Five Towns Field Club, to which Alderman Sutton belongs (p. 8), is presumably based on the North Staffordshire Naturalists' Field Club and Archaeological Society, founded in 1865. The *Staffordshire Sentinel*, which began weekly publication in 1854 and was a daily by the 1890s, was pleased to acknowledge in its review of *Anna* (September 1902) that it was the original of the *Staffordshire Signal* (p. 13).

APPENDIX 2: METHODISM IN *ANNA OF THE FIVE TOWNS*

Wesleyan Methodism is an essential context for understanding the action of *Anna of the Five Towns*. Bennett's Methodists are not, as in many nineteenth-century novels, marginalised characters, introduced into the narrative simply as targets of satire or humour, or incarnations of otherness, to be measured against a Church of England norm.[1] They occupy centre stage, and much of the novel's action is carried by scenes and set-pieces of chapel life: prayer-meetings, the Revival, the sewing meeting, the Sunday-school treat, the Bazaar. An ironical view of Methodism is present in the novel, and is particularly evident in the episode of the Revival, but the irony operates within a world that is largely Methodist, and the narrative carefully distinguishes between varieties of Methodism. These range from Sarah Vodrey, whose main interest in life is the variety of her own religious experience and who has 'never lived but in the fetters of slavery and fanaticism' (p. 187), to the 'wise and consoling heart' (p. 167) of Mrs Sutton, whose simple faith and sincerity do not prevent her from enjoying a materially comfortable life. Elsewhere, Methodism is represented by the 'naïve bliss' (p. 60) of those newly converted at the Revival; the organizational powers of Henry Mynors or the Revd Banks; the showy commercialism of the revivalist; and the malfeasance and despair of Titus Price.

The novel also offers a subtle portrait of Methodism in a particular historical phase, and Bennett places the action in the context of the establishment, growth and troubles of the sect over the 150 years of its history. The historical contextualizing is largely confined to one passage (pp. 20–1) when Bennett is sketching in Ephraim Tellwright's background. Ephraim is about sixty years old and was probably born around 1830, so his father will have been born in the early 1800s or even the 1790s, while his grandparents, who are 'of the Old Guard of Methodism', will have been associated with the Methodists while John Wesley (died 1791) was still alive. Ephraim's father inherits the family's 'tradition of holy fervour for the pure doctrine' and participates in the conflicts and schisms that assailed Methodism in the sixty years after Wesley's death.

The three examples of these troubles mentioned by Bennett are readily identified. In May and July 1807 camp meetings were held at Mow Cop, a hill to the north of the Potteries, in defiance of a ruling against such meetings at that year's Methodist Conference. The principal speakers were Hugh Bourne (1772–1852) and William Clowes (1780–1851), who believed that as the followers of Wesleyan Methodism had become more respectable, the movement had lost some of the drive and commitment of its early days. Both were eventually expelled from the Methodist Connexion and became the focus of breakaway movements which in 1812 united as The Society of Primitive Methodists. By 1814 the Revd Jabez Bunting (1779–1858) had emerged as the authoritarian leader of the Wesleyan Methodists. Samuel Warren (1781–1862) was a leading opponent of Bunting, rejecting his assumption of an almost papal authority and his creation of a ministerial élite, and arguing for an increase in local control by lay members. I have been unable to identify any affray in 1828, but in 1835 Bunting's plans to open a Theological Institute became a particular focus of conflict. Warren played a leading part in the opposition to the Institute, which some Methodists believed would further strengthen the power of the ministerial hierarchy. Warren was expelled from the Wesleyan Connexion in the same year, and although he was briefly a member of the newly formed Wesleyan Methodist Association, he eventually became an Anglican clergyman. The Revd James Everett (1784–1872) was the leader of the next phase of the opposition to Bunting, particularly disliking the growing influence of the ministry. A number of *Fly Sheets* attacking Bunting were published after 1845 and were almost certainly written either by Everett or by his close associates. He was expelled in 1849, and in 1857 founded the United Methodist Free Church. In the years 1850–5 Wesleyan Methodism lost 100,000 members, either by resignation or expulsion. Although Bourne and Clowes were first moved to defiance by issues of faith and practice, all three episodes had much to do with church government and the respective power of clergy and congregations as Methodism sought to establish its identity in the years after the death of its founder.

Bennett's family, on both sides, had a long history in Methodism and his father's family had been involved in an episode of local dissent and secession which was related to these larger issues. His paternal great-grandfather, Sampson Bennett, became a Wesleyan Methodist sometime between 1816 and 1820. At first the family worshipped at Swan Bank Chapel in Burslem – the 'Duck Bank' of the novel – to which was attached the powerful Burslem Sunday school. In 1828, the Wesleyan Methodist Church had ruled against the teaching of secular subjects on Sundays, and when in 1836 the Trustees decided to enforce this policy at Burslem a group of teachers refused to abide by this ruling and were expelled. This led to the establishment, in 1837, of Hill Top Chapel, where Bennett's grandfather John Bennett was a Trustee and Superintendent of the Sunday school. Eventually, however, the Bennetts moved back to Swan Bank, which had prospered in spite of the dispute and whose congregation included many prominent manufacturers and businessmen and their families. Bennett's maternal grandfather, Robert Longson, was a fervent Methodist, and Bennett often stayed with the Longsons and attended services in the Longson family pew. He also attended Sunday school and received his first schooling in the Infants' Department of Burslem Wesleyan Day School. In the 1870s Bennett's father, Enoch, was associated with Middleport Wesleyan Chapel and served as Superintendent of the Sunday school. By the 1880s, however, he was less committed to chapel life and distanced himself from the informal meetings held at the Waterloo Road house by the more devout Sarah Bennett.[2] Bennett was thus able to write about Methodism both from direct experience and family history.[3]

John Wesley himself would hardly have recognized or approved of the version of Methodist life represented by much of what takes place in and around Bursley Methodist Chapel. He always stressed the importance of itinerancy – the practice of peripatetic ministers moving around their circuit of chapels – and spent his whole ministry continually on the move, never becoming permanently associated with any particular chapel or community. But, as Robert Currie points out, even in Wesley's own lifetime his 'vertical' model of the structure of Methodism, with a direct line running from Wesley to the individual member, was being supplanted by a new 'horizontal' model based on chapel life.[4] Most Methodists, following Wesley's own precepts of diligence, honesty, thrift and obedience to the law, lived sober lives in settled communities and became increasingly attached to the activities of one particular chapel. Wesley distrusted this chapel loyalty, believing that members lost sight of the heavenly city in creating an earthly one. Indeed, he had foreseen the worldly entrapments that lay in wait for those following his own doctrines, writing in 1787: 'I do not see how it is possible in the nature of things for any revival of religion to continue long. For religion must necessarily produce both Industry and Frugality and these cannot but produce Riches. But as Riches increase so will Pride, Anger, and Love of the World in all its Branches.' Quoting this passage, J. L. and Barbara Hammond remark, '[a]s Methodism became a settled system it tended to take rather than give a standard. . . . Thus success and failure, achievement and defeat, had come to look very much the same inside and outside the chapel.'[5]

It is the Methodist culture that grew out of a development of these tendencies towards the settled chapel life based on prosperity and respectability that is depicted in *Anna*. From the 1870s onwards the very fabric of Methodist life was beginning to change. Traditionally, the class, a meeting held, as Bennett puts it, 'for the exchange of religious counsel and experience' (p. 122, footnote), had been the heart of religious life. But as a new, friendlier religion began to dominate, the class and with it the chapel became much more a place for socializing and shared entertainment. Revival and missions remained, but equally important to most members was the round of bazaars, fairs, Sunday school treats, sewing meetings and *conversaziones*. Robert Currie's description of this phase of Wesleyanism is readily applicable to *Anna*:

> Wesley's Christian Perfection was an ethic appropriate to the attempt to improve the unregenerate and ignorant through direction and control by an alien force: theologically, God; organizationally, the Methodist hierarchy. This ethic was accompanied by the complex structure of Christian doctrine and ritual. The promotion of perfection created the chapel community. During the nineteenth century, when ethic, doctrine and ritual were largely destroyed, the chapel community survived, though not unchanged.

> As the higher things Wesley offered to his followers were progressively eliminated from the Methodist horizon, the chapel community bulked larger and larger, not because it was expanding but because all else was contracting. . . . When secularization eroded ethic, doctrine and ritual, the chapel, the indestructible nucleus and residuum of the movement, remained.

Confirming the Hammonds' point about Methodist respectability, he goes on to say that Methodists 'eschewed everything drastic and extreme; they sought to avoid all conflicts; they held up the ideal of respectability and moderation in religion and life'.[6]

Along with this increasing respectability and desire for moderation there went a business and bureaucratic element. It is clear from the account of Ephraim's life that he has little relish for the doctrinal or evangelical side of Methodism. When he expounds 'the mystery of the Atonement' or grows 'garrulous with God', he does so because he thereby gains 'an unassailable position within the central group of the Society' (p. 20), and it is to the fiscal and organizational aspect of Methodism that he devotes his energies and talents: a telling image is Anna's early memory of her father counting the collection from an anniversary service (p. 20).[7] By the time of the action of *Anna* Ephraim seems no longer to attend chapel regularly and contributes to its funds only with reluctance. In the next generation, Henry Mynors, although he leads a class, conducts prayer meetings and plays a key part in the Revival, seems to be most valued in the chapel community for his combination of charm, business acumen and powers of organization and leadership.

At the heart of such religious experience as is portrayed in the novel lies Anna's crisis of belief. Although she plays her part in the work of the chapel, particularly as a Sunday school teacher, she feels herself at a distance from Methodist life. During the prayer-meeting, so firmly and skilfully conducted by Henry Mynors, Anna perceives that a kind of fervent idealism enters the room, an 'impassioned altruism' from which she is excluded. In part this is a matter of temperament: to stand up and declare her faith would be embarrassing for her. This temperamental reserve also explains her reluctance to visit the families of her Sunday school pupils – though her highly developed sense of duty and obedience to the dazzling Henry impel her to do so.

Similarly, she is anxious that the holiday with the Suttons might contain excessive piety.

But behind this temperamental resistance to the public expression of belief there lies, for Anna, a real dilemma, and one which is in many respects peculiarly Methodist. It is not really an issue of faith: if catechized, Anna would undoubtedly confirm her belief in the existence and power of God and of Christ's redemptive role; but in doing so she would lack 'that consciousness of personal relationship or of truth which comes to the whole personality and not to the mind and senses alone'.[8] Wesley's own strength of faith derived from the moment, on 24 May 1738, that he defined as his conversion, when he both experienced and accepted the reality of Christ's redemptive power as applied to himself, personally: 'I felt my heart strangely warmed. I felt I did trust in Christ, Christ alone, for salvation; and assurance was given me that He has taken away my sins, even mine, and saved me from the law of sin and death'.[9] It is this sense of 'assurance', to which Wesley hoped to bring his followers, that Anna finds difficult to attain, and Mrs Sutton perceives this uncertainty when she approaches Anna during the Revival service:

> 'I think I do believe,' [Anna] said weakly.
>
> 'You "think"? Are you sure? Are you not deceiving yourself? Belief is not with the lips: it is with the heart' (p. 55).

During the night following the Revival, Anna is tortured by the sense of her own pride, obstinacy and lack of faith. To a large extent the narrative underwrites her pain and desperate hope that attending the next morning's prayer meeting will bring her some relief. But her spiritual plight and quest for peace are also viewed with some irony, as in her determination that 'she would tell her father in the morning that she was convicted of sin, and, however hopelessly, seeking salvation; she would tell both her father and Agnes at breakfast' (p. 58). And the prayer meeting itself is also presented ironically, hardly offering the kind of spiritual uplift that she is seeking: poorly attended, the minister tired, the singing strained and the only signs of religious enthusiasm the 'ecstatic and naïve bliss' on the face of a youth 'saved' the previous evening and Sarah Vodrey who finds her 'sole diversion in the variety of her religious experiences' (p. 60). When Anna leaves the meeting it is 'like coming out of prison', and her feelings are of 'shame and discomfort' and a sense of having made herself ridiculous. On the night after Willie confesses his forgery Anna is again tortured by her lack of faith and reflects that she may be 'one of the souls foreordained to damnation' (p. 166). Here she seems to accept the doctrine of predestination, which held that God has determined his purpose from eternity, so that only the elect may enjoy eternal life. In the context of Methodist belief Anna is taking a harsh view of her situation, since Wesley himself preached a doctrine of salvation for all. Some branches of Methodism took a stricter view of the matter, but presumably not the easy-going society of which Anna is a member.

Mynors, however, offers a way out of Anna's dilemma. In his cool, rational and principled manner he suggests another route to faith, making it clear that his own experience of conversion has been entirely different from Mrs Sutton's and from John Wesley's: 'I – we – cannot promise you any sudden change of feeling, any sudden relief and certainty, such as some people experience. At least, I never had it' (p. 67). He offers instead a life based on a Christ-like example, a religion of works rather than faith, of behaviour rather than belief. Apart from its effect on Anna, such an admission from so prominent a member of the chapel, a man entrusted with the spiritual guidance of the young and a key role in the organization of the Revival, is in itself fascinating, and perhaps another dimension of Bennett's portrait of this late-nineteenth-century version of Methodism: a less strenuous form of conversion than that envisaged by its founder. For Anna, the effect is one of immense relief and gives her a focus for action. Her conversation with Mynors occurs in Chapter 6, entitled 'Willie', and it is of course in relation to Willie Price, the meek, the despised, the ultimately despairing scapegoat, that Anna is best able to exercise a Christ-like function. When she burns the forged bill of exchange she offers him the chance of salvation through penitence, although his shame and sense of loss are such that he cannot accept it. In her decision to do so, however, Anna challenges Henry's example, because she detects in his attitude towards Willie a 'condescending superiority' (p. 166) that she finds distasteful. She prefers to think of herself on equal terms with Willie, fraternizing, like Christ, with sinners. By the end of the novel, however, any sense of a continuing spiritual crisis has disappeared. As with so much else in her life, Anna accommodates herself to the realities of her situation and faces the future 'calmly and genially' (p. 199). It is surely significant that the book's final glimpse of chapel life is not a prayer-meeting but a bazaar, at which Anna is seen dutifully playing the role she will no doubt play at many similar events in the years to come.

References

1. See Valentine Cunningham, *Everywhere Spoken Against: Dissent in the Victorian Novel* (Oxford: Oxford University Press, 1975), for an excellent discussion of this issue.

2. In his essay 'The Making of Me' (1928), Bennett wrote: 'in ceremonial religious matters my father did not practise what he preached. When I was very young he gave up Sunday school entirely, and at no period did he attend chapel if he could decently help it' (*Sketches for Autobiography*, ed. James Hepburn (London: Allen & Unwin, 1979), p. 6).

3. Bennett's attitude to his Methodist background can be found in the essay 'My Religious Experience', extracts from which are reprinted in this book (pp. 209–11).

4. See Robert Currie, *Methodism Divided: a Study in the Sociology of Ecumenicalism* (London: Faber & Faber, 1968), p. 24.

5. J. L. and Barbara Hammond, *The Bleak Age* (Harmondsworth: Pelican Books, 1947), p. 137.

6. Currie, *Methodism Divided*, pp. 139–40.

7. See the general discussion of the role of money in the novel in the 'Introduction'.

8. Rupert E. Davies, *Methodism* (Harmondsworth: Penguin Books, 1963), p. 97.

9. *Selections from the Journal of John Wesley*, ed. Hugh Martin (London: SCM Press, 1955), p. 34.

BENNETT AND HIS CRITICS

It is often difficult to separate the critical history of any individual Bennett novel from the effect on his general reputation of the views of some of his contemporaries. On one level, these views relate to Bennett's style of life, derived from his considerable financial success as an author, playwright and journalist. For Lawrence, he was a 'sort of pig in clover',[1] while Ezra Pound portrayed him as Mr Nixon in 'the cream gilded cabin of his steam yacht', a shrewd player in the literary market and one of the enemies of literature guyed in *Hugh Selwyn Mauberley*:

> 'I never mentioned a man but with the view
> 'Of selling my own works.
> 'The tip's a good one, as for literature
> 'It gives no man a sinecure.'[2]

There was also in the reaction to Bennett an element of metropolitan snobbery towards a provincial writer, as in Clive Bell's memory of him in Paris in about 1904: 'he was the boy from Staffordshire who was making good and in his bowler hat and reach-me-downs he looked the part. He was at once pleased with himself and ashamed – we rather liked him, but we thought nothing of his writing.'[3]

The real damage to Bennett's reputation, however, was caused by the aesthetic terms of the modernist assault on his work, particularly in two of Virginia Woolf's essays, 'Modern Fiction', published in 1919, and 'Mr Bennett and Mrs Brown', the final version of which appeared in 1924. In both pieces, Virginia Woolf groups Bennett with Wells and Galsworthy, as 'Edwardian' writers, whose outlook and fictional technique is entirely different from that of her own generation (the 'Georgians'), among whom she names such of her contemporaries as Joyce, Forster and Conrad. In the earlier essay, Woolf charges Bennett and the others with an excessive reliance on material reality at the expense of the spirit of life:

> If we fasten ... one label on all these books, on which is one word, materialists, we mean by it that they write of unimportant things; that they spend immense skill and immense industry making the trivial and the transitory appear the true and the enduring. ... Life escapes; and perhaps without life nothing else is worth while.[4]

Woolf's argument repeats some of the terms of an earlier critique by Henry James. In his essay 'The New Novel' (1914) James comments on Bennett's accumulative method, particularly in *Clayhanger* (1910), finding in it a failure to go beyond the amassing of physical detail to create a satisfying aesthetic whole:

> When the author of *Clayhanger* has put down upon the table, in dense unconfused array, every fact required, every fact in any way invocable, to make the life of the *Five Towns* press upon us, and to make our sense of it, so full-fed, content us, we may very well go on for the time in the captive condition. ... Nothing at such moments – or rather at the end of them, when the end begins to threaten – may be of a more curious strain than the dawning unrest that suggests to us fairly our first critical comment: 'Yes, yes – but is this *all*?' These are the circumstances of the interest – we see, we see; but where is the interest itself, where and what is its centre, and how are we to measure it in relation to *that*?'[5]

Bennett himself actually precipitated the debate with Virginia Woolf with his remarks on her recently published novel, *Jacob's Room* (1923). His aesthetic ideas derive from an older, realistic tradition, but are flavoured by his intense reading of late-nineteenth-century French naturalism, and he defines artistic power as deriving from a combination of the aesthetic and the realistic: originality, in itself, is not enough:

> The foundation of good fiction is character creating, and nothing else. The characters must be so fully true that they possess even their own creator. Every deviation from truth, every omission of truth, necessarily impairs the emotional power and therefore weakens the interest. ...
>
> I have seldom read a cleverer book than Virginia Woolf's *Jacob's Room*. ... But the characters do not vitally survive in the

> mind because the author has been obsessed by details of originality and cleverness.[6]

Woolf's celebrated contention, at the beginning of 'Mr Bennett and Mrs Brown', apparently in answer to Bennett's charge, is that 'in or about December, 1910, human character changed'. This being so, Woolf believes that Bennett, Wells and Galsworthy have little to teach younger novelists about the making of fiction:

> Now it seems to me that to go to these men and ask them to teach you how to write a novel – how to create characters that are real – is precisely like going to a bootmaker and asking him to teach you how to make a watch. . . . [T]he Edwardians were never interested in character in itself; or in the book in itself. They were interested in something outside. Their books, then, were incomplete as books, and required that the reader should finish them, actively and practically, for himself. . . .
>
> That is what I mean by saying that the Edwardian tools are the wrong ones for us to use. They have laid an enormous stress on the fabric of things. They have given us a house in the hope that we may be able to deduce the human beings who live there. To give them their due, they have made that house much better worth living in. But if you hold that houses are in the first place about people, and only in the second about the houses they live in, that is the wrong way to set about it.[7]

Like James, Woolf argues that the mere accumulation of detail is not sufficient to produce significant art. The effect of such writing is less aesthetic than kinetic, rousing its readers to a desire for social action, rather than enhancing or illuminating their understanding of life.

The twin spectres of personal and artistic materialism continued to haunt Bennett's standing in the years after his death. The Marxist critic Ralph Fox saw Bennett as a victim of the decay of realism:

> Human personality . . . had disappeared from the contemporary novel, and with it the 'hero'. The process of killing off the hero was inevitable in the development of the nineteenth-century novel. The decay of realism compelled it. . . . Arnold Bennett, the faithful disciple of the French realists, wrote an excellent novel about his father and his own youth, and then, seized with the fatal desire to

write 'the history of a family' ruined his early work by two sequels. Similarly, he wrote one of the best novels of pre-war England about two old ladies whom he had known in the Potteries, and then descended to writing about a newspaper proprietor, an hotel, prostitution (yes, indeed, just like a hundred others!) and so on.[8]

Not surprisingly, both Leavises were dismissive of Bennett's work: Q. D. saw him as an example of a 'magazine outlook' in approach and subject matter, while F. R. disposed of his claims to art in a throwaway remark:

> The body of a magazine is now carefully selected to endorse the 'message' of the advertisements, and it looks as though a general infection has taken place. It would be impossible to find a more complete illustration of what might be called the magazine outlook of modern fiction than Bennett's last novel *Imperial Palace*. It is full of 'entrancing, perfect', and 'fabulously expensive' women, millionaires, luxurious living, and bluff man-of-the world horse-sense masquerading as psychology and insight.[9]

> . . . If Mark Twain lacked art in Arnold Bennett's sense (as Arnold Bennett pointed out), that only shows how little art in Arnold Bennett's sense matters, in comparison with art that is the answer of creative genius to the pressure of a profoundly felt and complex experience.[10]

Although Fox and the Leavises aim at the soft targets among Bennett's novels, which indeed have features in common with today's 'airport novels', it is clear that there is a deep underlying suspicion about his lack of seriousness.

These criticisms of Bennett's literary endeavour were to come later, when he was a famous writer. But *Anna of the Five Towns* was only Bennett's third novel, published when he was still comparatively unknown, and it marked a new direction in his work. On publication *Anna* was generally well received, and reviewers immediately identified a number of strengths in Bennett's work: the excellence and accuracy of the local colour, in particular the creation of the atmosphere of Methodism; the fine character-studies; and the admirable construction. As might be expected, the *Staffordshire Sentinel* laid emphasis on the Potteries setting, likening the novel's regional dimension to George Eliot, but the reviewer is also alive to the novel's qualities of character and plot, and sees that *Anna* represents an advance on Bennett's previous fiction:

> Anna ... is a remarkable 'creation', though the novel not only contains a great deal of local colour, but perhaps a substratum of local history ... but the real strength of the book lies in its study of character.... All Mr Bennett's characters move in a homely and limited circle, yet the story of their lives supplies an abundance of pathos, tragedy, and humour, and irresistibly compels one to read on. The people to whom the reader is introduced possess a vivid personality. At least, their personality is vividly drawn. They stand out boldly against the North Staffordshire background as might personal acquaintances. It never crosses the mind that they are not real people.... There is knowledge, and if not always sympathy, there is a reserve that excludes mere caricature.... We most heartily congratulate Mr Bennett upon his latest novel, which places him upon an infinitely higher plane than he previously occupied, and the Potteries may very well be proud of having produced so keen an observer, so trenchant and effective a writer, and a novelist who is gradually but, as we can scarcely doubt, surely winning his way to a recognised position among the authors of the day.[11]

Another provincial paper, the *Manchester Guardian*, noted the same qualities of authenticity and observation, together with an admirable restraint in the writing:

> ... the work of a capable and conscientious artist, one who has here recorded some life in the Potteries with unusual insight and fidelity to nature. The book cannot be called cheerful, but it is deeply interesting both as a local and a general study of human nature.... The greater womanliness of Anna compared with the chattering Beatrice is felt continually, although the author puts on no labels and uses no superfluous adjectives. The same forcible reserve and careful word-selection are used throughout, especially in the drawing of the chief character, the gruesome miser-father of Anna.[12]

The *Times Literary Supplement*, while praising Bennett's descriptive powers, had doubts about the overall effect of the novel: 'While the gross result of all this is incidentally tragic, the net result is surprisingly small – many will think too small.'[13] Other London reviewers, who praised the novel's descriptive qualities, had doubts about its denouement, and whether it is adequately prepared for in the preceding action. The *Academy* complained that:

> It is the sudden postulation of love between these two [Anna and Willie Price] at the very end of the story that, to our mind, is responsible for the reader's dissatisfaction with the completed drama. . . . We do not think that Anna would have done what she did, or that Willie Price would have done what he did. At any rate neither act seems proved, and we are led to wish that this complication had been introduced earlier in the story, had been of its stuff instead of its selvage.[14]

The *Spectator* had almost identical doubts, remarking that '[t]he tragedy is not according to nature but according to art'.[15]

Although after Bennett's death some critics continued to be influenced by the modernist view of him as a successful author but a poor artist, he retained a faithful readership, untroubled by the niceties of aesthetic debate, and found advocates for his work. Frank Swinnerton, a personal friend of Bennett, defended him against the diminishing metropolitan judgement of being a provincial writer:

> It is the simple-mindedness of Bennett that causes those who like to regard themselves as European to call him 'provincial'. He was in many respects the young man from the midlands. Whereas Gissing, also a provincial, had condemned the foul ugliness of cities, and Moore had hardly seemed to know what they looked like, so interested was he in clambering like an ant over the lives of wretched people, Bennett was delighted to embrace the beauties as well as the disfigurements of urban civilization. He not only saw the town, but he could see what it represented in the creative life of man. . . . [W]hile he was quite as sensitive to ugliness as any man I have ever met he was quite definitely a townsman. The country-side was pleasant, lovely, stuff to paint, exquisite to see; but there were not enough men and women, not enough houses, not enough of the movement and conflicts of human beings, to satisfy him. It was in people that he took all his interest; people who set their wits against the world, people who got on with their jobs, people who came to London and conquered it.[16]

Bennett himself was attracted by the idea of being a European writer and often complained that his books were better understood in France than in his own country. It is not surprising, therefore, that one of the earliest full-length studies of his work should be written by a French critic. George Lafourcade's book appeared in 1939, and made great claims for Bennett's status as an artist. *Anna of the Five Towns*, however, was not among Lafourcade's favourites:

> It must be granted that it lacks vitality, often tends to dullness complete and unrelieved. The style is heavy, even technical in the description of factories and local atmosphere, occasionally encumbered by explanatory foot-notes, a method which Bennett never used again. . . . The sense of oppression and ennui which soon becomes so strong in the reader is further emphasized by the numerous descriptive passages. These are in themselves remarkable and stand out very well. Chief among them are descriptions of industrial scenery and of the clay factories. . . . The trouble is that these descriptions nearly always read like digressions; they are external to the story and the art of blending them with the narrative . . . has not yet been mastered by Bennett. The book has all the sluggishness and something of the atmosphere of a novel by George Eliot. It often reads like a literary guide to the Five Towns and the surrounding country. At other times it has a didactic flavour. . . . At the same time it has some genuine artistic merit: the description of the revivalist meeting is a masterpiece of realism and irony, with some fine satirical touches. . . . [O]n the whole the novel is one of which Bennett should have been proud – a sincere and honest piece of work, not without promises of future greatness – a good, if somewhat stodgy, study of provincial life. It would have won a literary prize in France.[17]

That final comment seems to justify Bennett's view of the relative reception of his novels in France and England.

More recently, Bennett's reputation with academic critics has been further enhanced by the advocacy of some fellow practitioners, notably Angus Wilson, Margaret Drabble and John Wain, himself from the Potteries. Equally important in the recovery of Bennett's reputation has been a sense that Jamesian criteria are not the only ones by which fiction may be judged, and that some writers need to be rescued from a limiting judgement based on an aesthetic which emphasizes organicity, a concern with the rendering of subjective experience and technical innovation as the only marks of literary value. Furthermore,

Woolf's arguments may be seen not only as a justification of her own fictional practice, but also as representative of a new literary generation attempting its own definition of that highly contentious imponderable: life. Bennett may not be like life as Woolf knows and understands it; but Woolf herself, when she asks her readers to consider 'an ordinary mind on an ordinary day',[18] may be using 'ordinary' in a very special (extraordinary) sense.

Margaret Drabble's account of *Anna* certainly exemplifies a major shift in the terms of the debate about Bennett's work. She emphasizes the novel's similarities to what she regards as its model, Balzac's *Eugénie Grandet*, but shows how Bennett adapts the novel of *moeurs de province* for his own purposes:

> Both novels have young girls as their central characters, but both young girls are overshadowed by their miser fathers. Eugénie and Anna are both wooed for their wealth, and both fall in love unsuitably; both defy their fathers for their loved ones, and defy him in financial terms, the only terms he understands – Eugénie gives away her birthday gold (technically her own to do what she likes with) to her worthless cousin Charles, and Anna burns a bill of exchange to prevent prosecution of Willie Price, a defaulting tenant. . . . But Anna is not simply Eugénie rewritten in English terms – the debt is obvious, but in many ways Bennett has added to and altered his material. Indeed, much of the material in *Anna* is peculiarly Bennett's own: the Sunday School meetings, the Methodist preachers, the outings, the Methodist obsession with money and fiscal affairs – comparable, in terms of plot, to the French peasant Grandet's obsession, but quite different in origin and expression . . . Anna, also, is a very different character from Eugénie; she is much more spirited, more modern, more subtle. In fact, she is much more real.[19]

Nonetheless, if recent critics have been prepared to defend Bennett against the criticisms of James or Woolf, they do not refrain from adverse comment on his writing. Here, for instance, is John Lucas's finely nuanced comment on the long description of Bursley in the first chapter of the novel (pp. 13–14 of this edition):

> At best this is specious, at worst, plain silly. For Bennett has put the struggle in wrong – and irrelevant – terms. And whatever

> echoes of social Darwinism underlie the notion of 'ceaseless warfare of man and nature', they are quite incapable of providing the focus of what ought to be pinpointed as the real struggle: which is not the struggle between man and nature, but between man and man. Bennett's way of putting the matter reveals all too plainly that he has no real political awareness, no feeling for the ultimate complexities and ugliness of the system in and by means of which his characters struggle to survive and sometimes triumph. It is a failing and one that has significant and damaging consequences for much of his fiction.
>
> Yet the failing is partly offset by the fact that Bennett's readily sympathetic response to the strugglers themselves gives his fiction its especial distinction. Whatever the truth about Bennett as private man may be, there is no question of his recoiling in horror or disgust from the ugly world which as an imaginative writer he chooses to confront. On the contrary, he records it so fully and with such warmth of understanding that if we call his characteristic response to the ugliness one of acceptance we have immediately to add that such acceptance is in no way the product of complacency or ignorance.[20]

Elsewhere, however, Lucas has a different view of what Woolf found lacking in Bennett's work, particularly the credible presentation of Anna's feelings:

> [T]he novel is about how she more or less misses out on life. She has no way of realizing the large possibilities that love and money might seem to offer her. In the course of the novel we see her stirring into intellectual and emotional awakening; but the awakening isn't completed. And this is inevitable, because Anna has for so long been shut up that any offer of freedom – not matter how puny or illusory – will be enough to win her gratitude and acceptance. And what makes *Anna of the Five Towns* so distinguished and moving a novel is Bennett's ability to make credible the fact of Anna's prolonged confinement and the nature of her partial awakening.[21]

Peter Keating also comments on the rendering of Anna's experience, placing it in the context both of women's situation and of a pattern of generational conflict in fiction at the turn of the century:

Anna Tellwright's father Ephraim sits brooding in the front room 'unseen but felt, like an angry god behind a cloud . . . unappeased and dangerous'. Anna's great moment of personal challenge to his authority comes when she burns Willie Price's forged bill of exchange. Ephraim's response is characteristically violent: 'If thou breathes a word o' this to Henry Mynors or to any other man, I'll cut thy tongue out.' It is a triumph of sorts. Until then, Anna has believed that her father might well be capable of carrying out his terrifying threats, but 'she survived; she continued to breathe, eat, drink, and sleep; her father's power stopped short of annihilation'. Her consolation is that 'things could not be worse', but nor perhaps do they greatly improve. Her future husband, Henry Mynors, will not be violent to her or their children – the generations, in this respect as in so many others, are changing as Bennett is pointing out – but the marriage will be loveless. Her rebellion has only taught her how to endure. The father's job has been done. She is tamed, broken, habituated to the belief that 'a woman's life is always a renunciation, greater or less'.[22]

A recent powerful advocate of Bennett's work has been John Carey. His contentious study, *The Intellectuals and the Masses*, is intended to demonstrate that modernism represents a kind of élitist riposte by intellectuals – many of whom, Carey argues, harboured fantasies of mass extermination – to the advance of mass civilization and mass culture. Bennett emerges from Carey's book as a hero who seeks a middle way between the highbrow and the lowbrow, finds apt material for fiction in the lives of the masses, reaches a more adequate understanding of them than the modernists wished or were able to attain, and thus achieves a universality that eludes those of his contemporaries who were dismissive of his work. Furthermore, Carey's reading of the description of Bursley in Chapter 1 is rather different from John Lucas's; for Carey, it is Bennett's acceptance of natural processes, rather than the absence of a political dimension, that is most telling:

Bennett's biological perspective allowed him to take a tougher view than intellectuals about suburban sprawl and industrial squalor. They became marks of man's justifiable hostility to nature. For he saw that if nature means grass and trees, it also means cancer, bacteria and the torments of natural death, and in this guise it is obviously hateful. Besides, the desecration of landscape by houses and factories can itself be seen as a natural process, expressing man's industrializing and urbanizing instincts. Bennett offers both these justifications. . . .[23]

Finally, to end where this survey began, quotations from two recent critics who attempt to deal with Woolf's view of Bennett's work. First, David Trotter addresses the issues of observation and experience and asks questions – unasked by Virginia Woolf – as to the reasons for Bennett's choice of method; for he sees it as a choice, based on particular beliefs about understanding and representation, rather than as a limitation:

> Woolf's description of Bennett's method is accurate. But she didn't ask why he had chosen to represent character through circumstance. Indeed, she doesn't seem to regard it as a choice. Bennett was incapable of seeing Mrs Brown at all, however hard he peered. The distinction between generations then becomes a distinction not between equally valid methods, but between blindness and insight. . . . But in his novels he chose to disregard atmosphere, and render circumstance. Why? . . . 'Observation', Bennett wrote in 1898, 'can only be conducted from the outside'. . . He believed that understanding depended on a recognition of difference, not similarity. The irreducible differences between people, particularly between men and women, were for him the incentive, not the bar, to characterization. . . . James, Hueffer, Wells, Forster, Lawrence, Richardson, Woolf: all wrote about experiences akin to their own. To be aware is to be representable; to be representable is to be aware. But the understanding we have of the Baines sisters or Edwin Clayhanger is something we share with Bennett rather than the characters themselves. We know them as much by what they don't know as by what they do.[24]

Lyn Pykett's challenge to Virginia Woolf concentrates on a different aspect of the argument: Bennett's detailed materialism. Far from seeing this as an evasion of feeling or an attempt to render surface at the expense of depth, Pykett believes that Bennett's method requires readers to go beyond the surface detail and realize its true significance. It is as powerful an expression of the real strength and subtlety of Bennett's technique, both in *Anna of the Five Towns* and elsewhere, as one could hope to find:

Wells–Bennett–Galsworthy developed a new masculine realism, a forensic, scientific, or sociological realism derived from Zola (particularly in Bennett's case), as 'external realism of accumulated detail'. . . . As Virginia Woolf was to argue in her influential rejection of her literary elders, they placed 'enormous stress upon the fabric of things', expecting their readers to deduce the nature of its occupants from their descriptions of a house. Bennett's minutely detailed description of the dresser in the Tellwrights' kitchen in Chapter Seven of *Anna of the Five Towns* is a case in point, but one which I think gives us cause to question Woolf's dismissal of Bennett. The history of generations of Tellwright women, and the constraining pressure which that history exerts on the life of the current generation, are powerfully suggested by Bennett's description of this 'simple' and 'dignified' piece of furniture whose much-polished surface 'reflected the conscientious labour of generations'. The description of the dresser is not merely a catalogue of details, but is a crucial part of Bennett's evocation of the ordinary tragedy of Anna's life. It is addressed not simply to the reader's eye, but to his or her historical, social and moral understanding.[25]

References

(*Note*: Place of publication is London, unless otherwise indicated.)

1. Letter to Aldous Huxley, 27 March 1928, *The Letters of D. H. Lawrence*, vol. VI, 1927–28, ed. James T. Boulton and Margaret H. Boulton with Gerald M. Lacy (Cambridge: Cambridge University Press, 1991), p. 342.

2. Ezra Pound, 'Mr Nixon', *Collected Shorter Poems* (Faber & Faber, 1952), p. 212.

3. Clive Bell, *Old Friends: Personal Recollections* (Chatto & Windus, 1956); quoted in Margaret Drabble, *Arnold Bennett* (Weidenfeld & Nicolson, 1974), p. 108.

4. Virginia Woolf, 'Modern Fiction' (1919), *Collected Essays*, ed. Leonard Woolf (Chatto & Windus, 1966), vol. II, p. 105.

5. Henry James, 'The New Novel', *Notes on Novelists* (Dent, 1914), p. 258.

6. Arnold Bennett, 'Is the Novel Decaying?', *Cassell's Weekly*, 28

March 1923: 47; *Virginia Woolf: the Critical Heritage*, ed. Robin Majumdar and Allen McLaurin (Routledge & Kegan Paul, 1975), p. 112. Bennett's comments on *Jacob's Room* drew a number of responses before the publication of the final version of 'Mr Bennett and Mrs Brown'. As well as an earlier version of Woolf's essay there were replies from J. D. Beresford and Logan Pearsall Smith: these can be found in Majumdar and McLaurin's collection, pp. 115–19, 121–3 and 124–9, which also offers an interesting summary of the debate. A useful discussion of the issue can be found in Samuel Hynes, 'The Whole Contention Between Mr Bennett and Mrs Woolf', *Novel*, I (1967), 34–44, reprinted in *Edwardian Occasions: Essays on English Writing in the Early Twentieth Century* (Routledge & Kegan Paul, 1972), pp. 24–38.

7. Virginia Woolf, *Collected Essays*, vol. I, pp. 326–7, 332. Further exchanges in the debate followed, not least in Bennett's comments on Virginia Woolf's later novels, reprinted in the *Critical Heritage* volume.

8. Ralph Fox, *The Novel and the People* (1937; Lawrence & Wishart, 1979), pp. 91–2.

9. Q. D. Leavis, *Fiction and the Reading Public* (Chatto & Windus, 1939), pp. 198–9.

10. F. R. Leavis, 'Pudd'nhead Wilson' (1955) in *'Anna Karenina' and other Essays* (Chatto & Windus, 1967), p. 122.

11. Unsigned review, *Staffordshire Sentinel*, 15 September 1902; *Arnold Bennett: the Critical Heritage*, ed. James Hepburn (Routledge & Kegan Paul, 1981), pp. 155–6.

12. Unsigned review, *Manchester Guardian*, 26 September 1902; *Critical Heritage*, pp. 164–5.

13. Unsigned review, *Times Literary Supplement*, 26 September 1902; *Critical Heritage*, p. 165.

14. Unsigned review, *Academy*, 20 September 1902; *Critical Heritage*, p. 163.

15. Unsigned review, *Spectator*, 20 September 1902; *Critical Heritage*, p. 164.

16. Frank Swinnerton, *The Georgian Literary Scene* (1935: Dent, 1938), p. 140.

17. Georges Lafourcade, *Arnold Bennett: A Study* (Frederick Muller, 1939), pp. 96–9.

18. *Collected Essays*, II, p. 106.

19. Drabble, *Arnold Bennett*, p. 95.

20. John Lucas, *Arnold Bennett: A Study of his Fiction* (Methuen & Co., 1974), pp. 30–1.

21. Ibid., p. 40.

22. Peter Keating, *The Haunted Study: A Social History of the English Novel 1874–1914* (Secker & Warburg, 1989), p. 233.

23. John Carey, *The Intellectuals and the Masses: Pride and Prejudice among the Literary Intelligentsia, 1880–1939* (Faber & Faber, 1992), p. 173.

24. David Trotter, *The English Novel in History, 1895–1920* (Routledge, 1993), pp. 134–5.

25. Lyn Pykett, *Engendering Fictions: the English Novel in the Early Twentieth Century* (Edward Arnold, 1995), p. 72.

SUGGESTIONS FOR FURTHER READING

(*Note*: unless otherwise stated, the place of publication is London.)

Readers who have enjoyed *Anna of the Five Towns* may wish to read Bennett's other novels and short stories set in the Potteries: *Tales of the Five Towns* (1905); *Whom God Hath Joined* (1906); *The Grim Smile of the Five Towns* (1907); *The Old Wives' Tale* (1908); *Clayhanger* (1910) and its sequels *Hilda Lessways* (1911) and *These Twain* (1915); *Helen with the High Hand* (1910); *The Card* (1911); and *The Matador of the Five Towns* (1912). Of his novels not set in the Five Towns *Riceyman Steps* (1923) is undoubtedly the best.

The fullest bibliography is Anita Miller's *Arnold Bennett: an Annotated Bibliography 1887–1932* (New York and London: Garland, 1977). Bennett's journals, edited in three volumes by Desmond Flower (Cassell, 1932) give an excellent insight into his wide interests and working methods; there is also a one-volume selection edited by Frank Swinnerton (Harmondsworth: Penguin, 1954). His letters to his family, literary agent and friends have been edited in four volumes by James Hepburn (Oxford: Oxford University Press, 1966–86). *Sketches for Autobiography*, also edited by James Hepburn (Allen & Unwin, 1979), is an invaluable collection of essays and articles. His influential work as a critic and book reviewer can be found in *The Author's Craft and Other Critical Writings*, ed. Samuel Hynes (Lincoln: University of Nebraska Press, 1968), and *Arnold Bennett: The* Evening Standard *Years: 'Books and Persons' 1926–1931*, ed. Andrew Mylett (Chatto & Windus, 1974). His contemporary critical reputation is thoroughly covered in James Hepburn's *Arnold Bennett: the Critical Heritage* (Routledge & Kegan Paul, 1981). The debate between Bennett and Virginia Woolf is most familiar in Woolf's 'Mr Bennett and Mrs Brown' in *Collected Essays*, vol. 1, ed. Leonard Woolf (Chatto & Windus, 1966). Samuel Hynes has reviewed the controversy in 'The Whole Contention between Mr Bennett and Mrs Woolf' (*Novel*, 1 (1967): 34–44) which is reprinted in his *Edwardian Occasions: Essays on English Writing in the Early Twentieth Century* (Routledge & Kegan Paul, 1972).

Memoirs of Bennett include Marguerite Bennett's *My Arnold Bennett* (Ivor Nicolson & Watson, 1931) and Dorothy Cheston Bennett's *Arnold Bennett, a Portrait Done at Home* (Jonathan Cape, 1935). Reginald Pound's *Arnold Bennett* (Heinemann, 1952) emphasizes Bennett's career as a professional writer, but the best biography is Margaret Drabble's *Arnold Bennett* (Weidenfeld & Nicolson, 1974).

Bennett's use of locations and people from the Potteries is most exhaustively treated in Louis Tillier's *Studies in the Sources of Arnold Bennett's Novels* (Paris: Didier, 1969) and E. J. D. Warrillow's *Arnold Bennett and Stoke-on-Trent* (Stoke-on-Trent: Etruscan Publications, 1966). Warrillow's *A Sociological History of the City of Stoke-on-Trent* (Stoke-on-Trent: Etruscan Publications, 1977) is useful for general background, as is Harold Owen's *The Staffordshire Potter* (1901; Bath: Kingsmead Reprints, 1970). *Methodism Divided: A Study in the Sociology of Ecumenicalism* by R. C. Currie (Faber & Faber, 1968) provides information on the religious context.

General critical studies of Bennett's fiction include: Georges Lafourcade, *Arnold Bennett: a Study* (Frederick Muller, 1939); Walter Allen, *Arnold Bennett* (Home & Van Thal, 1948); James Hall, *Arnold Bennett: Primitivism and Taste* (Seattle: University of Washington Press, 1959); James Hepburn, *The Art of Arnold Bennett* (Bloomington: Indiana University Press, 1963); John Lucas, *Arnold Bennett: a Study of his Fiction* (Methuen, 1974); and Olga R. R. Broomfield, *Arnold Bennett* (Boston: Twayne, 1984).

There is a good chapter on Bennett in Douglas Hewitt's *English Fiction of the Early Modern Perod, 1890–1940* (Harlow: Longman, 1988); John Carey defends him in *The Intellectuals and the Masses: Pride and Prejudice Among the Literary Intelligentsia, 1880–1939* (Faber & Faber, 1992); and he is sympathetically discussed in Peter Keating's *The Haunted Study: a Social History of the English Novel, 1874–1914* (Secker & Warburg, 1992), David Trotter's *The English Novel in History, 1895–1920* (Routledge, 1993) and Lyn Pykett's *Engendering Fictions: the English Novel in the Early Twentieth Century* (Edward Arnold, 1995).

Studies of *Anna of the Five Towns* include: Donald D. Stone, 'The Art of Arnold Bennett: Transmutation and Empathy in *Anna of the Five Towns* and *Riceyman Steps*' in *Modernism Reconsidered*, ed. Robert Kiely (Cambridge, Mass.: Harvard University Press, 1983);

Mary Hamer, 'Jobs for the Girls: Arnold Bennett and Virginia Woolf', *Literature and History*, second series, 1: 2 (Autumn 1990): 48–61; and Linda R. Anderson, *Bennett, Wells and Conrad: Narrative in Transition* (New York: St Martin's Press, 1986).

TEXT SUMMARY

Chapter 1: The Kindling of Love

After Sunday school at Bursley Wesleyan Methodist Chapel, Anna Tellwright and her younger sister Agnes talk to other members of the congregation, including Willie Price, son of Titus Price, superintendent of the afternoon Sunday school, and Mrs Sutton, wife of the prosperous Alderman Sutton, and her daughter Beatrice. Anna has maternal feelings towards Willie and is aware of the contrast in style and manner between herself and Beatrice Sutton. Accompanied by Henry Mynors, a pottery manufacturer and superintendent of the morning Sunday school, they join the crowds visiting the new municipal park. From its highest terraces they survey the Five Towns, the centre of England's pottery manufacture. Anna realizes that Mynors is interested in her. She knows that their relationship will arouse much curiosity in Methodist circles, because Mynors is a rising businessman, while her father Ephraim Tellwright is known as a wealthy miser, and she is assumed to be an heiress.

Chapter 2: The Miser's Daughter

On the evening of the same Sunday, Anna sits at her bedroom window and reflects on her life and her realization that Henry loves her. Details are given of Tellwright's early life. He comes of old Methodist stock and has formerly been active in chapel life, as preacher and treasurer. Anna is his daughter by his first wife, who died when Anna was eight; Agnes is his daughter by his second wife, who died soon after Agnes was born. He has become extremely rich through shrewd investment, principally in property. A year before the novel begins he has returned to live in Bursley, where his family originated. Anna sees her nascent relationship with Mynors as a welcome contrast to her narrow and restricted life at home. She sees him approach the house, but he hesitates and does not knock at the door. When her usually reticent father shows some warmth towards her on his return from chapel she realizes the strength of her family ties.

Chapter 3: The Birthday

The next day is Anna's twenty-first birthday. Tellwright summons her to his study and much to her amazement reveals that on coming of age she inherits (from her mother under the terms of her grandfather's will) investments worth fifty thousand pounds. She learns that she owns the works rented by Titus Price and is horrified to discover that he is in arrears with the rent. On her father's instructions, she visits the bank to assume formal responsibility for her account and is treated with great respect by the manager. She then visits Price's works where, although her protective feelings for Willie are again aroused, she displays a hitherto unsuspected firmness with his father and obtains some money on account of the rent arrears. She learns from the Prices that her father and Mynors are planning to go into business together.

Chapter 4: A Visit

The Wesleyan Methodists are preparing for a Revival, to be led by a trumpet-playing revivalist. Anna attends a special meeting of Sunday school teachers, led by Mynors, during which she reflects on her own lack of a strong religious faith. After the meeting, Mynors accompanies Anna home for supper and a business discussion with her father. Again, Anna is conscious that Mynors is paying special attention to her.

Chapter 5: The Revival

Reluctantly but conscientiously, Anna visits the parents of her Sunday school pupils, trying (with little success) to persuade them to take part in the Revival. As she is preparing to attend the opening service of the Revival, her father tells her that Mynors is indeed seeking a business partner. Ephraim has no spare capital at present and suggests that it would be good experience for Anna to invest in Mynors' business. During the Revival service Anna feels her unworthiness and in spite of the revivalist's powerful exhortations and Mrs Sutton's gentler and kindly encouragement is unable to attain any sense of faith.

Chapter 6: Willie

After the service Anna is restless and troubled, despairing about her inability to find true faith, which she attributes to pride and obstinacy, and frustrated by her restricted life, although cheered by thoughts of Mynors. In the hope of finding some relief for her religious doubts, she decides to attend an early morning prayer meeting the next day. On her return from the meeting, where she had been disappointed not to see Mynors, she finds that she has forgotten to buy the bacon for breakfast, and that the delay in the meal has made her father very angry. In the afternoon, Mynors calls and it is agreed that Anna should become his business partner. He manages to allay some of Anna's religious anxieties. Meanwhile, unknown to Anna, Ephraim has written to Price demanding more money. Willie calls to discuss the note and Tellwright insists that as the property belongs to her, Anna should deal with him. In spite of her sympathy for Willie and her determination to live a more Christ-like life, Anna does not wish to anger her father and insists that Titus pay the sum demanded.

Chapter 7: The Sewing Meeting
Anna is invited to a sewing meeting at the Suttons' house, where she hears chapel gossip and is questioned by Miss Dickinson, another Sunday school teacher, about her business relationship with Mynors, which is common knowledge in the chapel. She also suspects that there is speculation about their personal relationship. At tea they are joined by Mrs Clayton Vernon, another prominent Methodist, Alderman Sutton, Mr Banks, the minister, and Mynors. As Anna is preparing to leave, Mrs Sutton again questions her about her religious faith and invites her to join the family for a holiday on the Isle of Man. Mynors accompanies Anna home, where he admires her kitchen and helps Agnes with her homework.

Chapter 8: On the Bank
Anna signs the contract for her partnership with Mynors, and he invites her to visit his works. He takes her round his manufactory, which contains a good deal of up-to-date machinery, and for the first time she witnesses and learns about the processes involved in making pottery. Remembering that her grandmother was a paintress, she tries her hand at painting a border on a plate. Meanwhile, without Anna's knowledge, Tellwright has sent the Prices a further demand, and returns from a day spent out of Bursley to find that Anna does not know if the Prices have responded, because she has been with Mynors. He is extremely angry and insists that she send a further note to the Prices.

Chapter 9: The Treat
Willie calls in response to the note to which, without consulting Anna, Tellwright has added a postscript saying the demand is final. Willie offers a bill of exchange signed by Mr Sutton and payable in three months. Tellwright agrees to accept it, although he intends to put further pressure on the Prices. Later that afternoon, Mrs Sutton visits, and she is soon joined by the Revd Banks, who is seeking contributions for the new Sunday school buildings. Tellwright cunningly agrees to

give the same amount as Price, but is dismayed and angry to discover that Price has offered to donate £25, and refuses to part with any money until Price has paid his contribution. Mrs Sutton, playing on Tellwright's fondness for her when they were young, has persuaded him to allow Anna to accompany the Suttons to the Isle of Man. Anna is delighted to learn that Mynors will also be a member of the party. The following week Agnes and Anna go on the Sunday school treat to Sneyd, a nearby stately home. Price, who is supposed to be in charge, arrives only at the last minute, and Mynors takes over responsibility for the party. When they arrive at Sneyd, Price busies himself organizing games and athletics, and seems in good spirits. His mood changes, however, when Willie arrives, clearly with bad news, and father and son leave without a word of explanation. Mynors again takes command, and when it begins to rain heavily during the picnic tea he arranges for the excursion train to take the party home early.

Chapter 10: The Isle

Although Anna is sure Mynors loves her, he has said nothing, and they meet regularly but not frequently. Her father, who has hitherto raised no objections to her going to the Isle of Man, is angry and obstructive when she asks him for money to buy clothes for the trip. Anna is reconciled to cancelling the holiday when the chance arrival of a postal order, which she cashes without her father's knowledge, enables her to buy what she needs. Tellwright is angered by her subterfuge, but powerless to intervene. The party sails to the Isle of Man from Liverpool and stays in Port Erin, a fishing village. Anna finds the holiday a welcome opportunity to be free of the duties and restrictions that dictate and hamper her everyday life, and relishes the sense of irresponsibility and the atmosphere of mild flirtatiousness between herself and Mynors. Beatrice seems moody and disturbed and it soon becomes apparent that she has influenza, from which she has suffered the previous winter. Anna proves herself to be a capable nurse, sustaining Mrs Sutton as well as caring for Beatrice. The Suttons have to prolong their stay until Beatrice is well. On the night before he and Anna are due to return to Bursley, Mynors at last declares his love and proposes marriage. Anna accepts, but asks him to say nothing to the Suttons.

Chapter 11: The Downfall

On the evening of their return to Bursley, Anna expects Henry to call on her father to discuss their engagement. When Mynors inexplicably fails to arrive, Anna herself tells her father what has happened. Although he makes a show of reluctance and says that Henry only wants Anna for her money, Tellwright raises no real objection to the engagement. At chapel next morning, Mynors' non-arrival is quickly explained: Titus Price has hanged himself, presumably because of his business difficulties. Mynors reassures Anna that she is not responsible for Price's death, since he was being pressed by many creditors, and the inquest confirms this view. After his father's funeral, Willie confesses to Anna that, at his father's request, he forged Mr Sutton's signature on the bill of exchange. Anna promises to help Willie and resolves to tell her father everything and ask for the return of the bill of exchange. But she anticipates Tellwright's refusal to collude in deceit and in the night she takes the bill from her father's desk and burns it. The next day she tells Willie that he is safe, but as she leaves the works she meets her father and is forced to confess to an amazed and outraged Tellwright.

Chapter 12: At the Priory

Ephraim punishes and humiliates Anna by giving the weekly housekeeping money to Agnes. Mynors takes Anna to tea with the Suttons, who have now returned from the Isle of Man, and are delighted at the news of the engagement. Although she has no passionate feelings for Mynors, Anna is prepared to do her duty and marry him, and they begin to make plans for their wedding. Mynors suggests that they should rent Priory House, which will soon be vacated by Willie. They are shown round the house by Sarah Vodrey, the Prices' faithful servant, and agree to rent it. Soon afterwards, Anna receives word that Sarah is ill and goes to nurse her. While she is there Willie, whom Anna still wishes to help, reveals that he is emigrating to Australia. Sarah dies the next day and the refurbishment of Priory House begins.

Chapter 13: The Bazaar

Anna and her father again argue when she asks him for money to buy household linen. Angrily, he hands over her bank-books. She tells Mynors that once they are married she wishes him to take charge of her financial affairs; Mynors is dazzled when he learns the extent of her wealth. Mynors tells her that he has discovered that Price embezzled money from the building fund and they agree to make good the missing sum between them. At the highly successful autumn bazaar Anna sees Willie for what she thinks is the last time, but finds no opportunity to give him the £100 note she has in her pocket.

Chapter 14: End of a Simple Soul

Early next morning Anna waits for Willie outside his house and gives him the envelope with the £100 note, telling him not to open it until he reaches Australia. As they part they realize that they love one another. Anna marries Mynors and although neither she nor anyone else hears from Willie again, she imagines him leading a successful life in Australia. In fact, racked by shame at his father's behaviour, Willie has committed suicide and lies at the bottom of an abandoned pit-shaft.

ACKNOWLEDGEMENTS

I am grateful to the following libraries and institutions for their help in the preparation of this edition: Douglas Library, Isle of Man (J. R. Bowring); Hallward Library, University of Nottingham; Hanley Library (Margaret Beard and Frank Edge); Liverpool Record Office (E. K. Parrott); Manx Museum and National Trust (Roger M. C. Sims). My thanks are also due to Dr Ian Sutton and Professor J. E. Thomas of the Department of Continuing Education at the University of Nottingham, who agreed to my release from other duties to start work on this edition. Several friends and colleagues in the Department were kind enough to help with specific queries for the explanatory notes: Dr Mark Dale (history and railways); Dr Phil Harris (diseases and medicine); Hilary and Philip Olleson, Hilary Sylvester and Ian Wells (music); and Barbara Watts (legal matters). Dr Lynda Prescott and other members of the Cultural Studies Seminar at the University of Bradford made useful comments on some of my annotations. Ann Hurford was very helpful in reading and discussing with me the Introduction and Appendices. Barbara Preston's experience of Nonconformist society was invaluable. Acknowledgement is also due to the copyright holders of the extracts reproduced in the Bennett and his Critics section of this book.